THE LIGHTNING TREE

THOMAS ALAN EBELT

Copyright © 2019 Thomas Alan Ebelt.

All rights reserved. No part of this book may be reproduced, stored, or transmitted by any means—whether auditory, graphic, mechanical, or electronic—without written permission of the author, except in the case of brief excerpts used in critical articles and reviews. Unauthorized reproduction of any part of this work is illegal and is punishable by law.

This is a work of fiction. All of the characters, names, incidents, organizations, and dialogue in this novel are either the products of the author's imagination or are used fictitiously.

ISBN: 978-1-6847-1308-0 (sc)
ISBN: 978-1-6847-1307-3 (e)

Because of the dynamic nature of the Internet, any web addresses or links contained in this book may have changed since publication and may no longer be valid. The views expressed in this work are solely those of the author and do not necessarily reflect the views of the publisher, and the publisher hereby disclaims any responsibility for them.

Any people depicted in stock imagery provided by Getty Images are models, and such images are being used for illustrative purposes only. Certain stock imagery © Getty Images.

Lulu Publishing Services rev. date: 11/19/2019

Also by Thomas Alan Ebelt

Blacksparrow (2014)
Whitefeather (2016)

CHAPTER 1

Gallup, New Mexico, 1937

Harold Borden stepped out of his beat-up, dusty car in the parking lot of Strong Mountain Trading Company. He checked his pocket to make sure the Spanish gold coin was still there before he walked in the front door and strode past the cashier's counter on his way back to the pawn section.

He could see Bobby Castor talking to an old Navajo woman, and he watched him hand her a pawn ticket, obviously for the squash blossom necklace lying on the counter. When the woman left, Harold stepped up and waited for Bobby to place the necklace in the vault and return.

Bobby said nothing as he approached. He knew Harold always acted self-conscious when he came in and saw his trappings of success. Unlike Harold, an old school mate, his own clothing was new and expensive, his blonde hair trimmed and neat. He had a big house in town and a new car to drive. Bobby didn't care that all of it came from the success of his father's business.

Harold swallowed a pang of jealousy, aware of his own shabby clothes and dirty baseball cap. He hated how Bobby acted as if he deserved all of his expensive things. His dad owned the business, but Bobby got to have the money. Instead of a nice, big house, Harold stayed in an old shack owned by his disabled uncle north of the tracks, or sometimes slept in his car out in the desert.

His thoughts turned to the gold coin in his pocket as he waited for Bobby to straighten up some papers behind the counter. Harold thought he was making him wait, and he remembered the old secrets they shared about things that happened when they were both in high school. It was something he held over Bobby, and he knew the man remembered.

"Bobby, I want to show you something, and I want to find out what it might be worth." This was code talk for the two men; Bobby Castor bought most of the native pottery and artifacts he dug up on the Reservation.

Bobby looked at the skinny man in the old clothes, the bad posture, and the stubble of a thin beard. "Is it outside in your car?"

"No, I've got it in my pocket." He reached into his dusty jeans, and set the gold coin on the counter.

Bobby glanced around, interested, but wary. He adjusted his round glasses, and picked up the coin. "Where did you get it?" he said without looking up.

When Harold didn't answer, Bobby lifted his head and glared at him. "If you're trying to fence something you stole, you can forget it."

"Now wait a minute, Bobby," Harold's voice took on a whiney tone. "It isn't stolen. Honest; I found it in the desert."

"Oh yeah? Where?"

Harold's eyes narrowed. "Uh-uh, I'm not saying anything, except there's more just like it; a lot more."

Bobby glared at his old school mate. "So, you think you're a rich man now? Gonna buy some nice clothes? Did you park your Cadillac outside? C'mon, let's take a look at it."

"Aw cut it out Bobby, you don't have to pick on me. If you don't want to buy it, just say so. I'll go somewhere else."

"Go ahead. No other trader in town will give you the time of day. They know pot hunting is illegal."

Harold frowned, and appeared uneasy.

Seeing Harold's discomfort, Bobby smiled through perfect, white teeth. "Lighten up; I'm just funning with you. Leave the coin with me and I'll see what I can find out about its value. Are you sure there's more of them?"

"Yeah I'm sure, and I'll come back tomorrow morning to pick it up unless you want to buy it." Harold turned away, and walked out before he said something else that might anger his old schoolmate.

Bobby watched him leave, and then took the coin back to his office, and picked up the phone. He called a collector he knew in Albuquerque, and described the gold coin in detail. When he hung-up, he held the shiny disk in front of him. "I'll be damned."

Harold, drove to his uncle's house on the north side of the tracks, and spent the day doing chores and running errands. That night, he lay in bed and thought about what he would do with the money from his newfound treasure.

He wasn't worried about Bobby or anyone else discovering its hidden location, but he was concerned about getting a fair price for it. The more he thought, he realized he didn't trust Bobby, even though he'd known him since grade school. Bobby was popular and good-looking, and for some reason, he chose Harold to be his sidekick and whipping boy. Bobby treated him well enough, but there were times, he made him out to be a fool. Harold resented it, but he was grateful to gain some acceptance from someone.

As he lay awake, he recalled the circumstances that caused he and Bobby to drift apart. He played the scenes back in his mind like a flickering movie.

It was the summer of 1913, and the boys on the baseball team met at their favorite spot in the boonies to drink beer. There were ten of them milling around; some playing catch and others just drinking and laughing. The sun was dropping behind a low ridge, and someone started a bonfire to ward off the evening chill.

It was the last few weeks of school, and everyone knew summer vacation would scatter most of them until classes began in their senior year. It was a time to celebrate. No one knew what would become of their lives after they graduated next year. Some would stay in Gallup, but others would scatter to the wind.

He still remembered everyone running up to Bobby's truck when he drove up. "Did you get the beer?" someone said.

While they wrestled a large keg from the back, Bobby walked around to the passenger door. "Come on out Stacy, no one's going to embarrass you. It's a party, and we're all here just to have some fun."

Stacy Toledo, a pretty, Navajo girl from school, looked around in alarm, "You said we would be alone. I don't want to be the only girl here; I just want to be with you, Bobby."

"But you are. Look, we'll just stay for a little while, and then go off by ourselves for the rest of the evening. You don't have to be back home tonight, do you?"

"No," not tonight."

"Okay then, let's just see what's going on." He grabbed her hand and pulled her along behind him.

Though barely sixteen, Stacy looked mature for her years. She was in love with Bobby Castor. He had good looks, and his family had money. They owned a trading company in town, and she knew she would never have money unless she found a way into white society. She hoped he would take her places, but this was not the kind of place she'd had in mind.

As they walked, the other boys began to notice her, and she clutched Bobby's arm for support. She felt nervous, and she wanted to believe he would protect her, but now, a warning voice whispered in her ear.

"Hey Bobby, what did you bring us besides the beer?"

Stacy's face burned at his words, and she shrank from the laughter that came from the others. "Let's go Bobby." She jerked at his arm, but he pulled her close.

"C'mon guys, ease off. She's a little shy. Let her be so she can relax. Hey, somebody bring us some beer."

With a large pitcher in one hand, and his arm around Stacy, he led her back to the truck. Pulling a blanket from the cab, they walked towards a stand of pinons at the edge of the clearing, and talked, and drank beer until darkness came.

Alone in his arms, she forgave him for his callus words earlier. They started making out, and at his urging, she drank more beer than she should have. Bobby's advances became more aggressive and insistent. Through a fog, she became aware that he was removing her clothing, and she started to struggle. She felt dizzy, and the young man was not about to be turned away. She finally gave in, and imagined how they would be together in the future.

Sometime later, he left her and returned to the campfire. The blaze was warm, and by then, everyone had consumed a large amount of beer.

"How was she Bobby?" one of the boys said with a smirk. "Are her tits big?"

"Yeah," said another. "Did you tell her you were going to marry her?"

Through some laughter, Bobby said, "I ain't marrying no Indian. And if you want to know how big they are, go see for yourself."

While a pack of half-drunk boys ran to the trees, a skinny, shy boy named Harold Borden remained at the fire with a concerned look on his face. "Bobby, you shouldn't have done that."

"Oh shut up runt. You might as well get some yourself. I'm going home."

"You're not going to leave her with all those jerks, are you? What's wrong with you? What do you think they're going to do to her?"

"Who cares; it's nothing she probably hasn't had already." Bobby marched to his truck, and drove away.

Harold sat alone keeping the fire going, and his throat ached as the sound of the girl's sobs came to his ears. He hated himself for not doing something to stop what went on.

In the darkness under the stars, after everyone else left, he listened to the sound coming from the edge of the clearing. He stood and made his way to the trees, and the sobbing stopped as he came nearer.

"I...I didn't come to hurt you. Everybody else is gone." When no reply came from the shadowy shape on the blanket, he said, "I'm sorry, I-I couldn't stop them. I figured I'd stay and take you home."

Stacy sobbed again, and Harold waiting for her to finish. I'll bring my car over and help you inside."

He returned, and parked near the trees with the lights pointed away from her. He got out and said, "Do you think you can walk to the car? If not, I'll carry you."

After some sniffles she said, "I can make it." Go back to the car. I'll be there in a minute."

When she opened the passenger door and stepped in, she sat as far away from Harold as possible. He could see her rumpled clothing and the outline of her face in the weak glow of the dash lights. Without speaking, Harold put the car in gear, and drove away.

She took a deep ragged breath, and said, "Thanks for not shining the lights on me. Can you take me out by Naschitti?"

The burden of what his friends had done bore down on his shoulders like a heavy weight. He said, "Yes."

Harold sighed, and fluffed up the pillow on his bed at his uncle's place. High school was long over, and he and Bobby saw less of each other as the years passed. Their only contact was when he found some piece of old pottery to sell for a few dollars.

Soon, with the thought of the gold coins returning, he drifted off to sleep.

CHAPTER 2

Harold Borden showed up at the trading company the next morning. "What can I do for you today?" Bobby said as the man approached the counter.

"Come on Bobby, you know why I'm here."

"Oh yeah, the coin. Now where did I put it?" He made an elaborate show of looking for it. "Oh here it is."

Harold didn't appreciate the kidding this morning. He wanted to make a deal for the coins and bring them in as quickly as he could from their hiding place. He scratched his whiskered jaw, and sucked on his broken tooth. "So what do you think? Can you give me a good price, or do I have to go somewhere else?" Harold surprised himself with his uncharacteristic boldness.

"Whoa now, how do I know this coin wasn't stolen from somewhere?"

"Because I told you I found it buried in the desert; and since when are you so picky about buying something from me?"

The man behind the counter narrowed his eyes. He hissed his reply. "Now listen to me you little shit. I've bought your crappy pottery for years; not because I needed to make some money, but because I wanted to help you. Now, if that doesn't mean anything, you can take your damn coin and get out of here."

Bobby knew he was taking a gamble on losing the chance to get his hands on the rest of the coins. Surprised by Harold's unusual boldness, he instinctively turned the tables on him. He had to make the man want to sell them for whatever price he was willing to pay.

Harold picked up the coin from the counter, and looked at it while he considered Bobby's words. He had no place else to sell them at no risk, and at a reasonable price.

"Okay Bobby, I'm sorry. It's just that I know they're valuable, and I've never been this close to so much money before." He let his words hang in the silence. "There's enough for both of us to make out real good this time."

Bobby smiled and said, "Yeah, that's what I'm thinking. When you bring them all in, we can figure out how much I owe you. How soon can you do it?"

"Well, there's quite a few, and they're heavy. I don't think it's a good idea to bring them all into the store at once."

"Good thinking. How about we meet south of town, instead, down that old trail where we used to party when we were in school? I can meet you there this afternoon. Make it about 4:30 so I can get off work and pick up some cash. It could add up to quite a lot, and you'll probably want to spend some of it right away."

"Yeah, I guess. How much do you figure each coin is worth?"

"Well, that depends on the condition, and how many there are. Relax, from what I learned, I think you'll be surprised."

Bobby Castor watched the sweat glisten on Harold's face as the man struggled with his feral instinct to be careful about trusting anyone, while considering what he could do when he was flush with money. "Okay," he said casting his eyes down to his dusty boots. "I'll meet you there at 4:30."

Bobby watched the man's narrow shoulders as he left the store. Then, he went to the storage area in back, and called to the man working there.

"Hey Louis, do you remember our old pal, Harold Borden?"

Louis Montoya, a dark, muscular man looked up. Moisture dripped from his forehead, down his broken nose, to his droopy mustache. He wiped his face with a rag and said, "Do you mean that little twerp from high-school?"

"Yeah. He's going to meet me this afternoon at our old party place south of town. I want you with me so we can pull off a little surprise. He thinks he hit the jackpot with some Spanish gold coins he found, and I'm thinking he might be upset when I tell him how little I'm going to pay for them. He might even get careless enough to drive his car off one of those cliffs out there."

"Louis grinned. Yeah, I hear it can be dangerous. All of a sudden, I have a feeling I'm going to come into some extra money."

CHAPTER 3

Harold Borden drove east from Gallup with the sun in his eyes. Cumulus clouds were gathering in the northwest, and though they were fair-weather formations, he suspected they would build into thunderheads before long and bring rain. That could present a problem on the trails to his destination.

His body tingled as he thought of the large stash of gold coins he had found yesterday. He had come upon them by accident while searching for signs of ancient habitation and gravesites to loot. In a low, cave-like opening in the rocks, he had discovered a large hoard of Spanish coins.

This morning, Bobby said he would pay a good price for as many as he could bring in, but Harold didn't know if he should trust his old school mate. Twenty years ago, as the captain of the baseball team, Bobby acted as if he was better than everyone else was, and Harold was often the butt of his jokes, just like now.

His thoughts returned to the money. Would the price be fair? Bobby said he would take care of him, and said to bring all the gold coins to a remote location off the highway south of town. He said it was to insure the privacy of their transaction, but did that really make sense?

Harold gnawed on that thought as he drove, and when he turned north off the highway at Thoreau, he cleared his mind, and dreamed about everything he could buy with the money. He stopped to pick up something for lunch, and drove north into the desert. The gravel road turned to dirt, and then into a rutted trail, meandering deep into the eroded hills and mesas of the Bisti.

The clouds were bunching up and becoming taller in the west now. Considering what rain would do to the two-track and the gullies he'd have to cross to get to the gold, he knew he had to hurry. There was still time to collect the bags of coins, and get out of the area before rain turned the trail into a greasy river. The more he thought about it, the faster he drove—no sense risking a chance of not getting back in time for their meeting.

When he reached the spot and stepped from the car, he turned his pale grey eyes to the clouds. He could smell rain as gusts of wind blew across the eerie landscape, pelting him with granules of sand. He took off his battered baseball hat, and dragged a forearm across his sunburned face as he looked around.

Looking older than his 42 years, his thin frame appeared undernourished and dried by the sun. Some called him a pothunter, and he knew he could face jail time if caught by the authorities on the Reservation.

He'd have to hurry. Taking his shovel and flashlight from the trunk, and hefting an old leather saddlebag over his shoulder, he started across the rocks toward the small cave he found.

Twenty minutes later, he stopped near his destination. Nothing moved except for a large crow circling above the rock formation. He had an odd feeling that eyes were watching him, and his heart began to beat faster as he wiped away the sweat that stung his eyes. He'd never felt a premonition as strong as this before, maybe it was the sound of the wind or the moisture in the air that spooked him. Finally, after taking a deep breath, he decided his jumpy nerves were the result of the excitement of finding the gold.

An odd-looking line of weathered, rock pillars lined a ridge ahead. Some called them hoodoos, and like silent spirits, they stood guard over an eroded plain of mushroom-shaped rocks with caps as big as truck tires. It reminded him of an alien landscape in a Flash Gordon movie he'd seen.

As he hiked further through the rocks and eroded channels, he looked for the shallow gully that hid the cave. Noticing his marker, he took a sweeping look around before he stepped down to the hidden entrance. He pulled away the brush that partially hid the opening, brought out his flashlight, and crawled inside. The low space widened to the size of a small room, and, as he played his flashlight along the walls, he saw a scrap of crumbling leather near the spot.

It was difficult to work in the low space. He dug until he found the first bag of coins, and began to fill the pouches of his saddlebag. When he pulled away the remains of the crumbling sack, he found another sack below it, also full of coins. He could hardly believe his good fortune. He dug further and uncovered another and another.

His heart beat like a heavy sledge as he worked in the dusty space, and soon, he began to feel lightheaded. He had a hard time catching his breath. Deciding it was time to get some fresh air; he crawled to the entrance, and thought he heard something outside. He listened to the sound of the wind, and willed his heart to slow down.

After several minutes, he decided the noise came from the gusts of blown sand, and he crawled outside to look around. He saw the dark clouds approaching, and knew he must hurry. It was impossible to carry more than two sacks of coins, so he covered up the rest, and erased all evidence of his digging.

He stood and lifted the heavy saddlebags to his shoulder, and with the wind whipping at his clothes, he began to walk back to his car. How much gold did he leave buried in the cave? Three more bags at least—maybe more.

When he stopped to rest with his heavy load, he realized it was beyond his ability to estimate the value of his treasure. He wiped the sweat from his face, and a dark thought crept into his mind. He began to doubt the wisdom of taking so much gold to his meeting with Bobby Castor. The spot was secluded, and he remembered the condescending attitude and the sneer on his face. Harold decided that the thought of the secret meeting did not set well with him at all.

Harold hefted his pack again, but before he could take a step, he heard a whispered voice. He turned just as a fierce gust of wind hit his face with sharp granules of sand. He dropped his bag and wiped at his tear-filled eyes, and when he could see again, he saw nothing but the rocks and the coming storm.

The desert was playing tricks on him. He grabbed his bags and started walking at a faster pace. After several minutes, a dark shape startled him when it darted across his path, and disappeared. He dropped the bags, and gripped his shovel like a weapon as he peered at the shadows in the rocks. Adrenalin surged through his body and he considered running the remaining distance to the car. When his fear gave him the signal to bolt, he ran but a short distance before he noticed the crouching shape in his path.

Partially hidden in shadow, it appeared larger than a coyote, and when he stopped to get a better look, he saw another shape rise from the shadows near it. This one stood in human form and stretched its arms. The figure wore a loincloth and an animal pelt over one shoulder. It stood watching him, and it lifted its head as if to catch the man's scent.

Harold couldn't tell if this apparition was male or female, but when a gust of wind blew back a corner of its garment and revealed a rounded breast, he was shocked to realize that the creature was a young woman. He saw sweat glistening on her muscular arms and legs, and he reacted to the animal confidence she displayed. Frozen with fear and indecision, he watched as the girl dropped to a crouch.

He knew his car sat a hundred yards beyond her, and his brain told him he could never reach safety without risking a confrontation. In pure terror, he dropped his saddlebags and ran in the opposite direction. He ran as if death was close behind, and he feared to look back and risk losing his footing.

Soon, the rumble of thunder came from the darkening sky. A gust of wind took his hat, and he felt raindrops as he ran. The rain came down even harder, and he slipped in the moist clay and fell.

He got up and ran again, and he lost his sense of time. A sharp pain began to grow in his side, and nearly crying from his exertion, his boots slipped on a wet rock and he fell hard across some gravel. Harold gasped as he struggled to regain his feet. He glanced frantically behind him, and saw nothing but the rocks and the rain.

The rain blurred the surrounding desert and lightning slashed and stabbed across the sky. He slipped several times in the wet clay, and he fell to his knees, only to get up and run again. When he could run no further, he fell against a tall boulder and slid to the ground. His eyes sought his pursuer in the wet curtain of gloom, but he saw nothing.

Laying there, catching his breath, he knew he should get moving, and try to circle back toward his car. He managed to stagger to his feet and began to walk again. He didn't think he outran the girl, but perhaps she just wanted to frighten him away. If so, she succeeded.

As the storm passed, Harold Borden found himself deep in the badlands, bleeding from several small wounds. With only a vague sense of where he was and how far he had come, he knew he could go no further. He collapsed against a rock near the edge of a ravine and closed his eyes.

Harold awoke with a start, and sensed a passage of time. He shivered as he saw the sun touching the irregular line of the horizon. The long shadows around him told him the desert was preparing for the night. He groaned and struggled to his feet, and some animal sense told him he wasn't alone. His eyes shifted to the left and right, seeking evidence of what his mind already knew.

A shadow came to life ten feet in front of him, and this time, he saw an old Navajo woman. She watched him but did not come closer. Harold reached down for a fist-sized rock, and another voice spoke.

"The rock will not help you. You should not have returned to take what is not yours."

It was the young girl. Harold stared for a moment, and when he turned back to the old woman, his vision blurred, and he saw the fearsome visage of a large wolf. Its eyes glared at him as they followed his movements.

His arms and legs were numb with fatigue, and he felt the rock slip from his hand. The fearsome animal moved toward him, and when Harold stumbled back and raised his hands to protect himself, he barely had time to open his mouth to scream as the animal rushed him and drove him over the edge of the ravine.

He hit the broken ground forty feet below, and lay silent and bloody. A thread of consciousness darted behind his sightless eyes, as a finger twitched and inched toward his shirt pocket. It found the object of its quest, and closed around the golden coin.

Harold Borden's body lost its heat in the cooling air, and soon, the hungry night dwellers came to investigate.

CHAPTER 4

"So where is he?" Louis Montoya blew smoke and flicked the butt of his cigarette away as he frowned at Bobby Castor. His dark, hooded eyes followed the line of pines back up the trail toward the Zuni Road.

"I said I don't know." Bobby's frustration showed in his voice. "He said he'd meet me here at 4:30 so I could give him the cash for his gold coins. That little bastard better not try to sell them to anyone else."

"They were Spanish gold, eh?" Montoya smoothed back his black mustache with his thumb, and watched the man pace.

"Yes, he showed me one, and said he had lots more." Bobby squinted as he looked along the rocks and scraggily junipers. His glasses reflected the sunlight as he turned.

Montoya lit another cigarette and exhaled. "So how does a little weasel like him come up with a stash of gold coins in the first place?"

"I don't know. He said he found them, but he wouldn't tell me where. He gritted his teeth as his hair blew across his forehead. "Hell, he's a pot hunter; where do you think he found them—in a tree? He said he'd get the rest of them and meet me right here."

"Well he either lost his nerve or changed his mind. Maybe he decided he didn't trust you enough to hand it over to you out here in the boonies. Maybe he figured you're too damn shady to meet you alone with all that gold." Montoya took another drag of his cigarette. "Do you remember when we use to party out here back in school? You'd bring the girls and the booze, and Harold would spend his time worrying about us getting caught. We sure had a lot of fun back then playing ball, and getting drunk at night.

Remember the time we all got together to celebrate, and you brought that Indian girl? What was her name?"

"Shut up Louis."

"I remember; it was Stacy. Boy did we all have a time with her; except for Harold. The chicken shit just sat by the fire and moped. Hell, he felt so bad he even drove her back to the Res. after we left."

"Will you shut *UP!*"

"Why, because your old man heard about it and whipped your ass? Too bad you never found out who squealed. Somebody did. Maybe it was Borden."

"He said he didn't, and I figured it was Coach Dallas. None of the other guys had the guts, and they'd end up getting in trouble, too."

"Not even Borden?"

"Especially not Borden; he's a wimp, and he knew I'd cut his nuts off. Damn it; if he doesn't show up in the next ten minutes, that's just what I might do when I catch up with him."

"He, he, he."

"Stop laughing like a fool." Bobby glared at the man. "What's so funny?"

"I remember your dad made you so mad when he hit you, you took a swing at him, and then he *really* wailed on you."

"That was twenty years ago; he wouldn't dare try it now."

"Oh yeah? He may be old, but he's still the he-wolf around here. Remember when he punched that newspaper reporter last year? The kid was big, but he sure backed down from your old man."

"Hell, he just didn't want to get in any trouble with his boss. Didn't I just tell you to shut up?"

Montoya ignored his words. "Do you know what I think?"

"Who cares, you don't even know *how* to think."

"Montoya hawked and spat. "What are we going to do if he doesn't show up?"

"I'll give him ten more minutes, and then I'll hunt the little turd down and take his gold away. Maybe I can make him disappear."

Montoya snorted. "While you're daydreaming, I have a better idea. What if I go out to his uncle's place tonight? That's where he stays when he's in town. If I find him, what do you want me to do—bring him back to your place to talk?"

"Yeah, and you don't have to bother being gentle about it."

CHAPTER 5

Sam Begay sat on the edge of his bed and yawned. His stomach still ached from the enchiladas he ate before taking in the movie at the Chief Theater in Gallup last night.

He took a deep breath, and dragged his fingers through his coarse, black hair. He still preferred it short, and he wished he'd stopped at the barbershop when he was in town. He'd kept it short for twenty years as a Navajo Law and Order officer, but now, a civilian in his early 40's, it just didn't seem that important.

He groaned as he stood and stretched, and then shuffled to the bathroom. Dark pupils stared back at him in the mirror. He noticed the puffy skin around his eyes, the pores prominent across his flat nose, and the meaty slabs of his cheeks. A few inches taller than six feet, he weighed about two-fifteen; twenty pounds less than a few years ago. At least he could feel good about that.

The sky was clear this morning. The Hopi and Zuni dancers had brought angry, male storms to the region the last two days, rather than the softer female rain that would nurture their crops. The heavy rain caused flooding, and it scoured deep gouges across the land of his people.

The disastrous effects of the dust bowl drought had already killed much of the grass and groundcover in the region, and he suspected this kind of climactic stress hundreds of years ago brought about the end of the Chaco Canyon civilization a dozen miles north, and the Mesa Verde cultures across the Colorado border. The people moved away and their cultures vanished, just like what was happening to some of his people now.

The Government had the idea of sending the starving families to the east and west, away from the reservation, but this effort was doomed to failure. Once uprooted from their ancestral lands and the cultural nurturing of their society, the People's spirits would die, just as the grass died without its grip on the soil.

The people were powerless to resist, and maybe that's what he'd liked about being a law officer. At least he had the authority to do something about the injustice he saw.

He left the house in old jeans and a western shirt, and he walked across the compound of the old Blacksparrow Mine. Adjusting his tan Stetson to block the bright sunlight, his boots made a shuffling sound on the packed dirt, already dried from yesterday's rain. The sharp calls of the jays in the trees along the mesa walls made him feel alive and part of this place.

He took a deep breath and sighed. Who could have ever imagined the inhuman things that had happened here two years ago? This place had been the base of a Nazi spy operation, and evil men had abducted scores of natives to work in their uranium mine. It all ended when Sam had recruited a rag-tag group of brave individuals to put an end to the atrocity.

He had made some close friends; Kip Combs, a young ex-Navy pilot who had his plane shot down, his girlfriend, Lisa Abbot, who was taken captive when she came looking for him, Diana Witherspoon and Val Tannen who met at an archeological dig in Chaco Canyon just before the spies abducted her and her archology students.

A year later when two Nazi spies returned to take their revenge, he and the others had stopped them for good. Now, he owned the old mining property; gifted to him by a secretive government man named Jack Whorten. He learned later, Val Tannin was his son.

There was one other man; an unlikely young Navajo he knew from his earlier days in law enforcement. Dan Yazzie came home from a short term in prison to learn of the deaths of his grandfather and daughter, and Sam had helped outfit him for his spirit journey of revenge. When Dan returned, he claimed he could talk to the spirits.

As Sam stood at one end of the half-mile wide, roughly circular open space, he still felt uncomfortable with the concept of owning the land. He took a look at the nearby buildings, and the others a half-mile away near an old railroad spur on the far side. An airstrip ran through the center of the area, and it ended at a disguised canyon in the cliff that once housed a giant dirigible.

The history of the events at Blacksparrow felt like a weight on his consciousness. His culture warned him that unlike the whites, his people believed no one could own the earth. A flea did not own a dog. A person owned a rifle, or a vehicle, but they did not own the land. He found that owning of Blacksparrow was like a prison, and he felt the weight of the invisible chains that shackled him to this place, keeping him from feeling free and at peace.

Finishing his tour, he approached the dining hall near his house with a question on his mind. Who was he? A man should know. He remembered studying his face in the mirror this morning. He looked like a forty-two year old Navajo. Maybe that was enough.

When he reached the front of the building, a memory he had been trying to push away for the last two months crept back into his consciousness— the woman who had betrayed his friends, and then died saving their lives.

He shook the painful thoughts away, and concentrated on the unusual footprints he noticed near the dining hall the past two days. It was a small thing, and it probably explained the missing food, but it disturbed his sense of cosmic balance. It tickled the hairs on the back of his neck, and whispered to him as he tried to concentrate on other things.

He found no new tracks this morning, and decided he might as well pick up some groceries at the trading post in Thoreau. Old Jake, the proprietor, had an unconventional way of thinking that sometimes made sense. Maybe he could help him sort out what was behind this footprint mystery.

CHAPTER 6

There were no other vehicles in the lot of the trading post, so Sam figured he could take his time shopping and chatting. The bell over the front door jingled, and the hinges creaked when he stepped into the cool interior. When his eyes became accustomed to the dim lighting, he made his way past the dusty shelves of merchandise to the back. The familiar, mixed fragrances of old varnish, and a dozen other unidentifiable things came to him.

Jake watched him from behind the counter, and he saw the old man's whiskery face and the old frayed shirt that sagged over his bony shoulders like a tent. Jake's large, gnarled hands rested on the counter near his cane.

"It's going to be another hot one today," Sam said. "Nice and cool in here though."

"Yeah, I guess," Jake's ragged voice said. "How are you getting along?"

Sam took a deep breath. He knew what Jake—his friend for many years—meant, but he didn't want to talk about it. He took another breath, knowing the old man would drag it out of him eventually. Jake was talking about Sally Whitefeather, of course, and the old man was going to make him admit that he was still in a fog over his loss and regret.

"I guess I'm okay. You know how it is." Sam made up his mind not to say anything more, and then he saw the odd look on Jake's whiskered face. "Something wrong Jake?"

It was the old man's turn to act uncomfortable. He leaned against the counter and looked away. "Ah…dang it Sam, sometimes you're just too

The Lightning Tree

damn savvy for your own good. You'll probably drag it out of me anyway, so I might as well tell you. It's my niece Helen back in Michigan."

Sam waited for Jake to gather his thoughts in the polite way of the Navajo; never forcing a person to speak before they were ready.

Jake scratched a whiskery cheek, took a deep breath, and held it for a few seconds before he blew it out. "She and her daughter are the only kin I have left."

Sam pursed his lips as he considered this. He kept silent, and waited for the rest of it.

She's my late, sister's girl, and she's been writing to me from time to time—just to be chatty, but yesterday I got a letter from her that bothered me."

Jake let the silence go on while he rubbed his nose. Sam waited, but Jake out-waited him this time.

"I don't remember you mentioning your niece before."

"Yeah, I know. Sam, I think something bad is going on with her and her old man."

Sam pursed his lips again and waited.

"She didn't give me all the details, but she said her husband has been staying out late, drinking, and carrying-on with his friends. Says he's been running with a bad crowd, and she thinks they're connected to the mob. Dang it, Sam, it just breaks my heart to tell you this, but—she said he's been getting more and more abusive. She says she can handle him knocking her around sometimes, but when he started doing the same thing to her daughter, she figured it was enough."

"Did she say what she planned to do about it?"

"No, and I'm tempted to tell her to move out here with me, but that would be a mistake."

Sam looked toward the curtained doorway to Jake's living quarters. "Where would you put them? It's pretty cramped back there."

"That isn't all. The big problem is; I'm not sure I could handle two women underfoot."

A few customers walked in as they talked, and when they came to the counter, Sam wandered back in the store to pick up the things he needed. The place was getting busier, and when he got back to the counter to check out, Jake had too much going on to talk.

He said "goodbye," and drove away thinking he would have to solve the footprint mystery himself. Just as well; he could use the distraction.

He thought about the pair of Keds sneakers he'd seen on a shelf in the trading post that matched the pattern of the tracks he'd found in the dried mud at the compound. The prints were small, like those of a boy or a young woman, and the tread appeared worn but still recognizable. He suspected the person who made them was still somewhere in the compound, and must have discovered a place to hole up. He didn't know where, but he would find out.

When he got back to Blacksparrow, he made a bologna sandwich and walked out on the porch to eat and think. No need to rush today; the mystery would keep. He looked down the row of buildings and considered the layout. Were there any clever places to hide? After finishing his sandwich, he decided to check the stable first.

He circled the shed and enclosure, and peered behind the bales of hay stacked against the back. Then he went inside and looked through the stalls for a sign of something out of place. Finding nothing that looked unusual, he shrugged his shoulders, and decided to saddle one of the horses and ride out toward Chaco Canyon. It would give the intruder a chance to come out of hiding and find something to eat, and who knows, some new tracks might betray a hiding place.

Sam returned a few hours later, and rode around the inside perimeter ignoring the noisy scrub jays that flew ahead of him. He found a few new prints on the far side of the compound, and stepped down to study them. He also found some dirty handprints—perhaps a young boy. He decided a female would keep her hands cleaner.

After twenty minutes of following the meandering tracks to the dining hall, they circled back to the cliffs and vanished like the previous ones he'd found. Sam shook his head, and backtracked until the trail led him in a circle.

He scratched his head, and let out his breath in frustration. Unsaddling his horse, he went back into the mess hall, and found dirty handprints around the sink, and more food missing.

Back outside, Sam circled the building and found more prints, some covering the ones just made. His eyes narrowed, and he resolved to solve this mystery *today*.

He ate a sandwich for lunch, and then followed the meandering tracks behind the buildings, to the far side of the compound again, where they stopped behind a tree near the cliff wall. He found a clue just above eye

The Lightning Tree

level—a small scuffmark on the bark of the tree. The boy must have climbed, and used a rope to get to the top of the cliff. He looked up the wall of rock wall, 200 feet to the top, and shook his head.

Turning to leave, he noticed something that didn't fit. Someone had sprinkled sand over a small area, trying to hide something by imitating the action of the wind. Another search near the wall provided him with a vague, partial print of a moccasin.

"Changed his shoes for moccasins and went off to his hiding place," he said to himself. "Tried to trick me into thinking he climbed up the cliff."

Sam smiled as he followed the vague tracks, only to lose them again.

He prepared supper late that afternoon, and by the time he had everything on the stove, he figured a way he could set a trap to catch the mysterious thief. The kitchen would be the logical place. He cleaned out the broom closet, and made sure he could fit inside and still watch the room through a crack in the door. Then, with a pot of stew simmering on the stove, he opened a window to make sure the aroma wafted outside.

He ate supper, and left the window open when he walked out to enjoy the sunset. He took his time, and when darkness came, he walked to his house beyond the dining hall, turned on a few lights, and left through the back door. He crept through the shadows behind the building to the mess hall, entered the kitchen by the back door, and squeezed into his hiding spot.

It took nearly an hour before his ears detected the stealthy approach of someone outside the partially opened window. He held his breath and listened to the sash scrape as someone raised it to gain entry to the kitchen.

Peering through the crack, he saw a shadowy head wearing a baseball cap, and a narrow set of shoulders in the open window. The small figure crawled inside and jumped to the floor, and in a moment, a match flared to life.

Sam knew the intruder would have to walk past his hiding place, and as he watched through the crack, he saw a hand and a face in the glow of the match. He didn't notice any weapon. Holding his breath until the dark shape passed close enough, he burst from the closet and wrapped his arms around the figure.

Whoever it was, let out a yelp of surprise, and squirmed and kicked as Sam carried him to the light switch. He clicked it on to see who he'd caught.

"Stop fighting and I'll let you go," he said, seeing the intruder was a young Navajo boy. "I'm not going to hurt you. I just want to find out who you are, and ask if you'd like something to eat."

That seemed to quiet the boy down, but when Sam relaxed his grip, the youngster bolted, and he had to catch him again.

"Look, I can tie you to a chair and feed you with a spoon, but wouldn't you rather just sit down while I get you a hot bowl of stew, and let you eat it by yourself?"

Fearful, dark eyes stared at him from a dirt-smudged face. "You're not mad at me? You promise not to hurt me?"

Sam saw fear and hunger in the boy's eyes—a good-looking lad, but in need of some cleaning up. He shook his head and smiled. "Son, I made this stew just so I could talk you into sitting down and telling me how you learned to backtrack and hide your prints so well. I found the place where you tried to make me to think you walked right up the cliff."

He saw the boy relax a bit, and a small, proud grin appeared. "You think I'm pretty good?"

"Yeah, I think you're pretty *darn* good."

Sam gave him a towel and a bar of soap, and he poured a bucket of water. When the boy finished washing, he said his name was Eric Nez. Sam pointed to where Eric could sit, and brought over a bowl of hot stew and two thick slices of bread. He pulled up another chair on the other side of the table and watched him eat.

The lad was skinny, and Sam could tell by the way he ate, that lack of food was probably the reason. When Eric finished his third bowl, Sam could see he was getting sleepy.

"Eric Nez, I know you're tired. Why don't we talk tomorrow? I'll get some blankets and show you where you can bunk for the night. Come morning, I'll make us some breakfast, and you can tell me how you learned to hide your tracks so well. How does bacon and eggs with fried potatoes sound?"

Eric's eyes were wide as he nodded his head. "Mister...?"

"You can call me Sam."

The hollow look in the boy's eyes held his. "Sam, why are you being so nice to me?"

Sam breathed a sigh and said, "Eric, where I come from, we don't call it 'being nice,' we just call it acting like a neighbor."

He showed Eric to the bunkhouse on the other side of the hall, and made up a cot he could use. When he left, he said to meet him back in the dining hall in the morning. Sam knew he was taking a risk that the youngster might bolt during the night, but he figured the promise of a good breakfast would make him stay.

CHAPTER 7

Sam had bacon and potatoes going the next morning, when he heard the front door open. He glanced from the kitchen and saw Eric standing inside the doorway. "Coffee or milk?"

"Can I have both?"

The boy attacked his plate of food as if he hadn't eaten in a week. Considering how much he'd put away last night, Sam marveled at how someone so small could eat so much. When breakfast was over, he cleared the table, and after refilling their cups, Eric answered Sam's questions.

"I lived with my mom and my grandfather out by Burnham. She hitched a ride to Farmington every week to work, and she stayed until the weekend when she came home. Grandfather was old, but he taught me how to track and hunt before he died.

After that, my mother said I was old enough to stay by myself while she was away, and one weekend, she didn't came home. I waited and waited, but I think she went away."

Sam had trouble finding his voice. "Do you know where she might have gone? How long ago was that?"

Eric shook his head and shrugged his shoulders. "She's been gone almost two months."

"Two months? You've been living by yourself for two months? How old are you, Eric?"

"Almost thirteen. Why?"

Sam heard the challenge in the boy's voice, and he could see the pride acquired from being on his own. "I just guessed you were older. What is your mother's name? Do you have any other relatives nearby?"

Eric shrugged his shoulders. "My mother's name is Rosemary Nez. She has a sister who used to live south of here somewhere, but that was a long time ago. I don't think I have any other relatives. I stayed home and snared rabbit and quail, and I harvested some plants for food. I'm a good hunter, and my grandfather taught me about the plants in the desert I could eat. I was sure hungry last night though. Don't worry; I can pay you for the food and the other things I took."

"Other things?"

Eric hung his head. "Yes: a flashlight and a blanket, and some matches—just little things."

"How would you pay me?"

"I've got money." The boy reached into a pocket of his ragged jeans and pulled out a big coin. He gave it to Sam. "Will that cover what I took and what I ate?"

Sam studied the unusual coin in his hand. The disk wasn't perfectly round, and it looked like a few pieces had been shaved off the edges. It was gold. One side had some odd writing, and there was a picture of a king and queen's head on the other side, both wearing crowns and facing each other. He was able to read some of the lettering; 'REGINA,' and 'FERNAND.' The rest was worn and he couldn't make any sense of it, but he did recognize the coin for what it was.

Diana Witherspoon, an archeologist from the University of New Mexico, had found a few just like it a year ago, on top the small mesa just north of Blacksparrow. She also found the bones and rusted armor of a Spanish soldier.

He handed the coin back to the boy. "Where did you find it?"

Eric appeared reluctant to take it back. He blurted out, "I found it by the body of a white man in the Bisti, but you can have it."

Sam held it in his hand and looked at each side again. "You found this near a body? I think you and I should saddle a couple of horses, and ride out there to take a good look. Eric, I used to be a law officer, and there are procedures that must be followed when a body is discovered. You don't need to worry though; I'll take care of it."

It was easier to get to the area on horseback rather than drive around to the primitive road, parking, and ending up walking from there. Sam saddled two horses, and he and the boy rode from the compound, skirting the smaller mesa to the north. Eric paid attention to the route they took toward the Bisti, and he pointed out the landmarks that would lead them to their destination.

They reached the edge of a flat plain of eroded rock and gravel by late morning. Ahead, a wall of weathered spires stood along the edge of a valley of odd sized gravel that littered the ground to the horizon. Sculpted stacks of rock stood like squat mushrooms in shades of reds and browns, and puffy, stratocumulus clouds hung low on the horizon. Higher in the sky, wispy feathers of cirrus hinted at a possible storm.

As they continued to ride, Sam noticed a lone buzzard soaring high in the air. He breathed deeply, savored the desert smell, and felt at home with the earth and sky.

Eric pointed to a distant grouping of rocks. "It's over there," he said.

They rode on until they came upon the body. Sam could tell it had been there for well over a week. The torn clothing and what was left of the gristle and bones would have to suffice to attempt to identify the victim and the cause of death. The last rain left few tracks to study.

Not wanting to risk the chance of rain erasing any remaining clues, Sam did as thorough an investigation as possible, while Eric watched from a dozen feet away.

The body was that of an Anglo male, and it lay face-up amid the scattered rocks at the base of a cliff. The eye sockets were empty, and the skull crushed in the back. Most of the skin was gone, and Sam noticed several tears in the clothing, and lacerations on the remaining tendon and bone. He saw evidence of some creature with strong jaws chewing a few of the bones. He also saw marks and scratches made by feathered predators and other smaller creatures.

He turned to Eric. "Where did you find the coin?"

"It was under his hand by your foot." Eric pointed to the outstretched, desiccated hand, and Sam crouched to look. He gently lifted the bones and then replaced them. "Does the body look the same as when you found it? Was it in the same position?"

"Yes." Eric swallowed and said, "Maybe it had more skin on it, and the bones weren't scattered as much. There were a lot more flies."

The Lightning Tree

Sam stood up. "How about tracks?" He glanced at the small impressions left by birds and other creatures, knowing the last rain probably wiped away most of the useful information."

"There were some, but they were from the animals."

Sam looked up. "Did you see any marks that looked like shoes or boots?"

Eric appeared shy. "No, but I saw some other tracks nearby when I got here."

Like any polite Navajo, Sam waited for Eric to explain.

"Moccasins," the boy said."

Sam knew that any soft depressions left before the last rain were gone now. He went to his saddlebag and brought back a folded sheet of canvas to cover the remains. He set rocks on the corners and edges to hold it in place.

"The man had to get here somehow," he said, looking around. "The road lies east about two miles. He may have come out here by himself in a car, or someone may have brought him here and killed him. Either way, it's some distance from the road. We'll ride back that way and see if we can find any other tracks or an abandoned vehicle. It might help us identify who he was. I don't see a wallet or any other personal items on the body. Did you see anything else when you found it?"

Eric shook his head, "No, just the coin."

A half-hour later, they found a dusty Ford sedan parked a hundred feet off the two-track. From the lack of any tire prints, it must have sat there since before the rain. Sam found the doors locked, and when he peered through the windows, he saw only trash on the floor.

"We'll take a quick look around here to see what else we can find. I'll jot down the plate number and see if I can find out who owns the car."

CHAPTER 8

When they got back to Blacksparrow that afternoon, Sam called the FBI field office in Gallup. Charlie Redman's voice came on the line, and Sam pictured his Dakota Indian friend sitting with his feet up behind his battered, wooden desk. He said, "Charlie, are you doing anything important right now?"

"Sam Begay, what a surprise. I haven't heard from you in a while."

"Well. I haven't had much to talk about until today."

"Uh-oh, here comes the part I don't like." Charlie grabbed a pad and pencil. "What is it, and what makes you think the FBI might be interested?"

"I need you to check out a license plate number for me."

"Why? Did some cute girl pass you on the highway in a sports car? If she did, she'd better be gorgeous if you expect me to go to all the trouble of checking out her license plate. Give it to me, and tell me why you want it."

Sam snorted at the other end of the line. "What's the matter Charlie? You've been drinking coffee and swatting flies all morning just hoping for something to happen. If you must know, I found an abandoned car out in the Bisti today, and the vehicle looks like it's been sitting there awhile. There's no sign of anyone around, but I did find a decomposed body a couple of miles away. There was no identification, but if you can track down the name of the owner of the car, it just might help us identify the corpse."

"Jeez Sam, where are you now?"

"I'm at Blacksparrow. I can meet you and the Medical Examiner on the road north of Crownpoint, and take you to where I found the car and the body. I'll bring along some horses in my trailer."

Sam hung up the phone and walked out on the covered porch of his house. Despite the gruesome nature of what he'd seen today, he felt his outlook on the world turning brighter. Maybe it was time to move on with his life. Here was a mystery, and death always unbalanced things. Fortunately, attempting to restore that balance was what he liked most about law enforcement.

True, he wasn't acting in an official capacity right now, but he did have a U. S. Marshal's badge, and the man from Washington who gave it to him, told him he could use it if he needed to. In fact, Jack Whorten had told him to call if he ever wanted to go back to work on a more permanent basis.

Eric helped hitch up the horse trailer and load the horses. They took sandwiches along, and drove from the compound to where they planned to meet Charlie and the M.E.

Within an hour, two cars followed his truck and trailer several miles down the two-track until he pulled off at the top of a hill. They stepped out of their vehicles, and Sam pointed to the abandoned car off the road a quarter of a mile ahead.

Richard Beeman, the Examiner; a tall, Anglo man in his mid-30s, with blonde hair and a sunburned face, looked around and said, "Every time I come out here I feel like I'm on another planet."

"You are Doc," Charlie said, adjusting his white Stetson. "It's called the Navajo Reservation. The scenery's great, but you can't find a decent laundry or a hamburger joint anywhere."

Charlie drank from his canteen, and said, "Know what I think, Sam? I think you're tired of spending all your time alone out here with the horses and coyotes. I think you want to get me involved in this just so I would ask you to come to Gallup tomorrow to finish your statement. Of course, while you're in town you'll expect me to take you to lunch; that way you can get a free meal out of it too. Maybe you figure you'll get a chance to see something female wearing a dress for a change, instead of fur from head to hoof."

Sam grinned. He liked Charlie, a tall, dark-haired, mixed-breed Indian from somewhere north near Canada. "Charlie, I don't remember you having a sense of humor before. It's a shame; I almost got to liking you."

"Bull," Charlie said, putting his canteen away. He and Sam walked up the trail to the abandoned car, looking for tracks or anything else that might be a clue. Doc Beeman and Eric followed several feet behind.

Sam said, "So how's Station Chief Decker treating you?"

"Oh, he's still got a bug up his ass. Probably from sitting behind that oak desk of his in Albuquerque—I hear it's infested with termites. He doesn't call much, but he does mention your name from time to time."

"Oh? I didn't realize he still cared about me."

"Sure does. I'd say you've made a lasting impression on him. He says you're a perfect example of someone with no regard for proper regulatory procedure."

"Well, I do put some effort into it."

"Effort hell, to hear Decker talk, you have a gift."

The two men reached the abandoned car without noticing anything out of the ordinary along the trail. Charlie found the doors locked, and broke through the passenger window. When he opened the door and stuck his head inside, he jerked back, recoiling from the stench of something rotten.

"Whew, let's get the doors open and air it out."

Charlie reached in, grabbed a greasy sack on the floor, and threw it from the car. It burst open when it hit the ground, and scattered some sliced meat, bread, and rotten fruit.

"Phew, why would anyone leave that in a hot car?"

Sam said, "Maybe he didn't intend to be gone very long."

Charlie found some papers in the glove box. "Harold Borden is the registered owner. Let's see what's in the trunk."

Sam already had it open. "Just like I thought, Charlie; some shovels, a pick, burlap sacks, and boxes. The guy was a pot hunter."

Charlie pushed up the brim of his Stetson and looked around. "Where did you find the corpse?"

"West of here, a couple of miles toward that gap in the mesas; we'll take the horses."

When the riders reached the spot, Charlie took photographs of the scene while the M.E. examined what was left of the body. It was late in the afternoon when they rode back to their vehicles with the remains wrapped in a tarp. Doc Beeman left first, and Sam and Eric loaded the horses in the trailer while Charlie took some notes.

He said, "I'll send someone out to tow Borden's car. I don't think anyone would want to sit inside and drive it very far, even with the windows open." He took Sam's and the boy's preliminary statements, and Sam said he would see him in Gallup Monday to answer any other questions.

Charlie said, "I just can't figure why the body was so far from the vehicle. Oh, by the way, someone discovered a body in town last week; an old, crippled man beat to death in his own home. A neighbor reported it after they looked in on him when they hadn't seen him for several days."

Sam looked at Charlie, his cop senses alert. "Are you going to tell me there's a connection?"

"I don't know. The old guy was beat up pretty bad, and his house was torn up as if someone was looking for something. His nephew is missing, and some folks think he might have done it. They say he lived with the old man, on and off."

"Oh? What are their names?"

"The old guy was Cal Taylor. He was in the merchant marine back in the war, and he took some shrapnel in his legs. The nephew was a loner; a local boy—early forty's. They say he never made much of himself. His name was Harold Borden."

Sam's eyes opened wide. "The same guy?"

"Yeah, they say he did some illegal pot hunting from time to time." Charlie tipped his hat back. "Funny thing; the old man didn't have much to steal, and the neighbors didn't think Borden was the kind of guy to beat up and kill someone. There is no evidence to indicate why anyone would tear up the house either, unless they were looking for something. The unofficial talk is that Borden argued with the old man and killed him."

Charlie looked at Sam for emphasis. "Some say that the old man may have had some money hidden away, but we found no evidence in the house. And now we find Borden with nothing on the body or in his car."

Sam didn't mention the gold coin Eric had found. He sensed there was a bigger mystery here than the two deaths, and he knew any evidence in the case would end up in a filing cabinet somewhere, forgotten or lost. He'd keep the coin for the time being, and let Charlie know if he found a connection.

When Charlie drove off, Sam took Eric aside and said, "I think before we go back, you and I should take a drive to your family's house so you can show me where you lived with your mother and grandfather."

Later that afternoon, in the hills south of Burnham, Sam parked his truck and trailer next to a small, log dwelling near a sculpted wall of sandstone. The rocks blocked the outline of the Ute Mountains to the north.

Eric appeared nervous. "You're not going to leave me here, are you?"

"Not unless you want me to. I think you'd be more comfortable at my place until we locate some of your relatives. I have plenty of room, and I can use the company. You said you had an aunt. Do you have any idea where she lives?"

"Not really." Eric looked at his feet, scraping a toe of his tennis shoe in the sand. "I haven't seen her since I was little. My mother said she ran off to live somewhere south of the highway to Albuquerque. She said she took up with a bad man, and she never came back to see us."

"Do you remember the man's name or his family clan?"

"No, and I don't think he was one of our people. Her last name is Tso, and my mother called her Sadie."

Sam didn't know many families in that area, but being near Thoreau, maybe Old Jake at the trading post heard the name before.

He walked around outside the small hogan, looked inside, and found nothing that went against Eric's story. He found a coat rack and some woman's clothing. They were a poor family. He found some papers with a name and took them outside to Eric.

"Is this your mother's name?" He avoided saying the name to keep from breaking the common taboo among the Navajo, of speaking the name of the deceased, fearing it would draw the attention of an evil Chindi spirit released upon the person's death.

Eric nodded.

"Where did you bury your grandfather?" Eric pointed toward the cliff, and Sam noticed the forlorn look on the boy's face. "Eric, I'm going to take a look up there, and when I return, we'll go back to my place and make supper. We can talk more about your family later. How does that sound?"

Eric nodded. "That sounds okay."

CHAPTER 9

Sam and Eric drove from Blacksparrow after breakfast Monday morning, and as they made their way southbound on the gravel road past Crownpoint, Sam was concerned about locating Eric's aunt. If they found her, he hoped she would be willing to make the boy welcome.

Remembering his own childhood, forced to leave his family to attend the government boarding schools, he knew the best place for someone his age was with his kin. He wanted Eric to have an anchor, rather than endure the cultural sapping experience of living in a white man's school.

There wasn't much information to go on. Eric said he had no other relatives except his Aunt Sadie, and his mother mentioned she lived south of the highway somewhere, but that was all he knew. Sam figured old Jake would know most of the people in the area, and perhaps he would remember someone by that name shopping at the trading post. It was a thin thread and a common name, but it was the logical place to start.

Driving into the parking lot, he saw a few families sitting in their vehicles in the shade of a lone tree. He parked near the building, and when he and Eric walked inside, Jake was just saying goodbye to a woman and her three children. Sam touched a finger to the brim of his hat as they passed in the aisle.

"Hey Jake, I brought you a new, potential customer."

Jake stood behind the counter with his thumbs hooked behind his red suspenders. He leaned forward and squinted at the boy. "He looks a mite young, but if he's got money, I can always use a new customer."

"Eric, this is Jake. Some folks call him 'old' Jake, and you can probably see why. Watch out for him; he's smarter and faster than he looks. He can make your money disappear quicker than a jackrabbit ducking in his hole."

Jake wore a long-suffering expression as he gripped his cane with gnarled fingers. "Boy, I learned my lesson the hard way. If you want any of that big Indian's money, you have to be quick. It's easier to wrestle the skin off a Florida gator than try to pry a nickel out of his hand."

Eric's attention focused on an odd, stuffed, creature on a shelf behind the counter. He turned to Sam and tugged at his sleeve. Sam knew Jake told yarns about the animal, and he wasn't about to put a damper on the old man's fun.

Jake turned and lifted the lid on the old, red, Coca Cola cooler behind him, fished around for a few seconds, and pulled out a wet bottle of Grape Nehi. He popped off the cap and toweled the water off before he set it on the counter in front of the boy. "This is just to show you how generous I really am, and how much I value a new customer."

Jake hooked his thumbs behind his suspenders again and winked at Sam. "I see you noticed that stuffed turkeysaurus behind me on the shelf. It's the only one I've ever seen—pretty rare since Sam chased them off with his fiddle playing. I won't bore you with the whole story, but if you catch Sam in a good mood, he might tell you about it."

Sam looked at Eric and rolled his eyes. He knew most customers saw the animal as a novelty item, just like the stuffed jackalope on a shelf near the door.

"Jake, I came to help Eric pick out some new duds, and while I'm here, I want to ask you a couple of questions. Do you know any Navajo woman around here by the name of Sadie Tso? She's probably around thirty years old. Eric says she's his aunt, and he thinks she might live somewhere south of the highway. His family name is Nez, and he hasn't seen her for a long time.

"Do you know if she took up with some guy and changed her name?"

Sam looked at Eric. Eric shrugged his shoulders.

Jake put his hand on his whiskery chin, and his lips and cheek muscles moved as he searched for an answer. "Tso's a common name, and if that's the clan she married to, I seem to remember a few families and a woman about her age coming in a few times a while back. They weren't a sociable lot as I recall. I think they live southeast of here—maybe this side of the Continental Divide, but I couldn't say for sure. It shouldn't be too hard to find her. Just stop at the first house you see out there and ask. You'll run across someone eventually who knows something."

Sam helped Eric pick out some clothes and sneakers, and had him change in the back room. Jake gave the boy a sack to carry his old stuff, and he couldn't help but smile at Eric's purple-stained lips, and how he looked in his new duds.

As he handed Sam his change, Eric walked toward the door. Jake touched Sam's arm and said in a low voice, "I need to tell you something." He looked to see if Eric was out of earshot. "I heard talk of some bad folk out that way. It always pays to be careful who you're talking to."

Sam nodded and walked out to join Eric.

It promised to be a hot day, and as they headed west, he hoped their search for his aunt would be successful. They ran into some roadwork on the highway, and as they slowed down for a section, Eric surprised Sam by asking, "Why didn't you give the policeman the gold coin when you took him to that body?"

Sam glanced at the boy. "I figured you'd notice. There are a couple of reasons: First, I didn't want that coin to disappear in an evidence file somewhere, and second, I think I might be able to use it to find the man's killer, if there was one."

An hour later, south of the highway on a rough two-track, they jostled in unison in the Ford truck as it squeaked and groaned over the uneven terrain. Stopping to ask for information and directions several times, they now drove up a long, winding incline. Sam said, "We might be getting close. The woman at the last house said some folks live just past the high ground ahead."

When they topped the ridge, a shallow canyon opened before them. Sam saw two houses on the right and one farther along on the left. Fifteen minutes later, he pulled into the first yard, and shut off the engine. He waited as good manners dictated, and a short while later, an old woman opened the door wearing a traditional skirt and velveteen blouse.

Sam walked up. "Ya-eeh-teh. I am Sam Begay, and I am looking for Sadie Tso. Her young nephew is in the truck, and I'm taking him to see her." When the woman didn't answer right away, he said. "A family member has passed away, and the boy has some things to tell her."

Without saying a word, the woman turned toward the house farther along on the left and twitched her lower lip as she lifted her chin. Sam nodded and walked back to the truck.

With the engine whining in protest, the vehicle jostled toward the house about a mile away. They drove up a rutted incline and saw the shoddy condition of the small dwelling. Piles of junk lay in the yard, and when they exchanged a glance, Sam said, "Wait in the truck until we know if this is the place we're looking for."

A woman opened the door a few minutes after they drove up, and she motioned for Sam to come up and talk. After a few minutes, he returned to the truck, started it up, and drove away.

"This woman says someone named Sadie lives with a man named Montoya on the other side of the ridge, but she couldn't say if they were home or not. We'll just have to see."

When they pulled up to the small house, Sam saw a new truck in the yard. Parts of an older one sat on its frame next to it. The door opened after a few minutes, and a woman's head peered out. She stepped outside, closed the door behind her, and waived for Sam to come up to the house.

She waited with her arms folded and a concerned expression on her face, and Sam could see a greenish bruise around her left eye. She tried to drag a wing of black hair over it as she glanced behind her.

"We came to speak to Sadie Tso about her sister and her nephew." He watched the woman's expression change from wariness to surprise and concern.

"I am Sadie."

"May we come in and talk?"

Her eyes showed alarm. "Talk outside. My man is sleeping—he works late."

Sam waived for Eric to join them. He introduced the boy and explained how he was alone since his mother disappeared and his grandfather passed away.

He watched the woman's face as Eric said a few words, lapsing into Navajo and back to English. He saw her expression soften, and then she held out her arms to the boy, and hugged him with tears in her eyes. Sam saw her expression turn back to concern. She let go of the boy and glanced back to the house, biting her lip as if trying to decide something.

They all were startled when the door flew open and an annoyed Hispanic man stepped out; his dark hair unkempt, legs unsteady, and his speech coarse and slurred.

"What's this all about? Who are these people, Sadie?"

"They came to bring me news about my family."

The man screwed up his face and said, "Well tell them to get the hell out of here. We got no interest in them or their news."

Sadie turned and caught the man by surprise. She pushed him back into the house and followed him. From where they stood outside the closed door, Sam and Eric could hear her let loose a blistering tirade.

A minute later, it got quiet, and the door opened. Sadie came out and said, "My sister's son is welcome in my house." She thanked Sam, and said she was sad not to have seen her sister and father before they passed.

Sam felt uneasy, and she noticed his warry expression. "He worked all night, and got drunk with his friends. He is tired, and will feel much better this evening. I will make him some stew, and he will apologize, and welcome the boy."

She took a deep breath and held it as Sam considered what she said. Something didn't sit right, but he put it off to his own feelings of guilt and sadness for having to say goodbye to the boy. He shook Eric's hand and said, "Go get your stuff."

She put her arm around the boy's shoulder when he returned with his bag. "Say goodbye to Mr. Begay, and come inside. I'll make you something to eat. Thank you for bringing my sister's boy to me, Mr. Begay."

Looking down at his feet, Eric said goodbye to Sam.

"I've enjoyed the time we've spent together, Eric," Sam said. "Be sure to come see me if you're ever around Blacksparrow."

He tipped his hat to Sadie, and glanced at the sun as he walked back to the truck. He could make it to Gallup by noon. Maybe he could catch Charlie before he left for lunch.

CHAPTER 10

Sam glanced at the cars in the parking lot of the new, El Rancho Hotel as he drove past. The place looked busy. The owners had ties to the moviemaking business, and they had it built to use as a base for the actors and crews filming western movies in the area. They needed a place to stay, and the people of Gallup got a classy new hotel and restaurant, as well as a chance to gawk at some Hollywood stars.

He drove past Charlie Redman's office, but his car was gone. Circling back to the El Rancho, Sam noticed Judge Reilly's car in front, and a few minutes later, he found the Judge sitting at a corner table, reading the paper while he ate.

"Care for some company?"

Two black eyebrows under a head of grey-white hair popped up from the article the Judge was reading, and he motioned for Sam to sit down. Shortly, a waitress appeared to take his order for a bowl of chili and a glass of lemonade.

The Judge set the paper down and spoke in his raspy voice. "I see you and that FBI Agent, Charlie Redman found a body north of Chaco Canyon. It says here that the animals got to him first." Never one to mince words, the Judge had no qualms about discussing indelicate matters over lunch.

"Judge, that's why I was glad to see your car in the parking lot. I have something I wanted to ask you."

"Oh?" Reilly's dark eyebrows lifted as he took a bite of his Ruben sandwich. He chewed, and spoke from the side of his mouth. "I hope it isn't about this damn blue suit I'm wearing today."

The Lightning Tree

Taken off guard by the Judge's response, Sam, was about to speak when the waitress arrived and served his chili and drink. He adjusted his napkin and picked up his spoon. "What's wrong with your suit?"

"You mean this expensive, damn, blue suit?" The Judge scowled and tore another bite from his sandwich.

Sam stirred his chili, and glanced at the suit. "It looks good on you. It makes you look important. Don't you like it?"

"Like it? I feel like a monkey dressed for the circus. It was Betty's idea. She bought it for my birthday, and when she noticed I hadn't worn it after a month, she made me put it on along with this stupid tie. I'm wearing it to keep peace in the family—you know how she can get."

Sam tasted his chili and decided to let it cool a bit. "Now Judge, Mrs. Reilly is one of the sweetest women you or I ever met."

Reilly glared at Sam. "Begay, you know damn well she used to be an attorney in Albuquerque before we got hitched. Not many people who know her would call her sweet."

Sam kept his head down to hide his smile, and slurped his hot chili. The last thing he wanted to do was step into this conversation any further than he already had.

"Oh, it's all right, Sam. I didn't mean to snarl at you like that. Hell, I have a closet full of suits, and you know what, I hardly ever wear any of them. If I want to impress someone, I'll do it in my courtroom in a Judge's robe. Take a look around, Sam, this is Gallup, New Mexico; the only jackasses who wear suits are the young-buck lawyers, some politicians, and the bankers and insurance agents."

Judge Reilly sat back and took a long drink of his ice tea. He set the glass down and smiled at Sam, one of his oldest friends. "What brings you to town today? And if you so much as breathe a word of what I said to the missus, I'll see that she starts picking out your clothes from now on."

Sam kept a straight face. He slurped some chili, set his spoon down, and dabbed his chin with his napkin. "She really made you wear it eh?"

The two men couldn't help but grin at each other. "She told me I'd wear it today, or she'd kick me out the door in my underwear."

"You're a brave man, Judge, and we both know you're darn lucky to have her."

They finished lunch with small talk about the weather, and after the waitress refilled their drinks, Sam said, "I want to ask your advice about something."

"Sure, just as long as it doesn't have anything to do with suits."

Sam smiled. "Nothing about that; it's about how I handled a situation with an orphan, Navajo boy I found hiding out around my place a few days ago. He says he's thirteen, and he's been living on his own for a few months since his mother disappeared."

"Hasn't he some other relatives?"

"Just an aunt, but he hadn't heard from her in years. We managed to find her living south of Continental Divide with her boyfriend. I left him with her, but I thought I'd check and see if that's within the legal guidelines. I'm a little concerned about the man living with her."

Reilly took a sip of ice tea and looked at Sam. "The way this country is right now, with all the poverty, and families barely getting by, I'll tell you off the record to let it stand, and don't worry about it. As long as the boy says she's kin, it's where he belongs."

They finished their drinks, and Judge Reilly paid the tab, while Sam left a tip. Outside, walking to their vehicles, Reilly said, "Just because it's where the boy belongs, Sam, it doesn't mean you can't stop by to look in on him. I wouldn't consider that to be out of line at all."

Sam said, "Thanks Judge, the next time I see Betty, I'll be sure to tell her that the suit looks good on you."

"You do that, Sam, and I swear you'll be the next one wearing it. It's been good seeing you again."

Sam drove past Charlie's office again, but his car was still gone. He drove to the barbershop, and read an old National Geographic magazine while he listened to the gossip about the new hotel and local politics.

When his turn came up, the barber made small talk while he worked the clippers. Sam's ears perked up when a customer came in and started talking about the old man the police found beaten to death at his home on the north side of town last week.

After he left the barber, he drove by the FBI office again and saw Charlie's government car parked out front. He walked in the door, and Charlie looked up at the counter.

"Sam Begay; I was just thinking about you."

Sam glanced at the vacant desk where he used to sit when he and Charlie worked together, and noted everything still looked about the same. He said, "Thinking about me?"

"Yeah. I expected to see you today. It's a shame it's too late for lunch."

"You weren't in, so I ate with Judge Reilly. I drove by afterward, and when I didn't see your car, I went to get a haircut. I figured to check back one more time before I left town. You said you wanted to go over your report on the body we found in the Bisti."

Redman leaned on the counter. "It's a coincidence you showed up just now."

"Why's that?

"Station Chief Decker just called from Albuquerque, and he bent my ear for fifteen minutes. Your name came up at least six or seven times."

"Why would he talk about me?"

"I don't know, but it was after he heard about you finding that body in the desert. For the first few minutes, all he could do was sputter and say things I shouldn't repeat. I could try to write it down for you, but I don't even know how to spell half of the words. There were a couple of short one's though."

Sam grimaced. "No, that's alright. I had a feeling he might get his nose bent when he found out I was involved."

Charlie went back to his desk and motioned for Sam to sit in the chair next to it. "I told Decker that all you did was call it in, and that a Navajo kid found the body. You know what I think? I think he wishes you would just move out of his jurisdiction and fade away."

"Well if he mentions it again, tell him that if I did move, it would be to Albuquerque so I could be closer to him."

Charlie shook his head, and pulled out a handful of papers from his desk. "I typed up the report on the body for you to read and sign. Seven pages; all of it required under J. Edger's new rules. That doesn't even include my follow-up report."

"I guess I know what you'll be busy with this afternoon." Sam's eyes lost focus for a moment. "It's a shame, because I wanted to talk to you about some things I've been shuffling around in my head."

Charlie set the papers back in the drawer. "What kind of things?"

Sam sat back. "Strange things; seemingly unrelated, but I'm not so sure. Maybe I shouldn't even tell you about it."

Charlie glared and leaned forward. "Don't think I'll let you leave that chair until you do."

"Okay. First, you have Harold Borden's body picked apart by scavengers in the desert. Second, his uncle is killed in town, and his house is torn up."

Sam lifted another finger, "Third—and I didn't tell you this—the Indian boy found a Spanish gold coin on Borden's body."

Charlie frowned. "That's interesting, but what's your point?"

"The point is this; Borden was a pot hunter. Chances are he found the coin somewhere in the desert."

"I still don't get it. How does this tie in with the murder of his uncle?"

"I don't know, but I think I'll take the coin around town to some of the traders and pawn dealers, and see if anyone recognizes it. Any objections?"

"Not from me. You know the people in this town better than I do, and you've been a law officer longer than I have. You still carry that U.S. Marshal's badge don't you?"

"Yeah, but it's not something I'm going to flash around. Do you think Chief Decker would mind if I just sort of worked around the edges of this case?"

"Sam, you and I both know he'd smoke through his eyeballs if he got wind of us even talking about it."

"So?"

"So I won't tell him if you don't."

Charlie's phone rang. He cleared his throat and picked up the receiver.

As Sam listened to Charlie's side of the conversation, he knew something was going on.

"Who is the woman? Lucy Tsosie? And the guy she shot at is her old man? Billy Tsosie? Is anyone hurt? Okay, okay, I'll get out there right away. Tell me how to get to the place. Uh-huh…turn left where? Out west of Tohatchi? How many miles? Just a minute."

Charlie covered the phone. Sam, do you know where the Tsosie clan lives west of Tohatchi?"

"Yeah, there's a couple dozen of them out there."

"Okay," Charlie spoke into the phone again. "I'll be out as quick as I can." He hung up and said, "Do you mind coming along? I might need some help finding the place, and with a lot of family around, it would be nice to have some backup. Do you have that badge with you?"

"Yeah."

"Good, pin it on and come with me."

As they walked out to Charlie's car, Sam said, "I don't think Chief ; to like this."

a, you've got a badge, and I'll tell him I had to take you along new the area."

The Lightning Tree

Charlie repeated the details of the call to Sam as they drove north out of town. A family argument got out of hand, and old-lady Tsosie chased her husband out of the house with a .22 rifle. No one was hurt yet, but the woman was cussing up a storm and firing shots in his direction.

They passed Yah-Ta-Hey and Mexican Springs, and when they turned west at Tohatchi, a truck sped past them on the narrow, dirt road, turned around, and followed Charlie's car. As they came up on the first houses, the truck's horn blared from behind them, and an arm waved out the window.

Charlie stopped, and a young man ran up from the truck. "Are you looking for Billy and Lucy Tsosie's place? It's on the right, just past the curve up ahead."

"Who are you?" Charlie said.

"I'm their nephew. I was visiting when they started arguing. She picked up a gun and went after him, and I took off to call for help."

"Okay, follow us, but stay back. I might want to talk to you later."

Charlie drove up the meandering two-track toward a hogan two hundred yards off the road. A shed and a corral stood to one side. When the two men stepped from the car, Charlie yelled to the house.

"Mrs. Tsosie? If you're in the house, come to the door without your rifle."

Charlie glanced at Sam as they waited. Sam scanned the yard and the surrounding rocks and trees. Neither man had their guns out yet.

It took five minutes before Lucy, a stout, middle-age woman, filled the doorway wearing a traditional, voluminous skirt and blouse.

Sam said to Charlie, "Do you mind if I do the talking? I think I know the family."

"Ya-tay Mrs. Tsosie, it's me, Sam Begay from Gallup. I remember you and Mr. Tsosie from the sing you had for your cousin three years ago." After Sam mentioned some of his family clan members, he said, "Is Billy in the house with you?"

The woman glanced to her left and pointed with her chin. "He's hiding by the bushes in those rocks."

"Do you mind if I come in and visit for a few minutes. It's hot out here, and a glass of water would sure be nice."

She looked at the two men, nodded her head, and went back inside.

Sam and Charlie walked up to the door. "Stay here," he said to Charlie, and entered the small house.

Charlie looked around outside, and motioned to the nephew to stay back. After ten minutes, Sam came out and said, "Wait here while I bring Billy back to the house."

Sam walked past the corral and called Billy's name as he approached the rocks. The man stuck up his head and waved.

"You have a nice place here, Mr. Tsosie; a wide view to the east, and shade from the afternoon sun."

Billy Tsosie nodded but didn't say anything.

"Lucy says you should come to the house now; she says she has some stew ready for you."

The man nodded again.

"She told me you took her grocery money and bought yourself a new hat."

Billy glanced at Sam with a forlorn look. Sam said, "Is it the same one you're wearing?"

Billy's mouth worked a little, but he said nothing. He took off his hat and showed Sam the small bullet hole through the front and back.

Sam held it up and peered through the holes. "She's a pretty good shot, huh?"

Billy nodded.

"Well, it's over then. She knows you want a new hat, and you know not to take her grocery money without asking."

Billy didn't talk much, but he knew how to nod his head.

"I'm glad you two worked it out. By the way, she said that my friend and I could sit down with you and have some of the stew she made. What do you say we go back and eat?"

The nephew joined them, and after they finished the stew and a plate of fry bread, Sam and Charlie said their goodbyes and walked to their car.

"So that's it?" Charlie said as he started the engine. "You just have a little chat with them and everything is fine?"

Sam raised an eyebrow and looked at Charlie. "Reasonable folks always seem to figure things out eventually."

Charlie gave Sam an incredulous look.

"Of course," Sam said, "when I told Mrs. Tsosie we wouldn't think of sampling her good cooking unless we could pay her what we were planning to spend at the restaurant for supper, she stuffed the money in her blouse, and asked me to tell her husband to come in and eat."

Charlie shook his head in amazement. "Sam, I'm begging you right now, please come back and work with me."

CHAPTER 11

"Did you read about the cops finding Borden's body and his car out in the Bisti?" Bobby Castor picked up the copy of the Gallup Independent and threw it in front of Louis Montoya.

Leaning against the back counter at the Strong Mountain Trading Post, Montoya said, "Found his body? Did they say anything about the gold coins?"

"No, and keep quiet; do you want someone to hear you? Just read the damn article."

Louis picked up the paper, read it, and tossed it down. "No wonder he never showed up for the meeting. I thought he chickened out just like back in school. It looks like someone saved us the trouble of getting rid of him."

"Yeah, but now we still don't know what he did with the gold. There's no mention of it. I talked to the reporter, and he said the scavengers picked the body clean. They had to identify him by the plates on his car they found a few miles away."

Montoya stroked his mustache as he glanced at the headline again. "It's a big story for the *Gallup Insignificant*, huh?" He grinned at his pun.

Bobby frowned. "There's a follow-up article inside about his uncle's death. It looks like they're suggesting that Borden may have killed him and ran away to commit suicide. The cops think Borden trashed the old man's house looking for money."

"I told you they would pin it on him."

Neither man noticed David Castor, Bobby's father, walk up the hallway behind them until he spoke. "You'd better hope they do. Both of you, in the back office, now—and bring the damn paper with you." Castor, a dignified looking man with a full head of grey hair and a stern look on his face, expected people to do what he told them to do.

The men followed him in silence, knowing his explosive temper when provoked. They didn't want to strike a match anywhere near the powder keg.

David Castor closed the door and followed the two men into the large, expensively appointed office. He gestured toward the chairs in front of the desk, and sat behind the polished, wooden surface. Nodding at the paper in front of them, he spoke softly—a very bad sign. "Tell me about Harold Borden and his uncle, Cal Taylor. You first, Bobby."

Bobby was used to his old man's temper. He spoke briefly, giving just the facts. "Borden came in last week with an old, Spanish, gold coin. He said he had a whole bag of them to sell. Louis and I set up a meeting the next day to buy them, but Borden never showed up. I sent Louis to see if his uncle knew where he was, and to see if he knew anything about the gold."

David Castor pursed his lips and turned to Montoya. He noticed the man was sweating and wouldn't meet his eyes. Castor opened the top drawer of the desk and pulled out a short-barreled .38 revolver. He made a show of checking the loaded cylinder before he placed it on the desk in front of him.

Montoya's eyes stayed on the gun. "It was after dark when I got there. I parked several blocks away and wore a mask. When I pushed the door open, I told the old guy I wanted to know where Harold was. He told me he hadn't seen him since morning. I asked him if he knew what he did with the gold coins, and he said he didn't know anything about any coins."

Montoya swallowed with difficulty. "I smacked him a few times to get him to talk, but he kept saying he didn't know where Harold or any gold was. He said he would call the cops if I didn't leave." Montoya licked his dry lips and glanced at Bobby before he continued.

"I pushed him, and told him he'd better tell me where he hid the stuff. He called me by my name, and I guess I pushed him again. He fell and hit his head. Can you believe it; the old fart cracked his skull on the edge of a table and died right there. I searched the place before I left, and I figured the cops would think Harold killed him. That's what the paper says."

David Castor put his hands together, touching the tips of his fingers as he considered what Montoya said. He took a deep breath and spoke in a mild, conversational tone. "Yesterday, I was in Santa Fe talking with some state officials I know. They think my chances of being elected Governor in a few years are good. Afterward, I drove down to Albuquerque to meet with some of my business partners. I gave them assurances that nothing would stand in the way of my winning the election."

Castor brushed a piece of lint from the lapel of his suit, and then reached with his right hand to nudge the barrel of the pistol so that it pointed toward Montoya. "It occurs to me that this is a time for caution and discretion. The people from the press can be...so annoying when they catch the scent of something improper. Even a two-bit, local reporter can draw in a pack of big dogs to bay at the shadows."

David Castor gave an exaggerated sigh. "So you see, when I hear about someone playing schoolboy games," he stared directly at his son, "especially now when everything I do will be scrutinized by my opponents *and* the press, I have to consider getting rid of anything or any*one* who may become a liability; clear the weeds from the garden, so to speak."

In a swift movement, David Castor picked up the gun and fired at the carved wooden Indian standing against the back wall behind the two men. Montoya dove to the floor while Bobby remained seated, griping the arms of his chair while a cloud of smoke hung in the room.

Montoya stayed down where he was, and David Castor ignored both of them. He inspected the firearm and placed it back on the desk. When he looked up, he nodded for Montoya to take his seat again.

"Understand me, both of you." Castor stood, leaning forward with his fingers on the desk and raked each man in turn with his cold, grey eyes. "I believe this recent, unfortunate death was brought about by a lapse in good judgement. It happens now and then." His voice took on a reasonable tone. "I suppose I should forgive you both, but then, I have my partners, and the delicate nature of our plans to take into consideration."

He picked up the gun again and pulled the hammer back. The cylinder clicked as it rotated. "Should anyone become aware of what you have done..." He paused for his words to sink in before he eased the hammer down. Pursing his lips, his expression turned contemplative. He sat back in his chair, and put the gun back in the top drawer.

"You two have no idea what my associates and I have gone through to orchestrate my political plans. I will tell you this; killing you both may create some unwanted scrutiny and perhaps, a moment's sadness, but after a few weeks, the deaths of two men whom several witnesses will report they saw drinking and arguing, would simply be considered a sad misunderstanding between friends. It would be a regrettable occurrence, but one quickly forgotten."

David took a deep breath. "I would give the appearance of being devastated, of course, and would say as much in my statement to the press." His expression turned deadly. "If I hear another word about gold coins, or treasure, or even a whisper about Harold Borden or his uncle from either of you…" He let the unspoken words form a picture in the minds of the two men. "Now get out of my sight."

Bobby glared at his father as he stood. Montoya followed him out the door and closed it quietly behind him.

David breathed deeply, opened another desk drawer, and pulled out a fat cigar. He clipped the end and held it between his teeth as he stood, and walked across the room to the carved, wooden Indian. He inspected the hole in the center of the forehead, and then lit the cigar and blew a thick cloud of smoke at the polished, wooden face.

CHAPTER 12

Wednesday, Sam returned to Gallup. He had the gold coin in his pocket, and he consulted a mental list he'd made of the local pawn shops and traders where someone might sell or pawn the coin. He had the whole day ahead of him, and he wanted to find out if anyone had seen a coin like it recently, of if they knew how much it might be worth.

It was a hot day with little wind. Traffic rumbled through town, churning up dust that slowly drifted east. It took him a few hours to work from the western end of town back to Charlie's office, and by then, his shirt stuck to his body like a second skin. Charlie wasn't in, so he continued on to his next stop. He found his first clue at the Strong Mountain Trading Company.

The cool building smelled of the varnish on the wooden floor and a hundred other things. It was a much bigger place than Jake's. Making his way past aisles of clothing, household goods, and tourist gee-haws, to the pawn section in the back, he recognized the blond man with glasses at the counter as Bobby Castor, the son of the owner.

Bobby recognized Sam. "Yah-ah-teh," he said with a thin smile.

Sam returned the greeting and got right down to business. It had been a long morning. "I came to ask if you've ever seen a coin like this one before." Sam put the gold disk on the counter and watched the man's eyes.

Bobby jumped as if it were a snake. He recovered quickly, but Sam had seen what he was hoping for.

"Wow, it isn't often that someone brings in something like this." Bobby made a show of looking at it closely. "It's old, and the writing is Spanish.

It might be worth quite a bit—certainly more than just the gold content. Where'd you get it?"

Sam ignored the question. "Do you have any idea how much the gold content would be worth?" All of his cop senses were alert and focused on the man.

Bobby hefted the disk, "Gold is going for around $35 an ounce; a troy ounce that is." He turned to a scale behind him and said, "About 14 grams. Depending on the purity, it might be worth as much as $17. As far as the collector's value, I wouldn't even want to guess; it could be a lot more."

"Do you know who I could talk to about what a collector might pay for it?" Sam noticed a few beads of sweat on the man's face.

"Nobody around here that I know of. You could try Albuquerque or Santa Fe."

Sam took the coin from Bobby's hand. "Okay, I guess I found out something. Thanks for your time."

"It's nice to see you again Mr. Begay. It's been a while. If you're looking to collect some other gold or silver items, I have some old pawn I'd be happy to show you."

"No, I just wanted to check on the coin. Thanks."

Sam walked out of the building knowing he had his first, real clue.

Bobby Castor left the counter and walked down a hall to the delivery area in the back.

When Louis Montoya heard his name called, he looked up from the boxes he was stacking. Bobby looked angry as he walked up. "What?"

"Do you remember a Navajo Cop who used to work with the FBI a few years ago?"

"Yeah, his name is Begay. Funny you should mention it."

"What do you mean, 'funny'?"

"Nothing important, but I saw him out by that gal's place I stay at past Continental Divide."

"When was that? Was he looking for you?" Bobby's blue eyes were intense.

"Hell no. He showed up the other day when I was hungover. He brought a kid with him, related to the girl I stay with. The little bastard is living with her now, and I'm about ready to get rid of both of them. Either that, or find a new place to hole up outside of town."

"Shit!"

"What? What's the problem?"

"The problem is Sam Begay. He had Borden's gold coin with him, and he wanted to know if I'd ever seen it before."

"How could you tell it was the same one?"

Bobby Castor felt like he was about to explode. "Because, you moron, I got a good look at it when Borden brought it in and had me check on the value. It had the same marks on it, and I'm telling you the Indian came right up to the damn counter and plopped down the same gold coin."

Taking off his glasses and wiping the sweat from his face, Bobby said, "When he set the coin in front of me, I almost jumped out of my shoes. How could he know I'd seen it before?"

"He probably didn't." Montoya smirked, and stroked his thick mustache. "He was just fishing."

"Well dammit, he almost hooked me. He'd better not connect this to your handiwork at Borden's uncle's house. I swear; if dad hears about it, he's liable to have his partners take you and I into the desert and cut our throats."

"Look Bobby, all it means is that he got the coin off Harold, or maybe he found it at his uncle's place. What I'd like to know is if he has an idea where the rest of the gold is hidden."

Bobby put his glasses back on. "Yeah, but dammit, this Indian is an ex-cop; he'll keep after this like a wolf smelling blood. We need to make sure he doesn't cause any trouble with anything else we've got going on."

"That's easy."

"What do you mean, 'easy'?"

"He could have an accident; a real *bad* one."

"An accident huh?"

"Sure, I hear people die every day on the highway. Sometimes they even run off the shoulder and end up in the bottom of a ravine. Pretty tragic; I mean, accidents like that."

If it wasn't for Bobby knowing his father's temper, he might have considered Montoya's suggestion. "No. Not after the way my old man blew up at us. I'm going to tell him what happened, and I'll let *him* decide what he wants to do."

"And what if this Indian cop comes back?"

"Dad will have to make that decision."

Montoya smirked, "Sure Bobby. He's the big man around here, isn't he." He turned to walk away, and Bobby reached out with his left hand, spun him around, and struck him across the jaw with his right. Montoya staggered back, but stayed on his feet. He rubbed his chin, and gave Bobby a wolfish grin.

"Your old man isn't going to live forever, but if you act up again, there's a good chance he might outlive you. If you lay a finger on me again, I'll guarantee it." The grin changed on Montoya's face to a cold glare.

Bobby frowned, but remained silent.

Montoya turned and spoke over his shoulder as he walked away. "Talk to your daddy, and if you ever try something with me again, I'll whip your ass ten times worse than I ever did back in high school."

CHAPTER 13

Sam stopped at the post office on his way back through town and saw Bob and Vicki Johnson, coming out the door. Vicki, a slender woman with blond hair, and her husband Bob; sunburned, stocky, and bowlegged, were a middle age couple who owned a small ranch up at McGaffey southeast of Gallup. Sam remembered someone telling him they were both pilots in their day.

They immediately recognized him, and Vicki said, "Hello, Mr. Begay, do you still remember us?"

Sam smiled. "Sure do; you're Kip Combs' Aunt and Uncle. It's good to see you again—it's been a couple of years, hasn't it?"

"Yep," Bob said, "back when that danged dirigible was flying around, giving us all fits. We appreciated the way you watched out for that daredevil nephew of ours."

"As I recall, he was doing his own share of watching out for the rest of us too," Sam said.

Vicki appeared thoughtful. "I haven't seen much of him this summer, have you?"

"Yes, as a matter of fact, about a month ago. He and Lisa Ann were helping her uncle do some work at the airbase down in Roswell. He said it was a hush-hush government thing, and he couldn't say anything."

Bob adjusted his Stetson and said, "He did mention something about working for a bigwig in Washington, but that was it."

Sam grinned and said, "Funny how things seem to quiet down when he isn't scaring the birds, or plowing up somebody's field with that airplane of his. I'll bet it's been quiet over at your place." His smile dropped when he noticed the couple exchange a look between them.

Bob said, "It's odd you should mention that, because we've been hearing an airplane flying low beyond the tree line after dusk, on and off for the last month or so. We haven't seen it, but we can hear the motor."

"It's all hills and forests out there, isn't it? Why would someone fly around that late in the day?"

"Who knows, but it's got us wondering. Of course, it could be some kind of forestry work. The CCC is pretty busy all over the state this year."

"I suppose," Sam said. "Maybe some rancher out there has a new hobby. Still, it does seem odd that it happens so late in the day."

"Vicki and Bob both laughed. "That's what we thought."

They chatted a few more minutes before saying their goodbyes. Sam checked his mail and drove past Charlie's vacant office before he headed to cover the businesses on the east end of town on his way back home.

An hour later, with no further luck with the gold coin, he headed back to Blacksparrow. He was tired, and grateful the sun was at his back. He thought of Bob and Vicki when he drove past the McGaffey road that climbed into the hills beyond the old Indian School. He envied them for having someone to share their thoughts and their days and nights.

He knew he was slipping into one of his moods. He had no family. Sure, he had a few friends, but most were off somewhere else. He sighed and pulled out a thought; he could go back into law enforcement and be around people all the time. He could help someone, but wouldn't he still be alone? One thing for certain, he wouldn't catch most people at their best if a badge brought them together.

He shook his head and realized he may never fill the void he felt inside him. It must be something like young Eric felt when he was alone for two months with no one to talk to, or to care if he woke up in the morning. At least the boy had someone now. His aunt seemed nice, but what about that brutal man she lived with?

Frowning, he realized he had nothing solid to support his concern. He shook it away and turned to his mental deck of clue cards. This was something he had learned to do over his twenty years as a B.I.A. law officer.

There were four cards laid out in his mind. A dead body in the desert was the first. He mulled over what he knew about that, and what he didn't.

The next card was the dead man's uncle; killed in town in his ransacked house. The old Spanish coin was the third card, and now he had a possible fit; a Gallup trader recognized the coin, but lied about it and said he didn't.

Four clues? Sam thought for moment and drew a fifth card. It didn't seem to fit anything in his hand. He envisioned the silhouette of an airplane flying over the secluded hills and forests south of McGaffey.

He drove past the high walls of red sandstone along the north side of the highway, and saw the faded, blue shape of Mount Taylor on the eastern horizon as he approached Thoreau. Turning north, he drove past the busy parking lot at Jake's trading post, and decided to stop some other time.

Charlie's words echoed in his mind for the hundredth time; "Please come back and work with me." Just thinking about it made his heart beat faster. He realized he also felt something else—a hard, twisted knot in his stomach.

He had difficulty sleeping that night, and he stepped out on the porch to watch the stars above the sandstone cliffs. The night peepers were out, and the flitting sound of the bats stirred his thoughts.

Something entered his mind like a pale moon peeking from a cloud. Every life has a purpose. For the past twenty years as a law officer, he knew what he stood for, and he knew his purpose.

He realized he'd lost that vital connection since quitting a few years ago. Sure, he'd made some friends since then, and done important things, but what was left after that? He imagined his days as a compass spinning without stopping to point anywhere.

That night in Gallup, Alan and Betsy Sandoval argued as they crossed the parking lot to their car. The Hispanic couple had stayed at the El Rancho after dinner, and they drank too much at the bar. While the small western band played in the corner, they had argued for an hour; she wanted to leave, but he didn't. By the time they pushed their way out the back door, their voices had increased by several decibels.

The couple reached the car, slammed the doors, and sped away with the tires spraying gravel. Betsy wanted to go home, but Alan wanted to crank the windows down and let the cool wind clear his mind. Neither of them noticed the old truck following them out of the parking lot.

The Lightning Tree

Aiming their Ford through town, Alan Sandoval turned north toward the Reservation. They argued some more, and neither noticed the headlights coming closer behind them.

A few miles past Yah-Ta-Hey, where the road cut through a section of sculpted rocks, Alan saw the lights and became annoyed by the bright reflection in his mirror. He cursed, and slowed down to allow the other vehicle to pass, but when it didn't, he stepped on the gas to pull away.

The two vehicles sped along, and the truck soon caught up to the Ford and nudged the rear bumper. Alan cursed, and Betsy, frightened by his erratic driving, began to scream at her husband to pull over. A red rage overcame him. He backhanded her, and spewed profanities as he slammed on the brakes.

The truck mashed into the back of his car, and he lost control as he slewed back and forth across the road. He avoided rolling the vehicle, but his path took him through a ditch into the rocks. The car bounced, and sideswiped a boulder on the driver's side. His wife's door flew open and she fell out, rolling along the ground, stopping face down in a shallow ditch. Blood oozed from a cut on her head, and covered the side of her face.

Through pure luck, Alan managed to stop the car just as it neared the edge of a deep gully. Dazed, banged up, and bleeding from his own cut on his forehead, he yelled something unintelligible as he tried to open his door.

In the blazing lights, a shadowy figure approached the dented driver's side and stuck a fist through the glass in the door. Alan tried to focus his eyes, but the dark form was gone. Alarmed at his raspy breathing, he heard a guttural snarl from the open passenger door. He barely had time to react when two large hands reached in, gripped the hair on his head, and bashed his skull into the steering wheel until his body went limp.

CHAPTER 14

Sam heard a ringing in the background of his dream. He listened but couldn't comprehend the meaning of it until the blanket of sleep lifted and he recognized the sound of the telephone in the other room. He sat up and searched for his slippers with his feet, and shuffled to the next room as the pale glow of dawn showed through the windows.

Collapsing in his desk chair, he took a deep breath and picked up the receiver. He was surprised at the ragged sound of his voice as he mumbled "hello."

"Sam, we've got another one."

He frowned as the words bounced around in his brain. When he finally recognized the voice, he jumped and said, "Charlie? What are you doing calling so early?"

"Do you remember those two weird killings last year; the ones with the small bits of wolf hair we found in the wrecked cars?"

"Yeah, why?"

"We've got another one. Can you come out to the scene, and help me figure out what happened?"

Sam blinked, took a deep breath, and yawned. "Where are you?"

"I'll be a couple of miles north of Yah-Ta-Hey on the highway."

"It'll take me almost an hour to get there, Charlie."

"So, I'll pick up coffee and donuts, and meet you in an hour. Sam, I need your help on this one."

"What about Chief Decker? Won't he be mad when he finds out I'm helping you?"

"Screw Decker; just get your Navajo ass out here."

Sam yawned again. "Okay, but the coffee better be hot—and I want donuts with frosting on them."

Sam hung up and went to the bathroom to splash water on his face. He walked out of the house fifteen minutes later, shivering in the chilly, morning air, and he started his truck just as the sun was peeking over the horizon.

An hour later, he pulled up behind Charlie's car on the side of the road north of Gallup. The medical examiner's van sat ahead of it, and he saw Charlie waving from the rocks a hundred feet off the highway. As he walked over, he noticed the tracks made by the dented car.

Nodding to Beeman, he said, "Morning Doc."

"Hi Sam, you can take a quick look, and then step back and let me do my job. Charlie says he won't let me take the body to the morgue until you look around first."

"Don't listen to him Sam," Charlie said as he walked up. "Beeman's in no hurry. He won't leave until the donuts are gone."

Sam said, "Now that I'm here, suppose you give me a quick run-down." He picked a donut from the box and listened to Charlie's narrative.

"The dead man behind the wheel is Alan Sandoval. He worked at the lumberyard in town. His wife Betty was with him. It looks like she fell from the car when it left the road. I found her wedged in a ditch thirty feet back. She's alive, but pretty banged up. The doc looked at her, and they took her to the hospital."

"Could she tell you anything?"

"No, she was unconscious when I found her. She woke up when they left, but she was in no condition to talk."

Sam finished his donut and wiped his hands on his pants. He watched the M.E. pick another donut from the box.

"Okay, Charlie, let's have a look."

Sam walked up to the car, and noticed the damage to the trunk lid and back bumper, and the left side. Charlie stepped away from the driver's door, and Sam peered into the front seat.

"The glass was broken, and the door jammed shut. I had to get in from the passenger side. I already dusted for prints around the doors and the interior. Come around and take a look."

Sam noticed several things as he examined the body lying across the seat. He walked around, entered through the passenger door, and looked at the dash, the seats, and the floor. He scanned every dark nook with a flashlight, and when he straightened up outside the car, he said. "The guy didn't die right away."

"Why do you say that?" Charlie said.

"Too much blood." Sam looked back at the tire tracks. "It only took a few seconds to get here from the road. The blood would have stopped if he died right away. His shirt looks torn as if someone grabbed him and gave him a good shaking. You can see how some of the buttons are missing." He showed Charlie two buttons he found under the seat. "It looks like his face made multiple contacts with the steering wheel and the dash."

"Couldn't that have come from the crash?"

"Maybe, but the ground is sandy."

Charlie frowned. "You don't think his wife could have done that to him, do you?"

"No, but we can check with her when she feels up to talking about it. As crazy as it sounds, I think someone came up to him after the car stopped, and beat his head against the wheel. Did you find any footprints around the car?"

"Uh, no…I haven't looked yet."

"Okay, I'll look. "Did you and the M.E. walk right up to the car?"

"Yeah, just to look inside and pronounce him dead."

"Let me see your boots. I'll check the M.E's too, so I'll know if I find something different.

Sam spent the next twenty minutes looking around the scene and back up to the road.

"Charlie said, "Did you find any other shoe prints?"

Sam stared at the ground and stooped down to get a closer look. "No but maybe something else."

"Like what?"

"Moccasins." He pointed to a few blurred scuffmarks near the tire tracks left by the car.

"Are you sure they're from the time of the crash?"

"Yep; there are a few touching the tire tracks. You might as well tell Doc Beeman he can take the body so he can do his autopsy."

The Lightning Tree

Sam walked around the scene again and back up to the road to walk up and down the side a few hundred yards each way before he returned to where Charlie waited.

"Did you find anything else?"

Sam nodded. "Yep; tracks from another vehicle with a couple of bald tires. Did Beeman have anything else to say about the condition of the body?"

"No, but I found something after we moved him out of the car." Charlie reached into his shirt pocket and brought out a folded envelope. He opened the flap and showed Sam the contents.

"Hair? It's not the man's. Did it come from the woman?"

"Nope. Wrong color."

"Do they own a dog?"

"I can check." Charlie frowned and said, "It looks like the same kind of animal hair we found in the car of the guy who died off the Zuni Road last year."

Sam looked at the tuft of hair and gave the envelope back to Charlie. He walked over to the Examiner's van. "Doc, did you find anything unusual about the remains of the body you brought back from the Bisti?"

"Do you mean in addition to the shredded clothing and the gnawed-on condition of the bones?"

"Yeah, how about any foreign matter, insect carcasses, rodent hair, stuff like that."

"Nothing you wouldn't expect, but I did find a few strands of hair that may have come from some animal, most likely, a coyote or some other predator. Why do you ask?"

"No reason, I guess it's a good thing we got here before something similar happened. By the way, did you keep that hair sample you found?"

"Sure, do you want to see it?"

"Yeah, Charlie can follow you back to pick it up, and I'll meet him in town. I'm going to stay here and look around some more."

Charlie was working on his second cup of coffee at the diner when Sam walked in. He pulled out a chair and sat down, and Charlie said, "It's the same color hair."

Sam motioned to the waitress for coffee, and he sat staring at his cup.

"What are you thinking about, Sam?"

"Nothing in particular, why?"

Charlie formed a slow smile. "I'll bet you're thinking about coming back to work, aren't you?"

Sam gave Charlie a level stare over the lip of his coffee cup. "If I do decide to come back, I'll ask for a job somewhere in Florida or maybe Michigan; someplace far away. My luck is, they'll put me right back here in Gallup, New Mexico with you."

Charlie looked at Sam with a big, satisfied grin on his face. "I know you want to come back."

Sam took a sip of coffee and said, "Maybe so, but you don't have to look so damn smug about it."

CHAPTER 15

Sam drove back to Gallup the next morning with a sense that things were starting to change around him. He felt restless. Charlie's new case was a compelling mystery, and the autopsy on the Borden body might shed some light, not only on the cause of his death, but also on the significance of the golden coin. He didn't want to admit it, but things were starting to bring back his sense of excitement and purpose.

His back ached from driving the hour-long trip from Blacksparrow to Gallup. If he did decide to go back into law enforcement, he should consider moving closer to town. Fixing up his old place east of town would make a lot of sense.

He'd left the house vacant for the last few years when he moved to Blacksparrow, and he knew it would take some work to make it livable again. If he moved, he'd also have to figure out what to do about his horses.

When he walked into the FBI office, Charlie was just sitting down at his desk with a cup of coffee. He looked up at Sam and said, "Coffee's on if you want some."

Sam glanced at his watch, estimated how long the pot must have been brewing, and said, "Sure." He swatted the dust off one of the chairs with his Stetson, dropped it on the seat, and walked to the back to get a cup.

He said, "Have you had a chance to talk to the Sandoval woman yet?"

"Charlie turned his head. "Nope, but I'm going to the hospital this morning. Want to come along?"

"Sure. How's she recovering?"

"Doctor says she'll be alright, but she's still bandaged up and weak. He said I could talk to her for a little while, and afterward, I'll have to head out to Window Rock."

"Sorry to hear that," Sam said from the back. "I was going to buy you lunch."

Charlie watched as Sam returned to the chair in front of his desk. "I'll bet. Maybe I should postpone my appointment with the tribal officials."

Sam sipped his hot coffee and said. "No, don't go to all that trouble because of me. I'm going out to my old place behind the hogback and see what kind of shape it's in."

"Are you going to sell it?"

"No, I thought I'd fix it up and stay closer to town during the week. If it works out, I might even sell Blacksparrow and move back permanently."

"Are you serious?"

"Yep. I have a lot of memories from the time I've spent out at Blacksparrow, Charlie, not all of them good. I figure maybe it's time to move on."

Twenty minutes later, Sam and Charlie walked into the hospital room and took off their hats. Mrs. Betsy Sandoval lay in the bed, propped up on some pillows, with a wide bandage wrapped around her head. She glanced at the two men, and Charlie winced as he saw her black eyes and the bruises on her face.

He cleared his throat and said, "Mrs. Sandoval, thank you for allowing me to visit you this morning. I'm Agent Redman with the FBI. I'm the officer who investigated the accident, and this is US Marshal, Sam Begay. Do you feel well enough to talk for a few minutes?"

She stared at both men and took a ragged breath. "Did you find out who did it?" Her voice was raspy and weak.

"Not yet ma'am, but we will. That's why I wanted to ask if you remember anything about the accident that might help us."

She took another breath and closed her eyes for a few seconds before she spoke. "We were arguing. We went out for dinner and drinks, and Alan wanted to drive to clear his head. We didn't notice the other vehicle coming up behind us until it rammed the back of our car. It was dark, and then the headlights were glaring through the back window."

She closed her eyes, and Charlie glanced at Sam. He said, "Could you see what kind of vehicle it was?"

Tears filled her eyes when she opened them. Her voice broke as she said, "No. The lights were so bright there was no way to tell, but I think it was a truck."

"Why do you think that, Mrs. Sandoval?"

She swallowed before she answered. "The lights were higher than the back of our car—they were shining right in the window."

"What happened next?"

"It kept ramming into our car. My husband lost control and went off the road, we hit something, and I banged my head. I don't remember anything else until I woke up in here…and they told me my husband was dead." She closed her eyes and turned her head away as tears fell down her face.

Charlie looked at Sam and back to the women. "Thank you, ma'am, I'm sorry I had to bother you at a time like this. I won't take any more of your time."

Before he could turn to go, Sam said, "Mrs. Sandoval, do you own a dog or some other animal with long hair?"

"No," She said, and winced with pain when she shook her head.

The two men left the hospital, and Charlie said, "I'll drop you off at your car on my way out to Window Rock. Are you going to stay around town today?"

"For a while, and then I'll head back to Blacksparrow."

Sam left Charlie's office, picked up a burrito and a soda, and drove east past the jagged ridge of upended rock that ran north and south along the eastern edge of town. A half-mile beyond, he turned down a two-track that ran south along the ridge, and soon pulled up to the small house he had locked and boarded up two years ago when he moved to Blacksparrow.

Shutting off the engine, he opened the door, and ate his lunch in the car. He studied the lines of the small frame house, and noticed a pile of tumbleweeds that had accumulated along one wall. A few of the boards tacked over the front windows had come loose and hung askew. The roof looked okay, but he'd know more when he went inside.

When he finished eating, he wadded up the wrapper, and downed the last swallow of grape soda before he stepped out of the car for a closer look. Everything looked secure. He glanced up at the power lines leading to the house, and he pulled a key from his wallet as he walked to the front door. The padlock looked rusty, but the key still worked.

It was dim and dusty inside, and he noticed signs that small animals had found their way in to spend the winter. As he walked through the half-empty rooms, he took note of the work he had to do to make the place livable again. It would take several days, and he'd have to bring in some furniture and bedding from Blacksparrow, but all in all, he could make the place livable enough to stay in by next week. He could put up a shed and a corral later, if he wanted to.

He stopped at Jake's trading post on the way back to Blacksparrow.

"Hi Sam," the old man said from the far end of the store as he watched his friend walk to the counter. "Did you have any luck finding that boy's kin?"

"Yep, we found his aunt. She seems pretty nice, but I didn't like the looks of her boyfriend."

"Why's that?"

"He's a drinker, and he seems to have a mean streak."

"Do you think the boy will be alright?"

"I hope so. His aunt seemed tough enough to hold her own, but…ah, Jake, I just don't know. I'm not sure I did the right thing."

Jake saw the concern on Sam's face, and said in a soft voice, "Sam, you can't save everyone all by yourself. If she's his kin, that's where he belongs."

Sam picked up a few supplies, muttered a few words about the weather as he left, and on the way home, Jake's words echoed in his mind.

CHAPTER 16

Sam gathered tools and supplies he would need to work on his house in Gallup, and Monday morning, he packed some food and a thermos of coffee. He made a phone call before he left Blacksparrow. It was early, but already after 9 a.m. on the East coast.

Jack Whorten's voice came on the line in his office in Washington DC. "Hi Sam, what's on your mind? Life isn't getting too dull and predictable for your tastes, is it?"

Whorten guessed right, but Sam wasn't going to give him the satisfaction of admitting it. "Jack, it's not that, it's just that my friend, Charlie Redman, the FBI guy in Gallup I worked with, has a few cases he hasn't been able to crack. I thought I might put in some spare time and give him a hand. He's helped me before, and I thought I'd see if I could return the favor."

Sam's words sounded a bit unusual, even to his own ears, but then, his relationship with Jack Whorten was much more so. He'd first met the man two years ago when he showed up in a grey suit from Washington to handle the aftermath of his big Nazi spy case at Blacksparrow. Jack made sure Sam got ownership of the place as a reward, but it came with a caveat; Sam had to agree to be available for an occasional assignment. Jack also gave him a U.S. Marshal's badge.

"I figured I'd check in with you, Jack, and see if it was okay to activate my U.S. Marshal status. I don't need to draw a regular paycheck, but some permanent position would be nice."

Without a pause, Whorten said, "Consider it done. Send me your reports with your expenses, and I'll add it to your salary. Just understand one thing."

"Yeah, Jack, I know; if you have an odd project come up, I'll drop everything and come running. That's fine with me."

The phone was silent for a few seconds before Jack's voice came back on the line. "Since you mentioned it, I don't have a real case for you right now, but I would like you to keep your eyes open for something."

Sam kept silent, and waited for the shoe to drop.

Jack said, "After your trip to Michigan last year, the Indian you met, Jason Bigwater, gave us the information he knew about mob activity from his contacts at the Graceland Ballroom in Lupton. The old Purple Gang and the Capone people are out of the picture now, but members of the Detroit mafia have taken up the slack. Some news has come across my desk, and it seems certain unsavory factions have an interest in something going on in New Mexico. I don't have anything definite, but I'd like you to keep your eyes and ears open for anything that might hint of mob activity."

"Sure, I'll do that."

"Good. Consider yourself on active duty. I'll let you know if anything else develops at this end. Sam this could turn out to be nothing, or it could be the tip of something very bad. Be careful, and knowing how things tend to happen around you, try to keep the body count down."

Sam snorted. "Sure Jack, 'body count?' Are you kidding?"

The line went silent for a few seconds before Jack said, "Sam, I never kid."

After he hung up the phone, Sam decided it would be nice to work on the Borden case while he stayed in town fixing up his old place. He could help Charlie on an informal basis, but he'd have to be careful not to let FBI Chief, Decker catch wind of it.

Sam loaded his truck, and when he reached Gallup, he put in a full day's work on his old place. His thoughts kept turning to the Borden case, and he saw the old, Spanish coin. By the end of the day, he crawled into his sleeping bag, and had no recollection of anything until he awoke the next morning.

Later in the week, he arranged to have the electricity hooked up, and a phone installed. He made a trip back to Blacksparrow to feed the horses, and by Thursday, after a lot of hard work, he did a walk-through of the house and decided he was ready to stay here.

Sure, the place needed a new roof, and a small garage and shed would be nice. He could leave the horses at the compound for time being, and check in on them during the week. Later, he could put up a corral, or board the horses when he decided to stay in town on a permanent basis.

Returning to Blacksparrow to bring another load to town, he stopped at the trading post in Thoreau to tell Jake of his plans.

"I've fixed up my old place outside of Gallup, and I plan to stay there most of the time. I'll still be coming back to Blacksparrow, though."

Jake said, "It seems like a lot of fuss and driving to me? How do you plan to keep up both places?"

"I don't know—maybe I'll sell Blacksparrow someday."

Jake scratched his whiskered cheek, and struggled to find the words he wanted. "Does that mean you won't be around here much?"

Sam had a rare look at Jake's true feelings, and he felt at a loss for words. "Jake, I'll still stop by, just like always. I'm considering going back into law enforcement, and it'll be my duty to check in just to make sure you aren't scalping the locals."

Jake gave Sam a mischievous grin. "No one has ever proven anything yet. Dang it Sam, it's just that—oh, maybe this'll free up some time for my other customers; you being such a nuisance and all."

Sam smiled. "Jake, stop trying to make a big deal out of this. I promise I'll still be around to look in on you. And besides, you have your business to run."

"Yeah, I guess."

Sam took a deep breath as drove away. Things change, and like it or not, people have to adjust. Solutions present themselves to those who look for them. Life is a moving stream, and if it were to stop, everything would settle to the bottom and rot. Knowing this made him feel more confident of his decision, but it didn't make him any happier.

CHAPTER 17

Late in the week, Sam drove to Blacksparrow again and spent the morning doing chores and planning what he would do when he returned to Gallup. He realized he would be putting more miles on his Ford truck, and he knew it wouldn't hold up for long. His old Chevy was his back-up car, but he doubted it would take hard use. He needed something reliable: something with good tires that could handle the reservation roads. He knew he'd have to do something soon.

He wanted to look into the Borden case again this afternoon. He'd check in with Charlie first, to see if anything new came up, and then go to the County and City Police to see what kind of information they had on the uncle, Calvin Taylor.

Returning to Gallup, he didn't see Charlie's car at his office, so he stopped at the police building. He showed his U.S. Marshal's badge, and asked to see their files on the death of Taylor. There wasn't much information, and when he left, he told the deputy he'd let them know if he came up with anything new.

He drove across the railroad tracks to the north side of town, parked his car near a small grocery store, and walked a few blocks toward the house belonging to the deceased, Cal Taylor. When he reached the narrow dirt track, he found six, small, frame houses, three on each side. A sandstone ridge stood to the north, and Churchrock rose before him as he walked toward the Taylor house at the end of the track on the left. He stopped at the dwelling just before it, and knocked on the door.

An old Hispanic man lived there. He said his name was Manuel Barraza, and he looked at least seventy years old, and was hard of hearing, and nearly blind without his glasses. He knew Harold Borden, and said the young man helped him from time to time when he needed something fixed around his place. He didn't see or hear anything when Borden's uncle was killed, and he said it was a shame now that the two men were dead, because he needed someone to fix his screen door.

It hung askew by one hinge, and Sam noticed the screws were missing from the top hinge. He asked the old man if he had some tools, and he looked in the shed next to the house until he found something to fix it. When he had the door back in working order, he walked to the next house to the west.

A young woman met him at the door with a crying baby in her arms. He noticed the room behind her was full of scattered clothes. She said her husband worked in Farmington during the week. They had little to do with their neighbors, and she hadn't seen or heard anything when Taylor was killed.

The house directly across the street looked in considerable disrepair. It was vacant and padlocked. Walking to the house east of it, he learned two brothers owned the last two houses on that side of the street. He talked to one of them who was single and out of work. From the look and smell of the man, he was an alcoholic. He told Sam that his younger brother and wife, used to live in the last house, and were now staying with her parents in Albuquerque, looking for work. He knew nothing of the dead man or his nephew, and said he was disgusted that the neighborhood seemed to be going downhill. Sam glanced up and down the short street and figured the downhill slide must have started over thirty years ago.

He walked back toward his car, and stepped into the corner grocery. He spoke to the couple who owned it, and they said they knew both, Borden and Taylor, but they didn't recall seeing or hearing anything unusual around the time the older man had died.

Disappointed that he'd found nothing useful, Sam drove back across the tracks to the post office and talked to the clerk behind the counter. He showed him his badge, and the man was able to give him some background on the uncle and nephew. Cal Taylor received a small pension check every month, but little else. He didn't recall Harold Borden ever getting mail, but he knew that he'd lived with his uncle for some time. He thought Harold had gone to school here, and he may have graduated.

It was nearly three o'clock when Sam drove past the FBI field office again, but still no Charlie. He parked his truck, debated if he should return home, and decided instead, to follow the small thread he picked up at the Post Office. He might as well visit the school and see if he could dig up some background information on Borden before he called it a day.

His thoughts turned to Eric Nez as he drove off. He should stop and find out how things were going on with his Aunt. The belligerent nature of the woman's boyfriend still bothered him, but she seemed genuinely happy to welcome Eric into her home.

He parked in front of the two-story, school building sitting on a low hill several blocks from the Post Office. The hallways were empty, and classes appeared to be over for the day. He walked upstairs to the principal's office, found the door open, and noticed a middle-aged woman at her desk. She was heavy set, with a round, florid face, and short, dark hair. When she looked up to greet him, he saw the shadow of a mustache on her lip.

"May I help you?" Her voice was pleasant, but the skeptical look on her face told him that she doubted if she could.

Sam showed her his badge, and she became more attentive. "I'm looking into the background of one of your students from twenty years ago. Do you keep records going back that far—perhaps some photos?"

She eyed him with even more skepticism. "I wouldn't be able to answer that; I've only worked here for a few years. You'll have to speak to Mr. Dallas, the Principal. He might know."

"Has he been with the school for a while?"

"Oh yes, Mr. Dallas has been Principal for eighteen years. He was a coach and a teacher before that."

"Is he here now? May I speak to him?"

"He's in his office. If you'll give me your name, I'll ask if he can see you." She got up, stepped around her desk like a swivel-hipped football player, and walked toward a closed door at the back of the room. Sam noticed the words "Edgar Dallas" and "Principal" painted on the pebble glass window.

She knocked, and stepped inside for a moment. When she came out, she retraced her route back to her desk and said, "Mr. Dallas doesn't usually see anyone without an appointment." She gave Sam a stern look, "I told him who you were, and he said he would make an exception. You may see him now."

Edgar Dallas turned out to be a tall, bespectacled man with a long, narrow nose, and an unforgiving look that Sam was sure could loosen the bowels of any student called in front of him for discipline.

"Mr. Begay?" The man's deep voice spoke with authority as he stood and stuck out his hand. "I'm Principal Dallas. Won't you have a seat?" He motioned to a worn, wooden chair in front of the desk.

"Thank you for seeing me on such short notice, Mr. Dallas. I won't take much of your time."

"Very well, what can I do for you, Mr. Begay?"

"I'm investigating the deaths of two men. One may have been a student here twenty years ago, and I'm wondering if you have records and student photographs that go back that far."

The man removed his glasses and looked mildly surprised. "Yes, I'm sure we have some records. Unfortunately, information that old is stored in the basement, and it may be difficult to locate the material you're looking for. We try to keep nearly everything, but the space we have for storage is limited."

Sam winced at the thought of digging through a dark room full of cobwebs and boxes of papers.

"Now, if you're just looking for photographs," Dallas said, "you may be in luck. We have group photos of every junior and senior class going back nearly twenty-five years."

"Would they be easier to locate?"

"Most certainly; the photos are in frames, and they adorn the walls of our library and main hallways. We also have photos of the athletic teams. If you'd like to see them, I could ask Mrs. Atkins to show you around the building."

It wasn't long before Sam stood in front of the class photos that Harold Borden appeared in; the junior year of 1912-13 and the senior year of 1913-14. The classes were small and only numbered 25 to 30 students. When he saw the photos of the athletic teams, he found Borden in a junior baseball photo, but not the senior one.

"Mrs. Atkins, would you have a copy of the two class photos and the two baseball teams available for my use?"

She appeared thoughtful and said. "We could check with Miss. Dobson. She's the librarian, and she might know. Would you like to have a seat while I ask her?"

Sam said he would, and thanked her. When the woman returned, she gave him directions to the library, and said Miss. Dobson would be happy to help him.

He found the Library sign on the wall with an arrow pointing to the left, and as he walked down the hall, the sound of his boots on the varnished wooden floor echoed off the walls and high ceiling. There was no way to be quiet. Entering the open door of the library, he smelled the scent of musty books, and children. An attractive, middle-aged woman stood behind the counter and looked up as he walked in.

"Excuse me; I'm looking for Miss. Dobson."

"That's me. Would you be Mr. Begay?"

Sam had expected someone younger, perhaps thin, with a pinched face, and an eccentric personality. Instead, he found an attractive, mature woman with glossy, reddish-brown hair. Reading glasses hung from her neck, and she had the sure smile of someone who knew and enjoyed her work.

"Pleased to meet you miss…ma'am," he said as he removed his Stetson.

She gave him a warm, tolerant smile and said, "Mrs. Atkins told me you were interested in copies of some of the old class pictures. Could you be a little more specific?"

"Yes ma'am, they would be the eleventh grade class from 1912-13 and the senior graduating class of 1913-14. Oh, and also the baseball teams for the same years."

"That's quite a long time ago. I have some extra yearbooks on the shelf, but not from that far back." She took off her glasses and put one of the earpieces in her mouth as she thought through the problem. "If I were to loan you our framed photos for a few days, would you be able to get a photographer to make copies for your use?"

Sam gave her a big smile. "Yes, that would be perfect. I know just the man who could do that for me. If I could borrow them today, I'll have them back to you sometime late Friday. May I?"

"You may, as long as you sign a receipt." She gave him a cautious smile in return. "If you bring them back late, you'll have to pay a fine. You don't even want to know what the penalty would be if you should lose or damage them in any way."

Sam grinned. "Miss Dobson, I assure you, I will guard them with my life while they are in my possession, and I will bring them back to you promptly, in the same condition I received them."

He left the schoolhouse with four framed photos and drove to the photography shop in town. He gave his instructions to the proprietor, who promised to have large copies made, and ready for him by Friday morning.

CHAPTER 18

Sam stayed in town Thursday night. Late Friday morning, with the heat in the car burning his hands when he placed them on the steering wheel, he drove to the photography shop to pick up the photos and the copies. Satisfied with the work, he paid the proprietor and drove the short distance to the school.

He found a few summer classes were in session when he walked inside the building, and he tried to step quietly down the hall to the library.

Miss Dobson examined the framed photos, took off her glasses, and smiled, apparently satisfied with their condition. "Thank you for returning them so promptly, Mr. Begay. I hope your copies came out alright."

"Yes ma'am they did. You were very kind to lend me the originals. I was wondering if you might be able to help me with something else."

She eyed him with a skeptical look. "And what might that be?"

"I want to interview some of the students in these photos. Do you know if any of them still live around here?"

She sighed, "If I were you, Mr. Begay, I would talk to the Alumni Secretary. She would be in contact with most of the past students, and would know who was still living in the area."

"That sounds like a great idea. That's just the person I want to talk to. Do you know where I might find her?"

"You might find her standing in front of you; it would be me. Are you going to tell me why I should consider giving you this information?"

Sam gave her a big, lopsided grin. "Well ma'am, it could be because you'd feel it was your civic duty to help an officer of the law, or it could be because you're curious to find out why I'm so interested. But then, it might be because I offered to buy you lunch to thank you for your time and gracious cooperation."

She twisted her lips and fiddled with her glasses as she considered his suggestion. "Very well, if you come back at 3:30 this afternoon, I'll bring out the alumni records and go through them with you."

"3:30 it is." He tipped his hat and turned to leave.

"Oh, Mr. Begay..."

"Yes?" He turned to see her wry smile and upraised eyebrow.

"Don't think it was just your charm, and the fact that you're a law officer; it was the offer for lunch."

Sam drove to Charlie's office wondering what he should think about Miss Dobson. She seemed a bit odd, but pleasant enough. He shook his head to chase his thought away, and saw Charlie's car parked on the street.

A few minutes later, sitting at his old desk with a cup of coffee, he spread out the copies of the photos. Charlie peered over his shoulder and said, "What's this all about, Sam?"

"These are the junior and senior classes when the deceased, Harold Borden, was a student. I'm going to check all the names to see if any of them are still around so I can talk to them. The school librarian is the alumni secretary, and she said she'd go through her records with me later today. She may have addresses for some of the people."

Charlie said, "Do you think Borden was still friends with some of his old classmates?"

"It's possible, even though he seems to have been a loner. I do know he talked to one of his classmates recently; Bobby Castor."

"Over at Strong Mountain Trading?" Charlie said.

"Yes, and he's the same guy who jumped when I showed him the gold coin, and tried to cover up with some fast talk."

Charlie said he had to leave again, but he gave Sam a key to the office. "You might as well use the office, but just remember, don't answer the phone. The last thing I need is for Chief Decker to call and hear your voice on the line."

When Charlie drove off, Sam wrote down the names of all the students in the photos. He found the junior and senior classes to be identical except for one girl who was missing from the senior photo. The two baseball teams were also the same, except for Harold Borden who didn't play on the senior team. These were the only two differences, and they seemed to have no apparent connection. He made a mental note to ask the Principal about the missing girl, Stacy Toledo.

Picking up a sack lunch at the diner, Sam spent most of the afternoon at his house east of town. He drove back to the school at 3:30, and Miss Dobson led him to a table where she'd set a storage box full of files.

"The older records are all here, but there isn't a lot of information. It was before I took over the secretary's job." She gave him a meaningful look.

Sam reached in his shirt pocket, "I made an alphabetical list of all the student's in the class photos so I could cross reference them."

He unfolded the paper, laid it in front of him, and started going through the oldest records first. They contained very few papers and notes. There was mention of four of the boys who died in action in World War I, and Sam made a notation on his list. He found memos about some of the girls who married and changed their names. Some married classmates, and there were several address changes noted. When they got to the folder for the 1923 graduating class, the records were much more complete and orderly.

"This is when I took over the secretary's position. I remember being horrified by the sloppy condition of the earlier records. It should be much easier going from this point forward."

Through the year 1931, there were three other deaths, two females and one male. Two were together when they ran into a train at a crossing, and there was even a newspaper clipping with an account of the accident.

"I must say, I'm impressed by the detailed records you kept, Miss Dobson."

"You can call me Joyce, Mr. Begay." She smiled.

"Thank you Joyce, and please call me Sam."

She opened the next folder and said, "Oh, I remember this boy; Robert Tibbits. He was so good-looking."

Sam noticed a clipping in the file—an obituary, and he made a note next to the name on his list.

"He was murdered," she said. "It was horrible; he was found hanging from a tree in his back yard."

Sam looked up from the article, "Do you remember why they said it was murder instead of suicide?"

"It was because his hands and feet were tied. They never did find out who killed him, or even why."

From that point on, Sam found at least one student death each year, a few of them women. There were newspaper clippings describing each one, and Sam read them all and made notations.

He closed the folder for 1936, and when he crossed out the sickness related deaths on his list, a chilly realization came to him. Starting in 1932, and for the next four years, at least one male, former student had died a violent death. The Tibbits boy was found hanging from a tree in 1932, Steven Sells died in 1933 from a rattlesnake bite, a car ran over John Damon in 1934, Melvin Stewart was shot and killed in 1935, and Orvil Baxter was found with his skull crushed in 1936.

Sam remembered Charlie taking him to the scene of Baxter's death out on the Zuni road. Charles Walker also died in 1936 in a lone, automobile accident, and now, in 1937, Peter Borden died from a fall off a cliff. Sam frowned at another name on the list, recalling the recent automobile accident where Alan Sandoval died, leaving his wife still recovering in the hospital.

What did it all mean? Some might be coincidence. Could there be another connection besides being schoolmates? Murder was a possibility in at least three of the cases, but the deaths all happened under different circumstances, and that would seem to rule out a serial killer.

Why was there at least one violent death each year? There should be local police files on the incidents, and he wanted to see what they would tell him.

Before he left, he checked the most current file for addresses of living classmates, and found two for the men. By coincidence, they lived locally. He made his notations and thanked Joyce for her time. He said he would call her next week to make good on his promise for lunch.

Charlie was working on reports when he returned to the office, and Sam sat at his old desk and began to write down his own notes.

"Any luck with the Alumni thing?" Charlie said.

"A little. Most of the newer records were detailed and complete. Here's the odd thing though; in each of the last five years, at least one male from the old senior class died by violent means."

"Anything else to tie them together?"

"No, the deaths happened by different means and in different locations. Funny thing though, you and I worked on four of them."

"Huh, how's that?"

Remember the Baxter guy who died out on the Zuni Road around the time I came back from my trip to Michigan last year?"

"Yeah."

And the guy with the knife wounds that drove off a cliff later that year?"

"Him too?"

"Yes, and Harold Borden, and just recently, Alan Sandoval."

"Gee."

"Charlie, I'm going to give this some thought tonight and see if anything comes to the surface. I have a feeling we're not going to like anything about this by the time we're done with it."

Sam's next stop was the Courthouse and jail. The Sheriff and City Police shared space inside the building. Manny Alvarez, the officer at the front desk, called the records clerk to escort Sam to the file room.

Sam had already pulled Charlie's FBI records on the four recent deaths, but he was more interested in the earlier ones. He read the list of names to the clerk: Melvin Stewart, John Damon, Steven Seller, and Robert Tibbits.

The deaths of Damon and Seller appeared to be accidental, while Stewart and Tibbits were listed as unsolved homicides. Sam read each file and found nothing new to consider. There was no mention of any kind of animal hair found on or near the bodies. He thanked the clerk, and left the Courthouse.

Late that afternoon, he returned to his house outside of town, and finished a few chores. After he ate supper, he cleared the dishes and set the envelope containing the class and baseball team photos on the table.

Looking for a fresh angle, he matched each deceased's name on his list with the face in the photos. As he studied the faces, he was surprised to find that nearly all of the baseball team members were deceased. That seemed odd. He looked at his notes on all the graduating classmate deaths. Four had died in action in WWI, but starting with Tibbits, the deaths were recent, and they represented all but two of the ball players.

Only two left alive from the entire team. How odd. The ball players represented a small group of students. How could this be just a coincidence?

He looked at the faces of the two boys still alive, and sat back in his chair. "Bobby Castor and Louis Montoya," he said aloud.

He had spoken to Bobby about the Borden coin, but he knew nothing about the dark-haired Hispanic boy, Louis Montoya. He decided to focus his efforts on the two ball players still alive. Were Castor and Montoya aware of the coincidence? Did they know anything about why this series of events happened? Did fear or guilt stalk their dreams?

CHAPTER 19

Eric Nez and his Aunt spent a quiet afternoon together in her small house in the hills along the Continental Divide. Louis Montoya, the man who stayed with her, had beaten her this morning before he left. Eric worried for her safety, and he tried to think of something he could do to protect his aunt.

"I will kill him if he attacks you again," he said when he brought her a bowl of soup. She winced as Eric propped pillows behind her back and helped her sit up in the sagging bed. He fed her with a spoon, and his anger burned inside him as he looked at the bruises on her arms and face.

Her skin was raw on one cheek where the man had hit her and dragged her across the plank floor. Her blackened eyes caught his, and they showed her sorrow. "No, he will just hurt you too. You cannot kill another man, no matter how evil he is. I will heal, and he will treat me better when he is sober."

Eric was upset, and he ached to take some kind of action. "He is a mad dog. He is not one of our people, and we owe him nothing!"

She touched his cheek and felt the heat of his anger. "Son of my sister, you are young, but you are brave. You must also be smart. I know now, I should not have taken you into this house with him around. He will not leave until he wishes to, so you must go. Find the one who brought you here, and ask if he will let you stay with him."

Eric's eyes misted with his strong emotions. "I am old enough to know the kind of evil inside this man who beats you. I am also old enough to kill a rabid dog that preys on women."

The Lightning Tree

Sadie winced as she took a deep breath. "He will be back tonight, and you must go before then. I will be all right. I will make his supper, and he will go to sleep with a full belly. I will feel better tomorrow, and he will be in a better mood."

She ate her soup, and slept while Eric straightened up the clutter in the house. He went outside and shook with anger, then he ran off into the desert where he could cry without his aunt hearing him. He must stop this evil man from hurting her. If he could knock Montoya unconscious, he could drag him from the house and tie him to a tree. He could then drive her away in the man's vehicle, and find Sam Begay's house where they would be safe.

Born from desperation, it wasn't much of a plan. Eric found three pieces of wood that would serve as clubs. He hid them in strategic places; one inside the house, and two outside. He also had his knife. He must be careful, for the man was strong and fast. When the need came to act, he must use the element of surprise.

He checked on his aunt through the afternoon, while listening for the sound of an approaching vehicle. When evening came, he heated more soup, and helped his aunt move to the table. She had just finished eating when Eric heard the sound of Montoya's truck.

"Leave quickly, she said, her voice desperate. "Hide outside until I find out if he has been drinking. If he is in a good mood, I will call for you."

Eric found a vantage spot behind some brush, and watched the truck skid to a stop in front of the house. His heart sank when he saw Montoya jump out, slam the door, and stagger toward the front step.

The boy's heart pounded in his throat as he picked up his club. He crept to a window to see what was happening inside, and heard nothing until he peered through the glass. He saw Montoya throw the woman to the floor. The man, obviously drunk, staggered, and kicked her as he screamed obscenities.

Knowing he must act now, Eric crept to the door, and with the sound of the man's cursing hiding any small noise, he lifted his club and rushed inside.

Something made Montoya turn just as Eric swung. The blow was a glancing one, and Montoya staggered back. He drew the machete hanging from his belt as an evil grin spread across his sweating face. He took a step toward the boy, but tripped on the woman's legs. She kicked him with desperation, and to Eric's horror, Montoya slashed at her with the heavy blade. He grunted and slashed again before he spun around and started toward the boy.

Blood covered his aunt's body, and he knew he was in no position to help her or fend off the heavy blade. He threw the club, and had the satisfaction of seeing it glance off the man's head as he turned and ran.

Having planned his escape route earlier, he ran sure-footed, while Montoya, slowed by alcohol and the uneven path, stumbled several times, and soon lost sight of his prey. He bellowed his drunken rage after a bad fall bloodied his nose and face, and he slowly got to his feet and staggered back to the house.

A hundred yards away, Eric stopped to catch his breath. He watched the house, and as the sun touched the western hills, he wondered what to do next. He jumped when he heard the sound of gunshots from the house—two muffled reports, then silence.

CHAPTER 20

That night, eighty miles north on the Reservation, a sharp wind blew through the dark canyons and snatched away the wood smoke rising from the top of a log hogan. An old Navajo woman sat inside, next to a kerosene lamp, hands clasped across her worn velveteen blouse. She mumbled a few unintelligible words as a much younger woman, partially in shadow, listened and watched her from a narrow bed across the room.

The old crone set her corncob pipe on the table and lifted a claw-like hand to scratch her earlobe as she spoke. "When I was a young girl less than half your age, I liked nothing better than to walk through the place where the spirits live. I was brave, and I thought nothing of the words my mother spoke to try to scare me away from there. I went because I collected the shiny black stones the whites call Apache tears."

"One day, I followed a rabbit through the strange hills, and I saw it shy away from a small cave. My curiosity drew me to explore the dark place, and when I lit a match and crawled inside, I could hear the whimpering of a young wolf. It lay next to its dead mother, and it was crying from hunger."

"I had no fear, and I picked up the animal and gave it some water. It drank from my hand, and I gave it some food. While it ate, I looked around the shadows of the cave and saw something yellow wink at me. I crawled over to it and found golden coins. When I came back to the baby wolf, it bit me, and I scurried from the cave and ran home."

"The next day, I came back with more food, but the young wolf was gone. I skinned the carcass of the she-wolf, and I made it into a talisman

I could wear to make me strong when I walked alone in the desert." The old woman glanced at the girl and saw a frown cross her brow.

"Grandmother, you told me I must protect the secret place of the golden coins from strangers who would steal them. I understand this, but you also told me we should spare the life of the white man who hunts for graves and old pottery. You said he would not suffer the same fate as the others. When I told you I saw him find the shiny coins, you said he would come back and steal them, and he must die. What has changed? Could we not just move the coins?"

The old woman looked at the worn leather wallet she had taken from the body of the pothunter. "Hush granddaughter, think no more of it. His fate would have joined the others soon enough." She stood on her thin, shaky legs, and stepped to the cast iron stove in the center of the room. As she tossed the wallet into the fire, anger flashed in her eyes. She could no longer use the man as a scapegoat, and she would have to alter her plans.

The young woman, still troubled, looked down at the dirt floor and said, "My brother asked again to see where the coins are hidden, but I told him he must seek your permission. He was very angry. Why do you not tell him?"

The crone's wrinkled face scowled. "My granddaughter, your brother has taken the ways of the white man. You have embraced the way of the People, while he has learned to think like the Balagaana who value the yellow metal above all else. It is unwise to trust him with the knowledge of the hiding place."

The old woman's eyes were narrow slits as she looked at the supple young woman Tessa was becoming. She must make her obey. "He is your brother, but he is like a white man. He has the same weaknesses: the desire for drink and woman, and the greed for money. You cannot forget this."

"When the last Balagaana has received the death he deserves, your task will be finished, and your mother will have her revenge. Do not forget how she suffered giving you and your brother life. She gave up her own, and it is fitting that her two children bring death to those who dishonored her. Sleep now, and talk no more."

Tessa hung her head in obedience. What will happen after that, Grandmother?"

The old woman picked up her pipe and struck a match, the skin of her sunken cheeks working like a bellows as she re-lit the tobacco. She exhaled a thick cloud of smoke. "Then, my precious granddaughter, I will go to my destiny, and you and your brother will leave this place."

CHAPTER 21

David Castor stepped out of his Cadillac in front of the covered porch spanning the length of his house. Located a few miles west of the El Morro Monument, he liked the secluded place, and he felt the stress of the day leaving his body as he walked up to the front door. Inside, he strode down a wide hallway to the suite of rooms he used when he was in town.

It was just after dusk, and he was tired from his long drive from Albuquerque. Enjoying the cool air inside the house, fragrant with the smell of pinon and leather, he dropped his briefcase on the desk and continued to the master bedroom to remove his suit and shoes.

He emerged a few moments later in a robe and soft leather slippers, and walked to the liquor cabinet to pour a tall glass of scotch. The strong drink braced him, and he sighed as he settled into his favorite chair. Running his fingers through his grey hair, he considered the weak links in his operation.

The most significant was his grown son Bobby. In his 40s, the boy was still a preening bully with the temperament of a petulant child. Seeking to mold him into a reliable link in his chain of influence, hoping to use him to help secure the office of Governor of the state, he now doubted that his son would ever live up to his expectations.

David had built his Gallup trading business as a young man, and he'd done it by ruthless, hard work and a keen eye on what he wanted to accomplish. He had forged his political connections the same way, and built a reputation for getting things done, and looking out for the common good of his associates. He knew if he hadn't, his bones would be lying in an unmarked grave in the desert somewhere.

Now, he felt annoyed by the heavy-handed way his associates on the west coast were treating him lately.

He groaned as he got up from the chair to refresh his drink. What should he do about his son? He knew Bobby wanted more control over the local operation as well as the trading post. He also knew that disaster would come of it. His son's only thoughts were of himself and his appetite for money and girls. He was not the kind of man his partners would ever trust to handle their delicate business matters.

David gulped half of the drink in one swallow. He relit his cigar, and began pacing. Hell, if the boy didn't wise up, he wouldn't outlive his old man. David, like his associates, was not the kind of man who ignored or forgave mistakes.

Twenty miles to the east, a small plane prepared to land under gathering stars. While spotters on the remote gravel road stayed alert for any sign of unwelcome traffic, a small crew spaced their vehicles on both sides of a section of the roadway with their lights on.

As the sound of the aircraft engine grew louder. Louis Montoya, his angry thoughts still of the stunt old man Castor pulled in the office at the trading company, signaled his men to get ready to unload the cargo as soon as the plane landed. What was that asshole trying to prove by firing his pistol in the room?

Bobby also seemed to be getting uppity lately. Where would the Castors be if he wasn't here to handle this part of their operation? Who else had the balls to handle the men who did this kind of work? Who else could keep them in line? Nobody, that's who. Montoya's self-talk did little to cool his temper. He threw down his cigarette and stepped back as the small aircraft touched down with a rush of prop noise, wind, and dust.

"Another big load boss?" a swarthy man said as he walked up.

"Big enough to buy your ass a million times over. Tell the boys to hurry up and unload the plane, and get the stuff hauled to our transfer site."

Montoya watched the trucks drive up to meet the aircraft. He glanced at his watch every few minutes, and after his men emptied the plane, he checked his watch again. The small aircraft taxied and flew off into the darkness, and Montoya made sure all the loaded vehicles left before he walked back to his own truck to follow the crew to their wooded site back in the hills.

The Lightning Tree

An hour later, he drove back to the road, traveled east, and turned up the driveway of a sprawling house with the porch lights shining through the trees.

Bobby Castor let him in, and led him to a large living room with wooden vigas spanning the ceiling. Navajo rugs hung on the adobe walls, and covered large sections of the slate floor. "Did everything go alright?" he said to Montoya.

"Yeah, the goods are stashed, but we had a small problem at the site that I had to take care of."

David Castor, now on his third glass of scotch, heard Montoya's comment as he entered the room. He sat down, and the men settled on opposite ends of the leather sofa across from him. The buzz from the scotch kept David relaxed as he listened to Montoya's report, and then asked him to explain the nature of the problem he mentioned when he walked in.

Montoya took a long pull from a bottle of beer Bobby handed him. "One of our boys thought he would go into business for himself. He took another long slug from his bottle, still avoiding the old man's eyes. Montoya belched and said, "He tried to get away with stashing some of the goods, but I caught on to him before he could pull it off."

Montoya smiled at his own cleverness. "I had the men tie him to a tree, and we had a nice talk before I chopped him with my machete. I told the others that since he tried to go into business with our crop, it was only fitting that we plant him on the spot."

Montoya tipped up his beer, and set the bottle down. "There was no need for either of you to bother with a small employee problem like that."

David nodded, and shared a glance with Bobby. "You might as well show our friend out. I'm sure he'll appreciate a chance to unwind after such an eventful evening." Turning to Montoya, David said, "If I have any questions, I'll have Bobby let you know."

David heard the door shut, and spoke when his son returned to the room. "I want you to interrogate everyone in that crew tonight. I want to know if anyone else has a different story about what went on."

"Bobby frowned. "And if someone does?"

"Bring him to me. In the meantime, have the boys load everything and move it to the storage barn south of town. Leave two good men to guard it, and tell them to stay put until you send someone to relieve them."

"Do you think there might be some kind of surveillance going on?"

David thought for a moment. "No, but anything is possible. I just think you or I should have had a chance to talk to the man before Montoya carved him up."

"Why? Don't you trust him?"

The elder Castor laid his eyes on his son. "With the kind of men backing this operation, and everything else I'm involved in, I'd be foolish to trust even you. And you'd be a damned idiot if you think I'd trust that low-life bastard, Montoya."

CHAPTER 22

Joyce Dobson was waiting outside of the school when Sam drove up Tuesday to take her to lunch. A light breeze rustled the leaves of two cottonwoods in front as she came down the steps wearing a colorful skirt and blouse, and met him halfway to the vehicle. She looked graceful and sure of herself, and he was glad she accepted his invitation.

He opened the passenger door for her, and said, "I thought we'd go to the El Rancho. It's early enough to miss the rush, so we should be able to get a good table." He grinned. "It isn't every day I get to take a pretty girl to lunch."

Joyce raised an eyebrow and gave Sam a sly, doubting smile. "And it's been a long time since I went to lunch with someone as nearsighted as you." She watched Sam's face turn red. "I can't remember the last time someone called me a girl, and it's been a while since I had a handsome man ask me to lunch."

Sam chuckled, and said, "I guess that makes us both old enough to know when someone's trying to pull their leg."

Joyce said, "Yes, but at least we're young enough to be flattered by it."

They both laughed, and chatted about the weather as they drove across town and pulled into the El Rancho parking lot. It was just starting to fill up, and Sam parked as close to the front door as he could. A few minutes later, they walked across the lobby, admiring the big fireplace and the two sweeping staircases on either side. Heavy, Spanish style furniture filled the room.

A waitress led them through the dining room, and seated them at a table covered with a white tablecloth. Sam noticed Judge Reilly several tables over and nodded his greeting. He suspected the younger man with the Judge was an attorney from out of town.

After the server came back with coffee and glasses of water, and took their lunch order, Joyce sipped her water as she looked around. "They say some movie people built this place to house their actors and crews while they film their westerns around the area. Isn't that exciting?"

Sam said, "Yes, and I hear they hired some locals and Reservation people as extras for some of the scenes. I guess they figure hiring real Indians will give their films an extra touch of authenticity."

They made small talk while they waited for their meal, and when Sam asked about her background, Joyce said she lived a quiet, but rewarding life as a librarian since her husband died in the Flu epidemic twenty years ago. She said she was a history buff, and she did some research for a writer or two in her free time.

Sam told her his family herded sheep, and he'd gone to a boarding school as a boy. After his parents passed away, he went to the University of New Mexico to study Law Enforcement.

Their meal came, and while they ate, Joyce said, "How is your investigation going with the old student photos? Or am I not supposed to ask?"

Sam swallowed a spoonful of hot, green chili stew, and used his napkin to dab his chin. "Oh, that's fine. I'm trying to track down some connections to a couple of recent deaths of former students. It's funny, the Junior and Senior year photos are identical except for two students; one of the girls in the Junior class and one boy on the junior baseball team."

"Really? Can I ask who they are, or is it confidential?"

"Oh, it's nothing like that; it's just that the boy missing on the senior ball team died just recently. His name was Harold Borden."

"Oh, I read about that. I didn't realize who he was, but I heard some people say he was a bit of a loner. Who was the missing girl from the senior class photo?"

"A Navajo girl named Stacy Toledo."

"Do you think it might mean something?"

Sam looked at Joyce as she leaned toward him with her chin resting in her hand. Her eyes sparkled with interest, and he had a fleeting picture of her as a young girl—inquisitive, intelligent, and very sure of herself.

When he caught himself staring, he snapped out of his thoughts and took another spoonful of stew.

"I don't know. It's too early to tell." He picked up his glass of water and finished it with a gulp. "It was a long time ago, and I don't expect anyone at the school would remember someone from that far back."

Joyce had a contemplative look on her face. She was enjoying Sam's company, and his shyness. "Mr. Dallas might remember. They say he used to be a teacher before he took the Principal's position. I think he even coached some of the ball teams."

"I guess it wouldn't hurt to ask him." Sam noticed Joyce's attention focusing on something beyond him on his left.

"Oh look," she said in a whispered voice as she leaned closer and touched his hand. "It's Rance Wilder, the silent movie star!"

Sam turned and recognized the distinguished looking man being seated at a table occupied by one of their local bigwigs, David Castor.

Joyce said, "I read somewhere that Mr. Wilder is in charge of a movie studio—maybe it's the same one that had this hotel built. Isn't it exciting?"

Sam couldn't help but smile. "We'll probably have movie stars around here all the time now. Pretty soon there will be so many, we'll be lucky to get a table in here."

Joyce smirked. "Don't be such a prune, Sam. This town could use some excitement, not to mention the extra revenue. Don't you like western movies?"

Sam shrugged his shoulders. "I guess growing up on the Reservation; I figure if you've seen one horse and one cactus, you've seen them all."

"Oh stop being silly." Her eyes sparkled with humor. "Do you live in town?"

"Yes I do. I have a place east of the hogback, but I also own an old mining property called Blacksparrow south of Chaco Canyon. It's in the middle of nowhere, but the access road is good, and there is even a small airfield on the property. I have a nice house and some horses, and I'm thinking of selling it."

"Selling it?" She stared into his eyes. "I'd like to see it sometime before you do." She straightened up suddenly and whispered, "Sam, I think this man wants to talk to you."

He turned around, and Judge Reilly stopped at the table. He nodded to Joyce, and said, "Hi Sam, I hate to interrupt you when you have a pretty girl at your table, but I wanted to ask you something." The judge smiled at Joyce.

Sam said, "Judge, this pretty girl is Joyce Dobson, our school librarian. Joyce, this distinguished looking old man is Judge Reilly."

Joyce held out her hand and the Judge took it. "The name is Daniel, ma'am. Pleased to meet you."

"The same to you, Judge—and I don't think you're old at all."

Judge Reilly smiled and said, "Sam I'm impressed by your good taste in women. I don't wish to interrupt your meal, but before you leave, could I have a few words with you in the lobby?"

"Sure Judge, we were just about to go."

"Good, I'll wait for you. It won't take but a minute."

Sam paid for lunch, and left a generous tip. Joyce said she wanted to freshen up, and he said, "I'll wait for you by the fireplace."

Sam took a seat next to the Judge in the lobby, and Reilly explained his problem. "Sam, Charlie Redman tells me you carry a U.S. Marshal's badge now. Is that right?"

Sam nodded, and cleared his throat. "It's kind of an honorary thing, Judge. I did some special work for the government a year ago."

"Well, are you a Marshal or not? If you are, I want to talk to you about some court work I need help with."

"What kind of help?"

Reilly leaned forward in his chair. "I need someone who knows the area and the Reservation to bring in fugitives from the Court. Half of my cases have to be dismissed because the defendants jump bail or just don't show up. I wouldn't ask for help, Sam, if I didn't need it."

Sam's thoughts ran around in his head as he considered what Reilly had in mind. He owed the Judge a favor for some help he'd given him a few years ago, and he was itching to shake off his so-called retirement. "Well, since you put it that way, Judge, and since I know how persistent you can be, I'll be happy to help. I guess I owe you that."

"Damn right you do." Judge Reilly gave him a conspiratorial smile. "That was some big doings out at that mine a few years back, wasn't it? Stop over to my office next week, and I'll show you what the job entails. I'll take whatever help you can give me, Sam."

The Judge had just left when Joyce joined Sam in the lobby. "He seems like a nice man," She said. "Have you known him long?"

"Sure, the Judge and I go way back. His wife used to be an attorney in Albuquerque before she married him and moved out here. They've both helped me over the years."

Sam noticed the inquisitive look on her face, and he smiled. "He wants me to locate and bring in some people who don't show up for their court dates."

"Are you going to help him?"

"I guess so. Say, you didn't use to be an attorney before you started working as the librarian, did you?"

Joyce laughed, "No, silly, why do you ask that?"

"I don't know, it just seems I've been through easier cross examinations on the witness stand." He grinned to show her he was kidding. "Remind me not to try to hide anything from you."

"Consider yourself reminded." It was her turn to smile, and it gave Sam a glimpse of the young girl she used to be. The moment lasted longer than either of them planned.

As they walked to the car, two distinguished looking men watched from the porch of the hotel. David Castor lit his cigar and tossed the match away. "Rance, from what we overheard, the place the Indian described out by Chaco Canyon might be worth looking into as a possible base for us—you could even use it as a filming location."

CHAPTER 23

Principal Edgar Dallas, wasn't in his office. His secretary Mrs. Atkins told Sam he was at a conference out of town and wouldn't be back until later in the week. She set an appointment for him on Friday afternoon.

As he drove away, Sam wasn't sure what he could accomplish for the rest of the week. He went over the clues he'd gathered, but could think of anything further to do until he spoke with the Principal on Friday.

A few miles east of town, he realized there was one thing. He could attempt to find out what was behind the airplane noises in the forest southeast of McGaffey. It might end up a waste of time, but he had nothing else to do. Maybe a few days in the wilderness on a horse might help him make some sense of his odd collection of clues.

He decided to drive out to Bob and Vicki Johnson's ranch at McGaffey tomorrow morning and see if they heard any more aircraft noises south of their ranch.

He rose with the sun the next morning, ate a quick breakfast before hitching up his horse trailer, and loaded it with his gear and two horses. He brought enough supplies to spend a few days in the wilderness.

Leaving Blacksparrow with the sun rising over the top of Mt. Taylor, he drove south to the highway, headed west toward Gallup, and turned south at Ft. Wingate to take the winding road up to McGaffey. As he drove past the vacant buildings of the old army fort, most recently put to use as an Indian school, he remembered the stories the old people told about the place.

The Lightning Tree

They called it Fort Fauntleroy back in the 1800s, and the white men used it during what they called the "Indian Wars." It was a staging area for sending the Navajo and some Apache people on a grueling 400-mile trek to a holding area south and east of Albuquerque late in the Civil War. Four years later, when they let the survivors return to their homes, they renamed the fort. The surviving Navajo people spoke of their cruel ordeal as the "Long Walk."

It was close to 10:00 a.m. when he pulled into the yard at the Johnson place and tooted the horn. He felt the cool breeze when he stepped out of the cab, and he took a deep breath as he gazed across the fields and meadows, bordered by walls of swaying pine and aspen.

"Sam Begay?" Vicki Johnson stepped out from the screen door of their farmhouse with a big smile. "Come in and have a cup of coffee and some pie. My goodness, what brings you all the way out here today? Bob's in the barn; would you mind calling him to come in?"

"I'm on my way," Bob said, moving in his bowlegged walk toward the truck. "What brings you all the way out here, Sam?"

"I figured I'd stop by and see if your missus made a fresh pie, and was looking for someone to help you eat it."

Bob said, "She made one yesterday. I hope you like apple."

The three made small talk in the kitchen over pie and coffee, and Vicki said, "By the way, Sam, just what is that nephew of mine, Kip, been doing that keeps him too busy to pay us a visit. It's been months since I've seen him."

Sam chuckled. "Probably the same things any young man does when he's not tied down with a wife and kids."

Vicki made a face, and when she shook her head, her hair still looked more blonde than grey. "I swear that young man is as wild and daring as I was before I met Bob and let him talk me into getting married."

Bob rolled his eyes and spoke in his slow, Texas drawl. "As I recall, you did most of the talking, and I doubt Kip even comes close to matching some of your old, harebrained, barnstorming stunts."

"Oh, pooh," She said, and gave Sam an exaggerated, conspiratorial wink.

As Vicki refilled their coffee cups, Sam said, "Have you heard any more planes flying around the area?"

Bob said, "Sure did; we heard one...was it last Saturday, Vicki?"

"I believe so. It was just after dark, and we could hear it in the distance. It seemed to come from the southeast, maybe along the divide. There was something odd about it though."

Sam set his cup down, "Like what?"

"Well, we could hear it coming in, and then the sound stopped. About 15 minutes later, we heard the engine again. Vicki glanced at Bob. "It almost sounded like it landed for a short time and then took off."

Sam frowned. "Where would someone have an airstrip in that direction? It's all state forest and reservation, and most of it is rocky and wooded."

"No place that I can think of," Bob said, "except for maybe a road. There are a few trails back there, but I doubt anyone could land a plane on them."

"What about the Ramah road?" Vicki said.

Bob said, "Could be. There isn't much traffic, especially east of Ramah, and it's the only road straight or wide enough for a landing. The gravel is in good shape most of the time."

Sam said, "I think I'll ride out that way. Maybe I'll get a chance to see the plane and find out what's going on."

"Do you think it might be involved in something illegal?" Vicki's eyes were wide with interest.

"There's only one way to find out for sure." Sam pushed his chair back from the table. "I doubt I'll find anything, and the odds are there's nothing sinister going on. The only problem is; I remember a few years back when you folks tipped us off about that dirigible flying over your place at night. I'm sure Kip told you what became of that."

Vicki and Bob exchange a meaningful glance, and Sam said, "I have a handful of odd clues I've been following for the past few weeks, and none of them seems to connect. This mystery plane is one of them, and I hope to find something, or scratch it off my list."

"Do you mind if I leave my truck and trailer here? I'll take the horses southeast along the Divide toward the Malpais, and then circle back toward El Morro and Ramah before I come back. I may be gone a few days, so don't worry."

"Not a problem; you can park next to the barn if you like."

They went outside, and Bob helped Sam unload the horses and stow his gear. An hour later, Sam rode through tall pines along an old two-track.

The sounds and smells of the woods and meadows worked like an elixir, and made him forget the concerns filling his mind for several weeks.

Checking his map, he left the trail down a wooded slope to follow a narrow valley. Swaying aspens bordered the lush grass, with their silver-green leaves flashing in the breeze. The air was fragrant with the smell of rich soil, wildflowers, and pine.

The horses made their way along a small meandering stream, keeping to the low country, and Sam figured if he were looking for tracks, he'd find them near water. He rode southeasterly, knowing he would eventually reach the Ramah Road.

When the ground turned rockier, and the canyon walls closed in, he followed a dry spillway of smooth, flat boulders that carried the snowmelt in the Spring. He eventually reached the top of a ridge and breathed the cool air as he looked east to Mt. Taylor to get his bearings. The hazy blue shape on the horizon marked the southeastern boundary of the traditional, tribal lands. It was sacred to his people, and they called it Tsoodzil. It was the home of Turquoise Girl as well as other old spirits.

Late in the day, continuing his trek south, he crossed the rugged spine of the Zuni Mountains—part of the Continental Divide. From this point, he could see the ancient, eroded rocks of El Morro further south. He let the horses rest, and then rode off into the lengthening shadows.

He saw nothing out of the ordinary all day, and no evidence of vehicle traffic or open space where a plane could land. Making camp at dusk against the shelter of a twenty-foot ridge, he picketed the horses in some grass, and built a small fire to heat coffee and a pot of beans. He looked forward to the slice of apple pie Vicki insisted he take along with him.

After he ate, he spread his bedroll underneath the pines, and with his senses attuned to the night, he watched the fireflies flashing in the darkness. He slept, and the lisping wind spoke to him in riddles about small planes, and the cargos they might carry.

The sun lit the tops of the aspens across the meadow when Sam awoke. Shivering in the chilly air, he started a fire, and finished off the beans and the last of the coffee before he started south toward the stretch of sandstone rocks along the road that ran past El Morro. The warm sun felt good on his shoulders, and he enjoyed feeling part of the wilderness, alive with birds and other small creatures. He wondered why he spent so much time indoors, when he could be outside in a beautiful place like this.

He let the horses water in a small stream, and he decided that if a plane landed somewhere out here, it would have to be at a rough, private airstrip or on a straight road. He knew of no airstrips, and there was only one good road. He would search there for unusual tire tracks or some other evidence that a plane landed recently.

Last night's sleep and the crisp morning air sharpened his senses and brought him luck. His path led him to a rutted two-track that bore the recent marks of more than one vehicle. He followed the tracks south to the eroded ridges north of El Morro, and continued to the gravel road. He would come back this way to explore the tracks, but first he wanted to see if he could find evidence of a plane landing nearby.

The village of Ramah, and the El Morro Monument lay to the west, so he headed east away from the settlement. He traveled along the roadway for several miles before he found what he was looking for.

The tire tracks were not from an automobile or a wagon. There were two, widely spaced tracks with another in the center, and it brought to mind the three-wheeled configuration on Kip's airplane. When he found a place where the third track vanished, he knew the single, front wheel only touched the ground when the plane moved slow enough after landing, or when it took off again.

This was what he was looking for; clear evidence that a plane had landed in a remote stretch of the roadway. But why?

He turned back when the tracks vanished, and he found where several automobiles pulled off the road and turned around. Had they met the plane? If so, it may have been to load something, or to haul it away.

Sam followed the automobile tracks to the trail where he first came across them. It was late morning now, and he thought of his appointment with Edgar Dallas tomorrow afternoon. Make it or not; he would run down this mystery first.

He returned to the trail, and followed the tracks back into the wilderness. There appeared to be three vehicles, probably small trucks. Around noon, he found where they turned around and parked in a sheltered spot along a ridge and some trees.

After giving the horses some water, he started walking around the entire area, making note of everything he saw. This may have been a staging area of some kind—a place to store and sort cargo. He found evidence of multiple campfires, and places where several people bedded down. He also saw where crates rested in the dirt before someone moved them.

After he searched in an ever-widening circle, and made a crude map of the area, he returned to collect some of the empty liquor bottles to check for fingerprints. He almost tripped over some loose brush, and his senses tingled. Moving the material aside, he found someone had disturbed the soil.

He kicked away more sticks and leaves, and uncovered a patch of soft, dark soil about three feet wide, and five feet long. His heart beat faster as he imagined what might lie beneath the surface.

Marking the location on his map, he finished his search, and came back with his camp shovel. Fifteen minutes later, he uncovered the body of a Hispanic male.

Sam spent another night under the stars, and by noon the next day, he returned to Johnson farm in McGaffey with the tarp-wrapped body tied to his packhorse. He spoke briefly with Bob and Vicki, and after instructing them to tell no one about what he'd found, he loaded the horses in the trailer, and drove away with his grisly cargo in the bed of the truck.

He called Charlie Redman when he reached Gallup, and told him to meet him at Doc Beeman's office.

CHAPTER 24

"Hi doc." Sam said when the M.E. stepped into the waiting room. "I've got something outside that I want you to take a look at. He motioned for him to follow, and showed him the tarp-covered shape in the bed of his truck. "Charlie Redman should be here any minute. Where do you want us to put this?"

"If it's what I think it is, pull to the back of the building. I'll get a cart and meet you."

Charlie Redman drove up a few minutes later and joined the two men inside. As Doc Beeman examined the body, Sam gave his narrative of how, when, and where he'd found it. Charlie took notes.

After his preliminary look at the corpse, Doc said. "You two might as well leave so I can do a thorough exam. I'll call Charlie when I'm finished."

"Thanks Doc., Sam and I will go back to my office and make out a report."

Outside the building, Sam said, "Charlie, do you mind if I stop at my place outside of town to drop off the horses and get cleaned up first. I've been out in the boonies for two days, and I'm not fit company in an enclosed space."

"Go ahead, I'll pick up lunch and meet you at the office, say around two o'clock."

"That'll work. I have some other things I want to do later in the afternoon."

Sam showed up before 2:00 and gave Charlie a full report while they ate lunch.

"You say the tracks you found on the road east of El Morro were made by an aircraft? How could you tell?"

"I know they weren't made by any automobile, unless it's one that's pretty wide and rolls on three wheels. It can also lift the third wheel and balance on two before it jumps up and floats over the road."

Charlie frowned. "Okay, but you did find automobile tracks going into the boonies to a camp site where you say some boxes and crates were stored temporarily. What do you think was inside them?"

"I can only guess, Charlie, but we both know there's a limit to how much weight a small plane can carry. I think it's safe to say if the landing was made after dark, that far from a town, and someone took the cargo into the woods, it had to be something illegal."

"And pretty valuable," Charlie said.

Sam nodded his head. "It appeared to have been an ongoing operation from the look of the site in the woods."

"And if you think they abandoned it now, what do you make of it?"

Sam grinned at Charlie. "I think we discovered a drug trafficking operation, and I think whoever is running it will need to find a new place to land a plane and store the goods for distribution."

"It makes sense, but what can we do about it now?"

"We'll figure out something, Charlie, but first, let's wait for Doc to give us his autopsy report, and see what information it adds to the case. In the meantime, I have a meeting with the school principal."

"How does that tie in with the case?"

"It doesn't as far as I know, but you never tell when something will jump out at you."

Twenty minutes later, Sam's boots echoed in the hall on his way to the Principal's office. He tipped his hat to Mrs. Atkins. "Nice to see you again ma'am. Mr. Dallas should be expecting me."

"Yes he is, Mr. Begay. If you'll have a seat, I'll see if he's ready to see you."

The woman showed her skill again by deftly twisting around the other desks to the Principal's door. She knocked and stepped in for a moment, then came out with a smile and motioned for Sam to come back.

"Have a seat Mr. Begay." Dallas motioned to the chair in front of his desk, and then removed his glasses and rubbed his long nose. "It's been a busy afternoon. We don't hold regular classes this time of year, but we still have summer students to teach and staff training to do. I hope I haven't made you wait long."

"Not at all," Sam said as he removed his hat and sat down. Edgar Dallas replaced his glasses. He looked the same as the first time they met. He had the same deep voice, but the unforgiving look was gone. Now, a smile crinkled the corners of his eyes.

"What can I help you with today? I hope Miss Dobson was able to find the class photos you were looking for."

Sam flicked a speck of dirt from his hat and raised his eyes. "Your people have been very helpful, and I hope I can impose just one more time by asking you for your recollections of a couple of matters."

"I'll do my best," Dallas said. His eyes big and innocent as he waited for Sam to speak.

"As I understand it, you have been the school Principal for several years."

"Yes, this is my eighteenth year."

"And you were a teacher before that?"

"Yes, I taught math and English."

"I understand you did some coaching, too."

"Yes I did. We only had a baseball team, but the boys were quite good. They were all close, being from such a small community. Is there something specific you would like to know?"

"Yes, as a matter of fact. I was the officer who discovered Harold Borden's body three weeks ago. In my investigation, I found that he was one of the ball players in his junior year, but not the senior year. Do you recall why that was?"

"I heard about the death, and I do remember a boy by that name. I don't recall him being an especially gifted player. Perhaps he quit after he realized he wasn't suited for the sport."

"Perhaps," Sam said. "You don't remember any specific incident or circumstances that may have caused him to drop out?"

Dallas' forehead crinkled. "Not that I can recall. It was twenty years ago, and I've seen hundreds of students since then."

"I see. By any chance, do you recall another student from back then; a Navajo girl named Stacey Toledo? She appeared in the junior class photo, but not the senior one."

Dallas shook his head and spoke after a brief silence. "I'm sorry, Mr. Begay, but you can't expect me to remember every student who has entered these doors."

Sam watched Dallas' face, and then smiled. "No, I guess not. She was the only junior student who didn't attend classes the senior year, and with Borden the only one missing from the ball team that year, I was hoping there might have been some connection that you were aware of."

After an awkward silence, Sam stood up and placed his Stetson on his head. "Thank you for your time, Mr. Dallas. You're right; it was a long time ago."

"I'm sorry I couldn't be of more help. If I think of something that might pertain to the two students, I'll be sure to get in touch with you."

Sam walked out the building certain of one thing; Edgar Dallas was hiding something.

CHAPTER 25

"There you are." Charlie sat back in his chair, as Sam walked into the FBI office Monday morning. "Doc Beeman just called and said he had the autopsy report ready for us.

How soon can we see him?"

"Right now. He said to get ahold of you and come over as soon as we can."

They drove to the clinic, and when they stepped into the lobby, a receptionist ushered them into the doctor's office to wait. As they sat, Charlie said to Sam, "Doc told me he had some interesting information for us."

The two made small talk until the M.E. walked in. Charlie said, "Hi Doc," and Sam nodded.

"First," Beeman said as he sat down, "I suppose you two want to know who the victim was. You're in luck." He reached into the top drawer of his desk. "I was able to get the City Police to help identify him. Here's a couple of recent photos for your records."

Sam and Charlie looked at the face of a tough-looking, young, Hispanic male.

"His name is Hector Nunez. The officer told me the man has been in and out of jail for a variety of offences; drunken disorderly, retail theft, breaking and entering, but nothing more serious than that. No known address, but they gave me the names of some people he's been seen with from time to time. I'll get to that in a minute."

He picked up a manila envelope, and dumped out two more photos and a smaller envelope.

"What's this?" Sam said.

"It's a couple of photos from the autopsy, and some notes I took. Also anything I found on the body except for his clothes. You'll notice the facial bruises, and a deep knife wound in the neck that killed him. It was a chopping blow, like from a big butcher knife or a machete—my guess would be the machete."

Sam passed the two photos to Charlie while Beeman handed him the small envelope, and said, "Take a look inside."

Sam thumbed it open and shook the contents into his hand. A few crumbled pieces of leafy material fell out. He sniffed it, passed the envelope to Charlie, and looked at Beeman. "Marijuana?"

"Yes, I found it inside the cuffs of his jeans. Does it mean anything to you?"

"Not much. Anyone wandering in the woods could pick up something like this. It grows almost anywhere."

"Yeah, that's what I thought, but I figured I'd save it for you. Other than that, the clothes and the body are clean of any other foreign material, except for the dirt from his grave."

"No wallet or jewelry?" Charlie said.

"Nope." Beeman put his hands behind his head and sat back with a smug look.

Sam watched him for a moment, and said, "Charlie, I think Doc is playing with us. He's probably getting back at us for taking up so much of his time lately, even though you did buy him donuts the other day."

The Doc sat forward in his chair. "Boys, forget the donuts, this one's going to cost you a steak. I did a toxicology study and found something in his system that might interest you." He picked up a sheet of paper and tossed it front of them. "Amphetamines; probably inhaled in the form of Benzedrine. Of course, it's legal over the counter."

Charlie picked up the paper and read it, and Doc Beeman said, "It's legal, but very big on the black market, too. Seems truck drivers and athletes have found a good use for it. I hear college kids use it to help cram for their exams. That's it gents. Try to stay out of trouble so I can get my other work done."

When they stood to leave, Sam said, "Wait a minute. You mentioned they gave you the names of the man's known acquaintances."

"Yes, three men. I wrote their names on the back of this envelope. The first two are Robert Silva, and Jerry Torrez, but they won't help you."

"Why's that," Charlie said as Beeman handed him the envelope.

"They both died in a house fire a year ago."

Sam said, "What about the third one?"

Charlie looked at the writing on the envelope. "Louis Montoya."

Beeman noticed Sam's reaction to hearing the name. "Is he alive?"

Turning, Sam said, "Who knows, Doc?"

Outside in the parking lot, Charlie stopped Sam. "You seemed surprised by the name of the last guy. Why?"

"Charlie, what if I told you that every boy on the old school ball team is dead, except for two of them, and one is Louis Montoya."

"Probably a coincidence." When Sam didn't respond, Charlie said, "Who's the other player?"

"Bobby Castor."

Charlie blinked with surprise. "Do you plan on staying around town today?"

"Yes, I have an appointment with Judge Reilly after lunch. He has some bench warrants for fugitives he wants me to round up for the court."

"Sounds like loads of fun. I've got some work to finish before I head out to Kayenta today. Maybe we can catch up later in the week. Are you staying at your house east of town now?"

"Part of the time. If you want to reach me, you might have to try both places."

Sam met Judge Reilly at his office after lunch. An efficient-looking secretary ushered him into his wood-paneled office in the back, and shut the door when she left, effectively silencing the noise of the clattering typewriter in the front.

The rich smell of polished wood came to him, and in a moment, the judge walked in from a library/conference room off to the side and shook his hand.

"I hope you're ready to go to work, Sam," he said in his raspy voice. "I have a mountain of files to sort through, but I pulled the one I want you to start with."

The judge waved him to a chair. "Have a seat. By the way, that friend of yours in Washington called and told me I was free to use as much of your time as you're willing to give me, but he said I'll have to let you go if he needs you. I told him he wasn't talking to some junior court appointee, but you can probably imagine what he said to that."

Sam winced. "I don't even want to guess, Judge."

"Never mind then. I know an old Washington insider when I hear one, and I'm not going to ask how you got hooked up with him. I'll put aside my Irish temper, and use as much of your time as you can give me; no questions asked."

Sam said, "He does have a knack of getting his way."

"Yes, and so does my wife, and I know better than to pick a fight with either one of them."

Reilly grabbed a folder from the top of the stack and tossed it in front of Sam. "Ever hear of a Mex guy around the area named Louis Montoya?"

Sam opened the file without saying a word, or betraying his surprise. He flipped through the contents, and was stunned when he saw the booking photo in the file. Now he knew what Montoya looked like, instead of having to guess from his teen-age picture in the old class photo. "The name rings a bell, Judge."

A short while later, stunned by the coincidence, he drove away. He'd seen the man last month in the doorway of Eric's Aunt's house by Continental Divide.

He remembered dropping the boy off, and not liking what he'd seen happen at the house. He'd been willing to think that everyone had a bad day now and then, but now, considering the information in the judge's file, he was very concerned about the safety of the woman and the boy. He'd been waiting for a convenient time to drive back and see how Eric was getting along, but now, it was a priority.

When he got into his truck, he felt under the seat for his revolver, and checked the loaded cylinders before he drove east toward Continental Divide. He would explain his visit as a courtesy call to see how Eric was getting along, but he doubted he would be welcomed if Montoya was around. Sam banged his fist on the steering wheel, and blamed himself for letting so much time go by.

Driving fast, he eventually turned off the highway onto the network of two-tracks that wove south into the hills along the divide. The old truck creaked and rattled over the uneven trail, and sweat dripped from Sam's forehead and cheeks in the hot cab. He felt his stomach knotting up as he drove closer to the house.

When he topped a rise, he saw the rough shack in the distance. There were no vehicles in the yard, and he might have to wait for the man to return. He would talk to the boy and his aunt first, and get some idea how they were getting along, then he'd ask when she expected Louis to come home.

He stopped in the yard, and stuffed his pistol under the seat while he waited for someone to come out. After five minutes, he got out of the truck and walked up to the door. There was no answer to his knock. He took a quick look along the low trees surrounding the house, and walked around behind the building.

As he passed two water barrels, he rapped a knuckle on the metal sides—almost empty. A small pile of split wood lay near the back wall, and he saw a garbage pile twenty feet from the house. His gut knotted up as he walked over to investigate the stench that came from the spot.

Chasing off a few scurrying rodents, he found broken glass, scattered cans, and spoiled scraps of food, all covered with a mat of flies. Turning to walk back to the building, he noticed a dust cloud from an approaching vehicle.

Just as he rounded the corner of the house, a dusty truck skidded to a stop behind his vehicle, and Louis Montoya jumped out with a rifle in his hand. Sam felt naked without his pistol. He held his hands open in front of him as Montoya walked up.

"What the hell are you snooping around here for? I told you to stay away. I should have taught you a lesson when I first laid eyes on you."

"No need to get upset, I just came to see the boy. I have some of his things in my truck."

Montoya backed up, keeping his rifle on Sam. He glanced into the cab of the truck and saw a bundle of clothing on the floor. Sam hoped he wouldn't look closer to see that the jeans and shirt were too large for Eric.

The man lowered his rifle and walked toward Sam. "I don't care what your reason is for coming here, when I tell you to stay away, I mean it."

Sam was ready for what came next. Montoya swung the rifle butt at his head, and Sam ducked, taking the glancing blow on his shoulder. His hat fell off, and before Montoya could swing the weapon again, Sam threw a handful of dirt at his face and tackled him. Montoya kicked like a wild man, and tried to get to his feet as Sam yanked the rifle out of his hands and threw it thirty feet away.

Montoya was quick, and ran for his truck. He jumped in and cranked the engine over before Sam could reach the door handle. By then the truck was moving and throwing dirt from the rear tires as it backed away. Sam grabbed for the man's shirt through the open window, and Montoya clipped him with his fist. Sam fell, and heard the truck brake and shift gears.

He knew Montoya wasn't finished with him. As the truck accelerated and bore down on him, he caught a glimpse of the wild face behind the wheel. Sam ran to his own truck, and leapt into the back to avoid the collision that crumpled part of the back bumper and fender of his old Ford. Montoya's truck kept going, towing a cloud of dust as it sped off.

Full of adrenalin, Sam jumped into the cab and started after him. It was easy following the dust cloud across the rough terrain. As he gave it gas, he hoped he wouldn't damage the worn suspension. He chased the other vehicle for over a mile before he lost sight of it around a bend, and as he slid around the corner, he saw the truck coming straight at him.

He glanced at the wall of rock on his left and at the last minute, swung the wheel to the right, and flew off the roadway into a dry wash as the other truck sped past. Sam tried to keep his momentum and make it back to the trail, but the rear tires sank in the soft sand and bogged down.

Two hours later, after changing a front tire with a blown sidewall, and digging himself out of the wash, he drove back to the shack to hunt for Montoya's rifle, but the man must have come back to retrieve it before he drove off.

An odd thought crossed his mind as he nursed his damaged vehicle back to the highway; Louis Montoya ran him off the road almost like the wolf hair killer might have done to his victims. Could Montoya be the killer? What was his connection to the other deaths? One thing was obvious; they were all high school teammates.

CHAPTER 26

After a short distance on the highway, Sam knew his truck had sustained more damage than the bumper and fender. The front end shimmied so badly at 30 miles an hour, he had to drive on the side of the road most of the way back to Gallup.

He thought he'd stop to see Benny Ortiz, an old acquaintance who owned an auto repair and blacksmith shop on the north side of town. The man had done some work for him in the past, and it looked like he needed his help again. Perhaps Benny could even beef up the frame and suspension to handle rougher, off-road use.

Sam made it into town and across the tracks to the north side. A few blocks past Mahoney, he turned left, then right, and parked in front of a cement block garage. A handful of old and damaged vehicles sat off to one side in front of a row of Russian olive bushes that kept a sagging picket fence from falling to the ground. As he walked up to the building, he heard the sound of hammering inside.

"Hey Benny," he called out when he noticed a stocky shape in front of a workbench at the back.

Benny turned, put his tools down, and said in a loud voice, "Well if it ain't some big Injun come all the way from the Res to see me. Hell, he looks like Sam Begay."

"Anybody ever tell you that you talk too much, Benny?" Sam grinned at his old friend. "It looks like you're still hammering on that same old piece of iron you were the last time I saw you."

The Lightning Tree

Wiping his hands on a grease rag, the barrel chested mechanic wiped a forearm across his brow. "Could be, but at least it's softer'n your head is, and it stays put when I take a swing at it. How have you been, Sam? Stayin' out of trouble?"

"Trying to," Sam said, "but it seems to know where to find me. You?"

"Just working hard, and getting fatter. My two boys have their own families now, and my Carmela, she never learned how to make smaller meals after they moved out. I don't have the heart to disappoint her, so I eat everything she puts in front of me. Benny smiled, I haven't seen you around since we welded all that iron on those pickups you and your friends brought in a couple of years ago. What's new?"

"It's a long story, Benny, but I want to ask if you still do some special work on vehicles?"

"Sure do. My boys have their own scrap business west of town, but I like to work on automobiles. What kind of a job do you have in mind?"

"My old Ford truck has seen some better days, especially since someone sideswiped me and ran me off the road today. I need to have someone fix a fender and the rear bumper, and take a look at the suspension."

"Does it still run O.K.?"

"Engine's not too bad, but it's a bit underpowered for what I'd like to do with it. The real problem is a bad shimmy since the accident."

Benny scratched the dark stubble on his cheeks. "Well, let's take a look at it, and then we can come back and talk."

The stocky man looked at the damage to the rear fender and bumper, and crawled under the truck. When the two walked back inside the garage, Sam said, "I don't care too much what it looks like, but I'd like to beef it up so it runs like a buffalo."

Benny chuckled, "Heck, I'll bolt a pair of horns on the hood if that's what you want, but it sounds like the other stuff might add some weight. I could stiffen the frame and put in some bigger springs. I might even locate a bigger engine I could swap out without too much trouble. I suppose you want it all done in a day or two."

"Could you?"

"Sure, if you don't mind driving a piece of crap that shivers like a dog when you take it out on the road. I'm a mechanic, Sam, not a miracle worker. If you want something that'll run like a buffalo and be reliable, I'll need at least a week."

"What do you think it'll cost me?"

"Depends on what I have to do, and if you're talking cash or trade."

"Since you put it that way, it just so happens I have some other vehicles back at my place north of Thoreau."

"What kind of shape are they in?"

"Some better than others. I have a back-up car, but there are four other sedans and trucks that need work to get them running and fit for the road."

"Hmm. I'll have to take a look at them. Do you have a ride home if you leave the truck?"

"No, but I guess I..."

"Don't worry about it; I can give you a ride home. We'll take my flat-bed trailer, and if we can come to terms, I'll take the old junkers back with me. We can go now if you want."

"Sure." Sam said.

Benny yelled out the back door of the shop. "Sonny? Come on in boy, I want you to meet a friend of mine." Benny turned to Sam. "I got me a young Navajo who's been helping me around the shop. I'll tell him where we're going, and he can watch things until I get back."

"Here he is. Sonny, this is Sam Begay. He wants me to do some special work on his truck out front."

The muscular young man nodded to Sam, and Sam nodded back. Sonny averted his eyes in the polite way of the Navajo, and Sam thought he saw some mixed blood. "Nice to meet you."

"Sonny, I'm going to take the flatbed out to Sam's place to look at some old vehicles. How far a drive is it, Sam?"

"It's out past Crownpoint, a few miles north on the Chaco Road. It'll probably take us an hour to get there."

"Okay Sonny, just lock the place up if I'm not back by closing time. I'll probably be bringing back a couple of cars."

Sonny nodded and went back to his work.

As they drove off, Benny said, "Is it the same place you and all them Indian boys were taking those trucks we welded that iron on a few years ago?"

"Yep, and the trucks sure did the job for us. It all turned out to be a hushed-up operation after some government authorities got involved, and I'm not supposed to talk about it."

Benny looked at Sam and sniffed. "With you involved, I don't doubt it was hush-hush." He chuckled. "You always did like to do things your own way."

They turned on to 66 and headed east out of town. An hour later, they drove through the Blacksparrow gate. Sam pointed to a row of vehicles parked next to one of the buildings. "The Chevy on the end is the one I still use; the others are yours if you want 'em."

A half-hour later, with a car and a pickup chained down on Bennie's trailer, he said to Sam, "I'll take the scrap vehicles in payment for the work on your truck. I'll pick the other two up when your truck is finished to your satisfaction."

Sam considered it a good trade, and it got rid of some of the clutter around the place.

That evening, as he finished supper at Blacksparrow, he found himself worrying about Eric Nez and his Aunt. What happened to them? The old house looked like it had been empty for a while. Were they in trouble, or just visiting somewhere? There was no doubt, now, that Louis Montoya could have injured the woman or the boy in a drunken rage. He had first-hand evidence of the man's violent temper. His growing concern nagged at him, and he had trouble sleeping that night.

His last thought before he drifted off, was that he had to take Louis Montoya into custody, and find out if the woman and boy were safe. The fact that Montoya was one of the old students in the class photos meant he might be a future victim in the wolf hair killings; he could even harbor a clue to the killer's motivation, or worse yet, it could mean something else.

CHAPTER 27

Sam phoned Charlie the next morning to see if he could meet him for lunch at the El Rancho.

"The El Rancho? That depends, are you buying or am I?"

"You are," Sam said. "I had something happen yesterday that I think you should know about. The good news is all it will cost you is lunch."

"Gee, how can I turn down a deal like that."

"You can't, so meet me at the El Rancho a quarter to noon and bring your money."

Charlie set the phone down and said, "Damn." Sam knew he couldn't pass up some juicy news, and if Sam wanted him to pay for it, it must be good.

When Sam walked inside the El Rancho Hotel, he saw Charlie waiting in one of the wood and leather chairs in the lobby. He walked up and said, "Hi Charlie, anything going on today?"

Charlie, looked up from a magazine and acted surprised to see him. "No, I just figured I'd come here and buy lunch for the first Navajo that walked up to me. It seems to be you, so you're in luck."

"Forget it," Sam said, "I'm buying. I have a hunch or two that I want your feedback on.

"You're buying me lunch just to hear what I think? What's going on, Sam, aren't you feeling well?"

"Charlie, if it'll make you feel better, I'll let you buy."

The Lightning Tree

"No, that's alright. If I have to listen to you, you might as well be the one paying for it."

The waitress seated the men at a booth near one end of the dining room. Charlie and Sam ordered chili and tortillas with ice tea. When the waitress left, Charlie said, "Okay, Sam, what have you got for me?"

Sam leaned across the table. "Charlie, this is the first time I've worked on a case with too many clues."

"Too many clues?" Charlie leaned forward, and his expression appeared doubtful. "More clues should make it easier to solve a case."

"Most of the time I might agree, but this time I have too many to make a clear picture. I can't even put them in any kind of order that makes sense. You know how I visualize each clue as a playing card, and then I shuffle them around to see what matches or fits into some kind of sequence, like a poker hand."

"Yeah, so what's the problem, besides you drawing a bad hand?"

"It's not that. I have more clues than I know what to do with."

"Maybe you're looking at multiple crimes. Maybe you need to set some of the clues aside and focus on one case."

The waitress arrived with their ice tea. Sam took a sip and looked around the restaurant while he thought about what Charlie said. He noticed David Castor and his friend, Rance Wilder across the room. David had his face turned away, but he could see the tan, chiseled face of Wilder, intent on something David was saying.

Charlie set his tea down and sat back. "What kind of clues are you having problems with?"

Sam leaned forward and said, "O.K. Here are the ones I have on the Borden case. One, we find his body in the middle of the Reservation, apparently killed in a fall. Two, a Spanish gold coin found with the body—simple so far, except that the man's uncle, whom he lived with in town, is found dead in his house, apparently killed around the same time."

He sat back as the waitress brought their chili and refilled their ice tea.

They both took a few tastes of the hot chili, and Sam set his spoon down and reached for a tortilla. "As I was saying, that's three clues, and it's still relatively simple, except a trader, Bobby Castor, recognized the coin when I showed it to him, and he lied about ever seeing it before. That's clue number four, and he also appeared shocked and surprised to see it."

Charlie said, "That doesn't mean that Castor could be connected to the deaths."

"Perhaps not, but I'm not through yet. "While I was looking for anyone who might have known Borden, I found out that he went to school in town, and he was in the same class as Bobby Castor, along with *each of the men killed* in your wolf hair cases or other suspicious accidents. Then I find that these same men also made up the entire high school baseball team."

"What are you saying, Sam? Do you think the gold coin is connected to the wolf hair killings, or are you saying that someone is killing off the old ball team players?"

"See what I mean, Charlie? Then, I drop off an orphan Indian boy at his aunt's place out by Continental Divide, and I find the man living with her is Louis Montoya."

"Isn't he the guy Doc Beeman mentioned?"

"Yes, and he is one of two surviving members of the ball team. I drove out to see how the kid was doing yesterday, and I found the house vacant. When I went to leave, Louis Montoya drove into the yard and braced me with a rifle. We scuffled, and he drove off. When I chased after him in my truck, he ran me off the road and got away."

Charlie said nothing, and Sam continued. "When I heard about some unusual airplane traffic over the wilderness southeast of McGaffey a while ago, I decided to investigate the area on horseback, I found tire tracks from a plane landing on the gravel road near El Morro. There were vehicle tracks too, so I followed them to a camp in the woods that looked like a transfer site, maybe for something illegal. That's where I found the recently buried body, and the M.E. told us that the police say the dead man is a local crook who was known to hang out with Louis Montoya. Charlie, every time I add another clue, I get a different hand."

Charlie put his spoon down, and slouched back in his seat again. "It sounds to me like you need to talk to Louis Montoya."

"That brings me to the Joker in the deck, Charlie. Judge Reilly just hired me to bring in some fugitives from old bench warrants. Guess who the first one he wants me to find is?"

Charlie shrugged his shoulders, and Sam leaned forward and said. "Louis Montoya."

Charlie said, "It sure is an unusual number of coincidences."

"Yeah, but other than the old bench warrant, and maybe an assault charge, what have I got on Montoya? And, who killed Borden and his uncle? Doc Beeman said there was a good chance that Borden died around the same time his uncle did, and they were found fifty miles apart as the crow flies—over rough canyon country."

"Maybe they were both killed to get at the gold coin," Charlie said, "or maybe there's more of them."

"Then how does Bobby Castor fit in? Montoya is a thug, but Castor is a local business owner with a father in state politics."

Charlie said, "Yeah, they would make strange bedfellows. But let's say Bobby Castor is crooked, and he's connected to the mystery airplane and the cargo."

Sam thought for a moment. "How does that connect to the school ball team, or the wolf hair killings, and what does that say about his dad?"

Charlie shrugged. "What if your clues are nothing but a bunch of odd coincidences?"

Sam picked up his glass of ice tea and finished it. "Charlie, you know how I hate coincidences."

They made small talk while the server took their dishes, and as they waited for their ticket, Sam didn't notice Castor and Wilder get up from their table and walk over to his.

"Excuse me, gentlemen, My name is Rance Wilder. My friend, Mr. Castor here, suggested that I introduce myself." He glanced at Charlie and back at Sam. "Mr. Begay, my movie studio has been looking for a suitable location to use as a field base for some filming. My friend mentioned overhearing that you own some land near Chaco Canyon, and he thinks it may be what I'm looking for. I'd like to talk to you about it, and possibly make some financial arrangements for the use of the property."

Sam couldn't help his jaw dropping in surprise at Wilder's words. Agonizing over the past several months about what to do with Blacksparrow, a possible solution found him.

"Mr. Begay, if you would be interested in discussing the subject, I could meet you later this afternoon—that is, if it would be convenient for you. I have a suite upstairs where we could talk—say, around 3:30?"

Sam cleared his throat. "It just so happens, Mr. Wilder, I might be interested in hearing your proposal. The time would be fine."

"Good, I'll look forward to seeing you. Just ask the front desk to ring me when you arrive."

Wilder and Castor walked off, and Sam and Charlie finished the last of their ice tea and got up to leave. The waitress returned, and Charlie went to pay the tab, but she told him Mr. Wilder had already paid for their meal along with a nice tip.

Charlie put his hat on and said, "How do you do it Sam?" You talk me into buying you lunch, and then you say you'll buy instead, and after that, you end up getting someone else you've never even met before to pay for it. No, don't say it—it's a gift, right?"

They drove back to Charlie's office, and sat across his desk while Charlie leafed through the mail he'd picked up on the way back. He tossed it in a drawer and said, "What do you think, Sam? You've been saying you didn't know what to do with that place for some time. You've got your house fixed up east of town now, so why not sell the old mine, or maybe lease it?"

Sam made a face. "It depends on what he plans to do out there, and how long he wants to use it. Some extra money wouldn't hurt, but I'll have to find out what he's willing to pay, first."

When Sam left the office, he set aside his thoughts about his meeting with Wilder later in the afternoon. He didn't tell Charlie about the mystery that weighed heaviest on his mind; what happened to Eric and his aunt?

CHAPTER 28

Sam walked into the lobby of the El Rancho hotel at 3:30 for his meeting, and he asked the desk clerk to call Mr. Wilder's room to let him know he had arrived.

The clerk made a call to the room, and when he hung up the phone, he smiled and said, "Mr. Wilder says to come right up. Turn left at the top of the stairs—suite 205."

Wilder met Sam at the door and invited him in. "Thank-you for coming Mr. Begay. May I call you Sam? And please, call me Rance."

Looking around the well-furnished room, Sam had never imagined such a spacious suite like this in Gallup. The furniture was of sturdy, hand carved wood, stained dark, and upholstered in leather like the Spanish style. The curtains were heavy with colorful designs, as were the bed covers in the adjoining room. Original southwestern paintings and Navajo rugs hung on the walls.

"Would you like something to drink? I had a pitcher of ice tea brought up a few minutes ago." Sam nodded, and the distinguished-looking man poured a glass for each of them. He beckoned Sam to sit on the couch while he chose a nearby chair.

After they both took a drink from their glasses, Wilder said, "I hope you don't mind if I get right to business, Mr. Begay. I'm sure you'll have some questions, but first let me explain what I'm looking for. My studio and some others, wish to capitalize on the current popularity of western movies. I'm not the first to discover the ideal landscape and weather in this part of the country." Wilder paused, and gave Sam a camera-practiced smile.

"A few of us put our resources together, and we built this hotel to cater to the actors and support people we bring in to make movies. Our work requires a large cast and crew, as well as truckloads of equipment. Once we start a project, we have to keep everything moving to meet deadlines and stay within our budgets."

Wilder set his glass down, "I don't mean to bore you with all of this information, but the point is; if I have a site where my people can set up and store equipment near the filming locations, I can save time and money. If your property fits our needs, I would consider leasing it for an attractive sum of money. Now tell me about this Blacksparrow place of yours."

Sam blinked and said, "Well there's nothing around for miles in all directions except for desert, canyons, tall buttes, and mesas. The Chaco Canyon ruins are located ten miles to the north." He went on to describe the buildings, airstrip, and the rail spur, as well as the general layout of the compound within the walls of the encircling mesa.

When Sam finished, Wilder said, "Do you have another place to stay while we do our filming?"

"Oh yes, I have a small house just outside of town here."

The man studied Sam for a moment. "Mr. Begay, I must say that I am eager to see this place you've described. I'd like to bring a few of my men with me to take a look at it. Would tomorrow morning be possible?"

Having agreed on the time to meet, Sam provided directions before he left the hotel and drove east out of town.

He stopped at his house to pick up a few things, and continued east toward Continental Divide. The knot of worry about the safety of Eric and his aunt had been building inside him all day. It looked like rain clouds forming when he turned south down a primitive road and followed the rough trail toward the woman's house. He hoped she and Eric had returned by now, and his eyes narrowed, hoping he would also find Louis Montoya. The man was the common link to nearly all of his clue cards, and he wanted very badly to speak with him.

His pistol lay on the seat next to him, and after a dusty, jarring ride, he saw the lone building ahead. He stopped to scan the desert around the place. Seeing no other vehicle, he drove up to the house. The pistol now rested in his belt behind his hip as he stepped from the car. "Hello the house. Is anybody home?"

Sam waited five minutes before he approached the front door. He kept looking around, but saw nothing moving. When he knocked, he didn't expect anyone to answer. The latch worked under his hand, and he nudged the door open. Peering into the dark room, he saw the place was vacant and in considerable disarray.

He closed the door and took a look around the outside of the house and yard. He found no recent tracks, or anything else to indicate where the boy and woman had gone. When he returned to the front door, he glanced at the surrounding hills before entering.

Clothes and blankets lie strewn about, chairs broken and upended. He found several empty whiskey bottles and dishes broken on the floor. "Anybody here?" He listened for an answer, but only heard the whistle of the wind outside.

He left the house and stood in the yard again, looking around for anything that appeared out of place. All he saw was trash, blowing sand, and a few small birds flitting through the brush. He took a deep breath, and walked to his car and drove away.

The next morning, a dusty Cadillac drove through the gates at Blacksparrow and honked the horn. Sam walked out to the porch of the dining hall and waived as the vehicle pulled up. He watched four men step out, and Rance Wilder introduced the three as Jim Taylor, one of his directors, Bill Paxton, a set builder, and Jerry Jones, in charge of logistics.

Rance said, "The scope and character of everything around this site exceeds my expectations, Sam. Can you take us on a walking tour of the place?"

"Sure, we can start here in the dining hall."

An hour later, after circling the compound, and walking through every building, all the while asking questions, they returned to the hall. Rance said, "Sam, would you mind if my associates and I talked among ourselves for a few moments?"

The men walked to the car and huddled while Sam went inside the building. He felt a shiver of apprehension at the thought of strangers taking over, but he also felt a sense of relief that his long-pondered problem of what to do with the place may have found a solution—if only a temporary one.

After ten minutes, Rance Wilder came inside the hall and sat down with Sam. "The boys tell me that this place will work for our purposes, providing we can make some modifications to some of the buildings, and set up a few sound stages inside the hangars. We don't wish to damage anything, but we do have to make the space work for our specific needs."

"I understand," Sam said. "Most of the structures are old and unused anyway. You could even tear down a few for that matter. I do want to keep the main house and dining hall intact, and of course, the big space inside the cliff wall where I store the equipment I own. You can use it for storage, too if you need it."

Wilder's smile lit up his face, and he nodded. "Of course, Sam, I'll want to keep the house and dining hall for our use too. That also goes for the smaller barracks next to it. We'll use one of the hangers for the aircraft we'll have coming in from time to time." He rolled his eyes. "These wealthy movie stars."

We may be able to use the rail spur at the far side to move some of our larger equipment, and, of course, we'll have several vehicles coming and going with our people, equipment, and supplies."

"Most of the crew and actors will be bussed back and forth to Gallup every day, but we'll keep a security crew on site at all times. I think we can find a good balance in protecting your property, Sam, and still modify things to suit our special needs."

Wilder looked at his manicured hands for a brief moment. "Sam, I'll have an agreement put in writing for your review and approval, but I think it's time we discussed the financial side of this arrangement. I'll tell you right now, my boys like what they see, and I don't mind paying a fair price to lease your property."

Sam cleared his throat. "How much do you think is reasonable?"

"I'm prepared to offer you $200.00 a month, providing we can sign a year's lease. With that, I'll want your assurances you won't spread any gossip around that would bring curious locals and tourists flocking to this place and disturbing our work. You're welcome, of course, to come and go within reason; after all it is your property, however, I would appreciate prior notification so we can accommodate you without disturbing our schedule."

Sam nodded his understanding, and Rance said. "I don't expect your answer right now, but I'd like to hear from you before the end of the week. If we can come to an agreement, I'll have my people prepare the lease for your review and signature. When that's done, I'll hand over a check for the first three months."

The Lightning Tree

Late that afternoon, Rance Wilder sat with David Castor in his house outside of Ramah. "Do you think the Indian will go for your offer?" Castor inspected his fat cigar, and blew a cloud of smoke toward the ceiling.

Wilder sipped wine from a large goblet. "Of course he will. It's probably more money than he's seen at one time before. He'll congratulate himself on how shrewd he was to negotiate for that much."

"You don't think you offered *too* much, do you? It might get him thinking, and wondering what's so valuable about the place. He's known as a pretty savvy cop."

"Don't worry. If he should become uncooperative, or a nuisance, my boys are very creative in staging accidents. Relax; I'm a rich studio executive, and a Hollywood movie star. I swim in money, and throw it around like water. I wouldn't be surprised if he tries to gouge more from me, either now or as time goes by, but it won't matter; you and I will be up to our necks in money."

Castor said, "Not to change the subject, but I've been hearing rumors about some legislation pending in Washington that would pertain to some of our activity. I hear the Feds are trying to enact a new law that would place a token tax on marihuana."

Rance said, "So, we can afford it."

"Yes, of course we can, but as soon as we or anyone else hands over payment, the Feds will come in and slip the cuffs on us."

"It figures. So, we stiff 'em on the tax. Who's going to know?"

Castor set his cigar down and said, "Try telling that to Al Capone. Don't forget how they got him on tax evasion."

"I see your point—and they call *us* crooks."

CHAPTER 29

Sam had a lot to think about after Rance Wilder and his associates drove away. He looked across the compound and tried to imagine what things would look like with some of the buildings gone. Did he really want to let a crew come in and make changes?

He decided to sleep on it. The lease money was a significant amount, and he'd be a fool not to take it. He made a list of what he would have to take care of before he turned the place over. He'd have to move all his personal things, groceries, horses, saddles, and tack. Would the movie crew want to rent the animals? No, he'd rather board them until he could build a corral at his place near Gallup. He could pay for it with some of the lease money.

When he drove from the compound the next morning, he realized he hadn't seen Old Jake in a while, and he knew how ornery the old coot could get when he thought he was being ignored. He'd have tell him about leasing Blacksparrow, and knowing how Jake liked to spread gossip, he'd have to play it down and swear him to silence, or have every curious tourist and local driving out to see how a movie is made.

The parking lot at the Trading Post was empty, and the bell sounded lonely as it jingled over the screen door when he walked in. As his eyes adjusted to the dim interior, he saw Jake leaning over the counter, reading something.

Sam's boots rapped on the wooden floor as he approached, but Jake still hadn't looked up. The old man finally mumbled something from the side of his mouth. "Hmmph, I thought you forgot all about your country friends now that you've decided to become a city Indian."

Sam pushed his Stetson back and sighed. "I wouldn't call Gallup a city, Jake, but I'll admit it doesn't have that country smell of horses and sheep, and some old fart leaning on a counter like it does here. What are you reading?"

"Jake was unimpressed. It's a Life magazine, if you must know. I like to keep up on current events." He looked at the date on the cover. Well, maybe not so current. It says here that they pretty much gave up on finding Amelia Earhart in the Pacific. They called in most of the ships and planes with nothing to show from the search. There's some other stuff about the Olympics last year. It says it was a historical moment for the country, and a poke in Hitler's eye for Jesse Owens to win four gold medals. Funny thing, the article says President Roosevelt didn't invite the boy to the White House to shake his hand, or even send him a telegram to congratulate him. Can you imagine that?"

Jake picked up his RC Cola and took a long swig. He set the bottle down, belched with some force, and started reading again.

Sam was just about to say something when Jake dropped the magazine and turned away as he woofed an explosive sneeze. He whipped out his handkerchief—a little too late, Sam noticed, and blew his nose with a honk that sounded like the horn on a model T.

Sam stood with a blank look on his face. "Too bad they don't have an Olympic event in belching and nose honking. You'd be a sure winner."

Jake sniffed and put his hanky away. "You think so?" Jake gave Sam a blank look.

Sam shook his head while Jake brushed the magazine to the side and said, "How's your place coming along in Gallup?"

"Just fine; I'm thinking I might put up a garage and a shed for some horses. I have some other news for you too. One of the movie companies working out of Gallup came to look at Blacksparrow. They think it would make a good location for filming some western movies, and they made an offer to lease the place. I've decided to take them up on it, and stay in Gallup. Maybe with the additional traffic from the movie crews, you'll be able to sell more of your overpriced souvenirs."

Jake rubbed his chin. "I might at that. I'll start marking up the prices as soon as you leave." Jake turned serious. "Sam, don't forget to stop by and see me from time to time."

Sam drove to Gallup to unload his things, and when he was done, he went to the El Rancho to leave a message for Rance Wilder. The man at the front desk said, "Mr. Wilder is in the dining room, would you like to speak to him?"

"Oh I..." Before Sam could finish his reply, He heard a voice he recognized.

"Sam Begay, I was hoping to hear from you today. Would you like to come up to my room so we can talk?"

Sam shook the man's hand. "That's not necessary, Mr. Wilder; I've decided to take your offer. If you'll have your people draw up the papers, we can seal our agreement, and you can get your stuff moved in."

"That's great news Sam, I'm certain this will work out for both of us. I'll have the papers drawn up by the end of the day. Can we meet tomorrow morning and see if we've covered everything to your satisfaction? Say 10:00 a.m.?"

Sam's next stop was Benny's garage. He noticed his Ford truck sitting on the rack inside the building. "Hey Benny, how's the work coming along?"

Bennie wiped his arm across his forehead as he turned from the workbench. "Making progress; I suspect I'll have it ready come Monday. The undercarriage is done, and the dents are bumped out. I yanked the engine and took it to the junkyard. My boys are working on one with a bit more horsepower that should fit under the hood. I've stiffened the frame to handle the extra weight, and I'm working on the brakes and suspension now."

"That's great, I just wanted to tell you I'm leasing out my property north of Thoreau, and you'll need to pick up the other junked vehicles before the new people move in. It sounds like they want to get started pretty soon."

"That's not a problem; I can come out this afternoon and haul the rest away."

Sam walked around the truck, and Benny said, "It's going to ride a little stiffer and sit taller than before, but you said you wanted it to run like a buffalo. I swear, Sam, you can bang up a vehicle as bad as my man Sonny does."

Sam smiled and said, "I had some help. How about him?"

The Lightning Tree

Benny pushed his ball cap back. "Does it all by himself, and doesn't talk about it, but I think he gets drunk and wrinkles up the fenders on any tree or rock that jumps out at him. It's amazing he can put it back together again, but he does."

"We all have some kind of gift, Benny. Say, you went to school here in Gallup, didn't you?"

"Sure did, graduated in '19, and so did the missus. Why?"

"Do you remember back when you were in the 9th or 10th grade about some kind of scandal involving the Junior and Senior baseball players?"

"Gee, that was a long time ago. We got married right away and started having kids. Everything else seems hazy that far back. I'll ask her and see if she remembers anything. What kind of scandal? Would it have to do with the police or some girls?"

"I'm not sure, but I do know it involves some of the Junior class boys. By the way, do you remember a student named Louis Montoya?"

"Now him, I remember. He always liked to pick on us underclassmen. Hell, he beat me up a few times when I tried to stop him from stealing my lunch. I got back at him though. I packed a tortilla with dog poop one day, and had my buddies hang around to back me up. Sure enough, he stole it and went off it eat it. Hoo-ee, he was mad. Seems he took a big bite before he realized what was inside it. Me and my friends stood him off, and he never bothered us again."

"As I remember, he fancied himself a girl-chaser, and he used to hang around with Bobby Castor. Bobby was the one who could get the girls. His daddy had money, and Bobby always had a new car and nice clothes. Do you have some special interest in Montoya, or can't you talk about it?"

"I'm just trying to find him, that's all."

"Well, I haven't seen him for some time, but it's likely he's still around. Say, how about I meet you at your place around 4:00?"

"That's good, I'll see you there."

Sam walked back to his car without noticing Sonny. The young Indian worker had been listening near the back door of the shop. His face looked thoughtful and wary.

CHAPTER 30

Back at Blacksparrow, Sam started gathering the remaining things he wanted to take to his place in Gallup. It might take a few trips, but he had the whole weekend to move. Benny Ortiz drove up a little after 4:00 p.m.

Sam helped him with the two old vehicles, and when they sat chained on the back of his truck and trailer, Benny said, "Did you mention you also needed some work done on your car?"

Sam pointed to his dented Chevy parked in front of the house. "It needs tires, brakes, and shocks. The engine's okay, and the interior is nice enough, but the body has some dents and dings. What do you think it might cost to make it look and run a bit nicer?"

"The tires, brakes, and shocks are easy, and I can do a quick job on the dents and paint. Do you still want to swap for the work?"

"Sure, if I could."

"How about, I take the bar stock and pipe lying on the rack next to the building to cover the cost of the repairs on the car? If it's okay with you, I'll load the stuff right now and take it with me."

"It's a deal."

A soft, female rain came the next morning; Sam's people call the heavy, lightning-shot storms, "male." He agreed with the concept, but in his experience with people, the naming didn't always ring true.

The showers passed by the time he got to the highway headed to Gallup, and he arrived at the El Rancho just before 10:00 a.m. He met with Rance and his assistant in his room, and after reviewing and signing the lease agreement, Sam said he would remove his personal stuff, and would be on hand Monday to turn over the place, and answer any last questions.

Rance seemed pleased, and he told Sam he wanted to start moving equipment to Blacksparrow no later than Monday afternoon.

Sam left the hotel, and checked on boarding arrangements for the horses at a place north of town. He decided to keep them there until he built a shelter and corral at his house.

On his way back to Blacksparrow that afternoon, he thought of Eric Nez again, and decided to drive out to his aunt's house one last time before giving up and presuming they moved away. With the recent rain, he should be able to tell if anyone else had been at the house since morning.

The wind was picking up, and sand and tumbleweed blew across the highway as he headed east toward Continental Divide. He turned off the highway, and drove south on the two-track. As he neared the house, he saw no tracks since the rain. Stopping at a place where he could see the building from a distance, he saw no vehicles.

The gusts of wind died down by the time he parked in the yard, and the packed earth showed no prints since the rain. He found the place as he remembered it; the door unlocked, and the interior scattered with blankets, bottles, and other debris. He walked outside and around the building again, and recognized the same rotten smell from the trash. It appeared some scavengers had dug into the pile, and scattered some discarded food.

Sam was halfway back to his truck when he stopped, turned around, and stared at the house. A moment later, he ran to the truck and pulled a shovel from behind the seat. He ran back to the trash pile, took a deep breath, and started digging.

The sweat dripped from his face, and his shirt stuck to his skin as he dug. After ten minutes, to his sorrow, he uncovered a small, pale hand and a bare arm.

An hour later, Sam, Charlie, and Doc. Beeman stood over the dirt-covered body of an Indian woman. A large amount of blood had dried around her neck and shoulders.

"Is she the boy's aunt?" Charlie said as he leaned on his shovel, breathing through a handkerchief tied around his mouth and nose.

Sam stood next to him, and said, "Yes, and I can only hope there isn't another body underneath hers."

They lifted the woman from the pit and laid her on a tarp so the Doc. could examine the wounds. Beeman said, "There are deep, multiple, cuts similar to the ones on the body you brought in from McGaffey, Sam."

Charlie and Sam looked at each other and started digging again. After fifteen minutes, they gave up.

"It looks like she's the only one buried here," Sam said to Charlie. "Let's help Beeman load the body, and get this hole filled in."

As the M.E. drove away, the two men made another thorough search of the area. Afterward, Charlie put his shovel in his car, and said, "If there's another body out here, it'll take a bulldozer at least a week to locate it."

"I don't think we'll find another one, Charlie. We might as well give it up, and head back to town to make out a report. Sam wiped his forehead and donned his Stetson. "I swear I won't rest until I have that son-of-a-bitch Montoya in chains."

"What about the boy?" Charlie said.

Sam took a ragged breath. "I don't know, but I'll find him." A knot sat in his stomach as he followed Charlie's car to the highway. What if he never saw Eric again?

By the time he and Charlie were sitting in his office, Sam was convinced Louis Montoya was the wolf hair killer.

"I thought you said Montoya and Castor are the last two potential *victims* of the wolf hair murderer? Now you're telling me you think Montoya is the killer?"

"A murder investigation is a fluid thing, Charlie. You have to keep an open mind to recognize the clues."

"What new clues do you have?"

"It's not so much that they're *new* clues, it's that I'm starting to recognize them *as* clues."

"Okay, Sam, what you mean."

"I mean, we know Montoya is wanted for skipping his court date, and I know him to be a vicious and unstable person, not just from when he ran me off the road, but also from his local police record. I'll bet he had a reputation back in high school, too. He's linked to the other murders by association; so, he's either a possible victim, or he's the killer. Think about it; how many others do we know who are tied to all the other victims, and are still around?"

Charlie said, "Just one; Bobby Castor."

"True," Sam said. "He's a well-off businessman. Why would he get his hands dirty, and risk connecting himself to a long string of killings, and such violent acts? He would risk being seen and identified, or tied to a beat-up vehicle, or maybe even injured. Why would he risk all that if he has virtually everything he could want?"

Charlie said, "Not to mention a father who's a well-known businessman and politician. The killings do seem to be the work of an especially, brutal man."

"Yes, and it leaves us with a big question and clue; why does the killer leave a tuft of wolf hair at the scene—or at least the ones you and I have investigated?"

"You said it might have something to do with a Navajo superstition."

"Yes, but the only Navajos we've come across in this whole case are the boy and his aunt."

"Tell me more about this superstition, Sam."

Sam scratched the back of his head. "It's like the old Salem witchcraft stories you read about in school. Superstitions are a way for primitive and vindictive people to blame their troubles on someone else." Sam leaned back in his chair. "Our legends say that the way to find a Navajo witch is to look for someone who has more than they need, while their kinfolk go hungry. It's about greed and revenge; things most Navajo people avoid."

"When a Navajo witch becomes powerful enough, they can become a skinwalker. They also call them shapeshifters, and they say the witch can take the form of an animal or a bird when they go out to do their evil deeds. Most of the time it's a wolf, and that's why you don't see my people wearing the skin of a wolf for clothing. Some tell stories of seeing a wolf running next to their car at night, peering into the window, or trying to open the door."

Charlie said, "Now that would scare the pants right off of me. I wonder if that guy I found outside his car down the Zuni road last year saw something like that."

"Hard to say," Sam said, "but I don't think Mr. and Mrs. Sandoval saw anything like that. She would have told us, and all she said she noticed were the lights of another vehicle ramming into the back of their car."

"Like Montoya did when he ran you off the road?"

"Yeah maybe."

CHAPTER 31

Two large trucks arrived at Blacksparrow Monday morning. Sam handed over a set of gate keys, and after helping orient them with the place, he drove away. He made a mental note to make sure his friends had his new phone number, and realized he still had mixed feelings about moving out.

He knew he had upset the balance of things when he took over ownership a few years ago. It went against the teachings of his people; land isn't owned, it is merely used. He was a caretaker, yet he had accepted payment from Rance Wilder. It was the white man's way, and this country belonged to the white man. It was their law. He wanted to do the right thing, and he reluctantly admitted that this was it. He would use the $600 advance rent to restore the balance of things when he spent it.

By the time he reached US 66 and headed west toward Gallup, the details of the convoluted case he was working on soon overshadowed his thoughts. There were murders to solve, and a killer, or killers to bring to justice.

He began flipping through each bit of evidence, studying each clue card as he tried to arrange them in some logical sequence. He still had too many cards, and too few connections to make a bet.

After unloading some things at his house outside Gallup, he drove to Benny's shop. His truck was parked in front of the garage, and he barely recognized it. Benny came out and watched Sam admiring the work.

"Benny, it looks almost like a military vehicle. I wouldn't be surprised if I could drive it up a wall."

The Lightning Tree

"Knowing you, Sam, I'd say you're more likely to drive it *through* a wall. I put in a new rear-end that will give you enough traction to get you through almost anything. If it doesn't, you might as well walk away and leave it, because it isn't coming out without a crane or a dozer. The frame shouldn't twist on you, and the engine has enough power to outrun a hot rod. It rides rough, but you'll get used to it. Here's the keys. I'll get started on your Chevy, and have it ready in a couple of days."

"What made you think to put a bumper guard on the front of the truck?"

"That was Sonny's idea. He said it would let you push a stalled vehicle without messing up the grill or the paint. By the way, I asked the missus if she remembered any kind of scandals back in high school involving the boys on the ball team and some girls. Do you know what she said? She told me there was always some kind of scandal going on with the boys and the girls, and it didn't matter if they were on the ball team or not."

Sam smiled. "Thanks Benny, I figured it was a long-shot." He glanced at the sun as he climbed into the cab of the truck. It was still an hour before noon, and he wanted to check with Charlie to see if he had heard from Doc. Beeman about the woman's autopsy.

A low rumble came from the engine as it idled, and he grinned at Benny before backing out of the lot and driving off. He noticed the seat belt, and he figured it might be handy on a chase over rough terrain.

Charlie was on the phone when Sam walked in the office. He went to the kitchen, and heard some of Charlie's side of the conversation. Finding a clean cup, he filled it with coffee, and came back to sit at his old desk.

Charlie set the receiver down, and Sam said, "Let me guess. That was Decker chewing you out because I found another body."

"You have a gift, Sam. According to him, you should have been born a bloodhound with the nose you have for trouble."

"It isn't that, Charlie. I just figure if I keep Decker distracted with my inscrutable, Navajo ways, it'll make it easier for you to do your job."

"Well, he just told me that keeping an eye on you is now part of my job." Charlie finished his coffee with a long gulp.

Sam made a face and said, "Have you heard from Beeman yet about the cuts on the woman's body?"

"Yeah. He confirmed they're similar to the ones on the body you brought back from El Morro. He said we have two examples of the same killer's work."

Sam took a deep breath. "And if Montoya is the killer, it makes me wonder how he fits in with the wolf hair and Borden cases. He's also one of the two, last living classmates on the ball team. That doesn't mean he's the killer, but he is the prime suspect in the other murders."

"C'mon Sam, the odds are he's our man."

"I'm still bothered by two things that don't add up," Sam said, "different killing methods, and no wolf hair found on the two buried bodies."

"Sam, they were dug up. Don't you think we might miss some animal hair?"

"I suppose, but it seems like the whole idea of the other killings were to make sure the tufts of hair were found with the bodies—at least the ones we investigated. We don't know for sure about the earlier ones, but it could simply be a matter of the investigating officer ignoring any hair they found, figuring it wasn't related to the incident. We'll never know, but there is a bigger fact we do know."

"What's that?"

"The two buried bodies weren't meant to be found; the others were."

Charlie sipped from his cup and said. "Yeah, but Montoya is still the best lead we've got. Hell, he's our only lead."

Sam stood up, and took his empty cup to the back. When he returned, he walked to the door and said, "I can't argue with that. Judge Reilly wants him too, and I'd better get to work."

"Yeah, me too. I'm off for Ft. Defiance. Say, have the movie people moved in at Blacksparrow yet?"

"They started this morning, and from their talk, there's a lot of equipment to move." He adjusted his hat and walked out to his truck. When Sam reached for his keys, he pulled out the gold coin he still carried. One golden coin; are there others? Someone must have thought there were. Why else ransack the old man's house and kill him? Did the killer know Borden was already lying dead in the Bisti?

He put the coin away. There was only one man he knew of who had seen the coin, other than Borden; Bobby Castor, and he had denied it.

As Sam drove off, he saw an unusual car pull away from the Post Office. It was a shiny, black convertible with big whitewall tires and lots of chrome on a low-slung body. He followed the car a short distance, and into the parking lot of Strong Mountain Trading Company. Sam parked alongside as the driver stepped out of the car.

Bobby Castor tried to hide his surprise, and put on a quick smile. "Good morning officer Begay, that's quite a tall truck you've got there."

"It just looks like that sitting next to your new sports car. It's a Cord 812, isn't it?"

"You do know your cars, officer. Have you seen one close up?"

"Nope, but it sure looks like a beauty."

"Rides like a dream too. Come over and take a good look. It has front wheel drive, independent suspension, and a semi-automatic four-speed. The engine only puts out 125 horsepower, so it'll never make a race car, but it sure handles nice."

"No running boards." Sam said.

"It doesn't need them. It's meant to be streamlined. Notice the headlights are recessed and hidden in the fenders."

Sam nodded and said, "She's a beauty alright."

"Yeah, but a temperamental one; the thing will pop out of gear sometimes on a rough road, and it has an occasional problem with vapor lock. Still, it'll turn heads when it goes by." Bobby grinned. "I guess that's the whole point, isn't it?"

Sam smiled. "Bobby, if you're going inside, I'd like to ask you about a couple of things."

"Sure, follow me through to the back so we can talk."

Standing at the pawn counter, Sam said, "When was the last time you saw Louis Montoya?"

Bobby face sagged. "It's been a while. I went to school with him, and we used to play ball together. I've seen him around from time to time, but not very often. He was in the store a few weeks ago."

"Did he want something, or did he talk about anything he'd been doing lately?"

"I don't recall anything specific. He might have come in to buy something, but he said he just stopped to talk about old times, and playing ball in school. I was busy, and we didn't talk very long. Are you looking for him?"

"Yes, I want to ask him about something he may have seen—nothing important. Do you remember him ever carrying a machete—you know; maybe on his belt like some guys carry a hunting knife?"

"No, and I don't think he was carrying one when I saw him."

Sam nodded and paused for a moment. "By the way, has anyone else come in with any Spanish gold coins like the one I showed you?"

Bobby grinned. "Nope, and I'd remember if they did. Have you sold it yet?"

Sam looked Bobby in the eyes. "No, I thought I'd hang on to it in case I ever came across any others like it. It might be nice to collect them." Bobby held his gaze until Sam tipped his hat and turned to walk away.

"If someone brings one in," Bobby said, "I'll be sure to let you know, officer. How do I get in touch with you?"

"Don't worry, I'll be around."

Bobby watched Sam walk down the aisle and out the front door. He jumped when a voice behind him said, "What was that all about?"

David Castor glared at his son. "What did he want?"

"Nothing much."

"Since when is it "nothing much" when a law officer wants to talk to you?"

"He pulled into the parking lot behind me when I got back from the Post Office. He was just admiring my car, is all."

"You're saying he followed you in just to talk about your damn car?"

"Look dad, he came in with an old gold coin a month ago. He wanted to get an idea what it was worth. He just asked me if I'd seen any more like it since then. He also wanted to know if I'd seen Louis Montoya lately."

"Why would he ask you about him? What did you say?"

"He knows we were in school together. I told him he stopped in a month ago, but other than that, I haven't seen him. What's the problem?"

"I don't know, but I don't like him snooping around, looking for one of our men. I want you to tell Montoya to stay low until we can find out why Begay is interested in him."

"Okay, but it's probably nothing."

"Boy, we have a lot of money riding on this operation. With the west coast people bankrolling part of it, and the Detroit guys wanting to keep an eye on their interests, I don't want to tell them *probably nothing*' if someone asks. Get in touch with Montoya, and find out what he knows. Then let me know. David glared at his son, turned, and walked to the back office.

Sixty miles to the northeast, Louis Montoya talked to the two men who drove a Ford delivery truck into the Blacksparrow compound. "Is that the last of it?"

The Lightning Tree

"Yeah, the warehouse south of town is empty, and the crew is cleaning it up."

"Good, put your load with the rest of it. When you're done, make sure the guard locks the doors."

He watched the men drive to the far edge of the compound where two gigantic doors, painted to match the sandstone walls of the mesa, stood open to reveal a cavernous hangar. He shook his head, still amazed how someone could build such a large enclosure by roofing over a natural cleft in the mesa wall. It looked big enough to hold a city street.

Montoya walked around the compound. The kitchen and dining hall were ready for use, and the security guards would stay in the nearby barracks, leaving the main house for the boss and any other visiting big shots.

Back in Gallup, David Castor looked up from his desk in the back of the trading post, and glared at his son. "If we pull this off, we'll be rolling in so much dough, even you won't be able to spend it all. You can have your fancy toys, but just remember that money is going to finance my campaign for Governor."

"I know!"

"Good, and if you're smart, you won't forget it. Make sure you tell Montoya to have his crew keep their eyes open for Begay or any other snoops while we ramp up our activity. I heard Detroit is sending out some out-of-town talent to help watch over their interests."

"If we bring in so many strangers, dad, how are we going to keep it from drawing the attention of the locals?"

"I'll worry about that. When we get everything rolling with the movie crews, you'll see that attention is just the thing we want; it'll be perfect cover to hide what we're really doing out there."

After the older Castor left through the back door, Bobby sat behind the desk and made a phone call.

"Guess who was just here asking about you."

"How do I know? The Queen of England? Maybe that cute little Indian girl I flirted with last night at the Commercial Club?"

"You got part of it right. It was an Indian, but *his* name was Sam Begay."

"Shit! Why is he looking for me?"

"He asked me if you carried a machete, and he knows we went to school together. Maybe he remembered you with that Indian gal out by Continental Divide. Maybe she talked."

"Nah, I took care of that."

"What do you mean?"

"I mean she isn't going to talk to him, or anyone else—ever."

"Jeez! What about the kid you said was staying with her? Did you shut him up too?"

There was a pause on the line. "Nah, the little shit ran off while I was busy with her. I checked back at the place a few times, but I haven't seen any sign of him. Don't worry; he doesn't know anything, and no one will ever find her."

"You'd better be right. Dad says you should stay out of sight so Begay doesn't find you."

"Look Bobby, that Indian cop is looking for me because I scuffled with him and ran him off the road. He doesn't know anything else. Besides, I've got a new gal in town who thinks I'm cute, and if you think I'm going to stay away from that, you're crazy."

"Don't be a smart-ass, Louis. Dad says for you to…"

"'Daddy says,' eh? Bobby, if you think I'm going to leave that little girl in town all by herself, you're crazy. I'd be sick with worry just thinking about how lonely she is."

CHAPTER 32

David Castor sat on the couch puffing on a cigar in Rance Wilder's room at the El Rancho Hotel. He reached to a large, glass ashtray to flick the ash, and said, "They should finish moving the stuff tonight so your movie crews can start setting up their equipment tomorrow."

"Good," Wilder said. "I'll have them start work on those old barracks on the far side by the tracks and have it looking like an old western town in no time. I might even bring in an old steam engine for some of the filming."

Castor took another puff of his cigar. "As long as we keep our work crews separated, we should be able to handle the goods with no one but the inside crew being the wiser. When your movie people arrive each morning, all the guards have to do is keep them away from the locked storage buildings at the back. They'll have free access through the rest of the compound except for the small bunkhouse the guards are using."

"When the crews come back to town after the filming each day, the guards will take over and light up the runway when the planes come in. There's no one nearby to get curious about aircraft coming and going, but if someone does, we'll tell 'em it's your eccentric movie people and their expensive toys. By the way, are you sure the lease documents you switched will stand up after we get rid of Begay?"

"They will David, and after he dies from some unfortunate accident, the place will automatically revert to me. We have an ideal setup." Wilder leveled his stare at Castor. "It's a good thing too; with the delays we suffered because of the El Morro situation, our partners want to see quick results."

Wilder's comment was not lost on Castor. "Rance, you know damn well they'll get it, but we can't predict when something unforeseen crops up. Just like your little problem last winter back in California when that con-artist Indian woman and her accomplice tried to blackmail you."

Wilder glared at Castor, and then smiled. "Yes, she was something to look at. Too bad, they disappeared before my men could bring them to me. They vanished without a trace, and I can only hope they're dead. By the way, I've been in contact with our associates in Detroit, and they'll be sending out a couple of men soon to keep an eye on their interests in the operation."

"I expected that," Castor said, "but I still don't like it."

"Nor do I, but I agreed to put up with their show of muscle. I don't expect them to send out any of their top talent, but the men should be capable."

"Fine, as long as they keep their mouths shut and stay out of the way."

"Exactly what I told them. It's nice to know that we think alike in these matters. Disagreements tend to be troublesome and wasteful."

Meanwhile, in a smoky, neighborhood bar in Detroit, Michigan, Bud Thomas ordered another round of Stroh's beer for him and his partner, Artie Buchman. Bud's narrow eyes and long face betrayed no emotion as he stroked his narrow mustache, and talked over the clack of pool balls.

"Tell you what, Artie, Let's go down to that club on Jackson. I'll call Sheila and ask if she and one of her girlfriends can meet us around eleven and show us a good time. I'll even let you buy the drinks."

Artie, sometimes called 'Artie the Bucket', was a heavy set contrast to his partner's lean shape. He looked around the room with squinty eyes, and his ruddy, round face gave him a look of innocence that contrasted with his reputation for fitting his enemies with concrete-filled buckets for shoes; thus his name. He grinned through a wide mouth of crooked teeth. "It's a deal, but won't your wife get mad if you come home late again?"

"If she does, I'll paste her in the kisser like last time. She knows better than to tell me what to do. Too bad she doesn't know how to treat me right like Sheila does."

"Okay, let's drink up. I'm getting a headache listening to the noise of those cue balls, and I got me a wad of cash to pay for booze and women for a week. I'm itchin' to get started—that is, if your wife'll let you stay out for the evening."

"Artie, I'd smack you if you weren't such a sweet and generous fella."

"Sure; just tell Sheila to find me a girl with some meat on her. I'm hungry tonight."

Across town, Bud's wife Helen stood inside the open door of their small, tract house, watching the stars. It was after midnight, cool and peaceful, with the muted rumble of cars somewhere beyond the dark shapes of the houses.

She had just made the biggest decision of her life, and she wondered if she and her daughter would ever feel safe again—safe from the brutal man her husband had become. She shivered, and felt alone and adrift like one of the points of light in the sky.

Her daughter Clara was a happy seven-year-old when she had first met Bud. Clara's father, her first husband, had died in a foundry accident the year before, and their money had run out.

Bud Thomas noticed her working at the restaurant one day, and she remembered thinking he had the most disarming smile she had ever seen. He acted bashful, though he found the courage to ask her on a date to see a movie.

He was friendly and attentive back then, and gentle with little Clara. He had a good job in a factory near the river, and when he asked her, she had consented to marry him. In a few years, they had bought this small house in an old, quiet neighborhood and moved from her apartment.

Work was steady, and they saved a little money, but then the strikes came, creating scores of unemployed men. The union busters came after that, and when the old Purple Gang broke up, the Chicago mob moved in to provide muscle to fight those who wanted to unionize and make a better life for their families.

She knew it was the long months of unemployment, and the way the loss of meaningful work can eat up a man, that changed Bud. She still worked at the restaurant, and he stayed home and became increasingly bitter. The gentleness he had once shown her and her daughter changed to frustration and rage. He began to drink heavily, depleting their meager savings, and driving a wedge between them.

Then one day he told her he had found a new job. He had joined the men recruited by the mob to battle the unions.

She didn't know what was happening at first, but soon, there was more money. Bud used it to by nicer clothes for himself, and later, she found out, booze and other women.

They argued constantly, and sometimes the smallest thing would set him off. She wore the marks of his brutality, and bore the abuse until her daughter, now a young teen, also became the target of his violent temper. Her daughter fought back one day, and he knocked her unconscious.

Helen decided that was enough, and when she started packing her bags, she discovered a large stash of money Bud had hidden from her. Astonished by the amount, she wondered what he could have done to earn so much money.

Soon, she realized how deeply her husband was involved with the mob. Thinking only of her daughter's safety, she wondered where they could go to get away from the monster Bud had become. She was certain he would try to find her.

She had an uncle in New Mexico, but he was more like a distant stranger she exchanged Christmas cards with each year. Besides, she couldn't imagine traveling to such a distant place she knew nothing about. She could move north to some small town where no one knew her, and decoy Bud to believe she and her daughter had taken a train out west. That could work. She had an old Christmas card somewhere she could plant as a fake clue to where they had gone.

Helen took a deep breath of cool air before she closed the door and walked to the bedroom. She undressed, pulled the blankets up to her chin, and lay with her eyes open.

"It'll be alright mom," Clara's small voice said in the darkness.

"Of course it will sweetheart. Go back to sleep." Helen sighed and closed her eyes. She pondered her act of defiance and desperation. She would take half of the money she found—it was her rightful share—and she would buy two tickets at the train station, and plant information to make it look as if they headed west to New Mexico.

As she waited for sleep to come, she thought of the woods and lakes up north where her parents had taken their vacations when she was a young girl. Clara would like it.

CHAPTER 33

Sam walked up the steps into the school building and down the hall toward the library. There were no children in the classrooms today, but he did see a few teachers and staff people working at their desks.

Joyce Dobson stood in front of a long shelf of books across the room, and noticed him when he walked in. Sam stopped at the counter, and she motioned for him to wait a moment. As he watched, she finished placing books on the shelves, and walked up to the front, smiling.

"Mr. Begay, to what do I owe the pleasure of this visit on such a beautiful day?"

"Would you believe, I'm looking for some pleasant company and conversation?"

She squinted one eye. "I don't know if I should believe such a story, coming from a suspicious-looking man like you." Her smile was full of mischief.

"Well, I was hoping you would, because I need to ask for your help again."

"Mr. Begay, why throw water on a girl's hopes? Look outside; the sun is shining, the birds are singing, and instead of working, I'd rather be out on a picnic." She sighed and gave him a thoughtful frown. "I guess the least I could do is ask what you have in mind. Does it have something to do with the class photos?"

"Sort of, and I need you to promise to keep it to yourself."

Joyce studied his face. "O.K. What do you need?"

"A favor and I'll gladly take you on a picnic if you help me."

"Take a look out that window, Mr. Begay. Make it today, and I'll do it. I'm off work in five minutes, and I haven't had anything to eat since a muffin for breakfast."

Sam grinned. He leaned against the counter and said, "You drive a hard bargain, but it's a deal. Do you remember when we talked about the missing Navajo girl from the senior class photo and the missing male student from the senior ball team photo? I have a hunch there was some sort of a scandal that took place in the junior year that involved the two students."

"Scandal? What kind?" Joyce leaned forward with her elbows on the counter.

"That's what I don't know. I was hoping, that since you have the alumni records, you might be able to contact a few of the old students, and ask them about it."

She said, "You think there is some connection between the Navajo girl and the boy?"

"Yes. I talked to Mr. Dallas about it, and he told me he was the ball coach back then, but he said he wasn't aware of anything unusual involving any of the players on the team and the girls in class. I'm hoping you can get in touch with some of the female students and ask them if they remember anything about a problem or a scandal back then."

Joyce made a face and said, "I have the phone numbers and addresses of several of them, and just to show you that you're not dealing with any ordinary school librarian, I've already made some calls."

"You have? What made you think to do that?"

"Mr. Begay, you might be an experienced officer of the law, but you are very naïve when it comes to understanding a woman's curiosity. I made the calls the same week we had lunch, just in case you ever asked about it."

"Did you take notes?"

Joyce rolled her eyes.

Sam couldn't help but laugh. "Of course you took notes. If you can get them for me, you'll have your picnic this afternoon. We can pick up something to eat and drink along the way."

Walking out to Sam's truck, Joyce said, "There may be some hope for you after all, Mr. Begay." She smiled with a hint of impish challenge.

A short while later with two boxed lunches on the seat between them, Sam drove east toward the hogback ridge. He told her there was a nice place off the road with a view of some interesting rock formations.

"I've never been back here before," she said. "It is pretty."

"I used to drive out and eat lunch here from time-to-time when I lived in town. Now that I'm back, I'm re-acquainting myself."

"What made you decide to move back to town?"

"I leased my other place south of Chaco Canyon to one of the movie outfits. They're going make some western films in the area."

"That sounds exciting," she said.

"To you and me, but I'm sure it's just a job to them. They offered me a lease deal, and I took them up on it."

He drove north off the highway, and crossed a narrow bridge spanning a wash that meandered back to some hills. "Just up ahead, there's a spot with some unusual, eroded sandstone. It's a nice place for a picnic."

He parked near some massive rocks where water and sand had scoured deep lines across the face of the sandstone. Oddly, the grain often ran at different angles on sections of the rock.

"See that?" Sam pointed. "It's proof that the rock tilted from time-to-time as water and sand gouged a path across it."

Joyce picked up the lunches while Sam pulled out a blanket from behind the seat. He led the way to a shaded spot, and spread the blanket on the ground. They ate as they sat and enjoyed the scenery and the sound of wind and the birds.

The warm breeze blew a wisp of hair across Joyce's cheek, and when she pushed it back, she said, "May I ask you why you're so interested in the old student classes?"

Sam finished chewing, swallowed, and put on a serious face. "I asked Mr. Dallas about what he knew about the missing student on the ball team and the girl who didn't attend the senior year classes, and I don't think he was truthful with his answer. He seemed evasive, and I believe he has a reason for it. I want to know what it is."

Joyce looked away at the rocks. "I guess I'd better tell you what I found out."

Sam took a drink of soda. "I was hoping you'd get around to telling me."

She frowned at him, and then smirked and said. "I was going to burst if I didn't. Here's what two of the women told me. It seems the boys on the baseball team had a reputation for drinking and partying in the boonies. Bobby Castor was the ringleader, and the other boys went along with whatever he said. I was told, that some of the girls joined them from time to time. They said, the boys would get drunk, and try to coax them into the back seat of their cars. I'm sure some of the girls were willing, but that wasn't the scandal. It was when the boys got together one time, and Bobby brought a Navajo girl along to liven up their party."

Sam listened, barely breathing, as Joyce spoke.

"The two women told me they heard about it from their boyfriends, who heard some of the team players talking about it. It seems that they all passed the girl around, and took turns. They teased one of the boys about it because he wouldn't join the rest of them." Joyce looked away, watching a hawk soar over the rocks.

Sam let a minute pass. "Did anyone mention who that boy was?"

She turned back to him. "Harold Borden; the one missing from the senior team, and the one they found dead in the desert last month."

Sam considered the implications of Joyce's story. He took a deep breath, looked at the position of the sun, and said, "I guess we'd better finish up and head back into town soon."

Later, back in the truck, he reached in his pocket and gave her a card. "If you hear about anything else, I want you to call me right away. If you can't reach me, call Charlie Redman at the FBI office. His number is there, too."

"The FBI? Am I getting myself into some kind of trouble by helping you?"

"No, Charlie's my friend, and all of this happened over twenty years ago. If I thought it might be dangerous, I wouldn't ask for your help. I just want you to be able to get a message to me if I'm not in town."

They drove back to Gallup, and Sam dropped Joyce off at her house in a quiet neighborhood near the school. On the way home, he thought of how she had surprised him today with her humor and easygoing nature—not to mention her intuition and initiative.

He stopped to pick up a few groceries, and examined the small worry moving around in the back of his mind. Was he putting her in danger by asking for her help? He couldn't see how, but he decided to be vigilant for anything that might hint of trouble.

Back home, the unknown whereabouts of Eric Nez soon crowded everything else out his mind. He sighed in frustration, and decided to take a walk down the path behind his house.

He had always considered the hogback ridge to be a privacy wall between the town and his little place in the desert. Here, alone in this quiet spot, surrounded by sandstone cliffs and junipers, his mind started working.

He hadn't made much progress in solving the wolf hair case, or for that matter, the relevance of the Spanish gold coin. He also knew Judge Reilly would be wondering why he hadn't brought Montoya into custody.

With the weekend coming in a few days, where would be the best place to find a man with drinking and women on his mind? In town at the bars, of course, and he decided he could start at the rough places along Railroad Avenue, Friday, as soon as the sun went down. He had a photo of Montoya to show around, and if he couldn't find him, he would at least get the word out that he was looking for him. Perhaps Montoya would hear about it and decide to try to find him instead.

He grimaced at the thought of having a homicidal killer on his trail, but if someone had to be the bait, he would rather it be him. Sam felt his blood warm at the thought of a stalking game, and leading a predator into a trap. He had to take some precautions, of course, and make sure he was ready for any surprise move.

CHAPTER 34

"Mr. Dallas wants to speak with you in his office Miss. Dobson. He's waiting."

Joyce Dobson saw the smug look on Mrs. Atkins' face. What could be so important or urgent for him to call for her in such a brusque manner? His secretary had always displayed a condescending attitude because of her position, but today she seemed to revel in the tone of her message.

"Very well, I'll be along directly, just let me…"

"He said he wants to see you *now*. Please come with me."

Joyce stared at the heavy-set woman for a few seconds, noting the smirk on her round, florid face. "Very well Mrs. Atkins."

The secretary followed Joyce down the hall and into the business office, then she pushed ahead to knock on the principal's door. "Mr. Dallas, Miss. Dobson is here."

"Show her in, and hold my calls until we've finished."

Joyce couldn't imagine why she'd been summoned in such a manner. Principal Dallas kept his eyes on a folder lying open in front of him, and didn't make eye contact with her as she entered.

"Please be seated Miss Dobson." A few moments later, he closed the file and set it aside. When he looked up, his expression displayed annoyance."

"Why have you called me here Mr. Dallas? Is something wrong?"

"Wrong? I don't know Miss Dobson, is there?"

"What do you mean?"

Dallas cleared his throat. Miss Dobson, the parents of this community have certain, shall I say, expectations of discretion and competence from our teachers and our staff—expectations that they feel are vital to the proper schooling of their children. The reason I summoned you here is that I feel these expectations are not being properly met by you."

"Mr. Dallas, what in the world are you talking about? Has someone complained? I haven't…"

"Now, now, I know some mistakes and misconceptions can occur from time-to-time; in fact, that's why I called you here. It has come to my attention that you have been fraternizing with a certain adult, Indian male. I know he has been here several times to see you, and I have reports of the two of you having lunch together at one of our local restaurants, and, as I hear it, causing a spectacle of yourselves. I am told that he picked you up at this school yesterday, and the two of you drove off to who-knows-where, or for what purpose."

"*Mr. Dallas!*" Joyce stood, struggling to hold back her anger and indignation. "Although the matter is certainly none of your business, we had a picnic lunch before he drove me home. As for causing 'a spectacle' at a restaurant; you need to check your source, because they are either blind or insane." She took a hankie from her pocket and dabbed at her eyes while Dallas watched her.

"No need to be upset, Miss Dobson; of course I know you wouldn't do anything to tarnish the reputation of this school, but I also know that tongues do wag. In our unique positions in this community, I expect all of our employees to adhere to high standards, and to set an example for our students and the parents of this community. You can consider this meeting as employee coaching. I'm just thinking of you and the good of this school. I would hate to let this matter pass, and possibly let it get out of hand."

Joyce was livid, but she managed to hold it back. "In that case sir, I'll strive to be more discreet in my *private* life."

"If you mean by 'discreet' that you'll avoid further contact with this particular Indian male, then I feel we have an understanding."

Joyce glared at Edgar Dallas. "You may feel what you wish." She stood, and walked out of the office.

Sam left his house that morning, and he missed the ringing phone. He drove to town with the windows open, enjoying the breeze on his way to pick up his car at Benny's garage. He saw it parked next to the building, and walked around it before he went inside to see Benny.

The stocky mechanic wiped grease from his hands, and nodded toward the vehicle. "New tires and brakes, and a tune up, and I found an old grill in good shape and swapped out the old one. Bumped out a few dents, too, and sprayed on a little paint. She's ready to go."

"I appreciate it Benny. I'll bring someone to pick it up a little later. Are we square?"

Benny shrugged his shoulders and said, "I suppose so, until you bang it up again or try to drive it up a tree. The keys are in it."

Sam stopped to see Charlie Redman next who told him that someone named Joyce Dobson called and wanted him to call her back.

"She said not to call her at school, or come by, but to call her at home later this afternoon or evening. She said it was important, and that she tried to reach you at your house earlier."

Sam frowned as he thought about the odd message.

Charlie said, "Are you two trying to line up a date?"

"Not that I'm aware of." Can you get away for a few minutes to help pick up my car from the shop, and drive it out to my place?"

"Sure, but we need to do it right now. I have to head down to Zuni as soon as I get back."

After they picked up the car, Sam dropped Charlie back at the office, and decided to take a drive north toward Burnham on the odd chance that Eric Nez may have hiked back to his old home after he left his aunt's place. He decided to call Miss Dobson at home, later.

By mid-day, Sam leaned against the fender of his truck in front of an empty, weathered hogan. He finished the sandwich he brought along, and drank some water as the blustery wind tugged at his hat.

He found no evidence of anyone having been in or near the house for some time. Where did that leave Eric to go besides Blacksparrow or the Thoreau Trading Post? He figured he would not return to his aunt's house, and if he showed up at the trading post, Jake would call him. Blacksparrow was busy with traffic and people, and Eric would not be welcome there.

Sam shook his head; waiting was not what he wanted to do right now. He was patient by nature, but he was also a man of action. What could have happened to the boy? He feared it was nothing good, and since he was in the area, he might as well ask around at the chapter house and any stores in the area to see if someone knew of him.

When he returned to Gallup several hours later, he replayed his conversations with a dozen people who knew of him, but no one recalled seeing him recently. Too tired to think, he fixed a quick meal and went to bed. He decided to call Joyce tomorrow morning, and fell asleep the instant his head hit the pillow.

Sometime during the night, a vague dream wound its way through his mind. At times it was vivid, and others not so. He carried a shovel over his shoulder, stopping at patches of soft earth to dig until his shoulders ached. In his sleep, he felt his skin covered with sweat as he lifted and tossed each load of dirt to the side. Sweat dripped in his eyes, and the sound of his labored breathing was like a mantra in his ears. As the hot sun beat down, he saw the shadow of his toiling body moving along the ground where he dug. Three feet down, he rested to catch his breath, and stepped to a different spot a short distance away to begin digging again.

Three feet down in a new spot, and still nothing. He wiped his brow and whimpered with frustration as he moved to yet another place. The sun was a hot fire burning the shirt off his back, but he kept digging. He approached three feet again, and gave a small cry of anguish as he felt the blade hit something dense. He made a low keening noise as he dropped to his knees in the hole, and began to dig at the loose soil with his bare hands.

As he worked with frenzied speed, he uncovered a small piece of cloth, and cried out as he redoubled his effort. He scooped up big handfuls of dirt and threw it out of the hole until he unearthed the thin body of an Indian boy lying face down. He gently cleared the soil away, and lifted the body to glance at the face he feared he would recognize.

"Ahhggg!" Sam jumped up in bed, kicking his legs, and he found the sheets tangled into a twisted knot. He took a deep lungful of air as he became cognizant of his whereabouts, and then he lay back to catch his breath. "Eric," he gasped.

He had to find the boy. He considered the daunting challenge of locating him, and he knew Montoya was his only source of information about what may have happened to him. The vivid dream had unnerved him. What if the man had caught the boy and killed him in the same manner as he had the woman?

Fully awake now, he realized that if Eric escaped from his aunt's house, Montoya may not have found him. The boy grew up learning how to survive on his own. He could hunt and track, and he was clever enough to hide his tracks to avoid detection—if he escaped.

What could he do in the next few days that would bring him closer to finding the boy, or the fugitive, Louis Montoya? Perhaps one thing would take care of the other. Montoya was his prime suspect in the wolf hair case, and he knew Judge Reilly would be getting impatient for some action on his bench warrant.

He decided to visit the bars along Railroad Avenue this weekend, thinking it to be the best place to pick up Montoya's trail. He would take the file photo of Montoya along, and make it known that he was looking for him. He may strike out, but eventually, someone would see the man, and remember that a big Indian named Sam Begay was looking for him. The odds were that his reputation and the years wearing a badge would get their attention, and Louis Montoya's.

CHAPTER 35

The phone startled Sam when it rang. He was half-awake and hadn't found the energy to climb out of bed to make coffee. Throwing off the sheet, he yawned, and shuffled to the other room. He picked up the receiver and said "hello," and was surprised at how ragged his voice sounded.

"Sam, why didn't you call me back yesterday? Where have you been?"

He glanced at the clock and saw how early it was. "Joyce, I got your message, but I was out of town until late, and I figured I'd call you this morning. Why did you say not to call you at school?"

"Sam, I had a meeting with Principal Dallas yesterday morning, and I'm still livid about what he said to me. I think it's important that you know about this because it may have something to do with the case you're working on."

Sam pulled out a chair from the kitchen table and searched for a pencil and a piece of paper. "What did he say? Are you alright?"

"Yes, I'm fine, but I'm angry as a hornet, and a little scared. I need to talk to you."

Sam was wide-awake now. "Do you want me to meet you somewhere?"

"Not right now. I have to leave for school, but I want to tell you what he said to me."

"Go ahead, I'm listening."

"Yesterday morning, Mr. Dallas' secretary told me he wanted to speak with me, and she insisted I come with her immediately. I can still see the smug look on her face, and I almost wanted to…oh never mind that. When I walked into his office, he had me sit in front of his desk while he glared at me. He seemed annoyed about something, and then he said how he felt that my *association with you* was causing a scandal at the school. Can you believe that? He said *concerned parents* were talking about me, and if I didn't stop seeing you, he would have to discharge me."

Sam was stunned. *"He said that?"*

"Yes, and I told him his concerned parents must be insane, because all I've ever done was talk to you a few times, and have lunch."

"Joyce, I wonder if this might have something to do with the information you've provided me for the case I'm following."

"He didn't mention anything about that, but the more I think about it, it's possible. Sam, I've worked at that school for over a ten years with nothing but excellent performance reviews—and now this? Your case *must* have something to do with it."

"Joyce, I don't know what to say. I'm sorry I inadvertently caused this to happen to you. I..."

"Oh just shut up, Sam. The thing that makes my blood boil is that he insinuated that my fraternizing with a Navajo man was somehow inappropriate and scandalous. I'm so mad I could bust a chair over his fat head and make him eat the pieces."

A brief grin crossed Sam's face. "Don't do anything like that yet." He thought for a moment. "Joyce, I think this might be the best clue so far."

"What do you mean?"

"I mean, I've had a hunch that he was holding something back since I asked him what he knew about events that occurred around the time those old class photos were taken. He claimed to have no recollection, but he was in a position to know everything."

"Like what?"

"Look Joyce, I'm not going to give him another reason to threaten you."

The line was silent for a moment. "Well, that's *very nice* of you, Sam, but don't even think I'll put up with that kind of answer. Besides, I already know how the Indian girl was mistreated by the boys on the ball team."

"Joyce, I don't want you to be in the way if someone tries to take aim at me. Now, that's not just a figure of speech. For your own protection, I can't involve you any further in this case than I already have. If you run across anything else that pertains to it, call me from your house. If I'm not home, call Charlie Redman. Let's bide our time, and be discreet when we talk."

The line went quiet. "Joyce? Are you there?"

"Yes Sam. You don't have to worry about being seen around me. I understand."

"Joyce?"

"I have to leave for work now. I have some reports, and a reading list to make up. I'll be sure to call if I hear of anything *important*."

"*Joyce!*"

"*What?*"

"Can you ride a horse?"

"*What?* What's that got to do with anything?"

"A lot. How about joining me for a horseback ride on Sunday?"

The line was silent for a few seconds. "Do you mean that?"

"Of course I do, Joyce."

"Good, because I'll be darned if that pompous bully is going to stop me from seeing whoever I want to. And for your information, Mr. Begay, I've been riding horses since I was a little girl."

Sam was smiling when he hung up the phone. *There* was a woman who could talk straight and say what she means.

He grinned as he put water on the stove for coffee, and while it heated, a few thoughts crept into his mind—the first being, "what in the world was he getting into?" He had a feeling Principal Dallas was neck-deep in a pile of something smelly, and if he gave the man a little more time, he just might lead him to whoever made the pile in the first place.

Sam knew all about the cultural tension between whites and the native population. Some of his people expressed similar thoughts. He also knew these things were not the basis for Dallas's words to Joyce. His words spoke of simple fear and intimidation, and there was purpose and logic behind them.

What was that purpose? What set off the actions of a killer like Louis Montoya? What was the logic behind the wolf hair murders?

CHAPTER 36

Bud Thomas woke with the house still in disarray. He could hear the late morning Detroit traffic as he sat on the bed in his rumpled clothes. Groaning from the splitting pain of a hangover, he tried to focus his eyes as he stood, and accidently bumped the table lamp. He winced and groaned when he heard the porcelain break. *"You bitch, where are you?"*

A half-hour later, with his face washed, his hair combed, and the remains of a pot of leftover coffee in him, he felt awake enough to think.

Helen and her daughter had not been home since early yesterday, and they were still missing. She had threated to leave after their argument two nights ago. Did she really go? Not if she knew what was good for her.

He looked around the kitchen, and saw the dirty dishes piled in the sink. Hell, she never left things messed up like this; maybe she thought he'd be gone for a few days, and she would have time to clean up later.

The smell of the garbage can under the sink made him sick, and he put on his shoes to take it downstairs. He lifted the paper sack out of the can, and the bottom split open, dumping the whole mess on the floor.

"Shit!" He screamed, willing himself not to explode and kick the mess across the room. He took a deep breath, found an empty bag, and started picking up the garbage.

Bud was nearly through, when he uncovered a crumpled piece of colored paper with some printing on it. A supermarket flyer, he thought. Curious enough to unfold it, he found a train schedule.

"What the...where did she get this?" He looked at the schedule of destinations, and arrival and departure times, and he saw where someone had underlined one of the departures; yesterday at 11:15 a.m. "Jeez," was all he could say. He saw it included a stop in Albuquerque, New Mexico, on Tuesday the 17, also underlined.

He was ready to explode when he saw a crumpled envelope and an old Christmas card. He brushed away a smear of coffee grounds and dried food, and saw it was from her uncle she used to talk about who lived in New Mexico. There wasn't much writing on the card, and the envelope was torn, without a full return address. He set the schedule and the card on the kitchen table, and finished cleaning up the trash.

Later, he was about to throw the card away, when he thought of something. He jumped from the chair in panic. "The money!" Dashing to the utility closet where he kept his tools, he pulled out the metal toolbox and lifted out the heavy tray. He found the package of wrapped bills, and discovered it was light. When he tore it open, he counted $2,500; exactly half of what should be there. *She took his MONEY!*

An hour later, Bud Thomas pushed the station clerk into the back room while Artie stood guard in front of the ticket window. The train station was quiet this time in the afternoon. Bud shoved the man against the wall, and pulled a knife from his pocket, releasing the catch on the spring-loaded blade as he brought it up to the man's face.

The clerk's eyes bulged as Bud asked him again if he recalled a woman and her daughter leave on the Friday train.

"M-m-m-mister, I swear I don't remember a woman and a young girl that age buying a ticket. If you're looking for someone who boarded a train on Friday, all I can tell you is the direction it was going."

"So tell me smart guy. If they left between 7:00 a.m. and 7:00 p.m, where would they go?"

"Well, here's the schedule. There were two trains taking on passengers during that time; one heading east to New York, and the other, west to Los Angeles."

"That's more like it," Bud said. "Now, if you're smart, you'll forget all about me and what we talked about."

"M-m-mister, I've already forgotten everything since before you showed up, and I'm not likely to remember anything else except going home tonight."

Bud smiled at the clerk and stared at him with his dead eyes. "Since you decided to be helpful, I'll forget about your uncooperative attitude at the ticket window. Here's a ten spot. Take the missus out to dinner and celebrate your good sense. I was never here—ain't that so?"

"Y-y-yes, that's right…I never saw you."

Bud walked away, and Artie joined him as they left the station.

"Did he tell you anything?"

"Yeah, he said he didn't see or hear nothing except the $10 bill I gave him to keep quiet."

"What should we do now?"

Bud wasn't sure. He needed to think about the connection between the train schedule, and his wife's uncle from New Mexico. "Artie, do you think the boss would let us go on vacation so I can hunt down that thieving bitch?"

"Ha," Artie said, "I think if you ever told him something like that, he'd probably ask for your shoe size so he could have me make up a custom pair of cement overshoes for you."

"Yeah, that's what I thought."

All Bud knew was that Helen and her daughter left for parts unknown with $2,500 of his money; possibly west to New Mexico. "Artie, what I can't understand is where she got the nerve to do something like that? Nobody steals from Bud Thomas—nobody!"

Later that afternoon, Bud and Artie drove down an alley behind a certain dry cleaner's business, and entered the back of the building next door.

Inside, Mr. Richard Denocotti, a heavy-set man wearing a suit that looked like it cost more than most peoples' automobiles, pondered how to best keep tabs on the growing, joint operation out west. He needed to send a couple of good boys to watch over his interests, but not necessarily his best people. A knock came on his door, and Billy Fig, his right hand man, stuck his head in. "Boss, the two guys you wanted to talk to about that job out west just walked in."

"How well do you know them, Billy?"

"I've seen them around. They're a couple of Joey's boys, and they look smart enough. Joey said one of them practically begged to take the job when he heard it would take him to New Mexico."

Denocotti looked thoughtful for a moment. "Ok, send them in."

Bud & Artie took a seat on the couch near the desk, and after looking the two over, Denocotti said, "Bud Thomas, eh? I hear you're a good man with a gun. I also hear your friend Artie is the one who fitted those two Irish boys with concrete shoes last month. Joey thinks you're both smart enough to follow orders."

Bud said, "We know enough to do what we're told to."

Denocotti nodded to Fig, and began to explain what he expected of the two men. "I need you to be my eyes and ears in the operation west of Albuquerque." As he explained further, and asked a few questions, he decided he liked what he saw in the two men. He told them they had the job, and Fig would arrange for a Cadillac they could drive out there.

Bud and Artie left, and Denocotti turned to his assistant, "When they pick up the car, make sure they understand that I'll have my eye on them. Tell them if they want to keep breathing, they'd better not disappoint me."

CHAPTER 37

Sam picked up Joyce Dobson at her place Sunday morning. The weather was perfect—not too hot with a mild breeze.

She met him at the door wearing jeans, western boots and hat, and a checkered blouse. She'd prepared some food to take along, and Sam smiled and said, "You look prepared to do some riding. When was the last time you were on a horse?"

"It was years ago, she said, lifting her hat and brushing her red-brown hair back. I grew up in the country, and riding a horse is just like riding a bicycle; it all comes back pretty quick. You said you have your own horses; where do you keep them?"

"North of town right now; the same place I store my trailer and other gear. After I hitch up the trailer and load the horses, I thought we'd drive north, and then head east on the back roads toward the Bisti."

Joyce Dobson was smiling. "I've never been out that way. What's it like?

It's pretty country, but rugged too. They say it's a place where the spirits live."

Do you go out there very often?" she said as Sam carried the basket of food and walked with her to the truck.

"It's been a while," he said, remembering young Eric leading him to the body of Harold Borden over a month ago.

"Well it looks like you picked a good day." She looked at the sky and gave him a big smile.

As they drove away, Sam wondered if he'd found a friend. He liked her, and he thought she was an attractive woman, and a joy to talk with. She had a confidence that seemed to come from knowing who she was, and what she wanted out of life. That left him to wonder what she saw in him, if anything. Did she want something more than a library full of books to keep her company? Did she yearn for an adventure and some excitement? She seemed to take to the mystery surrounding the old school classmates without much prompting.

One thing for certain; it wasn't his good looks and charming personality that fed her interest, but she did consent to come with him today.

Within an hour, they drove east of the highway down a dusty two-track toward a ragged line of hills. They jostled over rough terrain that ran through an area of large boulders and eroded rock while Joyce looked out the window, turning to smile at him every now and then.

She said, "How did you ever become a U.S. Marshal, Sam?"

He glanced at her and turned back to watch the road. "It's a long story." He turned down a two-track branching to the right, while trying to think of a simple way to answer her question. The trail wound toward a low ridge above a plain of odd-looking rocks.

After the uncomfortable silence, she said, "I'm sorry. If it's something you would rather not talk about, that's okay."

"No, no it's nothing like that, it's just a…long story. Some of it, complicated."

"So tell me anyway, I've got time to listen."

He gave her a glance as he steered around the ruts in the road. "I suppose I might as well. You're likely to drag it out of me sooner or later."

She giggled when she saw his lopsided grin. "Sam, you must think I'm a pest."

"No, it's not that; it's more like persistence. You have a gift."

Joyce beamed a big smile at him. "It's refreshing to speak to a man with enough intelligence to know when to humor a girl. So tell me."

"Okay, you win. You're the darnedest woman I've ever met." He shook his head.

"Start talking then, and stop changing the subject." She rested her arm across the back of the seat and poked him on the shoulder.

He rolled his eyes and gave an exaggerated sigh, and grinned. "When I finished school, I got a chance to attend the University of New Mexico to study law enforcement. After I graduated, I joined the Bureau of Indian

Affairs Law and Order Division and worked alongside the local FBI agent in Gallup. The agents came and went, but I stuck around for twenty years before I quit two years ago."

"Is that when you became a U.S. Marshal?"

"No, not right away. I was approached by someone in Washington to do some special work, and I got a Marshal's badge to make it official."

"Okay, that covers your job. What else do you do to keep busy when you're not working?"

"I have a small ranch south of Chaco Canyon. I just leased it to one of the movie studios to use as a base for filming some western movies."

"That sounds exciting. Will you get a chance to watch them make a movie?"

"I guess I could, but they just took over recently, and I think they'd rather not be bothered for a while so they can set up their equipment and start their work."

Joyce took a deep breath of fragrant desert air as she looked at the rugged landscape around them. "Everything seems so strange and wonderful out here. Thank you for inviting me today, Sam."

As they drove across a dry, sandy wash, Sam said, "This is part of the Chaco Wash that runs through Chaco Canyon. Have you ever been out there?"

"Oh yes, a few times. I think it's beautiful and haunting. Oh look at that odd line of rocks up ahead!"

"My people call them hoodoos—big medicine some say."

"I've seen some pictures before—and I remember some that looked like giant mushrooms. Look over there; it looks like a row of rock teepees, or a line of people standing in long robes."

"Yes, and some people call them fairy chimneys and goblins."

She was quiet as she took in the unusual scenery, and then she said, "Sam, why did you ask me to come with you today?"

Approaching a place to climb up the other side of the wash, and startled by her question, he felt his face growing warm as he concentrated on keeping traction in the sand.

On top of the bank, he slowed and stopped. "I guess I asked you because I think you make a pretty good friend, and I didn't like how Principal Dallas talked to you." They both were silent as they looked at the scenery around them. Sam said, "Why did *you* come with *me* today?"

The Lightning Tree

She looked frankly into his eyes. "Because, I think you're a good man, and believe in what you're doing. I don't know many people like you, Sam, and I enjoy being around you."

He felt his face warming, and he was afraid he would blush—it only made it worse.

She giggled at his discomfort. "Also, because you blush easier than anyone else I've ever met."

Sam tried to hide his smile, and drove a quarter-mile further before he pulled off the trail and parked. They got out and saddled the horses, and when Sam strapped on his sidearm, he noticed Joyce's wary glance. He said, "It's always a good thing to be prepared when you go into the desert."

He was pleased to discover that she really did know how to handle a horse. They followed a winding trail along the top of the wash, and stopped near a layered wall of rock about two miles from the truck.

"Chaco Canyon lies east of here, and we'll ride a bit northeast to get a better look at the rock formations." He took a drink from his canteen and Joyce did the same. "We should reach the place in about a half-hour. Do you want to take a break now?"

"No, I can wait."

They crossed another seasonal wash as they rode into the hills. The route cut through a canyon and around several unusual rock masses showing evidence of ancient erosion. Entering a broad, gravel-strewn plain, they found themselves surrounded by the most unusual rock formations Joyce had ever seen. She asked if they could stop to explore, and they both dismounted while she walked around the eerie, alien place. "I can almost imagine I'm on another planet," She said. "It wouldn't surprise me to see Flash Gordon land a rocket ship here any minute now."

Sam chuckled and led the way to a spot with a few cottonwoods and some grass where they could picket the horses.

Ten minutes later, they sat on a blanket with the basket of food they brought, and ate sandwiches while they watched cotton-ball clouds make fuzzy shadows across the desert.

"Sam, have you ever been married?"

He stopped chewing for a second, then finished, and swallowed before he answered. "Almost, when I was younger—we figured it would be a mistake, and called it off. You?"

"Yes, a long time ago. We were in love, and we moved out here from the Midwest. He died a year later during the flu epidemic."

"I'm sorry. Have you thought of getting married again?"

She looked into the distance before she turned back to Sam. "No, what about you? Haven't you fallen in love with anyone else?"

He thought of a woman from his recent past. "Almost, but it didn't work out. She turned out to be a professional thief."

Joyce was shocked. "That must have been awful. What happened to her—or would you rather not talk about it?"

"She died after saving my life and several of my friends. I decided to remember her for that."

"How long ago was it?"

"A few months ago."

Joyce was surprised by his candor, speaking about something so recent and difficult to talk about. She respected him for his open honesty, but felt sorry for drawing him out to mention it.

"Sam I…didn't mean to pry into your past."

He shrugged and looked at the horizon. "Joyce, we're both old enough to know that life is seldom a smooth path. It zig-zags and shakes us up, but we're both a couple of survivors. We've been tested, and we know what we want out of life." He paused for a moment. "At least that's how I think of it."

Their eyes held for a moment until he broke the silence. "Besides, you know how to ride a horse, and you're not the kind to kowtow to anyone who tries to bully you. I think you're a rare person, and someone I'm pleased to call a friend."

A smile grew across Joyce's face. "I am your friend, Sam. And if I ever have to put that pompous, old windbag, Edgar Dallas, in his place, I hope you'll come and watch me."

Sam laughed. "Be sure to let me know; it'll be my pleasure." He couldn't help but smile as he looked at the huge grin on her face.

"Good," she said, "and if I can ever take care of someone who's pestering you, just say the word."

Out of sight, atop the canyon wall, a slender, Navajo female wearing an animal pelt across her shoulders, crouched as she watched the two people below. She took a quick breath when she saw the woman lean forward and touch the man's face.

CHAPTER 38

The old Navajo woman sat in her battered, wooden rocker under a brush arbor watching the sun paint the clouds on the western horizon. She gazed across the line of mesas and hills, and when she noticed her great granddaughter step from the hogan with a bowl of food, she smiled and lifted a claw-like hand.

She took the offered bowl and spoon, and without speaking, she began to eat the meaty stew. She was aware of the girl watching her, and when she finished, she set the bowl and spoon aside and wiped her wrist across her chin. Her old bones were aching, and she knew her time would come soon. There were still things to do, and she feared her failing strength might require a faster resolution to her long-awaited revenge.

Tessa took the bowl and spoon, and said, "Grandmother, my brother tells me he wants to finish his task now."

The old crone spun around in the rocker, her face twisted in rage. "Tell your brother that I will let him know when *I am ready!* I too feel that the time is long in coming!" She took a ragged breath, quieted down, and spoke softly. "Tell me girl, have you seen anyone else near the place of the yellow coins?"

The girl saw the birthmark on the old woman's neck as she turned, and she mentioned nothing of the Navajo man and *Belagaana* woman she saw earlier. It would bring danger to the couple if the old woman knew of it. Tessa hung her head. "No grandmother, I have traveled there every day since they took the pot hunter's body, and I have seen only the small creatures that live nearby."

The old woman scratched her ear and squinted at the girl. "Has your brother asked about the hidden place again?"

Tessa avoided her eyes. She didn't need to tell her that he had. "He knows you have forbidden me to tell him, but he asks me why you have not told him yourself. He says you do not trust him."

"Trust him? Does he think I am so senile that I would trust a man with my treasure? I would rather lie with a serpent, or coax a scorpion to crawl upon my leg!"

The old woman hawked and spat to the side. "Listen child; a man can be very clever. He will speak softly to a woman, and undo her dress while he steals from her. Your mother learned this when she was at the white man's school. They laughed and mocked her as they stole her dignity. Your brother is no different. If he finds the yellow coins, he will take them."

"But, he has told me that it is not so." Tessie leaned forward and wiped the spittle from the old woman's chin.

"Obey me child, and be silent."

"But...he is my brother."

"Enough! Stop this prattle, and leave me."

The old woman watched as the girl walked back to the hogan. She sat and rocked, feeling her fatigue as she gazed upon the distant mesas under the setting sun. Her long journey would soon be finished. What she had waited so long to possess, would be hers. Her greatest danger did not come from Tessa's brother, but from something else. She sensed the presence of a spirit, and she knew it for what it was. She feared it, because it knew of her past.

Tessa sat on her narrow bed inside the hogan, with turmoil and fear clutching her thoughts. She feared the old woman would find out about the man and woman she had seen today. She remembered feeling an odd stirring in her heart as she watched them talk and eat, and when they left, she had seen him take her hand and help her on her horse.

He did not act as grandmother said men did. Did she speak truth, or did her words hide something else—perhaps a deception?

That evening, an hour's drive south of Gallup, Bobby Castor turned his black Cord up the driveway of his father's house outside of Ramah. The headlights caught the long building, sitting beyond several large cottonwoods, while streaks of a red and orange sunset faded behind the distant hills.

He considered his father's words on the phone earlier, and he felt increasingly annoyed by the fury behind them. Bobby had heard similar ones from him most of his life, and he felt he was forever doing something to displease his father. It was time to stand up to the old man and put an end to it. He shut off the engine, and gritted his teeth as he walked to the front door.

Entering without knocking, he saw a light in the living room.

"About time you got here," his father said. David Castor sat in his favorite chair with a half-full glass, and Bobby said, "I'm here. What do you want from me? All that stuff happened back in high school, what do you expect me to do about it now? Besides, we both know the girl wasn't as innocent as she appeared to be."

David scowled, "For one thing, you can admit what an ass you were, and then you can help me come up with some ideas on how to stop this meddling, Indian, U.S Marshal from turning over more dirt."

"Do you have any beer?"

"It's in the kitchen."

Bobby could feel the heat on his face as he left the room. He opened a chilled bottle, took a long slug, and belched as he walked back to confront his father. "What did Dallas have to say?"

"He called after I came back from Santa Fe, and he told me he'd been trying to reach me all weekend. He said a Navajo Marshal talked to him, and hinted that he knew all about the scandal at the school twenty years ago. It seems the librarian helped him dig up some old information."

"Are you talking about Sam Begay?"

"Yes, the same cop who came into the store to talk to you about Louis Montoya last week. It's been twenty years, and now this shit floats to the surface!"

"What do you expect me to do about it?" Bobby's anger came out, and the old man leapt out of his chair.

"Boy, if you open your mouth like that again, I'll drag you outside and teach you some manners." He glared at his son. "I expect you to shut-up, that's what. It looks like your daddy has to change your diaper again before the stink gets bad enough to cost me the Governor's nomination. Sit down and tell me everything you know about Begay."

"I already told you most of it; he came in the store with an old, Spanish gold coin, and asked if I'd seen any like it, and what it might be worth. Then he asked if I'd seen Borden lately. The other day, he came back, and asked about Montoya."

"Montoya? Nothing else? No mention of the girl in school?"

"No! Did Dallas say the cop asked about her?"

"No he didn't. He thinks Begay is fishing. He knows something happened, but he's still guessing about it. The problem is, he'll keep on guessing, and talking to people until he finds out something. Bobby, if he ties you to any of this, I can kiss the Governor's mansion in Santa Fe goodbye. And if that happens, my partners in California and Michigan are likely to flush me and you down the toilet."

Bobby chugged the rest of his beer and put the bottle on the table. He glared at his father and said, "Then we'll make the problem go away."

"Yes we will, and we need to do it soon, and as quietly as possible. I'm going to be up-front with Rance Wilder, and I'll ask him to approve how we handle this thing. He has the connections, and he may want to put an end to this meddling Navajo Marshal in his own way."

CHAPTER 39

After Sam dropped Joyce off at her house late that afternoon, she had put away her picnic basket, changed her clothes, and looked for something to keep her occupied for the evening—maybe a book.

She prepared a light supper, and thought about her horseback ride with Sam. You are a strange man Mr. Begay, she thought. So concerned with your work and so sincere with your talk; if someone didn't know you better, they'd dismiss you as a naive hick. She knew better, and she could almost hear the wheels turning inside his head. He was good at hiding it, but she was even better at sensing such things.

He was interested in her. Was she interested in him? Of course, how often did a girl her age get a chance to spend time with someone with such an exciting occupation?

She saw how Sam put up barriers to protect his feelings and his secrets. She sensed how he hid the burdens he carried, and masked the scars—mental and otherwise. Joyce knew she shouldn't look beyond what she already saw and surmised, but she also knew she couldn't help but want to peel back more of his hard, outer layer and learn what was inside.

On the way home, Sam had thought about what he could do about the veiled threats Principal Dallas made to Joyce. She had asked him to let her handle it for now, but in case she couldn't, he was ready to bring light to the man's involvement in covering up the old scandal. It was always good to have some options.

It was time to focus on his search for Louis Montoya, but Joyce's words kept interrupting his thoughts. He wasn't sure how to act around her. What were his intentions? He didn't want to complicate his life right now, but he also didn't want to let someone like her drift away.

He remembered her touching his arm and shoulder when they spoke. Was it just her way? Maybe she was interested in a little excitement, and helping him on his case provided her with that. He doubted her interest was more than that. Friends; that's all they were. Shared interests and easy conversation made good friends. A few laughs made it even better, and if it ever turned out to be more, well, sometimes things happened that way.

Back at his place east of town, he cleaned up, made some coffee, and consulted his notes from his search for Louis Montoya last week.

He'd visited the bars in town, and showed the man's photograph to the owners and employees. He'd made it known that he wanted to talk to the man, and that he would be around to check back with them, but, as of late last Saturday, after two more visits, he'd driven home without a clue to the man's whereabouts. Most said they recognized him, but they hadn't seen him in some time.

Shrugging off his unsuccessful efforts to find the man, he decided to delve into what he knew about Montoya's character. Other than being an unstable hothead and killer, a womanizer, and a drinker, what motivated him? Was it greed, ego, revenge, or something else? Did any of it have to do with the old school scandal or the wolf hair killings?

He considered another mystery. What would cause a girl like Stacy Toledo to leave school? Did she get sick? Were there other problems? Maybe her family moved away, or maybe she just lost interest in school. Perhaps she suffered an accident and died.

Harold Borden quit the ball team. Did he suffer from an injury, lose interest, or maybe have a falling-out with his friends? Could the occurrences, somehow be related?

As his thoughts wandered, he remembered something drawing his attention today. It was an odd, uncanny feeling. He remembered how he felt eyes on him as he and Joyce had their picnic lunch. He saw nothing, but he felt something or someone watching them.

Sam shook his head, and returned to his primary problem. If Montoya were Navajo, people would say he was out of *hozho*—the balance of things. They would say a dark wind blows within him, twisting his thoughts and actions. He would be someone to avoid until he came back into harmony.

What if it was something worse. He could be a *coyote*; a trickster, someone who deliberately places hardships on people to hurt them or make them die. Or even worse yet, a *skinwalker*; a witch who could walk in the guise of an animal, like a wolf, and use revenge and greed to feed the need to kill.

Putting all that aside, Montoya was still someone to avoid, unless it was your job to bring him to justice. After all, the man was the closest connection to the rash of wolf hair killings, not to mention the missing Navajo boy and the death of his aunt. Montoya may also be involved in the death of Borden's uncle, or Borden himself. The gold coin? What better motivation was there than greed?

As evening approached, Sam's thoughts turned even darker. He thought of young Eric, and acknowledged that he brought the boy to the place where an evil man like Montoya could endanger his life. Guilt washed over him, and Sam vowed he would bring anyone responsible for harming the boy to swift justice.

The streetlights were on in Gallup when Bobby Castor returned from his dad's house to Strong Mountain Trading Co. As he pulled around the back of the building, he noticed Louis Montoya's dented truck next to the small circle of light above the back door, He parked the Cord, and Louis walked over as he stepped out.

"What are you doing in town?" Bobby said, releasing some of the pent-up anger from his meeting with his father. "Dad told you to lay low at Blacksparrow with the rest of the crew."

"I got bored, and I needed some money to buy booze. I figured you might stop back here to make sure the employees locked up when they left. Don't worry, I'll stay out of trouble. It's Sunday; I'm going to hook up with a girlfriend, and I'll be back at the mine before anyone misses me."

"Dammit, will you listen to me? We want you to stay out of town, away from Sam Begay. Do you want him to catch you and throw you in jail?"

Montoya glared at him. "So it's *we*, not just your dad? Bobby that Navajo cop won't even know my Mexican ass was around. Make with some bucks before I get mad and take it from you."

The two men faced off for a moment, and Louis smirked and said, "Never mind, I'll knock over a gas station and get my own cash."

"Dammit Louis, here, take the money. Just get out of my sight and don't cause any trouble. If dad hears about this, I'll let you deal with your own stupid actions."

Montoya took the money and grinned. "Bobby, if I was you, I'd watch the smart-talk. You like to keep your hands clean, but I don't mind getting mine dirty—or bloody. If you push me, I'll push back hard. The same goes for that lawman if he tries anything."

Bobby fumed as he watched Montoya jump in his truck and throw gravel as he fishtailed out of the parking lot.

CHAPTER 40

Louis Montoya woke Monday morning, hung-over and angry. He searched the foggy landscape of his brain and recalled the smell of the beer joints in town last night, and walking through the alleys full of broken bottles, and drunks sleeping off their cheap booze. Born part Indian, he felt at home with the noise and the slurred native tongues of the revelers.

He'd started spending his money at one end of the strip, and made his way east. A couple of women had caught his eye, and they'd kept him company as long as he paid for their drinks. Several hours later, he'd left with a Hispanic girl he'd been with a few times before.

This morning, he sat up in bed to the sound of a work crew running some equipment down the street. He swung his feet to the floor and started to get dressed, and when the girl woke and tugged at his shirt, he pushed her away.

She raised herself on one elbow. "You shouldn't have hit me last night, Louis. My cheek is still sore, and my mouth is cut inside."

"Shut up or I'll smack you again. Sleep it off. I'll be back tonight, and if you clean yourself up, I might take you with me. If not, there are plenty of other women to help me spend my money."

"It's not right for you to treat me like this," she said, anger sharpening her tongue. "If my brother knew about it, he'd blacken both your eyes and make you beg me to forgive you."

"Yeah, well that spic ain't around, so shut up. You're lucky I don't knock you cross-eyed for sassing me. Make yourself pretty tonight, or I might leave you in an alley with the rest of the trash." Her curses followed him out the door, and he drove through town with a hollow feeling in his stomach.

Louis decided to blame the meddling Indian cop for his bad mood. Sure, Castor told him to stay away from town, but he'd be damned if he'd let Begay's meddling keep him from coming and going as he pleased. The Indian cop was long overdue for a bad accident—definitely fatal. After that, old man Castor would have no reason to tell him to stay out of town. As if he would anyway. He didn't like being cooped up and told what to do. He'd be back tonight, and maybe find some other girl in a good mood.

Sam Begay finished supper, and as dusk fell, he put on a jacket to hide the fact that he was carrying his .38 revolver under his armpit. He preferred his big, Colt .45, but the size made concealment a problem. In the mirror, he looked like any country Indian in town for an evening of drinking.

Jumping in his old Chevy sedan, he drove to town and parked south of the main drag. He watched the groups of revelers on the sidewalk and joined them as they walked past the bars along Railroad Avenue. There were four establishments along two blocks, and he entered one, stepped up to the bar, and ordered a beer while he looked around the room for Montoya. After a half-an-hour, he left and did the same thing at the next bar.

A few hours later, he left the fourth bar, and still hadn't seen his quarry. It was getting late, and the crowd was louder and more raucous. There were several fights already, and he stayed back and let the bouncers eject the unruly customers. He left and went to revisit the first bar.

A block away, on the dark sidewalk between streetlights, a muscular man with a shaggy mustache, and a cigarette hanging from his lips, shuffled up to the noisy bar. He avoided the drunks outside the door, and shouldered into the smoky room, unaware that Sam had entered the place ten minutes earlier.

Louis Montoya was having a bad night. He'd started drinking before he came to town, and now, after spending most of his money, his brain was thoroughly twisted. He was angry because none of the girls seemed to have any interest in him tonight. He blamed the bitch from last night for putting out the word on him. In addition, he'd misplaced a wad of money a half-hour ago, and he suspected someone stole it when he wasn't looking.

Weaving through the crowd, he moved to the far side of the room without noticing Sam standing behind a group of people. Montoya felt ready to explode at the first provocation. He looked at the booths and tables for anyone he knew.

Sam watched him while staying out of sight, looking for a place he could take him without causing too much of a scene. He nodded to the bartender, having already told him who he was looking for, and what he planned to do. He moved a few steps closer, behind some people where he could watch Montoya in a mirror, and waited to see if the man might come to him.

It looked like Montoya would join a group of Navajos several tables away, but one of the women began to curse in a loud, drunken voice, and the three men at the table stood and stared Montoya down until he swore and moved on.

He passed beyond Sam's view around a wall at the end of the bar, and Sam became uneasy. That section contained a few booths and the bathrooms next to an exit door. He looked at his watch and decided to give Montoya a few minutes to come back before he followed and took a chance on the man seeing him.

When Montoya didn't return, Sam walked around the bar and glanced past the booths, ready to avert his face if he saw his quarry. Montoya wasn't there. He gazed past the bathrooms and saw the back door standing open. Montoya must have bolted, or maybe he just left to visit another bar. Sam moved quickly to the door, and stepped down into the dark alley. He looked left and right, but couldn't see any moving shape.

He exhaled in frustration. Just as he turned to go back inside to check the bathrooms, someone jumped from the doorway and slammed him into the garbage cans along the wall.

Sam fell backward and hit his head, and through a fog, he noticed a shadowy shape standing over him. He tried to get up, but the shadow kicked him with heavy boots. Sam rolled, and when the man stepped forward for another kick, he swept his assailant's leg and knocked him to the ground. He recognized Montoya, and he grappled with him, trading blows, until Montoya landed a lucky punch and pushed away.

They both got to their feet, and Montoya waved the knife in his hand. "I've got you now lawman; I'm going to gut you and let you bleed out in the garbage."

The man lunged, and Sam dodged the blade and spun around, looking for something to use as a weapon. He didn't want to draw his gun unless it was necessary. He found a broken chair leg and edged closer to the man.

Sidestepping Montoya's next charge, he swung the length of wood at the blade, and hit the man's wrist with a solid blow that knocked the knife across the alley. Montoya, stunned by the pain and the loss of his knife, took Sam's next blow across his left ear and sank to his knees.

He surprised Sam by shaking it off, and the next instant, he picked up an empty bottle and hurled it at Sam's head. Sam ducked and lifted his arm to ward off a blow. He lost his balance, and as he recovered, he saw Montoya turn and run. Giving chase, the two ran down the alley; the clop of Montoya's boots sounding loud compared to the softer pad of Sam's shoes.

It isn't easy to run in high-heeled, western boots. Made more for protecting your feet and keeping them in the stirrups, they can be awkward when running; especially on broken ground. Sam knew he had an edge, but the long-legged Montoya maintained his lead. The rhythmic noise of their feet, and the huffing sound of their breathing, echoed down the dark alley and into the street. Sam was glad for the weight he'd lost this year, but Montoya was a surprisingly good runner.

As they approached a cross street, both men were nearing the end of their endurance. Sam was gaining when Montoya dashed into traffic and narrowly avoided the bumper of a passing truck. Sam came out, and ran into a group of drunken men. Two of them went down, and Sam lost his balance and fell to the pavement. When he looked up, Montoya was gone, and the men were shouting and cursing, ready to take out their anger out on him.

Out of breath, and with blood welling from his skinned hands and knees, Sam reached for his .38 and fired a round into the air. "U.S. Marshal," he gasped. "Back away."

The men scattered, leaving Sam to take stock of his injuries. He cursed his bad luck, and limped several blocks back to his vehicle. On his drive home, he was too upset thinking about his failure to apprehend Montoya, to notice the vehicle following at a discreet distance.

Montoya drove with his face twisted in an evil snarl. He was angry; not because he had lost his knife, but because he had become sick when he reached his own vehicle. His chest still hurt from running, and the smell of his own vomit filled the cab of the truck. No one could do this to him and get away with it.

The Lightning Tree

He followed Begay, and hoped he would lead him to where he lived. Then he would show what it felt like to have someone hunting him for a change. Montoya knew many ways to kill a man, and some were very painful.

Sam turn off the highway east of town past the hogback, and Montoya turned off his headlights and followed at a safe distance. He stopped when he saw Begay pull up to a small house, and he waited for the Indian to go inside before he stepped from his own vehicle.

The night sounds of the bats and crickets were all he could hear from where he stood a few hundred feet from the house. The place was secluded, and it would be a perfect spot to kill someone. This far from town, no one would hear the screams of agony while he took his time to inflict pain before the final, slow death to his enemy. He imagined several ways to do it, and he would savor every moment as the man pleaded for his life.

But, not tonight. Tonight he had his injuries to tend. Montoya let the heat of his rage dissipate in the cool, night air, and he walked back to his truck and drove away.

CHAPTER 41

A thousand miles away, the headlights of a black Cadillac blazed a tunnel through the muggy air full of swarming insects. Bud Thomas drove with intensity, passing slower drivers, and ignoring the splattered carnage on the windshield as the big vehicle tore through the night. His friend Artie slept in the back seat, farting every time they hit a bump.

"Dammit Artie, do I have get someone to sew your ass shut so I can breathe some fresh air in here? The smell of your armpits is bad enough."

Artie mumbled "O.K." and farted again, just because he could.

They took turns driving, and stopped at a motel once to shower and catch up on their sleep. By Wednesday night, they arrived in Albuquerque through Tijeras Canyon with the lights of the city spread out across the Rio Grande valley. They found a motel, and planned to check the train station and bus depot tomorrow morning before driving on to their destination a hundred miles west of the city.

Bud was up first, and while Artie cleaned up and shaved, he went outside to have a smoke. Bright sunlight warmed the chilly air as he walked around the black Cadillac eying the bug guts smeared across the front bumper and grill. Remnants of the multi-colored carnage smeared along the curve of the fenders and hood, and even across the spare tire covers mounted on the running boards.

He noted where the ark of the wiper blades scraped through most of the crud on the split windshield, and when he reached the back of the Caddy, he cringed to see blue paint and a deep scrape across the back bumper and trunk.

"Son of a..." Bud turned to look at the half-dozen cars still parked in front of the units. He strode past each vehicle, looking for any sign of damage that would match the dents in the Caddy, but he found none. With no hope of locating the other vehicle and driver, he frowned and walked back to the room.

Artie was slicking down his dark hair in the mirror when he heard Bud come in and swear. "What's the matter?"

"Some dim-wit creased the back of the Caddy last night while we were sleeping. It's O.K. to drive, but Mr. Denocotti isn't going to like it when he sees it."

"So? It wasn't our fault, we were asleep."

"Sure, and how am I supposed to tell him that? His instructions were to drive straight through."

"He didn't say anything to me about that." Artie said.

"Denocotti won't care who he told, or didn't tell," Bud said. "We'll both end up with lead poisoning if we don't fix it before we take it back."

"Then we'll fix it. It can't cost that much."

"Maybe not, but I'd sure like to get hold of the dummy who did it, and mess up *his* grill."

Artie laughed. "Just like that watchman over at the factory last week? Hell, the guy with the car doesn't know how lucky he is."

Bud swore again and opened the door to walk out. "Hurry up; it's starting to get hot already."

They drove across town, stopped at a restaurant for breakfast, and Bud used the pay phone to call the train station. When he came back to the table, he said. "We may be in luck. The next train is due in an hour, and there won't be another one headed west for a few more days. The one before it came through three days ago, so it's doubtful Helen and the kid were on that one. We'll check the passengers on this train, and I'll ask the attendant if he remembers seeing them on the other one.

Bud knew his chances were slim in locating the women, but Helen had taken *his* money, and he would't stand for it. He clenched his fists and contemplated what he would do to her if he found her.

It was around lunchtime when Bud parked the dusty Cadillac in front of the Thoreau Trading Post. He waited in the car while Artie went in to pick up a couple of packs of smokes.

Checking the directions on the map he brought along, he figured they would reach their destination within a half-hour. He reached to open the door to let in some air, and started to wipe away the sweat from his forehead and neck when he heard a crunching sound. The big car jerked on its springs, and when he snapped his head around, he saw the back of an old pickup truck through the rear windows. The blood rose to his face as he grabbed the door handle and jumped out to the sound of gears grinding and someone goosing a gas pedal.

Inside the building, Old Jake was too busy notice anything outside, and he didn't see Sam Begay's truck pull off the highway and drive toward the trading post.

"Just what the hell is going on?" Bud Thomas roared as he strode up to the driver's door of the truck. He saw a young Navajo boy desperately struggling to put the transmission into gear and pull away. "Not so fast you little twerp." Bud jerked the door open, pulled the young lad out of the cab, and threw him to the ground. He reached down to grab boy's neck, and walked him to the Caddy to show him the damage to the rear end. There was a new dent and scrape, but most of the impact appeared to be in the same spot as the earlier damage.

"Okay kid, I hope you've got enough money to cover the cost of fixing this expensive, car you just hit."

The boy struggled to get away, and Bud slapped him to the ground. He jerked him back on his feet, and turned to glare at the two women watching from the cab of the truck. "You two stay put, or I'll give you some of the same thing he's getting." He shook the boy and slapped him again, unaware of the vehicle driving into the lot.

Noticing the one-sided struggle, Sam pulled up next to the black Cadillac, and hit the horn as he stepped out. "U.S. Marshal. Let go of the boy and put your hands on the roof of the car."

Bud glared at the big Indian, and then smiled and let go of the kid. "Officer, you've got this all wrong. This juvenile delinquent backed into my car, and I was asking him who was going to pay for the damage. I had to coax him a bit to get him to talk."

A predatory look crossed Sam's face. "I guess you're in luck then, because when we're done here, we'll know exactly who is going to pay for what. Let's see your driver's license, and suppose you tell me exactly what happened."

Bud held his words as he pulled out his license. "It's pretty plain to see, officer. This Indian kid smashed into the back of my car. I hope he's got the money to fix it."

Sam jotted down a few notes, and handed back the driver's license. He said something to the boy in Navajo as he stepped over to look at the damage. The boy replied briefly, and Sam took a closer look; then turned to inspect the bumper of the old truck. When he walked back to the owner of the car, he said, "Mr. Thomas, it appears you're mistaken."

"Mistaken? What are you talking about? Are you trying to tell me this kid *didn't* hit my car?"

"Oh, no. I can see where the back of the truck scraped your bent bumper. I can also see where a blue automobile hit the same spot not too long ago, causing most of the damage. I have a dilemma on my hands. I believe in a person taking full responsibility for their actions, but it's clear the truck only scraped your already damaged bumper and trunk, I don't see any sense in him paying for something you already needed to repair."

He stepped a little closer to Bud and said in a softer voice, "I'm concerned that you would try to pull a swindle on this boy. Being Navajo *and* a U.S. Marshal, I'm trained to stay calm in situations like this, but it just makes me mad to see you ruff up the boy like you did. It makes my hot, Indian blood start to boil, and I have a hard time controlling my temper when that happens."

Sam took a deep breath. "I can feel it happening right now, so maybe it's best that you give this youngster a twenty dollar bill, and apologize for the trouble you caused. After that, you and I can talk about what we should do about you lying to an officer of the law.

Sam watched as Bud grit his teeth. He saw the sweat on his brow, and the reluctant smile that crossed his face. Bud reached in his pocket and pulled a twenty from his money clip. "Here kid, sorry about the roughing up. You're pretty tough, and you'll make a good fighter someday. Buy something nice for your mother, okay?"

Bud turned to Sam, "Sorry officer, I guess I'm just having a bad day. I didn't notice the damage this morning when I left the motel. It was my mistake, and I didn't mean any disrespect."

Just then, Artie walk out of the building and stopped when he saw his partner standing in front of the big Indian. "Something wrong Bud?"

Sam glanced at Artie and back at Bud. "Nothing wrong here. Your friend and I were just talking about the nice weather we're having. Have a good day gents."

Sam tipped his hat and stood next to his truck until the Caddy drove away. Once inside the building, he waited until his eyes adjusted to the dim light before he walked up to the counter.

"Hiya Sam," Jake called out, "how's living in town suiting you?"

"Just fine Jake. Got any Grape Nehi?"

"Sure do; in fact I'll join you." Jake went through his ritual of fishing two bottles out of the old, red Coca-Cola cooler. He popped the caps and toweled the water from each bottle before handing one to Sam. "Here's to you," he said, and took a long slug from his bottle.

Sam did the same, and they both stood there in silence.

"What happened outside, Sam? I saw you talking to one of those boys with the black car."

"Nothing much; some Anglo was cuffing a young Navajo kid. The guy outweighed the boy by about a hundred twenty pounds, and I thought the fight was a bit one-sided. It seems the kid backed into a part of the car that was already damaged, and the guy wanted him to pay to fix all of it."

"What did you do?"

"Wasn't much I could do. I was about to offer to take them both to a Judge so they could argue their cases, but the guy decided to forget about the damage. He even gave the kid a $20 bill, and apologized for the misunderstanding."

Jake glanced out the window at the dust settling in the lot. "I know the family. The boy's dad was a trick roper in the rodeo. Not as well-known as Will Roger's was, but he was darn good. It's a shame the family is struggling now." Jake noticed Sam appeared distracted. "Are you working on a case today?"

Sam knew Jake could read him like an Indian reads footprints. "I'm working, but I'm not sure if it's one case, or several. There is something I need to ask you, though."

The old storekeeper leaned forward on the counter, and Sam said, "Jake, you haven't by chance seen that young boy, Eric Nez around here, have you?"

No, the one time I did, he was with you when you went out to look for his aunt. Why? Did something happen?"

"Yes, something bad. I found his aunt, and dropped him off, but I didn't like the looks of her boyfriend who was staying with her. He was drunk and abusive, and I hoped it wouldn't be a full-time problem. I figured to check back to find out, but when I did, the woman and the boy were missing. The guy showed up, and he tried to get rough with me. He ran my truck off the road, and when I made it back to the place a few days later, the house was vacant.

I waited a few more days and checked again, but the house looked abandoned. I searched around the yard and found where someone buried the woman's body, but I didn't find any sign of the boy."

Jake's face dropped. "No wonder you look distracted. Is he still missing?"

"Yes. The only good news is, I know he can take care of himself. He's smart, and he's been on his own before. The bad news is, I still can't find the guy who ran me off the road. I think he's responsible for the woman's death, as well as another murder out by Ramah."

"Gee Sam, I'll keep an eye out for the youngster. Who's the guy you're looking for, in case I see him?"

"He's a bad one, Jake. I'll give you his name and description, but you have to promise not to do anything except call me if you see or hear of him. He's not someone you want to tangle with."

Sam glanced out the window to the parking lot. "By the way, did the guy who came in from the Caddy say anything about what they were doing around here?"

"Nope, but he did ask for some directions and road conditions."

"To where?"

"North of here, to a place called Blacksparrow."

"Blacksparrow? Those guys looked like hoods, and their car had Michigan plates. When were you going to tell me about this, Jake?"

"I was getting around to it. I know how ornery you are when you get riled up. I figured to hold back until I caught you in a more pleasant state of mind."

Sam drove back to Gallup thinking of Eric, and wondering what he could do to find Louis Montoya. He forgot about the two men in the car for now, and realized he had no connection to Montoya except for the downtown bars. That left him nothing to do until nightfall.

Halfway home, he remembered Jake saying one of the hoods asked for directions for Blacksparrow, and it occurred to him that he had a sudden desire to see how a working crew filmed a western movie. He decided to talk to Rance Wilder, and arrange for a courtesy visit to Blacksparrow.

CHAPTER 42

David Castor and Rance Wilder drank coffee after a late breakfast in the dining hall at Blacksparrow. Their driver dropped them off so they could be on hand to meet the two representatives of their partners in Detroit.

While they waited, Castor asked one of the security men to tell Louis Montoya he wanted to speak with him. When Louis showed up, Castor signaled the cook to stay in the kitchen. Wilder noticed, with amusement, that Montoya's expression was one of uncertainty.

Castor spoke as soon as the man sat down. "I understand there was a disturbance in Gallup earlier this week, and I heard you were seen in the bars after I *instructed* you to stay out of town." He paused to let that sink in. "Not only did you disobey my orders, it seems you've also caught the attention of a certain Navajo, U.S. Marshal."

Montoya blinked. "I can take care of myself. Begay didn't have a chance of catching me."

"I see," said Castor after a meaningful glance at Wilder. "The way I heard it, he almost *did* capture you, but that's not my point. My point is *I instructed you to stay out of town.*"

Montoya looked uneasy as Castor continued in a reasonable voice. "There was a time when I was inclined to be lenient with you, Louis. I felt it was somewhat useful to have a man around with a violent reputation, thinking it would help keep the other men in line. Things have changed. Since acquiring this site, there are other considerations, and other decision makers. Frankly, my partners feel that an act of insubordination such as yours is—how shall I say it—unacceptable."

Castor glanced again at Rance Wilder who sipped from his coffee cup. "We expect the arrival of two men from Detroit today," Castor said. "I will give them specific instructions concerning you, Louis. In the interest of the success of our venture, after I make introductions, I will instruct them to kill you if you set one foot outside the gates without specific permission from me." Castor glared at Montoya as his words settled in. "You *will* do as you are told, Louis, or you will be dead; it's that simple."

Montoya sat silent and stony-faced until Rance Wilder said, "Why don't you join us for lunch, Mr. Montoya. Our out of town guests should be here soon, and we can all get acquainted."

Later that day, back in Gallup, Rance Wilder returned Sam Begay's call to the El Rancho. He agreed to Sam's request for a tour, and arranged for time on Saturday morning when most of the crew was away from the compound.

Wilder informed Castor at the hotel that evening. "Sit down David, there's no need to be nervous. Begay was bound to ask for a walk-through at some point; after all, it is his property."

"Yes, it's just that I'm worried about him seeing something that could arouse his suspicion."

"Don't worry David. When I agreed to the visit, I told him I hoped he would be pleased with what our crew had done. I also told him I expected him to honor his promise to allow the actors and crew to complete their future work without unnecessary interruptions."

"It still bothers me," Castor said.

Wilder sipped from his glass of Scotch. "It was a reasonable request, David, and it gave me a chance to remind him to keep his part of our bargain. It should insure that he stays away for the rest of the summer, or at least until we plan a more permanent solution to his meddling.

Castor said, "We'll have to keep Montoya and the two Detroit men out of sight. After hearing what happened to those two in the parking lot of the trading post, I don't want Begay anywhere near them."

Saturday morning, having no luck in locating Louis Montoya, Sam arrived at Blacksparrow for his site tour. He drove past the gate and parked near the dining hall.

"He's here," Montoya said as he watched from the barracks building just past the hall.

The Lightning Tree

Artie stepped over and looked out the window. "Bud, come here and take a look, it's the Indian cop who gave you a hard time at the trading post."

Bud muttered something profane as he got up and peered through the glass. "Uppity damn Indian, I should have bounced him off the ground a few times, and kicked his face in for good measure."

Montoya despised the two men in their slick clothes and greased back hair. Annoyed by their superior attitudes, He said, "Don't worry; the way this Navajo cop keeps showing up where he isn't wanted, you'll get another chance."

"It sounds like you have your own beef with this cop," Artie said."

Montoya glared out the window. "He's been sniffing around my back trail for over a month, and the sonofabitch tried to grab me at a bar in Gallup this week. I've about had enough of him."

Artie gave his partner a knowing smirk. "So why didn't you take care of him? Maybe he's too tough for you."

Montoya spun around, and pulled the big machete he carried in a sheath strapped to his belt. "You city boys with your smart mouths need to understand something; you're in *man* country now. We cast bigger shadows here, and we use bigger guns and bigger knives than you fancy cousins do back east."

Bud appeared bored. "Are you scared Artie? Cause if you are, I'll be happy to put him somewhere where he won't bother you."

"Nah," Artie said, "He don't bother me; he's kind of fun to have around for laughs."

Bud looked at Montoya with cold, dead eyes. "Sonny, where we come from, you're just a greaser. The only thing big about you is how much you crap when the law is after you—and just so you know, a dumb move like you just made can get you a job feeding the worms."

Artie said, "Maybe we can give him a chance to show us who casts a bigger shadow, but all I can tell from here is that he's got a bigger mouth."

The machete was still in Montoya's hand. His eyes blazed with anger, when Artie, standing by the window, hissed, and said, "Freeze, they're walking this way. Get back from the windows until they pass the building."

A man from the movie crew walked with Sam, past the barracks, on the way to the stable and the old aircraft hangars.

"You can see we enlarged the corral to handle the extra riding stock. By the way, everybody calls me Oats, because I'm the one who feeds the horses." He chuckled, and took off his hat to scratch his crop of sandy, unkempt hair. "We left the dining hall and the sleeping quarters intact like you said, but when we get to the hangers, you'll see we're using them for interior sets, and a place to store some of our equipment."

Sam nodded as they walked, grinning at the man's bowlegged gait. "It looks like you did a good job on the corral."

"Yep, I've been at this kind of work for some time, Mr. Begay. Most of the horses and crew are a few miles north of here today, doing some filming. I don't expect them back until near dark. Right now, we have a crew putting up sets on the north side of the compound by the tracks. We'll walk over in a few minutes."

Sam glanced at the stacks of building material and equipment jammed into the two small hangars, and stepping back outside, they walked toward the fake, western town site across the way. He had to admit the place had the look of a well-run operation.

He paid attention to the parked vehicles as they walked, looking for the black Cadillac he'd seen at Jakes the other day, but it was either hidden or wasn't around. As they crossed the dirt airstrip bisecting the compound east to west, he noticed tire marks of aircraft that had recently used the runway.

"Do you have a lot of planes coming in here?"

"Sure do. We truck most of our equipment, but some of it has to be flown in quick, and then shuffled out to some other place when we're done. It's a complicated operation just keeping track of everything. Of course, some of the movies stars like to fly their own planes in to do their parts, and then leave right afterward to go back to their beach houses and mansions in California. Some life, huh?"

Oats gave Sam a toothy grin, and Sam shook his head and smiled. Crossing the compound to the line of buildings and sheds along the north wall, Sam said, "It looks like an old western town now."

"It does, don't it?" Oats grinned again. "It's a bit of old Hollywood magic; we set up some storefronts and fake walls to cover up the old stuff."

As the three men watched Oats and Begay walk to the far side of the compound, Artie said to Bud, "For a minute there, I thought the old

The Lightning Tree

fart was going to let the Indian walk through the building where we hid our car."

"Yeah," Bud said, "He'd remember the Caddy for sure. How about your truck, Montoya, does he know it by sight?"

"I should hope so. I ran his Navajo ass off a trail a month ago, and I almost got him another time."

Artie said, "I suspect he might like to have a little chat with you, eh?"

"The next time I see him, I'll let him talk before I fix him for good with my machete."

"It sounds as if you like to put that big knife to work from time to time," Artie said.

Montoya smirked. "Last month, I used it to take care of a woman who woke me while I was sleeping off a drunk. I was getting tired of her, anyway. Before that, I caught one of my crew trying to steal part of a shipment. I don't consider it work." Montoya grinned at the two men. "How do you city boys get your exercise? Do you wear fancy clothes and go dancing?"

Bud smiled, mildly impressed by the blade work Montoya described. "Nothing as strenuous as that, I use a small knife so I can get in close and personal. I like it when it gets…colorful. Now, Artie here, is an artist. He needs to wear an apron to keep his clothes clean when he works. He specializes in cement overshoes. By the way, I'm thinking of a certain woman I know, and if I ever catch up with her, I just might try my hand with a heavier blade like yours."

Sam and Oats walked around the sets, watching the carpenters work. Sam tipped his hat up. "It sure looks real enough from here."

Oats smiled. "Some lumber framing, cardboard and cloth; paint it up, and it looks like the Golden Slipper Emporium."

As they headed around the line of made-up buildings, Sam froze as he noticed something on the ground near his feet. He glanced up at the mesa wall, and nonchalantly looked again at the footprints in the sand near his boots. They were small, and they bore the distinctive tread of a pair of Keds sneakers. They were recent, and he knew it meant that Eric Nez had escaped from Montoya at his aunt's house, and somehow made it back to Blacksparrow. But where was he now? Believing the boy was hiding somewhere nearby, he tried to figure how long he may have been here. It couldn't be more than two weeks.

He felt relief and concern. How could he find the boy and get him to safety without the people here knowing about it? His's heart beat faster; he had to find a way, but how?

As they walked back to the other side of the compound, Sam kept Oats talking, and afterward, thanked him for the informative tour.

"It was a pleasure Mr. Begay. I hope you're happy with the modifications we've made to suit our needs. We sure don't want to damage anything permanent."

Sam shook his hand. "I'll let you go back to your work, and I'll head back to Gallup."

He walked to his vehicle, pulled himself in behind the wheel, and froze. Someone had placed a rolled up blanket on the floor of the passenger side, and as he stared at it, he saw it move.

Not sure what to do, Sam said in a quiet voice, "Whoever or whatever you are, stay still until I drive away from the compound." He started up the truck, and drove toward the gate. As he approached, Oats moved the barrier away, and waved Sam through.

CHAPTER 43

"Okay, we're past the gate now. You can take the blanket off, but don't stick your head up yet." When Sam saw Eric's dirty face and bashful smile, he said, "Boy, I don't know whether to give you a hug, or boot you in the seat of your pants. You had me worried, but I'm sure glad to see you. Are you hurt?"

Eric said, "No, I can take care of myself, remember?"

"I remember, but you must be crazy to come back here and hide out with all these strangers around."

"I wondered where you were, but I figured you'd come back sooner or later."

"Are you hungry or thirsty?"

"No, they have lots of food, and it was easy to take as much as I wanted."

Sam looked at the boy. "How long have you been hiding out?"

"A couple of weeks, I guess. I kept waiting for you to come back. Why did it take you so long?"

"Eric, it's a long story. I moved out and leased the place after I took you to your aunt's house. I've been looking all over for you since I had a run-in with her boyfriend. I was worried something might have happened to you." Sam felt his stomach knot as he thought about the woman's body buried behind the house. How could he tell Eric?

Eric spoke so softly that Sam asked him to repeat it. "The bad man hurt my aunt. You're not going to take me back there are you?"

"No. We're going to my place outside of Gallup. I'll make you some food, and set up a place where you can sleep. You can sit up now. Are you tired? You can sleep on the way if you like. We can talk later."

Eric yawned, and said, "Sam, I'm sure glad you showed up."

Later, with Eric asleep in the other room, Sam sat at the table and wrote down his thoughts and questions. He remembered what Old Jake said about the out-of-town man asking for directions to Blacksparrow. He looked at the clock, and phoned Charlie Redman.

"Charlie, I was hoping I'd catch you. Can you check out another license plate for me?"

"What now? Don't tell me you found another abandoned car somewhere."

Sam snorted. "Relax, it's nothing like that. I had a chat with some tough-looking men at the Thoreau Trading Post last week, and I wonder if you could check the registration on their car. It's a Michigan plate."

"Sure, but I'll have to do it Monday."

"That's fine. I'm in no rush, just curious."

"Yeah...just curious." Charlie's words were full of sarcasm.

Sam let Eric sleep as late as he wanted through the weekend, knowing the boy needed his rest. Bit by bit he quizzed him about what he saw and did at Blacksparrow. When the phone rang Monday, he picked it up and heard Charlie Redman's voice on the line.

"Sam, this is Charlie. I have the info on the plate number of that Caddy you asked about. The car is registered to a firm called "Arrow Security in Detroit. I hope that helps. Is there anything more you want to tell me about it?"

Sam knew his friend was fishing for information. "Charlie, I jotted it down when I saw it at the trading post in Thoreau. I really don't know where this will lead, but if something comes up, I'll call you."

He set the phone down and turned to see Eric walking into the kitchen. "What do you say we go into town and pick up some restaurant food, and eat it back here?"

After they returned to the house and ate, Sam made a map of the Blacksparrow compound, and had Eric point out where he saw the men store the cargo from the planes, and where the guards patrolled and slept. He said he was planning to scout the place after dark, and he wanted Eric to stay with Jake at the trading post for a few days. Sam wasn't sure the boy would like the idea, but Eric didn't seem to mind.

The two were in Sam's truck heading east an hour later. It was a hot day, and neither spoke much; content to sip from their bottles of Grape Nehi soda, and gaze at the scenery. When Sam turned into the parking lot at the trading post, he drove under a tree that offered some shade.

He shut off the engine, and turned to Eric. "There's something I forgot to ask you. While you were at Blacksparrow, did you notice a black Cadillac with two city men driving it?"

"Uh huh, and I heard them talking a few times. They said mean things, and made fun of the some of the others working there. I saw them hide their car before you came, and I also saw the other man."

"What other man?"

Eric looked down and acted uneasy. His voice was soft and hesitant. "You know, the man who was living with my aunt. Sam, I think he did something bad to her."

Sam was almost afraid to speak. "Eric, his name is Louis Montoya. Did you notice him carrying a big knife?"

"Yes, only it wasn't the kind for whittling, it was made for chopping. He carried it in a leather holster on his belt."

Sam stared at the boy. "They call it a machete, Eric, and…I think he killed your aunt with it."

Eric looked out the window and spoke in a small voice. "I know."

A red haze filled Sam's eyes as he thought of what he would do when he came face-to-face with Montoya. He took a deep breath and said, "It's a hot day. Let's go inside, and I'll treat you to another cold Nehi."

Eric looked forlorn, but nodded his head.

When Sam's eyes adjusted to the dim lighting enough to see the old man behind the counter, he said, "Jake, do you remember my friend, Eric?"

"I sure do. I was wondering when you'd bring him back to see me again."

"Well, here he is. Suppose you fish out two Grape Nehi's for my friend and I."

Jake wiped the water off two bottles with a dishtowel, and popped the caps before he pushed them in front of Sam and Eric. "Nice to see you again young fella."

Eric appeared bashful, and Sam said, "We need to get him some extra clothes and a good pair of boots."

Sam and Eric went to the clothing section to pick up the items, and while Eric changed into his new clothing, Sam spoke to Jake and asked if the boy could stay with him for a while until he could pin down what was going on at Blacksparrow.

"That's fine with me, Sam. It'll be nice to have someone around to talk to. I have a chocolate pie in the back I'll share with him, and if he wants to earn some money, I can use a little help in the store."

The boy walked up wearing his new clothes, and Sam took him aside to talk. "Eric, I'm going to ask you stay here with Jake while I go out to Blacksparrow tonight. I want you to help Jake watch out for any of the men from out there if they show up in the store. He'll need your help to recognize them. I'll be busy for a few days, but I'll check in with you by phone. Eric, there's no telling what might happen in the next few weeks, and I want you safe, and in a position to help Jake if he needs it."

Eric nodded his understanding, and Sam said, "Jake told me there might be a paying job for you, if you want it. He also said he'd tell you some stories about when he and I first met. Some people think old Jake is a grouchy old guy, and he sounds like it sometimes, but I know he cares more for people than he lets on. I've even seen him charge less for groceries when he knows a customer can't afford to buy enough to feed their family. He knows he can't just give it to them, because they won't take it, so he tells them he has a special price on some things."

Eric appeared thoughtful, as Sam continued. "Now take that pie he has in the back room for example; I know there isn't *anything* old Jake likes better than chocolate pie, but do you know what he told me? He said he didn't want it."

"Why did he say that?"

"Because I think he figured you might like it, and he wanted you to have as much as you wanted to eat."

"But why would he do that? He doesn't even know me very well." Eric's face showed his lack of understanding.

"I don't know, sometimes white men get like that when they're old. It's like they lose their common sense. I wouldn't worry about it though, I figure he knows where he can get more when he wants it. Maybe he thinks he might make a new friend or a customer out of you."

Eric thought this over and nodded at Sam. "I think Jake is pretty smart."

Sam chuckled. "I think so too."

Oates raised his voice, and stood with his fists on his hips as he spoke to Montoya and the two Michigan thugs. "I tell you, I think he had someone in the truck with him when he left. I saw him talking when he drove away, and I remember seeing something like a blanket on the floor of the truck."

"Maybe he was just talking to himself," Bud said.

Montoya said, "No, I believe he's right. I saw some odd prints where Begay parked his truck. I think we had a stowaway inside the compound, and I remember the cook complaining about some missing food. It had to be a kid to make such small prints. As a matter of fact, I think they look familiar."

Artie said. "So what? How can a kid cause us a problem?"

Bud shrugged. "Other than knowing you and I are here, he must have seen the planes landing and taking off at night. He might even have been nosey enough to check out the cargos."

Montoya looked distracted. "I think we'd better turn this place upside down right now, and make sure we don't have any other hidden surprises."

Over the next several hours, the men searched every small nook where someone could hide. By late afternoon, Montoya discovered an empty crate with a blanket inside. He didn't tell the others that he had a suspicion of who the hidden person was; after all, how many youngsters knew about this place, and wore those kinds of shoes?

"Look," he said, "I'm going to town to tell Castor about this. Don't mention it to anyone else until I get back."

Bud said, "Hold it; you're not leaving this place until the boss says otherwise. Those were his words."

"So what? He needs to hear about this first-hand, and if you don't like it, you can take it up with me when I get back." Montoya turned, and drove away with a heavy foot on the gas.

Artie sneezed from the dust, and Bud said, "That's alright, let him go. I'll call the boss and tell him who's coming to see him, and why. I'm betting we'll get our chance to step on this guy sooner than later."

"You think?"

CHAPTER 44

Sam drove back to Gallup to pick up some dark clothing and a few other things he would need for a night in the desert. He stopped at Charlie's office first, found him working at his desk, and told him of his suspicions about the activities at Blacksparrow.

Charlie shook his head. "Not again Sam, that place has been a magnet for trouble ever since you moved in—and even before that.

"I know. I'm telling you because I want you to know what's going on in case I get into some trouble. There isn't anything more you need to worry about right now, except that I'm going out there."

He left Gallup before dark, turned off 66 at Thoreau, and continued north past the Crownpoint turn-off. Taking a primitive trail into the desert, he left the track, and followed a sandy arroyo that angled toward Blacksparrow. When he found a suitable place to park his truck, he waited for darkness before hiking closer to the compound. He found a place to watch for aircraft, with a good view inside the gate, and he settled down to wait.

That evening, Louis Montoya sat on the couch across from David Castor at his house east of Ramah.

Castor stubbed out his cigar and took a sip from his glass of scotch. "You say Begay drove away with someone stowed in his truck? How do you know for sure, and who do you think it was?"

Louis took a pull from his bottle of beer. "The guard at the gate said he saw something. Also, the cook has been complaining that he's noticed some food missing over the past few weeks."

"So, why should someone having a midnight snack be so mysterious?"

"Mr. Castor, I'm thinking it's something worse than that. I think we had a hidden spy in the compound."

"Castor jumped forward in his chair, glaring at the man. "Tell me why you think that!"

Montoya fidgeted, obviously uneasy about saying anything more. "It was like this. About a month ago, Begay came driving up to a gal's house south of Continental Divide where I was staying. He brought this Indian kid with him, and it turned out the woman was the boy's aunt. I told her I didn't want him around, but she wanted the boy to stay. After Begay left, I figured he would come back again to check up on the kid, so I told her to send him somewhere else. She didn't like that, and I was getting tired of her attitude. We argued, and she came at me with a knife."

Montoya looked away and Castor knew the man was hiding something. "I don't understand, Louis; why would the boy run away and follow you to Blacksparrow? Did you check back with the woman? Are you still seeing her?"

"Well, not any more, she's...dead."

Castor wrinkled his nose and glared at the man, certain Montoya was the reason for the woman's demise. "I suppose you have first-hand knowledge of this?" When Montoya didn't reply, he said, "So you think this boy was hiding out at the movie site?"

"I can't say for sure, but I think he may have tried to find Begay. After all, he was the one who brought him to stay with his aunt in the first place."

"I see." Castor bit off the end of another cigar and made a big show of lighting it. While he sat back with his eyes focused on the heavy vigas supporting the ceiling, he said, "So, this boy knows you, and Sam Begay is looking for you; I suppose that means the two of them are talking about *you* right now. I guess that also means *you* would be the one responsible for tipping the law onto our operation at Blacksparrow."

Louis Montoya jumped from his chair, his face a mask of fear. "Mr. Castor, it's not like that at all!"

"No? Then please, Louis, tell me how it is." Castors soft voice did not match the intense look on his face.

"Look Mr. Castor, that Indian cop has been sniffing around the edges of our operation even before we moved. He's probably still trying to figure things out; that's why he must have asked for a tour of the place. Heck, the two guys from Detroit told me they had a run-in with him in the parking lot of the trading post in Thoreau when they first came to town. Maybe he was checking up on them."

Castor set his cigar down and picked up his glass. He rattled the ice as he considered Montoya's words. "So you're saying it could be just a coincidence?"

"That's what I think, but it's not for me to say. If you think we should do something about it, I can tell you where he lives east of Gallup. Maybe you could have some of the boys pay him a visit."

"Louis, I think you've done enough thinking for today. I want you to go back to Blacksparrow and tell the boys to keep their eyes open. I'll make arrangements to resolve this problem, and until I do, I want everyone to stay put, *INCLUDING YOU!* Is that clear?"

"Yes sir, Mr. Castor, whatever you say."

David Castor smiled. "Good, Louis, that's the most intelligent thing I've heard come out of your mouth yet."

As Montoya drove away, Castor picked up the phone and called the El Rancho Hotel. When Rance Wilder came on the line, he said, "We may have a serious problem, and I'd like to discuss it with you in person, tonight."

When the sun dropped beyond the mesas, the heat of the day quickly left the desert. Sam shivered and muttered to himself, "Next time I'll bring a warmer coat." Thankful for the thermos of hot coffee he sat and remained watchful.

It was well after midnight when he heard the distant moaning of an aircraft. This could be it. He wouldn't be able to see much in the darkness, but if they lit up the compound when the aircraft landed, he should be able to see what was going on.

He stayed behind cover and waited. He saw no lights from the plane yet, but he could hear it circling the area. When the lights came on inside the gates, they outlined the small runway through the center of the compound, and he knew the craft was about to land. He brought out his field glasses to get a closer look.

After the small plane touched down a few moments later, he crawled to within 500 feet of the entrance and watched the activity inside. He couldn't make out the number on the tail of the aircraft, but he saw several people moving next to it. Unfortunately, he couldn't make out who they were, but he did note where they unloaded the cargo. When the plane was getting ready to take-off again, he returned to his hiding place, and barely made it before the aircraft roared into the sky.

He decided to stick around to see if any more activity took place, and a little over an hour later, another plane circled the starry sky before it landed. The crew followed the same procedure, but this plane appeared to take on some cargo before flying off.

There were no other landings that night, and when the first pale blush of daylight appeared over the tops of the mesas, Sam made his way to the truck and drove back to Gallup.

He slept until late afternoon, cleaned up, and made something to eat before calling Joyce Dobson.

"Sam Begay? Yes, I do seem to remember a big guy who took me for a horseback ride some time ago. I think his name was Sam…or was it Steve…I'm not sure."

Sam was getting used to her quirks by now. "You'd better remember me, after all that money I spent to lay out a gourmet luncheon in the middle of the desert."

"Then it *is* you," she said. "It's about time you called. I was beginning to think you'd forgotten all the witty conversation I was making to try to get your attention."

Sam couldn't help but smile. "Now Joyce, you know darned well I was paying attention to you."

"Good. I just wanted to hear you say it." She laughed. "You must have been pretty busy to keep from calling me before now."

"It was pure agony, Joyce, but being a desert Indian, I've learned to suffer in silence. Seriously, I've been busy, but I wanted to check with you to make sure Principal Dallas isn't giving you any more trouble."

"No, he seems to be avoiding me, but I can tell he's watching what I do. Sam, I'm sorry I teased you. You can relax. I like you, but I'm happy with my life and my career; I'm just glad you're part of it, that's all. Besides, a little excitement is good now and then, and I can always use a friend. Just don't think you can get away with ignoring me again."

"Joyce, you are something else. Don't worry; I have no intention of trying such a foolish thing."

"Good. You can tell me more about it another time, but I have some information I dug up on your case, and I thought you'd like to hear it."

"Sure. What is it?"

"Remember when you said you had a hard time tying things together because the old classmates died in different ways."

"Yes, that's right. There were a few that were similar, but I haven't found anything to link them except for the boys being on the same baseball team. Did you come across something else?"

"Yes, in a way. I don't know how important it might be, but you can decide. I was plotting out the dates they died on a calendar to help me keep track of it all, and I stumbled upon something odd. The deaths all occurred at different times in the year, but I did find an odd coincidence." Joyce paused for effect. "They all happened around a full moon. Hearing silence on the other end, she added, I'm not saying Lon Chaney is running loose somewhere, turning into a wolf man, and killing people, but it does seem to be an unusual coincidence."

"Sam? Are you still there? Sam?"

"I'm here. I was just thinking of something else. Joyce, don't mention this to anyone, but I found some small tufts of wolf hair near the bodies of the more recent victims."

"Oh-my-gosh," she said in a whispered voice.

CHAPTER 45

Eric and Jake worked and talked in the store throughout the day, and quickly became friends. Jake was impressed with the boy's ingenuity, and Eric liked to listen to his tall stories.

The old man put him to work cleaning and stocking the shelves, and when Eric asked about the unusual stuffed animal on the shelf behind the back counter, he told him it was a Turkeysaurus. He said Sam gave it to him.

Eric stared at the large, bird-like creature covered with short feathers. It stood over two feet tall on muscular legs, and it was easily six feet long from its elongated snout, full of sharp teeth, to its long tail ending in a feathered knob. The animal had wings, but the claws that protruded from one of the joints, made them appear also to function as arms.

A smile transformed Jakes face as he noticed Eric's intense interest. Eager to spin his favorite yarn, he said, "Most folks don't believe it, but Sam Begay caught that one out by his place north of here. It seems one of his friends shot it after it broke into one of the buildings, and he had it stuffed, and gave it to me. He called it a Turkeysaurus—pretty rare too."

Eric smirked and said, "Come on Jake, I'm not that dumb. I'll bet it's just a prop for teasing the tourists, like that Jackalope by the front door."

Jake huffed and stuck out his chest. "Now son, that Jackalope is real, too. You being from the Reservation, maybe you've never heard of some things that live in other parts of this country. Nope, it's a Turkeysaurus, and Sam told me a young lady ended its days with a shotgun. He said it was just a small one, and he's seen one bigger than a horse, and another even larger."

Eric shook his head as he went back to his work, though he did sneak a sideways glance at the thing through the day.

Resting during the afternoon and evening in Gallup, Sam thought about Joyce Dobson's words about the deaths of the ball team players during a full moon. He paced inside the house that night after doing dishes, and when he went to bed, he tossed and turned to disturbing dreams.

He awoke the next morning with his mind made up to drive out to McGaffey to see Bob and Vicky Johnson, and find out if they were still hearing sounds of aircraft flying over the wilderness south of their place. If they were, it could mean there were other operations like the one at Blacksparrow.

After breakfast, he drove out to their place, and by the time he returned to Gallup, he had a good idea of what may have transpired.

The Johnsons had not heard aircraft since his last visit when he rode from their place on horseback, and returned with the body he found in the wilderness. This gave him one last thing to check to make sure the smugglers had changed the location of their operation—probably to his place south of Chaco Canyon.

Passing through Gallup, and then driving south on the Zuni Road, he turned east toward Ramah, and continued through the small town, to the same section of road where he'd found the tracks of a small plane landing and taking off. After checking twenty miles of gravel road all the way to the Malpais, he found no evidence of tracks now. Heading back, he drove down the two-track where he'd uncovered the body in the woods, but he saw no evidence a vehicle had used the trail for some time.

He drove back toward Ramah, and noticed the sprawling house owned by David Castor. It got him thinking; Wilder and Castor were friends and business associates. If Wilder was running a smuggling operation at Blacksparrow using small planes, and Castor lived near where he believed an earlier operation also used planes, what were the chances the two were connected?

On a whim, he stopped at a gas station in Ramah to inquire if anyone had mentioned hearing any low-flying aircraft in the area recently. The boy working the pumps remembered hearing some a while back, but nothing for the last month. A few other locals told him the same thing, and when he returned to Gallup, a dark cloud of suspicion filled his mind.

By the time he drove to his house, he had to admit that his fears were true. The two men were behind an ongoing smuggling business, and they were using his property near Chaco Canyon as a new base for their operations.

He lacked only one thing to present his suspicions to the FBI Station Chief Decker—proof.

He could hear Decker now; *("Airplanes, you say? Flying over the mountains? You saw landing tracks where? On the road? They're not there anymore? You found a body several miles away in the woods? Now airplanes are landing at your place out by Chaco Canyon, a hundred miles north of there? The people say they're flying actors and movie equipment for their filming? These are the same people who built that new hotel in Gallup? You say they are smuggling what? And you have no proof to back-up your story?")*

Sam said aloud what he thought Chief Decker's next words would be; *"Get out of my office."* The other agents would shake their heads and say, "Sam Begay used to be a good cop; just a Navajo policeman, mind you, but a good one. He's a US Marshal now, and I have no idea how that happened."

That evening, David Castor and Rance Wilder had drinks at the Cattleman's Club in downtown Albuquerque. They spoke in low voices as they sipped the expensive liquor, and discussed their plans for tomorrow.

Rance said, "Are you sure we're doing the right thing to invite the head of the FBI office to join us for a round of golf tomorrow?"

Castor chuckled, "Don't worry. It's the best part of the whole plan. First, he and I have been playing golf together on and off for a couple of years now. Second, Thad Decker is a big fan of yours. You should have seen his eyes light up when I mentioned you would be joining us for golf tomorrow. Third, he seems to have some kind of a feud going on with Sam Begay. I found that out when I was telling him about the way the Indian was harassing my son Bobby in Gallup. When I mentioned how you told me you were concerned about Sam interfering with your movie making, I swear his face turned beet-red."

Rance sipped his whiskey as David Castor continued. "I suggested he try to sort out his problems with Begay, but the way Decker talked; he'd just as soon Begay moved to another planet."

"Interesting," Wilder said. "That means if we can arrange the Indian's unfortunate 'accident' in a plausible fashion, we should be able to gain enough leverage to sway Decker, and set him up for blackmail. Who knows what might be possible after that?"

Castor smiled, and said, "Yes." He took a long pull from his drink. "With Decker being a fan of yours, we may be able to convince him to tell his people to keep their noses out of our business at Blacksparrow altogether. If he ever does become suspicious, we can use it to keep him in line by threatening to implicate him. We could also make him out to be an accomplice in Begay's demise."

He set his glass down. "I think the two boys from Michigan should be the ones to take care of the Indian. I'm told they both have impressive credentials."

Wilder smiled, "David, I do enjoy how your devious mind works. Let's order dinner and prepare to enjoy a nice steak while the bartender refreshes our drinks."

CHAPTER 46

As Sam sought to push aside his concerns about recent events, a soft female rain came during the night. It made a soothing sound on the roof, and it lulled him to sleep.

When daybreak came, he stepped outside, shirtless, and breathed the fresh smell of the desert. He took in the moist, fragrant air, and greeted the new day. On the way back to the kitchen to heat water for coffee, he discovered a puddle of water on the floor.

There was a leak somewhere, and he debated whether to take care of it now, or wait until later. It didn't rain very often, but he knew if he put it off, the job would ultimately become more extensive and costly. Rather than waste time worrying about it, he put a ladder against the house, and climbed to the roof to check it out.

It turned out to be a tear in the roof covering, and he knew he could fix it with a can of tar and a few nails. He drank a cup of coffee first, and then drove down his muddy two-track to the highway, and headed to town.

After he picked up a can of tar, he decided to see if Charlie was around. Maybe he could talk him into springing for breakfast. He could tell him about his trip yesterday, and bounce some thoughts off him. He could usually count on his friend to come up with a few different angles and ideas, and if not, at least to reinforce the ones he already had.

Charlie wasn't at his office. He drove past his house to see if he was running late for work, but his car was gone from the driveway. Sam sighed, and decided to skip breakfast. As he returned to the house, a strange lethargy came over him. It was probably too wet to make repairs right now, and with clear skies expected for the next several days, he decided to put off the job until tomorrow.

When David Castor and Rance Wilder returned to Blacksparrow late that afternoon from their golf game in Albuquerque, the foreman gave them some bad news. He told them that one of the men reported seeing someone snooping on their operation last night from outside the gates, and they found vehicle tracks when they checked the place this morning. Both men felt uneasy, and David called his son in Gallup to see if he was aware of anything else unusual.

"It's funny you called. I heard from a few of the locals in Ramah about Sam Begay asking questions out there yesterday. He was asking if they heard aircraft flying around the area recently."

David hung up the phone and told Rance, and they summoned Montoya and the two Detroit hoods to the main house to talk. David was certain that the person snooping at Blacksparrow was Sam Begay.

After explaining to the men that they wanted Begay dead, Rance asked the Michigan boys if they felt they could take care of the job. Montoya argued that he was more familiar with the man and the area, and he knew where the lawman lived. He didn't mention he had his own score to settle.

"Look, this cop is savvy, and I think the safest and surest way to get this done is with a rifle at his house outside of town. It's secluded, and a distance shot is less risky than a face-to-face confrontation with a handgun." He didn't tell them that he wanted his own revenge on the Navajo cop.

After some heated conversation and posturing between Montoya and the two Detroit hoods, Castor and Wilder agreed to let Montoya do the job.

Early the next morning, Louis Montoya pulled down the two-track and parked his vehicle some distance from Sam's house. He shivered in the chilly air as he approached, and about seventy-five yards from the house, he crouched in a shallow crevice behind some rocks, and waited for the man to step outside. He had an unobstructed view of the building, and the place gave him a clean shot at his target when the stepped outside.

Hours later, in the growing heat of the day, he groaned, and wiped the sweat from his face as he tried to get comfortable.

The Lightning Tree

He thought of Castor's blunt promise to have the two Michigan hoods kill him if he didn't finish the job like he was told to. Smug bastard; he'd show them who had the cajones and the smarts to get rid of the cop. After this job, he'd ask for an apology.

He still remembered old man Castor grandstanding in his office a while back, and firing his pistol at the wooden Indian—what an asshole. Getting rid of Begay would buy him some respect.

The morning crept on; he was sweating, and his water canteen was running low. It was hours since he first drove up the trail and settled in his position. Was he going to stay in the house all day? Noticing the ladder next to the house, and what looked like some roofing supplies next to it, he remembered it rained yesterday. Maybe the Indian planned to go up on the roof to do some work. With his patience nearly gone, Montoya considered an alternate plan of approaching the house and busting down the door if Begay didn't come out soon.

It was late morning when Sam rolled out of bed. He put on some old clothes, drank a cup of coffee, and set out his tools before he stepped outside to climb the ladder to the roof.

Montoya's muscles were screaming, and he was ready to succumb to his impatience, when he saw Sam step from the front door. He shifted his position to prepare for a killing shot, and as he hunkered down, and shouldered his hunting rifle to take aim, the big Indian picked up the ladder and carried it to the other side of the house.

"What?" he hissed and lifted his eyes from the sights. "No, no, no! Shit!"

As he fumed and waited for a shot, Begay appeared again and took his tools and a can of tar around the building. Montoya prepared for a shot when the man appeared again, but after several minutes of waiting, he decided to move to a vantage point on the other side of the building. Just as he took his first steps, he noticed the head and torso of the man appear on top of the roof.

Smiling, he settled back into his first position. He had a good upper torso shot, and if he missed with his first round, he could rush the house, and trap the man on the roof. That would give him plenty of time to fire again and complete his job.

A few moments later, Begay stood and stretched his back as Montoya lined up his sights. He watched the man take his hat off, and wipe his brow with a forearm. When he saw the Indian look around at the hogback ridge to the west, and roll his head to work out the kinks, he presented Montoya with a perfect target.

The sharp report and echo filled Montoya's ears as he felt the jolt of the rifle on his shoulder. He saw Begay lurch forward and drop out of sight.

A wave of relief and exuberance washed over Montoya. He rose to his feet, and started across the rough ground toward the house to see if the body fell. He approached with caution, and from a distance, saw the still form lying on the ground near the ladder with blood on his head and shirt. As he waited to determine if there was any movement, he heard the sound of a vehicle coming up the trail to the house.

Montoya debated putting another shot into the body, but after weighing his chances of slipping away undetected; he ducked out of sight and crawled back to his vehicle. Before he jumped into the truck, he peered through the gnarled trees and brush toward the house. He couldn't make out anything, and when he heard the sound a horn, he figured the other vehicle just pulled up to the house. This was a good time to leave.

He resisted the urge to speed away, and he drove slowly and quietly to the highway, and headed back to report his success. Because of the long fall from the roof that likely broke the Indian's neck, and the amount of blood he saw on Begay's head, Montoya was certain that the man was dead. However, halfway back to Blacksparrow, doubt began to creep into his mind like a poisonous, crawling insect.

CHAPTER 47

Consciousness came to Sam like a delirious dream. When he woke, he was unsure where he was or even when. He struggled to open his eyes, and decided to keep them closed while he listened to the odd mechanical noises and the occasional soft pad of someone walking nearby.

Distant voices came to his ears, but they were too faint to make any sense of what was said. Perhaps he was dreaming. The air smelled of soap and medicine, and when he attempted to move, he felt constrained—tied up. There was a dull pain in his head. Where was he?

He heard a door close, and someone was talking. The words became clearer, and he realized the voice was speaking to him.

"Sam? Can you hear me? If you can, say something or move your fingers."

My fingers? Words formed in his mind, but he could not speak them.

"Please Mr. Begay, if you can hear my voice, try to move or say something so I'll know."

Okay, I think my hand is moving…

"That's good. You moved your fingers. Now stay here while I get someone who wants to speak with you."

Stay here? Do they expect me to run away? Where am I? When he heard a door shut, he tried to open his eyes, and succeeded. His eyelids fluttered, and he struggled to bring things into focus as he peered across the room. A curtain hung along one side of his bed. *Is this a hospital?*

The door opened, and as he turned his head, a familiar voice spoke his name. He recognized the blurred features of Charlie Redman.

"Thank you nurse," Charlie said, "would you mind leaving us alone for a few minutes. I'll try not to tire him too much."

The door shut, and Charlie said. "Sam? It's me, Charlie. They tell me it should be okay to talk to you for a few minutes. I brought you here to the Rehoboth Mission Hospital yesterday. You've been under sedation and unconscious most of the time since then. Don't try to move. I found you on the ground beside your house, and it looked like you fell from the roof. Do you remember anything about what happened?"

Sam struggled to make his lips move, and when he touched them with the tip of his tongue they felt cracked and swollen. All he could manage was to mumble, "Am I…going…to live?"

"The doctor says yes, but it'll be a few days before he can decide when he can release you. He says you're lucky to be alive with the wound on your head. He told me your brains could have leaked out, and I told him you should be O.K. because your head is mostly bone anyway."

Sam's swollen lips moved again. "Thanks."

"You're welcome," Charlie said. "The doc told me not to make you talk too much—can you remember anything at all?"

"I think someone shot me, and I fell."

"Doc says he had to close a long gouge on the top of your head, and your arms and legs are scraped up pretty bad from the fall. When I found you, your body was covered with blood. Doc asked me if I knew anyone who had a reason to try to kill you, and I told him, I could only think of a dozen or so."

Sam's lips formed a crooked smile. "I always knew I could count on you."

"I was on my way out to see you yesterday after Decker called and gave me an earful about his golfing buddies saying you were bothering them at the movie site at Blacksparrow. When I drove up to your house, I heard a shot, and I found you on the ground, and brought you to the Hospital. Thank goodness, it was close by. After that, I went back to your place to take a good look around.

"By the way, Decker called again this morning, and I told him what happened. He said to tell you to stop taking up valuable space in the hospital, and he wants you to call him as soon as you feel up to it. He says he has something important to discuss with you, and it didn't sound like he was mad or anything. Look, I should let you rest. I'll come back tomorrow and see if you can remember anything else."

As Sam closed his eyes, Charlie said, "Sam I'll catch whoever did this. You just concentrate on getting well, okay?" Charlie left, and when the nurse showed up, she noticed her patient was asleep.

CHAPTER 48

Sam felt well enough to go home on Friday, a week after he regained consciousness from his gunshot wound. The doctor released him to Charlie Redman, who drove him from the hospital.

Pulling up to Sam's house, Charlie said, "I picked up some canned soup and sandwich fixings from the grocery. It should be enough to get you by until you feel like shopping on your own."

While Sam got comfortable in a chair in the living room, Charlie opened up a can of soup and put it on the stove.

"Do you feel like talking, Sam? I'd like to fill in a few details for my report. I have the part where you went up on the roof to patch a leak, and how you fell, but I'd like to go over it all again to fill in some details before I leave you to rest. Do you remember hearing more than one gunshot, or anything else before you fell?"

Sam closed his eyes for a moment and said, "No, I don't. You said you were driving up to the house and may have heard the shot; did you see or hear a vehicle taking off?"

Charlie nodded. "I may have heard something, but when I found you, I was too busy trying to get you into my car and rush you to the hospital. I did go back to the house, and took a good look around. I found tracks and marks from the butt of a rifle where someone may have waited to get a shot at you. I also saw tire tracks on top of mine closer to the highway. The shooter must have left while I was hauling you to my car."

While Sam added this information to his clue cards, he massaged his temple, and winced when he touched a sore spot.

The Lightning Tree

"You still look tired Sam. I'll pour you some soup, and make a sandwich before I leave you. Take it easy. You can call me tomorrow if you think of anything else. I should be at the office all day unless someone decides to rob a bank, or kill someone on the Res."

The soup tasted good, and Sam listened to Charlie drive away as he ate lunch, grateful for the taste of something besides hospital food. When he was finished, he set the dishes in the sink, and returned to the couch to sleep.

A little before dark, he awoke with a dull headache. He opened another can of soup, and went to bed after he ate. Tomorrow would come soon enough, and he would have the whole weekend to rest and regain his strength. He would sleep and let his thoughts swim around in his head. Maybe by morning, they would align and make some sense.

The next morning, he felt hungry and clear-headed. Standing in the front doorway, listening to the sounds, the smell of the desert made the house smell musty. He opened the windows, but there wasn't much of a breeze. After drinking a glass of water, he ate some toast, and realized he was too tired to do anything else. He lay on the couch and slept.

That morning in Gallup, Charlie Redman sat behind his desk, finishing reports for the week. He groaned when the phone rang.

"Agent Redman speaking."

"Redman, this is Decker. I want to talk with you about your friend, Sam Begay."

Redman sat up. "Yes sir, how can I help you?"

"I read your report about what happened last week, and I wanted to find out if he's home from the hospital."

"Yes sir, I brought him back yesterday, and I went over the details of the shooting with him. It'll be in my report today. He still seems weak, and I suspect he's resting."

"Good, I hope he stays in bed for a few more days. I called because I wanted to ask you what you know about his recent activities."

Charlie frowned. "Recent activities? Like what sir?"

"Like what kind of cases he's been working on—and don't try to tell me you don't know. You two talk like a couple of schoolgirls when you're together."

"Well, he did mention he was bringing in some fugitives on bench warrants for Judge Reilly. He also showed me an old Spanish gold coin that might be connected to the body he found in the desert last month. He mentioned looking into some old school records on the guy."

"Did he say anything about how he came to know Rance Wilder, the movie producer who's doing some filming out there?"

"Yes he did. In fact, he told me he leased his Blacksparrow property to him. He said Wilder was going to make western movies out there."

The line was silent for a moment, until Decker said, "That must be how they met."

Charlie was curious now. "Is there something else you want me to ask him?"

"No, no, I was just curious. I played golf with Wilder and one of your local businessmen, David Castor, last week. Sam's name came up, and I figured you might know something."

"Sure, Sam told me about them." Charlie could barely keep from asking why his boss was interested.

After a pause, Decker said. "Well, that's all I wanted to know. Make sure you mail your report today."

"Yes sir I will." Charlie heard a click as the phone hung up. Wondering what Decker really had on his mind, he sighed, and thought it seemed unusual for the man to mention Sam's name without raising his voice. No use wasting time thinking about it now, he had reports to finish before noon.

Rance Wilder and David Castor ate a lunch in his suite at the El Rancho Hotel, and discussed the perplexing turn of events. "So why haven't we heard anything?"

Wilder swallowed a forkful of chicken enchilada, and washed it down with iced tea before he spoke. "Yes, it is strange. There hasn't been any mention of Begay's death in the papers, and someone should have found his body found by now."

"I don't like it," Castor said, scooping up some beans with a piece of tortilla. "Montoya mentioned a car showing up at Begay's house right after he shot the man off his roof, and he said it looked like that FBI agent friend of his. If you ask me, Montoya was damn lucky to get away."

"Then, why have we heard no word about the body? The local news should have picked up the story—hell; a dead cop would make the front page in Albuquerque, and here in Gallup, they'd probably run a special edition!"

The Lightning Tree

Castor swallowed his food, and looked at Wilder with an odd expression on his face. "What if he's not dead? What if he's lying in a hospital somewhere?"

"Wilder frowned and slowly shook his head. If he is, he's had a week to recuperate. It would have to be here in town, and easy enough to check."

"What if he's not here, or what if the cops are sitting on the story?"

"David, it's a simple thing; all we do is have someone call the hospital and ask."

"Okay, I'll make the call when I'm done eating. Rance, this whole thing is starting to put me on edge. We shouldn't have let Montoya finish the job. He's a weak link, and I think we need to get rid of him."

"I'll defer to your judgement, David. Perhaps we should deal with it now, rather than later. It's time you started putting pressure on our friendly FBI Chief in Albuquerque. Thad Decker is a rather boorish golfer, but I believe the time we spent developing rapport with him was a wise investment. Dozens of golf club members saw him in our company, and by now, our associate will have placed a substantial sum of money in Decker's bank account. We'll give him a little more time to discover his mysterious windfall before we have a frank conversation with him. Blackmail is such an interesting tool for persuasion, don't you agree David?"

After lunch, David Castor called St. Mary's Hospital to inquire about a certain patient. "You're sure no such person was admitted to the hospital this past week? How about someone being treated and released? Nothing there either?" No, no, that's alright. My mistake."

David put down the phone and looked at Rance's quizzical expression. "No record. Wait a minute, there's an Indian Hospital outside of town called the Rehoboth Mission. It's close to his place, and maybe that's where he went. I'll try there."

A few minutes later, David put down the phone. "He left the hospital yesterday, and he's probably at home. That incompetent bastard Montoya, wait 'till I get my hands on him."

Rance looked at David with his icy, blue eyes. "Where is he now?"

"He'd better be at Blacksparrow, and I think we should get over there as soon as we can."

"I agree David, the sooner the better. We'll can discuss what to do with him on the way out there."

CHAPTER 49

A week after the shooting, Louis Montoya was still strutting around, bragging to the other men at the Blacksparrow compound about shooting Begay from the roof of his house. Bud and Artie had heard enough, and were about to shut him up when one of the men called Bud to the phone to speak with David Castor.

The conversation was brief, and Bud eyes lit up. After he hung up, he talked to Artie. "The boss says Begay didn't die. He says he spent a week in the hospital, and now he's back home."

An evil grin spread across Artie's face. "Well I'll be. That shit-heel Montoya was spreading crap all this time. I even heard him bragging to some of the boys while you were on the phone. What do you say we rub his nose in it?"

Bud chuckled. "As much as I'd like to, we'd better wait for Castor and Wilder to get here. They want to talk with him first."

"Ah c'mon Bud, we can have a little fun—you know, lead him on a bit."

"Nope. I'm just supposed to tell him to stick around so Mr. Castor can talk with him when he gets here."

When Castor's Cadillac pulled into Blacksparrow, Artie nudged Bud's shoulder, and nodded to where Montoya was lazing around on the porch, talking to a couple of men. They all watched the car pull up to the building, and saw Castor and Wilder gesture to Montoya to join them inside.

The Lightning Tree

The two Detroit hoods exchanged a knowing smirk, and waited for the fireworks to start. After several minutes, a man left the building and came over and said, "Castor wants to see you both right now."

The two were just stepping onto the porch when the door burst open, and an angry Louis Montoya shoved past them and strode toward the bunkhouse.

"Sheesh, some people are so impolite," Artie said over his shoulder. They stepped inside, and Castor waved them to the table.

"We've decided to let you take over the job Mr. Montoya bungled. We want you to get rid of Begay, and we want it done now. Your employer back east said good things about you two, and we figure it's time to give you the chance to show us how you do things in the city. Have a seat and we'll explain what we want done."

Fifteen minutes later, Castor waved to a kitchen worker and told him to find out what was taking Montoya so long to make, and bring them a map to Begay's house in Gallup. He returned a few minutes later with unpleasant news.

"*WHAT?* Montoya left?"

"Yessir, one of the boys said he drove off right after he came out of the hall. He told one of the guys he had a job to finish, and then he jumped in his truck and took off."

Wilder looked at Castor, and then turned to the Detroit hoods. "There's nothing to do right now, but regardless of what happens—even if that greaser finishes the job on Begay, I want you two to make Montoya scream like rabbit before he dies. Then I want you to dump his filthy body where even the coyotes can't find him."

At his house outside of Gallup, Sam Begay woke from his nap thinking Louis Montoya was the logical person behind the attempt on his life. If that was true, there was also a strong possibility that he was the wolf hair killer. He didn't have strong proof yet, but Montoya was the only real suspect.

He got up from the sofa, stretched, and noticed the sun touching the saw-tooth ridge of the hogback to the west of his house. This would be a nice time for a walk as the heat of the day left the desert. It might even help him clarify his thoughts. He drank a glass of water, and put on his boots. Maybe, he would be hungry enough to fix some supper when he got back.

Leaving the stuffy air in the house, he walked down a narrow path toward the ridge, and smiled as he saw the smudge of red behind it. He felt at peace with the setting sun. A little over a half-mile from the house, he found the place in the rocks where a small spring nourished some vegetation, and created a cool oasis for the desert dwellers.

He felt a burdon lift from his shoulders, and in spite of his aches and pains, his mind felt clearer. He knew walking always helped him think.

The weight of the mystery behind the people who leased Blacksparrow soon darkened his mood. Was there truth behind the explanation about why the planes landed at night? Were they moving equipment and people to accommodate their filming schedules, or did the activity cover something else going on? What was the involvement of Rance Wilder and David Castor in the strange things Eric Nez saw at the compound?

He decided to talk to Charlie on Monday, and try to come up with a way to prove or disprove his suspicions.

With the dark, saw-tooth outline of the ridge standing against the salmon sky, he breathed the familiar smells of the desert. This place was a part of him; it helped define who he was, and what he valued. It welcomed him as one who belonged here; it accepted him.

As he walked, he scared up an occasional jackrabbit and a few quail, and when the shadows deepened, he sensed the smaller creatures scurrying about on their nocturnal search for food and moisture. Arid and barren as it was, this place was full of life and diversity.

It was cooler now, and he was glad he took a jacket along for the walk back. Donning the garment, he stopped to listen, and heard the sounds of Gallup, muffled by the ridge between him and the town. The sound reminded him of his obligations, and his place in society.

He looked at the stars, and then north to the flickering lights of the traffic on US 66 nearly two miles away. Mostly hidden by the irregular lay of the land and vegetation, he noticed two lights wink in the distance. They disappeared, and then winked again, and it took him a moment to realize that a vehicle was driving up the bumpy, two-track toward his house. It was time to get back.

He could barely make out the dim path at his feet as the lights came closer. Was it a visitor, or maybe just a couple pulling off the highway to find a quiet place to park?

The sound of the peeping insects and the scuffing of his shoes filled his ears as he continued toward his house. The exertion warmed him, and

The Lightning Tree

he blocked out everything else until the night erupted in a blinding flash of light and a violent explosion. The concussion of the blast knocked him down, and he lay there waiting for his eyes to adjust to the night again.

There was a big fire, and he knew it was coming from where his house stood. With his heart pounding, he ran, tripping twice before he slowed down and paid attention to his surroundings. There was no need to hurry; he could tell by the size of the fire that the place was a total loss.

Unseen by Sam, a dark figure sprinted down the two-track away from the fire. When the man reached his parked truck, he started the engine, and spun around without looking back.

Louis Montoya, though still out of breath from running, yelled and whooped as he reached the highway and headed east. He stood on the gas, and bounced in the seat with joy and relief. As he sped away, he didn't notice a second vehicle pulling onto the highway a quarter mile behind him. Soon, the headlights were bright in his mirror.

Annoyed more than concerned, he looked up. It couldn't be Begay—or could it? He hit the gas pedal in panic, but soon decided that someone from the house couldn't have made it to the highway this quickly. Besides, he had seen the fire engulf both vehicles parked next to the building. It had to be some other traveler on the road.

He tried to relax, and slowed down to let the other driver overtake him and pass, but after a few miles, the other vehicle was still there. Montoya slowed even more, and the lights came closer, but they didn't pass.

"What the..." Was the other driver sleepy, or was he deliberately toying with him? Louis hit the gas again and pulled away, but the lights soon closed the gap, and stayed behind him.

"Damn!" He screamed and hit the brakes. Tires squalled as he fought the wheel and pulled to the side of the road. The other headlights illuminated the cloud of dust that drifted over Montoya's truck, and when he looked back, they were shining in his rear window. The other driver had stopped along the shoulder about a hundred feet back.

Louis, enraged beyond reason for someone toying with him, jammed the truck in reverse, and hit the gas. He tried to ram the other vehicle, but soon realized the other driver was also backing up, maintaining the distance behind him. Screaming vile obscenities, he stopped and reached in the glove box for his .38. He stuck his head out the window, and fired four shots. The lights went out, and he threw the revolver on the seat, put the vehicle in gear, and tore off into the night.

After a few miles, the lights caught up with him again, maintaining the same distance behind as before. Montoya was sweating and worried. He saw the sign for Fort Wingate coming up, and he thought of the hills and tricky curves along the narrow road that led to the farms and cabins at McGaffey beyond it. Perhaps he could out-drive his pursuer on the twisty, gravel road. Maybe he could set a trap somewhere. Who was this guy? It couldn't be Begay, could it?

He stood on his brakes at the last minute, took the turnoff, and stomped on the gas, speeding past the old buildings and up the winding gravel road to the top of the ridge. He took bold chances, coming close to losing traction several times in the darkness above the ravines. Whenever he glanced back, to his dismay, the lights of the other vehicle were still on his tail.

On top of the ridge, he speeded up to the next set of curves, hoping to find a flat space to duck off the road and let his pursuer drive past. He was sweating with panic. If he couldn't outrun the other guy, maybe he could let him get him close enough so he could hit the brakes and try to force him off a curve.

When Montoya reached the end of a strait section, the other vehicle was far enough back, that he could slip around the next curve and duck off the road somewhere. As soon as he was out of sight, he found his spot and braked hard, darting off the road, and spinning around, hoping to ram the other vehicle as it sped by.

He wasn't quick enough. The other truck was too fast, and he missed his chance. Rather than pursue, he decided to cut and run. Montoya roared back toward the main highway, hoping to get far enough ahead to lose his pursuer, but when the lights popped up in his rear view mirror again, he knew the other truck had more horsepower than his.

With headlights glaring, the other vehicle closed the gap, and tapped the back of Montoya's truck. Louis screamed his frustration, and kept his foot on the gas as they approached the road snaking down the hillside. The other driver bumped the back of his truck again, urging him to go faster.

As they speed into the curves, a desperate, Louis Montoya fumbled for his pistol, but it dropped to the floor out of reach. It was just as well, he had his hands full just trying to keep his truck on the road. He hit the next set of curves too fast, slewing sideways, drifting around toward the next switchback.

The other driver tapped his bumper again, and like a nightmare in slow motion, Montoya felt his back tires break lose in the hairpin curves. As he tried to drift through the turn, he had a fleeting sense he had lost his desperate gamble. Clutching the wheel with white knuckles, and cursing at the top of his lungs, he felt another sharp nudge as the blood drained from his face.

The truck fishtailed right, and then left on the sharp, sloping curve, and when the vehicle swapped ends, it kissed the rock face, and skidded through the guardrail into open space.

CHAPTER 50

Charlie Redman kept hearing a noise, like someone hammering. When he found his way out of his dream, he realized the noise was someone knocking on his front door. He groaned as he dragged himself out of bed, muttered something coarse, and put on his slippers and stumbled downstairs. He hit the light switch, and peered through the window at Sam Begay standing under the porch light.

"Charlie, let me in—and turn off the darn light. It's me."

Charlie groaned and unlocked the door. He held it open, and said, "Sam, what are you doing here in the middle of night? Can't it wait until morning?"

A car drove off as Sam stepped inside and said, "I'm sorry to bother you Charlie. I know it's late."

"Come inside and shut the door. Did someone just drive away?"

"Yeah, they gave me a lift. Can you put me up for the night?"

Charlie blinked his eyes when he saw the condition of Sam's clothing. "What happened to you?"

Sam sighed, and looked at his friend with weary eyes. "Charlie, someone firebombed my house, and there was nothing left by the time the fire department showed up. My two vehicles are gone, too."

"Holy cow, are you alright?"

"Yeah I guess. I went out walking along the hogback just before dark, and I was coming back to the house when it blew up. There was a big explosion and fireball."

The Lightning Tree

Charlie motioned to a chair. "Sit down. Are you all right? Do you want some coffee?"

"No, but I could use some water."

As Charlie went into the kitchen, he spoke over his shoulder. "It sounds like you were lucky to be out walking when it happened."

"Yeah, I guess."

Charlie came back with a glass of water. "What makes you think it was firebombed? Maybe something happened to the wiring, or something else."

Sam gulped the water, and took a deep breath. "I saw lights from a vehicle on the trail leading up to the house, and I didn't think much of it. I figured it was a young couple, or some kids drinking. Less than ten minutes later, everything blew up." Sam took another drink of water and said, "I ran toward the house, and tripped, and tore the knees out of my pants. When I got up, I heard an engine start, and I saw lights racing back toward the highway."

Sam took a deep breath and said, "My truck and car are gutted, and my house is nothing but a pile of charcoal. Everything is a total loss. I looked around for footprints, and I saw where a good-sized man in work boots come up to the house, poured gasoline on everything, and set it on fire. He dropped the gas can when he ran back to his vehicle, and from the length of his stride, I'd say he was about 5 foot 10, and weighed around 175 to 185 pounds."

"Who would do such a thing?"

"That's what I'm wondering. Someone called the fire department, and the Sheriff showed up after the truck arrived. After they doused the fire, I had the officer drop me off here. Can you put me up for the night?"

"Sure." Charlie saw the deep fatigue on his friend's face. "Why don't you plan on staying here until you can figure out what you're going to do. I have an extra room with a bed you can use."

"Thanks Charlie. All I want to do right now is sleep. I'm dead tired."

Sam woke the next morning to the sound of the phone ringing. When Charlie didn't answer it, he crawled out of bed and followed the noise to the kitchen. He picked up the receiver, and Charlie's voice came on the line. "Sam, I'm sorry if I woke you, but there's been an accident up on the McGaffey Road past the old Fort and Indian school. It must have happened last night some time, and I thought you might want to come with me and have a look at the scene. I'll stop at the house in ten minutes to pick you up."

Sam was dressed and waiting at the door when Charlie's car pull in the driveway. He jumped in the passenger side, and Charlie said, "There's coffee in the thermos, and a box of donuts on the back seat. I figured you'd need it to get your brain working this morning."

Charlie told him about the accident as they drove away. "Someone reported it this morning. They think the pickup truck lost control coming down the curves on the hill too fast. I asked the officer to keep everyone away from the scene so you and I could have a good look around. I'm not saying this has anything to do with the fire at your place, but I don't like coincidences any more than you do. I remember the last accident you and I investigated north of town, and I want to make sure this one isn't related."

"Are you saying you think it might be tied to the wolf hair deaths?"

"No, but the officer at the scene told me there were skid marks from two vehicles. It could have been some kids hot rodding, but I'm not going to bet on anything until we check it out."

A half-hour later, they arrived at the scene of the accident. The road wound up the mesa, following the contours of the ridge, and a mile up the incline, they saw a section of twisted guardrail torn away. A tow truck sat nearby on the side of the road lowering a cable down the ravine.

They parked, and Charlie talked to the man with the tow truck. He climbed down the hill with him to look around and helped hook a cable to the wrecked vehicle. Sam stayed behind and watched from the road.

Charlie looked inside the cab. There was a body stuck behind the wheel, broken and bloody; obviously brutalized by the fall. There was nothing else to do but leave it in the cab and bring it up with the wreck.

Sam gave Charlie a hand when he came up the hill, and waited for him to catch his breath while the wrecker driver started pulling the vehicle up the embankment. He left Charlie to supervise, and started walking along the shoulder of the road, taking note of the skid marks, and looking for anything that might be a clue to the cause of the accident.

When the wrecker dragged the battered pickup onto the side of the road, Sam returned and glanced into the cab. He identified the driver, half-suspecting who it was, but still surprised to see the broken body of Louis Montoya.

"What a mess, eh?" Charlie said. "Do you recognize him?"

Sam squinted as he looked across the rough terrain. "Yes, and also the truck. Come walk up the road with me. I want you to see something."

When they reached a certain spot at the side of the road, Sam pointed at two stacked rocks, the bottom one a little bigger than the one on top. "Kind of an odd-looking thing to be just lying there, isn't it?" He gestured with his head. "Pick up the bottom one and take a look at what's underneath."

Charlie wore a puzzled expression. He lifted the rocks and stared for a moment before he reached down and picked up a thick tuft of hair. He looked at Sam. "It's wolf hair, isn't it?"

They returned to Charlie's place an hour later, and fixed some sandwiches. While they ate, Charlie mentioned that Chief Decker had called him late Friday. "He didn't say much—just talked about reports and stuff, but he did ask what kind of case you were working on lately, and if I knew how you came to know David Castor and Rance Wilder. I told him you leased your Blacksparrow property to them to use as a base to film some western movies, but that was all I knew."

Sam stopped chewing. "That's odd. How would he hear about that? There must be more than simple curiosity on his mind to spark his interest."

"Like what?"

"I don't know—and that's what bothers me."

Charlie took another bite of his sandwich and changed the subject. "I noticed you picked up some broken glass and stuff you found on the side of the road away from the accident."

"Yes, I found some pieces of tail lights and some headlight glass. I figured I'd check it against the broken stuff on the truck, and see if any of it matches."

Sam, people have been losing stuff off their cars along that road for years."

"Yeah I guess, but I'm going to save the pieces anyway, just in case I get a chance to check it against some other vehicle I come across. By the way, the boots on Montoya's body match the prints I found out by my place. I'm certain he's the one who set the fire. The only thing I don't believe is that he left that tuft of hair under the rock on the side of the road. The wolf hair killer staged that clue for us to find, and it means that Louis Montoya isn't the killer."

Charlie stopped chewing, and considered the implication.

"Charlie, something suspicious is going on at Blacksparrow. When I went out there for a tour, that missing Indian boy, Eric Nez, stowed away in my truck when I drove away. He told me he was hiding inside the compound for several days. I went back there to watch the place at night, and I saw a couple planes come in, drop some cargo, and leave. The people who leased the place had an explanation for it, but I'm not so sure about it now. Something just isn't right."

"Why's that?"

"Almost two weeks ago, I ran into two sharp-dressed hoods in front of the trading post in Thoreau, and I found out they were asking directions to Blacksparrow. Then, when Eric and I talked as we drove away from the place, he told me about seeing the two men out there."

"So?" Charlie chewed and swallowed a bite of sandwich.

"A week ago, someone, shot me off my roof, and now, a week later, someone firebombed it, and I think he ended up dead in a ravine."

"You think it was Montoya?"

"Who else? Eric told me he also saw Montoya at Blacksparrow."

"Well, he won't be bothering you again," Charlie said.

"Charlie, you're missing the point. They're all connected to the Blacksparrow movie people, and I've seen some very suspicious activity out there involving aircraft landing after dark. There is one other thing; Jack Whorten, that government guy from Washington you met a while back, called and told me to be on the lookout for mob activity in the area. Charlie, I think I found their smuggling operation."

Charlie put down his sandwich. "What should we do?"

"That's a good question. I don't want to do anything until I can get hard proof of what they're up to." Sam looked thoughtful for a moment. "I want to cast a wide enough net to catch whoever is behind it all."

"How do we do that?"

"I don't know. They guard the place too well to slip in through the front gate. I'm not ready to try anything yet, but with the kind of people involved in this operation, I'm sure we'll need some help."

They finished eating in silence, and then Charlie said, "It makes me wonder about Chief Decker's call. Why did he ask if I knew about you having anything to do with Rance Wilder and David Castor?"

CHAPTER 51

Sam spent the rest of the afternoon at Charlie's trying to put some notes together. Frustrated that his records were lost in the fire as well as his personal belongings, he did his best to list the information he could remember on the wolf hair killings. It gave him a chance to refresh his memory and look at things from another angle.

The list of suspects for the killings was smaller now, and Bobby Castor was the last living student from the school team. Everything seemed to focus on the players. Was it something they did—or knew? He didn't think of Bobby as a killer, and if he wasn't, he was most likely the next, and last, victim. So who was the killer?

He also had something else to investigate, and that involved David Castor and Rance Wilder, as well as the two men in the Cadillac. Perhaps they all were involved in the clandestine activity at Blacksparrow.

Charlie walked into the kitchen. "You have a frustrated look on your face Sam. Is something stuck in your craw?"

Sam sat back in his chair. "Charlie, I just realized that every mess I've been in over the last few years involves Blacksparrow. It's like a curse. First; the Nazi spies, and everything that happened with it, and then that ancient ruin we found underneath the mesa, not to mention those creatures, and now, some Hollywood big shots with mob connections are up to something. When I'm done with this, Charlie, I'm going to close the place and forget I ever heard of it."

Charlie opened a beer. He gestured to Sam, who shook his head and said, "I'll stick to coffee. I want to run these wolf hair clues to the ground before I take a break."

"Okay," Charlie said. "Where do you stand with it?"

"Well, with Montoya dead, Bobby Castor is the last living ball player. That makes him the last person who might have first-hand knowledge of what went on twenty years ago. Edgar Dallas, the school principal, was the coach at the time, and he and Bobby's father might know something, but Stacy Toledo would be the only one who would know for sure, and no one has heard from her since."

Charlie took a long swig of beer. "Maybe she's dead. The odds are, all you have are the three living witnesses. I'd concentrate on putting the pressure on them, and try to find out what happened to her."

"And if the three prove to be tough nuts to crack?"

Charlie belched. "Then find something you can use to crack their nuts." Charlie smirked and said, "I'm going to get groceries. See you later."

While Sam finished his notes, he thought of calling call Joyce Dobson to tell her what happened this past week, and where he was staying. He enjoyed her company, and she was a useful source of information. As he picked up the phone, he realized he might be pulling her deeper into a very dangerous case, and all he could do to protect her was to keep a closer eye on her. Fortunately, he would enjoy that part."

"Sam Begay! Am I glad you called."

"Why? Is something wrong?" He could barely hide the concern from his voice.

"I hope not, I baked a cherry pie, and I called earlier to see if you'd like to come over for a slice. Your phone was out of order. Did you just get it fixed?"

"Uh...no Joyce, somebody set fire to my house last night."

"What? Are you serious? You're not hurt are you?"

"No, I'm alright, but the place is a total loss, as well as my two vehicles."

"Oh Sam! Where are you calling from? Do you have a place to stay?"

"I'm over at Charlie Redman's house for the time being. He said I could stay until I get things figured out."

Are you close by? Why don't you both come over for supper and some pie?"

"Well, he's out right now. I could ask him when he gets back."

"He's a bachelor, isn't he? Do you think he'd pass up a chance for a home-cooked meal and some fresh baked pie?"

Sam grinned. "Not Charlie. I guess I'd like you both to meet anyway. When do you want us there?"

Charlie and Sam showed up at Joyce's house a little after 5:30. She met them at the door wearing a colorful summer dress. Her hair looked soft, and Sam was surprised to see her without her glasses. He looked around at the comfortable furnishing in her house, and was instantly at ease.

Charlie seemed to feel the same way, and after introductions, he said, "Sam tried to talk me out of coming along—something about three's a crowd—but when I mentioned I was the one with the car, he agreed to put up with me." Charlie's grin and Sam's exaggerated expression told her these two men were good friends and used to teasing each other.

Joyce said, "Sam, if you need to borrow a car for a while, I have an old one in the garage you can use. It runs, but you might have to put some new tires on it."

Sam thought about it, and when it appeared he might decline the offer, she said, "It's just taking up space. I don't use it, and it's not much to look at, but it beats walking or hitching a ride."

Sam and Charlie exchanged a speculative look, and went to the garage to look at the car while Joyce finished preparing dinner. When they came back to the house, Sam said, "We got it started, but it needs a tune-up. I'll come by tomorrow and do something about the tires. Thanks for the offer Joyce, it'll sure help."

"Forget it; it'll be nice to have the extra room in the garage again. Why don't you boys wash up, and I'll finish setting the table so we can eat."

Sam and Charlie ate like hungry bears, and Joyce chuckled as they cleared their plates and took seconds. "My gosh, it makes a woman proud to know someone likes her cooking."

Sam put down his napkin and sat back in his chair. "Careful what you say Joyce; Charlie will volunteer to show up every night if it makes you feel that good. I might start feeling jealous, and suspicious of his intentions. After all, I saw you first."

They all chuckled, and after cleaning off the table, Joyce poured coffee. "Now that I've fed you, you're going to have to tell me what happened to your house Sam."

Sam took a deep breath, and glanced at Charlie. "I guess I might as well tell you everything."

Joyce eyed both of the men. "Good, because after you do, I'll tell you something I found out yesterday."

Sam turned to Charlie and said, "Joyce has been doing some research for me on the wolf hair victims. I think we can tell her what we know about the case."

Sam talked about the firebombing, and about the wrecked automobile and the body they found off the McGaffey road, he also explained the string of deaths of the old baseball team players. "That leaves Bobby Castor as the last living ballplayer, and he may be the next victim, or even the killer. What did you find out?"

Joyce refilled their coffee cups, and sat down. "Do you remember when I said I'd talk to some of the old alumni students about what they remembered about the old ball team?" She glanced at both men, and saw that she had their attention. "I had a phone call from the sister of one of the players back then. Her name is Betty Summers, and her brother was Jesse Summers."

Sam recollected the name on the list he made. "Jesse died in the war, didn't he?"

"Yes, but before that, he told his older sister what happened one night when all the teammates got together at their old party spot south of town. It seems Stacy Toledo was living with the Castors while she went to school." She noted Sam's surprise and continued. "The girl was in some kind of sponsored student program. Jesse told her that all the boys were drinking when Bobby brought Stacy to their party. He said she was the only girl there, and she wasn't happy about it. Everyone knew she had a crush on Bobby, and when it got dark, he took her in the woods and had sex with her. Jessie told her, that when Bobby was done, he invited the rest of the boys to do the same."

Joyce lowered her eyes and took a quick sip of coffee. "Betty's brother told her that he and the others participated, except for one boy who refused.

Betty told me she said she was so angry with her brother that she threated to tell her parents. He begged her not to, and he talked her out of it. He told her he felt so bad he just had to tell someone about it."

Both men stared at Joyce. Sam cleared his throat. "Did her brother tell her who the boy was that didn't participate?"

"Yes. Harold Borden. He stayed after everyone else left, and he drove her back to her home on the Reservation."

Charlie looked at Sam. "Borden was the pot hunter you and the boy found dead out in the Bisti."

Sam nodded. "Joyce, you told me you checked the dates of the prior killings, and you said they occurred around a full moon, right?"

"Yes. We joked about Lon Chaney and the wolf man—why?"

"Just a crazy coincidence. Have you ever heard about Navajo witches?"

"Just vaguely, why?"

"A powerful Navajo witch is sometimes called a skinwalker. They are pure evil, and supposed to have the power to change their shape and take on a different form when they do their killing."

"Do you mean like a wolf?"

Sam nodded his head. "Charlie and I have investigated the deaths of the last five ball players, and we found a tuft of wolf hair on or near each of the bodies, except for Peter Borden."

Charlie said, "That could have been because his body had been in the desert for so long, and ravaged by predators."

Joyce grimaced, and then appeared thoughtful. "I was just thinking of something else. This whole thing might explain why the Navajo girl didn't attend school the next year."

Charlie said, "And if Borden was angry at his friends for what they did, that could be why he didn't go out for the team the next year."

Joyce looked at the frown on Sam's face. "What's the matter?"

"I was just thinking. What if the Indian girl is the killer?"

Charlie shook his head. "I don't think a woman would be capable of doing the brutal things we saw when we found the bodies. She may have had a part in it, but I'll bet someone else is behind the physical violence."

"Like one of her family members?" Sam looked at the wide eyes staring at him.

CHAPTER 52

The first thing Sam did Monday morning was to drive Joyce's car to Benny's garage for new tires and a tune-up. He told him the bad news about his other two vehicles destroyed in the fire, and walked a few blocks to a small restaurant for breakfast while he waited. He was in no hurry. Lingering over the newspaper and several cups of coffee, he thought about what he wanted to accomplish this week.

With Louis Montoya out of the picture, he needed to let Judge Reilly know he could close his file. He wanted to talk to David and Bobby Castor, as well as Principal Dallas, but before he did that, he wanted to give Joyce a chance to check the old school records for any information on where Stacy Toledo's family lived on the reservation.

Stacy would be the most logical source of information about the wolf hair murders, but if he couldn't find her, all he could do was put more pressure on the others to find out what they knew.

He took his time walking back to the garage, visiting with some of the locals he knew along the way. He found Benny leaning elbow-deep under the hood of the old Ford when he walked up. Benny turned his head and said, "I'm almost finished—just a few things before I calculate how much of your money I'll be taking home to the missus tonight."

"Shucks Benny, I figured you knew that when you first saw me drive in the lot. Take your time; I'll just poke around in the yard, and listen to what the birds have to say about you."

Sam walked out the back door of the shop, and glanced at the dozen-or-so cars lying haphazardly in the tall weeds, all showing signs of

The Lightning Tree

several missing parts. Ducking into a smaller, attached building, he walked around two vehicles awaiting repairs. He thought he recognized one as the battered truck owned by Sonny, Benny's worker. The right front fender was crumpled, and the front tire had a deep gouge in the tread. He also noticed the crumpled bumper guard protecting the grill of the truck. As he walked past, something red in the grill winked at him. Stooping to reach through the bent metal, he picked out a small piece of broken, red plastic about the size of a quarter. He almost tossed it away, but on a hunch, he put it in his pocket.

Walking back to the main garage, he found Benny wiping his hands on a shop rag.

"She's all finished Sam—sorry to hear about you losing your other vehicles in the fire. This one should run pretty good now."

"Benny, is that your helper's truck in the next building?"

"Yes, the darn fool said he tried to blaze a trail out in the boonies after dark, and a boulder jumped out at him. He was lucky he didn't mash the radiator. As it was, he barely limped into work this morning. I sent him out to my boys' scrap yard for parts a little while ago."

Sam paid Benny for his work, drove back across the tracks, and parked in front of Judge Reilly's office. After a few minutes, the Judge called Sam back to his office, and gestured to one of the chairs in front of his desk.

"About time you checked in, Sam. I've been wondering how you were coming along with that fugitive I asked you to find. I heard about your house burning over the weekend, and I'm glad to see you're alright.

"That's why I came to see you, Judge. I finally caught up with Montoya, but I'm afraid he's not in any condition to appear in court."

"Why's that? The man has been running free for too long. It's time he had his day in front of the bench."

"I know, but when I found him, he was dead inside his truck at the bottom of a ravine. I figure he was the one who firebombed my house, earlier."

Judge Reilly eyes bugged out. He snorted, and pulled out a file from his desk. Well, he was a bad one. It's probably best that he's gone. Don't your people have a special thing they call it when someone does terrible things like he did?"

"They say a dark wind blows inside him, Judge. Most folks on the Res. prefer to give a man a chance to make amends and return to harmony, but I think Montoya has been acting like he has no relatives for too long."

"No relatives?"

"It means he has no family to dishonor, and it means he has acted without concern that his relatives may bear the stigma of his actions."

"There's a lot of good sense to that. He was a bad seed, and we're better off without him."

"Judge, I need to lay off any other cases for a while. I have some other business I need to attend to, and it might take me some time to straighten it out. I hope you understand, and I'll let you know when I'm through."

"Sure, it's not a problem Sam. You'll have to find some other place to live, and housing is tight in this town—always has been. Just let me know when you're ready to take on some work again."

The Judge stood, and they shook hands. "I notice you've been working on your Anglo handshake, Sam. You almost have it. Here, let me show you something. Now, lock the web between your thumb and finger with the other guy before you make a grip; without it, some yay-hoo can grab your fingers and grind your knuckles to powder before you get your hand back. It works the other way around, too."

Sam grunted in reply, and walked out to his car. He figured it was a good time take it for a drive and see how Eric was doing with old Jake in Thoreau.

He pulled into the parking around lunchtime. The screen door creaked as he pushed it open, and he noticed the bell was missing. Halfway to the counter, he saw Jake filling a cardboard box with groceries for a young Navajo family.

Sam tipped his hat as the customers walked past, and he heard a loud sneeze from the counter. "Allergies again, Jake?"

Jake honked into his handkerchief, and tucked it in his back pocket. "Yep, it's a bad summer for it. Glad you showed up today; that boy is fitting right in, and doing a man's work. How was your weekend?"

"Not so good."

Jake waited for Sam to explain, and he finally said, "Are you going to tell me about it, or do I have to get one of those Navajo women to come over and loosen your tongue? I swear, I know a few who can make a rock talk just by looking sideways at it."

"Well, my house burned down, and it melted my two vehicles. I caught up with the guy who torched it, and he's dead. Is that ok? I thought I'd check in with Eric so he wouldn't think I forgot about him."

Old Jake took Sam's story to be nothing more than the usual hyperbole. "He's putting some boxes away right now. The crowd is thinning out; why don't you call him in, and join us for lunch?"

Eric noticed Sam as soon as he stepped behind the building. He ran up and said, "Sam, I was hoping you'd come by to see me. We're stocking shelves today."

When they stepped inside, Jake smiled and said, "The boy's got all the makings of a good storekeeper."

Eric turned to Sam with a big smile on his face. "See, I told you I knew how to do the work in here."

They ate sandwiches in the back room, and Jake left the curtain open to watch the front of the store. After lunch, he went out front, and Sam and Eric stayed at the table to talk.

"Eric, I want to tell you something very important. That man who beat you, and killed your Aunt, is dead. You don't have to worry about him anymore."

Eric looked at Sam with big eyes, and said, "Did you kill him?"

Sam shook his head. "No, it happened by his own actions. He was out of balance with this world for too long, and he couldn't find his path back to harmony."

CHAPTER 53

Sam returned to Gallup, and spent the afternoon poking through the charred ruins of his house and two vehicles. He found a few things he could salvage, but most of his belongings were gone. By some miracle, he located his wallet and badge, along with his medicine pouch under some debris that must have protected it, but everything else was burnt, melted, or shattered. It could have been worse—someone might have had to pull his charred body from the ashes.

He ran some errands, and gave thought to rebuilding the place. After all, he did like the location and the view. Maybe he could build something a bit larger.

On his way through town, his thoughts turned to a conversation he had with Eric. He knew how the boy gained entry to the Blacksparrow compound after dark, and he wondered if he could do the same thing. He didn't want to attempt a take-over without backup, in case he ran into trouble, but he also wanted some proof about what was going on before he brought in the FBI.

All he could do right now was to gather some equipment and dark clothing. He would talk to Charlie about it, and when the time came for action, Charlie could bring in some other agents. Stopping at the bank before it closed, he withdrew some cash, and then drove to Charlie's office.

"Hi Sam." Charlie leaned back in his chair, with papers scattered across the top of his desk. "Any chance you could talk Joyce into having us over for supper again?"

"Forget it Charlie, if we ask her for another invite so soon, she's liable to get spooked and tell us both to stay away."

Charlie sat forward and shuffled his papers. "Yeah, that's what I figured. What have you been up to?"

Sam sat down in the chair in front of Charlie's desk. "I put new tires on the car, and I had it tuned up. I also withdrew some cash from the bank so I could cover my share of food and expenses. Say, what did you do with that box of junk I picked up on the McGaffey road near the wreck?"

"It's in the back room by the door."

Sam got up and brought it to the vacant desk next to Charlie's. He started rummaging through the broken pieces of plastic and metal, and pulled out all the red plastic he could find. Then, he took the small piece he found in the grill of the truck at Benny's, and tried to match it with the other stuff.

"Charlie said, "What are you doing?"

"I'm trying to see if any of this stuff matches the small piece I found today. Tomorrow, I'll go out to where they hauled the wreck and see if anything fits what's left on the truck."

After a few more minutes of fumbling, he said, "No match." He put the box down, and Charlie said, "Hungry? I'll buy."

Later that evening, Rance Wilder and David Castor talked in his room at the El Rancho. The air was thick with cigar smoke, and they both had sour expressions on their faces.

"Dammit, I just don't like it," Castor said, "Begay is bound to be as skittish as a rabbit in a dog pen. I'm sure he knows something is going on. The two hoods from Detroit believe he suspects they're around somewhere. Apparently, they had a run-in with him at the trading post by the highway when they first came to Blacksparrow.

"Do they think he may know they're staying at the movie set? They hid out with Montoya when we let him take his tour of the place."

"Yes," Castor said, "but don't forget about that stowaway. One of our men saw someone else in Begay's truck when he drove away. Montoya's dead, but what if Begay comes looking for the other two guys?"

Rance concentrated on his cigar as he thought. "You're right. With the new merchandise we're bringing in, we can't afford to take any chances. We either get rid of him for good, or shut down the operation long enough for him to lose interest in the place."

"You know damn well we can't do that. Our partners would make us carve our own headstones if we even suggested it. Like it or not, Rance, we have to get rid of Begay, the sooner the better. Maybe we can set some kind of a trap."

Rance Wilder looked at David. "He's bound to be skittish with all that's happened, but let's sit down with Bud and Artie and put our heads together to find a solution to our Sam Begay problem. In the meantime, we'll increase security at the site, and keep everyone on alert."

"I just thought of something," David Castor said as he looked at the ceiling. "What if we could get our F.B.I. acquaintance, Thad Decker, to order Begay to stay out of our hair?"

"Rance snorted, how in the world could we do that?"

"I'm not sure, but I know he doesn't like the Indian. I could make a discreet suggestion, but I think money and blackmail would be more effective. Remember, we didn't include Decker in our golf outing just to enjoy his company. If you or I are ever suspected of anything, we can remind him that his presence in our company may also implicate him. In fact, we can take some steps to guarantee it."

Rance Wilder chuckled at Castor's suggestion. "David, I do enjoy the way you think. Imagine having our own F.B.I. official in our pocket—the business opportunities would be significant."

The phone was ringing when Sam and Charlie walked into his house. Charlie picked it up and said, "Hello? Sure," and he handed it to Sam. "It's Joyce for you."

"Hi Joyce, what's up?"

"Sam, I found out something important about the Toledo girl, and I knew you'd want to hear about it right away. Listen; Principal Dallas caught me looking through some old records in the basement storage area. I told him I was trying to find some information for my alumni files, but he seemed very suspicious."

"Joyce, I hope this doesn't get you into trouble."

"It better not. It's none of his concern if I need something for my alumni duties. Anyway, I found some old information on Stacy Toldeo. Do you have a pencil and paper?"

Sam rummaged around and found a pen and a scrap of paper. "Okay shoot."

"First of all, the only home address I could find for her was in care of the Newcomb Chapter House."

Sam said, "Did it give any names of a parent or relative?"

"No, it just showed hers; but there was something else even more interesting. Want to hear it?"

"Joyce, you are making me crazy."

"I can't help it; I'm so excited about this. I found another address she used while she stayed in Gallup to attend school. Guess what; it's the home of David and Priscilla Castor. I'll bet you're surprised."

Sam paused for a moment. "You win the bet. I know the family, and I also know his wife died years ago."

"Well? Did I do good?"

"Joyce, you are a terrific detective, and a number-one snoop."

He heard her giggle, and said, "Joyce, did you find out anything else?"

"No that's it. I hope it helps. Do you want me to do something else?"

"Yeah, forget about all of this for the time being. Put it out of your mind, and stay out of trouble. I don't want Edgar Dallas getting more suspicious than he already is. I'll do some checking on this end, and let you know if I need more information." The line went silent for a few seconds. He swallowed and said, "By the way, can I buy you dinner Friday night? That is if I don't have to bring Charlie along."

"Well, if you insist—but only if you show up on time."

CHAPTER 54

The next morning, Sam told Charlie he would probably spend most of the day on the Res. north of Gallup, but first he wanted to arrange to have his two burnt vehicles hauled away from his home site. He took the box of junk he found on the roadside with him, and while he was there, he would take a closer look at Montoya's wrecked truck at the scrapyard.

Sam drove to the yard west of town, and spoke to one of Benny's sons. He explained what he needed done with his burned vehicles, and gave directions to his place. Before he left, he found Montoya's wrecked truck and checked it over. Most of the glass was shattered or missing, but he did find part of one taillight still attached. He compared it to the broken pieces he carried along, but he couldn't determine if any had been part of this truck. To his further dismay, the small red piece he found on Sonny's truck didn't match either.

He made his way back to his car and headed toward town. Turning north toward Shiprock, he soon passed Yah-Ta-Hey and Mexican Springs. The desert was full of color from the recent rains, and the moisture brought out the deeper hues of the layers of rock on the mesas. It was pretty country.

Within an hour of driving, he turned into the parking lot of the Newcomb Chapter House. The building served as a community center, similar to the town halls in other parts of the country. It was also a place for families in the remote areas to pick up their mail.

He glanced at the vehicles parked around the building out of habit, and when he walked inside, he introduced himself to the woman in charge of the mail. She wore a nametag that said her name was Ruth Toadlena. He told her he needed to locate someone, and her round face took on a thoughtful frown as he said the name, Stacy Toledo. She went to her desk and took out a spiral notebook, and after flipping through several pages, she came back to the counter and said, "I don't have anyone by that name getting their mail here. Do you know if she is married, or if she uses another name?"

"Not that I'm aware of, but I guess it's possible. She would be in her mid-30s, but I don't know much else about her. I do know she attended school in Gallup twenty years ago."

Ruth looked thoughtful. "Let me ask Sadie Betoni. She's been around longer than I have; maybe she's heard of her."

Sam poured himself some coffee from a pot on a table as the woman walked off. He put a dime in the can next to the paper cups, and waited. She was gone long enough for him to finish most of his coffee, and when he saw her returning with an older woman, he gulped the last of it down and tossed the cup in a trashcan.

The older woman, probably in her sixties, moved with a limp. Ruth said, "Mr. Begay, this is Sadie Betoni. She turned to the woman and spoke in Navajo, introducing Sam.

Sam spoke in his native tongue to the older woman, and started by naming some of his family clan members, in the traditional Navajo way of greeting a stranger. She responded in the same polite way, and after they talked for several minutes, he learned she knew nothing of Stacy Toledo, though she said she knew of some other families with that name who lived west of Window Rock, near Ganado, in Arizona.

Sam thanked her for her time, and noticed the Toadlena woman wave to him from her desk. An old man and woman stood near her, and they watched him as he walked over.

"Mr. Begay, this is Hosteen Joe and his wife Betty. They've lived around here for most of their lives, and Mr. Joe says he thinks he remembers some Toledo clan living east of here. He said he hasn't seen or heard of them in twenty years, and he never knew exactly where they lived."

After a short conversation with the couple, Sam realized their information wasn't going to help. He had an odd feeling that the couple was a bit uncomfortable talking to him. It wasn't uncommon, considering the difference in generations, and him being a stranger. He said a polite 'thank-you,' and before he left the building, he stepped over to Ruth

Toadlena and said, "Just by chance, there is someone else I'm looking for. Do you know a young woman named Rosemary Nez?" Sam mentioned the name of Eric's missing mother, hoping to clear up the mystery surrounding her disappearance some months ago.

Ruth said, "Yes. She used to come here to look for a ride to Farmington every week where she worked, but I haven't seen her since late spring."

"Do you know if she rode with the same people each time?"

Ruth pursed her lips and appeared thoughtful. "I don't think so. Sometimes she would start walking, and catch a ride along the way."

When Sam walked outside to his car, he took a deep breath, and tried to ignore the dull ache he felt in his heart for the missing woman's son, Eric Nez.

He drove off to continue his original search. There weren't many primitive roads heading east from the highway, but he knew they all connected to a web of two-tracks reaching dozens of miles into the hills. He headed east, stopping at all the dwellings he came across to ask if anyone knew of the Toledo place.

Hours later, after a long, hot day of driving down the rutted gravel and primitive two-tracks, climbing ridges and traversing dry washes, dodging jackrabbits and the occasional roadrunner, he decided to call it quits. The sun was sinking behind the Chuska Mountains as he headed south toward Gallup. Behind him, the sun covered the tip of the weathered, volcanic monolith called Shiprock.

During the afternoon, he had stopped at dozens of small houses and weathered hogans—some vacant, others in alarming disrepair, and inhabited by very poor people. Most he talked to were warry of strangers, and they acted suspicious and uncomfortable talking about another family.

He had no new clues, and only one minor finding that tickled the back of his brain. He remembered stopping at an old hogan. No one was home, and a padlock hung in the door latch. He'd looked around the yard and noticed some tire tracks before returning to his car. He studied the worn tread, and noticed an odd, jagged cut in one of the tires that looked like a lightning bolt.

He drove away without thinking of it again until he drew nearer to Gallup. As he passed the eroded rocks just north of Ya-Ta-Hey, he remembered. Many people drove on worn tires these days. Cuts, and patches, and blowouts were a common thing. Why did this particular mark tickle his memory?

That night at Charlie's house, he talked about the day on the Reservation, and what Joyce learned about Stacy Toledo using the Castor's address while she stayed in town to attend school.

"Wow," said Charlie, "that could put a new slant on things. It certainly ties the two students together. What are you going to do?"

"I'm going to see Bobby Castor in the morning, and ask him how it feels to be the last living ball player involved in the rape of Stacy Toledo."

"You never were very good at being subtle, Sam. What do you expect him to do or say?"

"I have no idea. I'll let him surprise me. Maybe he might piss his pants; after all, he is the last living teammate. He's arrogant, perhaps even a bully, but a serial killer? It just doesn't feel right."

Charlie lounged back in his chair, his stocking feet resting an ottoman. He took a swig of beer and said. "Where does it leave you if he's not the killer? Wouldn't it make him the next victim?"

Sam made a face. "If he is, then who is the killer? Charlie, let's get a piece of paper, and list every crazy idea we can think of about this."

Fifteen minutes later Sam finished the last of his beer, and looked at the list they made. "Some of these names are so doubtful; I might as well write down my own name. Charlie, this whole case makes me crazy enough to strangle someone, myself."

Charlie said. "Who do you think looks the most plausible?"

"I would say Edgar Dallas, their old coach. He could still be angry about something connected to what happened."

Charlie said, "You might as well consider David Castor, too. He might be worried about protecting his political image."

Sam was quiet as he looked through the list. "What do you think about Stacy Toledo?"

"What? Do you believe these killings have a woman's touch behind them?"

"No," Sam said, "but maybe she has a boyfriend or a husband, and maybe *he* has a screw loose."

"After all this time?" Charlie got up to get another beer. "So how do we find her? You said you had no luck today."

Sam sighed and set the list down. "I don't know Charlie, I feel like I'm looking for a needle in a haystack, and I think someone forgot to bring the needle."

Sam woke in the middle of the night, and couldn't get back to sleep. He questioned what he was trying to accomplish, and asked himself what he could do about it right now? How could he satisfy his need to make something right, and to solve the wolf hair murders?

He knew the statistics of how many killings happened each year in this part of the country. He also knew how a serial killer usually uses the same method to accomplish his (or her) misdeeds. This case was different; the string of deaths didn't fit the statistics, and the deaths of the old classmates had few similarities except for the more recent ones. Considering the time span of the murders, it was as if the killer had changed his or her methods. Did that mean there were two killers—or a family of killers?

His upbringing had taught him that everything was connected, but in this case, the only connection was the players on the school team. They had done something to bring about their deaths. Rape is a violent crime, and it was, most likely, behind the violent nature of the deaths. Actions create equal and opposite reactions.

CHAPTER 55

Sam woke after a restless night of half-remembered dreams. Montoya, his main suspect in the wolf hair cases was dead. Not sure what to do next, he remembered one thing that seemed out of place, the gold coin. How did it fit into all of this? He had no answer, but he knew someone who might be able to help, Diana Witherspoon, a friend and teacher at the University of New Mexico in Albuquerque.

Remembering how she had found a similar coin near Blacksparrow over a year ago, he decided to call her this week. He dressed, and found Charlie's note in the kitchen stating he was on his way to investigate some reports of thefts on the Zuni Reservation.

Sam left the house, and stopped at a diner for breakfast and coffee before he drove to Strong Mountain Trading. Remembering how Bobby appeared uncomfortable when he first showed him the gold coin, Sam figured the man knew more about it than he admitted. He drove around the back of the building, and saw Bobby Castor's black Cord before he parked in the lot and went inside.

As before, he noticed the difference between this larger establishment, and the smaller, older businesses like Jake's in Thoreau. The lighting was better, and everything looked clean. The shelves were filled with merchandise meant to satisfy the tastes of tourists, as well as the locals, and Reservation customers.

Working his way to the back, he didn't see Bobby, but he knew he had to be around somewhere. He rang the bell at the pawn counter, and waited.

A moment later, Bobby came out, and Sam noticed his eyes widening, before narrowing into slits behind his round glasses.

After a deep breath, Bobby formed a half-smile, and approached the counter. "Sam Begay, what brings you here today? Do you have more of those gold coins? I might be interested in buying them."

Sam kept him off balance by not smiling. "I decided to keep it, but I have something else I want to talk to you about."

Bobby waited stone faced.

"Bobby, you and I might be thinking the same thing right now." Sam matched Bobby's own blank expression.

After a long, awkward silence, Bobby swallowed and said, "I'm not sure I know what you mean, Mr. Begay. What same thing would you and I be thinking?"

"I'd say we're both thinking about how it feels for you to be the last living player from your old high school baseball team, of course."

"What?"

Sam leaned on the counter. "You must have read about it in the paper. Your old pal Louis Montoya died last weekend, and that makes you the last living player. It doesn't take much imagination to figure that either you're the killer, or the next victim. I'm just wondering which one you are."

Bobby's face turned pale, then red. "I'm no killer! Who do you think you are, accusing me of such a thing? I'll have a lawyer on you so fast you won't have time to blink."

Sam noticed spittle on the corner of Bobby's mouth, and he looked him over before he spoke. "I'm sure you could, but the way I'm thinking, if you're not the killer, it means you're the next victim. I know a lot of attorneys; and most are pretty handy with a pen and some fancy words, but I never met one who would volunteer to be a bodyguard for their client."

The two men stared at each other. "Bobby, I would think someone in your position might want to cooperate with someone like me, especially when I want to keep you alive."

"You make it sound like your concern for my well-being is the *only* reason you came in today." Bobby's voice dripped with sarcasm.

"Think what you wish." Sam face showed his sincerity. "My job is to keep people safe, and to bring law-breakers to justice. I want to stop these killings, and believe it or not, I think someone has you in their sights."

Sam saw a mixture of distrust and fear cross Bobby's face. It appeared he wanted to say something, but decided not to.

"Officer, if I ever feel I need your help, I'll let you know. In the meantime, I have a business to run, and I'm busy. Is there anything else on your mind?"

"Nope; I'm just trying to do my best to keep the people in this community safe." Sam stared into Bobby's eyes for a long moment before he turned to leave. He stopped and turned back. "By the way, do you recall going to school with a Navajo girl named Stacy Toledo?"

Bobby froze, and his jaw went slack, "I-I'm not...it was a long time ago."

Sam smiled, nodded, and walked out to his car.

As he left, David Castor appeared in the hallway behind his son. "In the back office with me, now."

The two men settled into their chairs across the big desk. David leaned back with his eyes on the ceiling, and Bobby spoke first. "Did you hear what he said to me? He as much as accused me of killing that bastard, Montoya. When I called his bluff, he said he was just concerned about my safety. Can you believe that?"

David lowered his eyes on Bobby and said, "He told you he knows you were involved with Montoya, and he's going to find the truth one way or another. I want you to forget about that for the time being. Right now, I'm more concerned about something else he said. "How did he find out about Stacy Toledo?"

Anger flashed across Bobby's face. He bit off his words. "Don't mention her name in front of me." He stood and kicked his chair away. "Don't you *ever talk* about her in front of *me*." He glared at his father, and then strode out of the office.

David appeared calm. He took a deep breath, looked at his fingernails, and tilted his head back to gaze at the ceiling again.

The phone rang in the front office of the school. A moment later, Mrs. Atkins knocked on Principal Dallas' door, opened it, and said, "It's Mr. Castor for you, sir."

Edgar Dallas wiped his hand across his jaws, and took a deep breath before he picked up the phone. "Yes David?"

CHAPTER 56

Using the extra set of keys Charlie gave him, Sam used the office phone to make calls to several chapter houses on the Reservation north and west of Gallup. Some knew of a few Toledo families in their area, but they didn't recall anyone with the first name of Stacy.

After drawing a blank, he decided to call Diana Witherspoon at the University of New Mexico in Albuquerque, and was fortunate to catch her between classes.

"Sam Begay, this is a pleasant surprise. You haven't run into some kind of trouble out at your place again, have you?"

Sam smiled as he spoke. "I'm not sure yet, but something is bound to come up sooner or later."

Diana laughed at her end of the line. "I hope not for your sake, Sam. It's good to hear your voice. To what do I owe this special call?"

"First, to see how you and that boyfriend of yours are doing, and then I wanted to pick your brain about something."

"Val and I are getting along fine; he's back in Washington with his dad this week—some sort of hush-hush assignment. I'm teaching, and finishing my paper on what we discovered out by your place a while back. What can I help you with?"

"It has to do with that Spanish gold coin you found. I wanted to ask if you ever figured out how it got there. I know the Spanish explorers marched through the area 400 years ago, but did you ever read anything about them losing a large number of gold coins? I'm not going treasure hunting, but a young boy found a coin out in the Bisti, similar to the

The Lightning Tree

one you did, and I wondered if there's a historical record of Coronado, or anyone else, losing things like that."

"Hmm. Not really, but several Spanish expeditions trudged all over this state for years, stealing, fighting, and raising a fuss with the natives. There's no doubt they had gold with them, and it's not much of a stretch to believe some of it was lost here and there. I do know Coronado used to carry a large amount of gold with him to pay his men, but nothing specific about a lost treasure. Is that what you're up to?"

Sam chuckled. "No, but if I do something like that, you'll be the first to know about it. An old coin showed up as a clue in a series of deaths I'm investigating, and I'm just running down possibilities, is all."

"Well, I'm sorry I can't help much, Sam, but I'm glad to hear your voice again. Let me know if anything interesting comes up. It might turn out to be something I'd like to look into."

"I will, and tell that boyfriend of yours to stay safe."

Sam picked up groceries, and spent the rest of the day running errands. After Charlie returned from Window Rock, he was in and out of the office finishing reports, and taking papers to the courthouse. He told Sam he had to leave again, and would eat something along the way.

The phone was ringing at Charlie's house when Sam walked in the door late that afternoon. He set his things down and picked up the receiver.

"Sam, it's about time you got home. This is Joyce, and do I have some information for you."

"Hi Joyce I was just thinking of calling, and asking you out for dinner."

"That sounds good, but why not come over here tonight instead. I'm making some Mexican food, and one of my neighbors is coming over."

"Oh?"

"I think you'll want to speak with her. Her name is June Barraza. She's the one who gave me her old car—the one you're using right now. We were talking over the fence today, and she told me she used to work for the Castor family around the time his wife passed away. She said she cleaned their house and fixed some of the meals. She also told me she remembers a Navajo girl staying with them while she attended school here. Guess what her name was?" Joyce paused for effect. "Stacy Toledo. I thought you might want to talk to June and hear what she has to say. She'll be over for dinner around 5:30. Can you make it?"

"Joyce, did I ever tell you I think you're an incredibly good detective? Of *course* I'll be there."

When Sam arrived, Joyce led him though the living room, and into the kitchen where the smell of spicy Mexican food filled the room. He noticed a stout, grey haired woman sitting at the dining table with a glass of iced tea.

"Sam, this is Mrs. June Barraza, my neighbor. June, this is Sam Begay, the U.S. Marshal I told you about. He's here as a friend, but he's also looking for information about Stacy Toledo."

"Pleased to meet you Mrs. Barraza." Sam set his hat on an empty chair and sat at the table as Joyce brought him a glass of ice tea.

Joyce said, "June, while I finish getting supper ready, why don't you tell Sam what you told me." She stepped away and left the two to talk.

June looked at him with amused interest. "Mr. Begay, I believe I met you once when my husband Arthur was still alive. Do you remember about ten years ago when we had all that flooding on the north side of the tracks?"

"Yes I do. It came on real fast, and a number of businesses and homes got flooded pretty bad."

"Do you remember helping a couple who were in their car and almost got swept away by the water? They had a little dog with them."

Sam began to smile. "Yes I do. I remember helping a nice gentleman and his young wife out of their stranded vehicle and up to higher ground."

"Yes, and you went back to get Rusty, our little dog. That man was my late husband, Mr. Begay, and I want to thank you for calling me young. Mr. Barraza was a little older than I was, but he was always so adventurous. He acted just like an excited little boy sometimes. My Arthur passed away five years ago, and I still miss him every day."

"I'm very sorry to hear of your loss," Sam said. "It's quite a coincidence, us meeting again after all these years."

"Yes it is, and Joyce thinks I can help you with some information about when I was keeping house for the Castor family. Now Mr. Begay, I'm not one to gossip, but some of the things that went on in that house just didn't sit well with a simple woman like me. Joyce tells me you're a good man, and now that I know who you are, I'm certain of it. She said you're looking into an incident going back twenty years, and the Castors might be involved."

"Yes that's right. First of all, can you tell me how you came to work in the Castor household?"

"I sure can. It was just before the war, and money was tight. I told my husband I was approached by Mr. Castor to help care for his wife at home. She was a sickly and troubled woman, and I think most of her problems came from drinking. She could be quite difficult to get along with at times, but I managed. I helped with most of the meals and the cleaning.

Mr. Castor seemed so busy all the time, and his son Bobbie never did help around the house. After a while, it got so it took most of my time, and I told him I was going to have to cut back. That's when he took in a young Navajo girl to help with the cooking and chores in the evening. Her name was Stacy Toledo."

Just then, Joyce said, "Supper's ready. Stay where you are. I'll set the table and bring in the food."

"Nonsense dear," June said, "I'll help set the table. Mr. Begay, would you like some more ice tea?"

The three made small talk during dinner, and when the dishes were cleared away, Joyce poured coffee and sat down to listen to June relate the rest of her story.

"How long did you work for the Castors?" Sam said.

"A few years, but I quit two months after Mrs. Castor died."

"Oh? Do you remember how she died?"

"Yes, and it was strange; she used to have these spells sometimes—almost as if she was another person. She would argue with Mr. Castor like someone possessed by the devil. Oh, the things she would say!"

"Like what, Mrs. Barraza?"

"Oh, she would cuss and scream at him, and throw things. Sometimes, when she was drinking, she couldn't walk and would fall on her bottom and couldn't get back on her feet. I guess that's how she fell over the railing one night and broke her neck. It was a sad thing."

Sam said, "It sounds like she was a tortured woman—like something was eating her inside."

"I thought that too. It wasn't long after she died, that I found out something that might have been what tipped her over the edge, so to speak."

Sam and Joyce exchanged a wary look as June continued.

"I told Mr. Castor I would be late coming over one morning because I had a doctor appointment. The nurse cancelled at the last minute, so I changed clothes and went over to the Castor house to do my chores. I had my own key, and when I stepped into the house, I could hear voices upstairs. It was Mr. Castor and the Indian girl talking, but it sounded odd. It was like they were working on something, and I thought they were moving furniture. I didn't think much of it until the girl started shouting. Her voice sounded desperate and excited, and I went up the stairs to see if I could help."

June paused, and Sam waited for her to continue."

She looked at Joyce before finishing the last of her coffee. "What happened was I caught David in bed with the girl, and the noise I heard was the headboard banging against the wall. When I walked in, the two of them were grunting like a couple of farm animals."

"I was so shocked, I almost tripped going back down the stairs. Bobby must have left for school already, and I didn't know what to do, so I made myself busy in the kitchen. I think Mr. Castor saw me in the hallway."

Sam and Joyce both sipped from their coffee cups to hide their amused expressions, and Joyce put her cup down and said, "I'll get desert." She rose, and stepped away.

Mrs. Barraza said, "It wasn't long after that, Bobby was getting into some bad arguments with his father. They would yell, and I even saw the two of them take a few swings at each other. It was right at the end of the school year, when I decided to stop working for the family. I told Mr. Castor I had to quit, and he paid me right away.

Not long after that, I found out the Navajo girl left, too, and Mr. Castor hired another housekeeper."

"Are you sure the girl's name was Stacy Toledo?" Sam said.

"Oh yes. She and I talked from time to time. She seemed to be a nice girl. She was bright, but shy, and she kept to herself most of the time. When school was over, she must have moved back with her family on the Reservation. The new housekeeper told me she heard the girl left without any notice."

Sam appeared thoughtful. "Did you ever hear what part of the Reservation she was from?"

"No, she didn't talk much about that. I got the impression she lived north toward Farmington somewhere, but I never knew where. I hope this helps you in some way Mr. Begay?"

The Lightning Tree

"Yes it does, Mrs. Barraza. In fact it probably explains why the girl didn't attend senior classes that fall."

Joyce brought desert from the kitchen; a special treat she called flan, and they made small talk while they ate.

When Sam left the house, Mrs. Barraza said to Joyce, "It looks like you found a good use for that old car of mine."

Joyce blushed and said, "His burnt up recently when his house caught fire. I figured I wasn't driving it, so it might as well be put to some good use."

June grinned. "I wonder who is going to end up getting the best use of it; you or him?"

"Why June, what do you mean by that?"

Joyce's innocent expression made the other woman laugh. "Oh nothing; I just figured you might have found a way to use it to help keep you warm at night."

Joyce raised an eyebrow and frowned. "June Barraza! You have a devious mind." "It's not like that at all!"

"Not yet, dear." June grinned in a knowing way.

On the drive back to Charlie's house, Sam mulled over the information Mrs. Barraza gave him, and he knew it was the clue he was looking for. With it, he might be able to smoke out the motivation behind the deaths of the ball players. Once he had that, the identity of the killer would become clear.

Now, he knew why Bobby Castor didn't want to acknowledge any closer tie to Stacy Toledo. As he waited for sleep that night, he sorted through his mental clue cards, selecting those that no longer applied to the case. Montoya's death, and Eric Nez showing up, solved a portion of the mystery, but he still had a killer to find, and the connection to the old school ball team to pin down.

He had an explanation of why the Navajo girl stopped going to school. Was this part of the killer's motive? He closed his eyes for a moment and opened them. He also had to find out what the old Spanish coin had to do with it, if anything.

CHAPTER 57

Edgar Dallas dreaded coming to work this morning. He rushed past Mrs. Atkins desk, and shut the door to his office with David Castor's angry words still ringing in his ear. He took a deep breath to calm himself, and wiped his face with his handkerchief, regretting ever helping the man with the cover-up so many years ago.

Why couldn't this lie buried in the past? Why did it have to rise to the surface now after all these years? What good could come from it? Twenty years ago, times were different; people were different. Why drag up something that he couldn't do anything about?

He took several deep breaths and felt his frustration fade. The only thing he could do now was locate any remaining threads, and get rid of them.

He and David Castor both knew Joyce Dobson was the source of the information. She had disobeyed his orders to stop looking into past events, and he must discipline her.

He could fire her, but he hated to lose someone with her skills and experience. Still, he would not tolerate an employee who ignored his orders, especially when it could uncover something that would put him in an embarrassing position.

If it wasn't for Castor's habit of rewarding friends with lavish gifts, he would tell the man to butt out of the school's business. Blackmail; that's what it was. He thought of Castor's heated words; 'Shut Joyce Dobson up, or fire her. If you don't, your position with the school could be at risk.'

The more he thought about it, the angrier he got, but the fear of possible repercussions sent a chill through him.

With the doors closed for the day at Strong Mountain Trading, David Castor sat at his desk and stubbed out his cigar in a glass ashtray, while his son Bobby slouched in a chair.

"I've been thinking some more about this after I talked to Edgar Dallas yesterday. Begay knows you and Montoya were involved in something back in school, but what I don't understand is how he found a connection to Stacy Toledo."

"So what? She could just as easily have accused you of forcing yourself on her while she was living under *your* roof. She was pregnant before I ever touched her. Hell, you should be grateful I made her run back home to the Reservation."

"David Castor glared across the desk. "Listen to me you little shit; your stunt with your friends almost cost me a blot on my reputation, and ruined my chances of running for Governor. As it is, we're both fortunate that I didn't beat you within an inch of your life for what *you* did."

"You could have tried *old man*. In fact, any time you want to now is fine with me. It was *your* fault that mom died. You didn't push her off the stairs, but you treated her like shit. She started drinking because of you, and I blame *you* for her death. What's so funny?"

David's smile hid his anger. "You never even came close to figuring it out; I slept with that girl because she was infatuated with *you*. Oh, I could see it. You should thank me for not letting you make the bad choice of taking up with her. I did you a favor boy, but now that I see what a whiney little shit you've become, I wish your mother never gave birth to you in the first place."

Bobby stood up and kicked his chair over. He glared at his father and approached the desk with clenched his fists.

The older man was not impressed. "Posture all you want, but don't ever think of crossing me." David paused while the two glared at each other. "I told Dallas to shut the school librarian up or else. She has to be the leak, and we'll see if he's successful. As far as Begay goes, I'll be less subtle with him. Now get out of here while I'm in a good enough mood to let you walk out."

Bobby's face was beet-red with anger as he left. David heard the back door slam, and then a car start up and race away. He picked up the phone, and when the hotel clerk answered, he asked for Rance Wilder's room.

"Rance, it looks like we have another reason to find a permanent solution to our Indian problem. Do you have any ideas?"

After a short pause, Rance Wilder said, "Yes, I've given it some thought already, and I'll see what I can do. I'll talk to you later."

Joyce called Sam that afternoon, and reached him at the FBI office. Charlie was out, and Sam was mulling over what he had learned last night from Mrs. Barraza.

"Sam I'm so glad I found you."

When she paused, he knew something serious was bothering her. "What is it Joyce?"

She took a deep breath and said, "Edgar Dallas called me into his office this morning. He was very abrupt and angry, and he gave me two days off without pay. He said he learned I was still helping you with information on a case you were working on, and he said he had no choice but to discipline me for disobeying his instructions. Sam, I'm so upset I don't know whether to scream or cry."

"Are you alright?" He could feel his adrenaline building inside like a bank of storm clouds. "Do you want me to come over?"

"Oh I'm fine. I've had my cry, and now I'm just mad! Oh that man—what I'd like to say to him!"

"Joyce, why don't you let me take you to dinner this evening? That way we can both get mad together. I want you to tell me everything that happened, and if you feel like crying, I've got a dry shoulder you can use."

She sniffed and said, "Now, you're going to make me cry again, and I don't want to." She sniffled a bit more. "I don't know how I'm going to look when you pick me up."

Sam said, "You'll look just fine. I'll pick you up at 6:00. Put on a smile, but keep the mad. I want to hear everything about it. Deal?"

"Deal."

Sam hung up the phone thinking it may be time to have another conversation with Edgar Dallas. He would wait until tomorrow morning, and regardless of what Joyce told him tonight, he had several things to discuss with the man.

The Lightning Tree

Joyce had her smile on when he picked her up at the house. She wore a colorful dress, and had her hair made up pretty. He gave her a quick hug at the door and walked her to the car. He said, "I don't want to butt into your business, but right now, Edgar Dallas is on the top of my list of least favorite people."

It was a warm evening, and the restaurant was filling up with the dinner crowd. He asked for a booth so they could talk with a little privacy, and they had just ordered a glass of wine before their meal, when Rance Wilder walked in. He noticed Sam, and waved as he came over to their booth.

He nodded to Joyce and turned to Sam. "I'm glad I ran across you. I've been meaning to ask for your help with one of my filming projects. I don't want to keep you from your lovely dinner guest, but could we speak for a few moments before you leave this evening?"

Sam glanced at Joyce and said, "Mr. Wilder, this is Joyce Dobson. Joyce, Rance Wilder, the movie producer who leased my property out by Chaco Canyon. Would you mind if he and I talked for a moment right now at the table?"

Joyce smiled. "Not at all; in fact I'd love to hear more about the movie business."

"Good," Sam said. "Pull up a chair Mr. Wilder, and tell me what you have in mind."

Rance beamed a big smile at Joyce, and pulled over a chair and sat down. "I'm in a bit of a bind, Sam. Our current filming is ahead of schedule, and I want to keep the pace going. Our next phase involves a group of extras, and I need someone to help me find thirty young Indian men who can ride horses, and understand enough English to take direction. I'd like to hire them for about ten days. They'll earn regular wages while they work, and food and lodging will be taken care of. Is this something you could help me with?"

"I guess I could."

"Good, what I'd like to suggest, is you and I take a drive out to Blacksparrow on Saturday so you can help my people scout the area for the best locations for what we want to film. I'll pay you a consulting fee for your time. After that, you can start locating the Indian riders. Can you meet me here Saturday morning? We can drive out in my car."

CHAPTER 58

Friday morning, Sam called the school from Charlie's office and asked to speak with Edgar Dallas. He gave his name to the secretary, and waited while she checked to see if he was available. He couldn't see the frown on her face, but he did notice her cold and aloof manner. A few minutes later, she came back on the line.

"Mr. Dallas is just leaving, and he'll be away from his office for the rest of the day. Perhaps you could call back next week. He may have some time available, but you'll have to call first and check."

Sam hung up the phone. The school was less than ten minutes away, and he wanted to talk to the man right now.

Joyce Dobson's words ran through his mind as he drove to the school. He parked, walked inside to the Principal's office, and listened to Mrs. Atkins tell him Mr. Dallas already left for the day. She appeared nervous and started to say something else, but Sam was already on his way out the door.

He hurried to his car and drove across town to where Dallas lived. It wasn't far, and when he could see the house a short distance up the street, he noticed a car pulling into the garage. Sam parked, and waited for the door to close before he walked up to the front porch and rang the bell.

Edgar Dallas opened the door, and Sam saw surprise turn to dismay on the man's face.

"Mr. Dallas, I'm sorry to bother you at home, and I apologize in advance for what I have to say to you."

The man's demeanor turned to indignation and belligerence. "Now see here officer Begay, I have no time to speak with you right now, and I'm not even sure I ever want to see you here again."

Sam shook his head, and put his hands in his pockets. "That's a shame; you see I hoped to get this resolved face to face instead of going through official channels. If I go that route, I'm afraid it would draw things out for both of us, and of course, that would mean the newspapers would pick it up. I just hoped to make it easier, is all."

Dallas glared and appeared uneasy. "What are you talking about?"

"Oh, I asked Miss. Dobson, in her official capacity as the alumni secretary for the school, to help me get in touch with some of the old students. You see, I needed help in locating the family of one of the graduates who was killed recently. I can't divulge the details—family privacy and all."

"You won't tell me who it was?"

"I'd rather not say. It could muddy up things later. We might have to go in front of a judge."

Dallas was fidgeting, trying to decide if Begay was trying to hoodwink him or not. "Just what is it you want from me? Miss. Dobson ignored my explicit instructions, but yes, she is the secretary, and she is in charge of alumni duties."

"Yes, and I respect the discretion she showed in helping me. You have a dedicated employee, and I figured I'd talk to you before you made a mistake you would regret later."

"Oh? Perhaps I may have expressed my concerns in haste."

"I understand," Sam said. "We all want to do the right thing. May I come in?"

The man hesitated, but Sam reached for the handle of the screen door, and Dallas stepped aside to let him in. They stood facing each other in the entryway.

Sam said, "That's what I always strive to do; the right thing. I want you to understand, so you can do the right thing."

Dallas still had an uncertain look on his face. "If you would speak more directly, Mr. Begay, perhaps I would understand exactly what it is you want from me."

Staring directly into the man's eyes, his own face a mask of stone, Sam said, "I want you to help me stop the killings. I want you to tell me exactly what you know about the events surrounding the rape of a junior high school girl named Stacy Toledo twenty years ago."

Sam could tell Dallas was expecting this. He watched his eyes blink as the man tried to compose the proper reaction on his face.

"I...do remember a little about it. I was the ball coach back then, and I heard some locker room talk and rumors. I heard the girl went back to the reservation, and I don't believe she attended school the next year. I heard nothing more about it, and I assumed she had no interest in continuing her schooling."

"So, you figured if she didn't stay in town and speak up about it, she had no interest in pursuing the matter?"

"Here now, that isn't what I said. I won't have you insinuating I didn't make myself available to hear both sides of the story. I spoke to Mr. Castor, the father of the team captain, and he told me he talked to his son about it. He assured me that this sort of occurrence would never happen again. As I understood it, the whole thing was more boy-girl mischief than rape, and he told me his son knew the difference."

"Did he also know his son brought alcohol to their party?"

Dallas was obviously concerned. "I do remember someone saying that they all went somewhere south of town to drink beer. I suspect she may have had some, and the boys may have...taken advantage of her."

Sam frowned and said, "As I hear it, ten boys raped her, all except for the one who drove her home after everyone else left." He paused and glared at Decker. "Who told you to drop the issue? Was it David Castor? He would have wanted to protect his son. Sam could see he struck the right chord. "I wouldn't be surprised if he called you recently to talk about his concerns."

"Now look, Begay, that's all I know. Anything else is my own business, and none of yours. I will choose who I talk to in the course of my work."

Sam nodded, his face turning sad. "That's what I was talking about earlier; trying to avoid a misunderstanding. Most of us want to do the right thing, but sometimes we make mistakes—just like the one you're making now."

"Mistakes? What are you talking about?"

With intensity burning in his eyes, Sam said, "I'm talking about nine murders over the last five years, Mr. Dallas, and I'd like your help in stopping the next one. Of course, I could get a subpoena and start gathering statements from other students and your staff at the school. I could even have my FBI counterparts start checking your bank records for any large sums of money deposited that might indicate a bribe—or you could just tell me what happened. I came here to give you the opportunity to make the right decision. After all, it was twenty years ago, and all I want is the truth so I have a better chance of stopping more killings."

They glared at each other for several seconds before Dallas looked down and took a deep breath. "I guess misunderstandings happen sometimes. David Castor called yesterday. He asked if I knew why you were talking to someone at the school, and asking about an incident that happened so long ago. He was angry, and he said he wouldn't stand for any invasion of his, or some other family's privacy concerning an event involving their minor children at the time."

Sam nodded. "I understand. Go on."

"It happened like you said. The Navajo girl left town, and the parents of the other students wanted to leave it at that. Nothing ever came of it; that is until you started asking around."

"Edgar, I'm glad you did the right thing and told me about this. By the way, speaking of the right thing, I believe a phone call from you to Miss Dobson this morning would be in order. An apology and a personal request to return to her duties at no loss in pay would seem appropriate."

"Yes, I think so. I'll do it right now." Dallas lifted his eyes to Sam. "Thank you for helping me do the right thing."

When Sam walked in Charlie's office a bit later, he sat behind his old desk and called Joyce Dobson.

"Oh, Sam, it's you. You'll never guess who just called me."

"Edgar Dallas?"

"W-why yes. How did you know that? He apologized to me for everything, and he said he was looking forward to seeing me back to work on Monday. Did you have something to do with this?" She paused for Sam to answer, and then thought better of it. "No, forget I asked. I don't want to know."

"If you say so, Joyce."

"Sam, there's something else I want to tell you. I was thinking last night, and, this might sound a little far-fetched, but what if Stacy Toledo became pregnant after the rape?"

"That's possible—what are you getting at?"

"Well, if she had a child, it would be around twenty years old now. And if the boy or girl knew what happened to their mother, is it possible they might think of taking some kind of revenge?"

"You're saying he or she would be old enough to take things into their own hands if they wanted to?"

"That's right. If I was her daughter, and I knew what they did to my mother, I might decide to punish each one of them for what they did to her. I'm not saying *I'd* kill anyone, but someone else might."

Joyce waited for Sam's response. "Are you still there?"

"Yes, I was thinking. By the way, remind me never to get on your bad side."

After he hung up, Sam leaned back and thought about her words. Stacy Toledo could have become pregnant, and if so, her child would be old enough now to take some kind of revenge. Motivation was there, but would it be strong enough to drive someone to kill so many people? It sounded far-fetched, and it was not the traditional way of his people. Still, it was the most plausible explanation he had since starting his investigation.

If only he could find Stacy. She would be the most likely suspect. If she had a strong son, she might encourage him to take the path of revenge for her. Knowing of the event, he may even do it of his own accord. A healthy, motivated daughter could do the same thing, but somehow, the brutal deaths seemed more likely to be something a male would do.

Still, it just didn't seem like the sort of path his people would take, except for a special kind of witch they call a skinwalker.

CHAPTER 59

When Charlie got home that evening, Sam told him of his conversation with Principal Dallas. He also mentioned Joyce Dobson's suggestion that the wolf hair killings might be an act of revenge by one of Stacy Toledo's family.

Charlie said, "It sounds a little far-fetched, but I guess it's possible. Maybe, with Montoya dead, it's all over. Who else do we have as a possible murderer?"

Sam said, "Good question, I still have a hard time believing a traditional Navajo is the killer. Harmony and balance with nature is a big part of our traditional life—they call it *hozho*. If someone disturbs that balance by word or deed, most Navajo would stay away, and give that person time to get well again."

"If nothing else," Charlie said, "Joyce's suggestion *could* fit the events. Of course that presumes Bobby Castor isn't the killer. There are a couple of other things, too."

"Do you mean the tufts of wolf hair and the gold coin? It's common for a white man to covet gold, and most would think nothing of handling a wolf pelt, but it's not what a traditional Navajo would do. They would avoid the wolf skin, and greed would seldom enter into it. There is only one kind of Navajo who would lust for gold and feel comfortable with the skin of a wolf, and that's a skinwalker; a Navajo witch."

"Charlie nodded. "With Montoya dead, and Castor the only ball player left alive, we could presume he's either the killer or the next victim. It should be easy to chart his whereabouts when the more recent killings took place, so let's do it. At least we'll know for certain either way if he could be our killer."

"Are you volunteering to check it out?"

"Sure, the 'I' in FBI still stands for investigation, doesn't it?"

Sam grinned. "I've heard other words used from time to time."

"Spare me," Charlie said. "I'll list dates and approximate times of death of the recent victims, and see if I can compare it to Bobby's whereabouts. He's pretty well known, and he's on the town council. There's a good chance I can confirm his schedule, and match the times. In fact, I'll see if I can do the same with his dad."

"Okay, and if they both have alibi's, who does that leave us?"

Charlie snorted. "Some habitual, drunk driver with a bad attitude and bad luck, that's who; unless we find Stacy Toledo, or a family member who's a witch."

Sam scratched the back of his head. "I guess I should do some thinking about the Navajo witch angle. By the way, I'm going out to Blacksparrow in the morning with Rance Wilder. He wants me to help his crew scout out some filming locations."

"Do you think that's a wise thing to do?"

Sam saw the concerned look on Charlie's face. "Don't worry, I should be fine, and it'll give me a chance to look around the place some more. By the way, Wilder also asked me to hunt up some local Navajos to work as extras for a few weeks. When I get back to town, I'll head out on the Res. and talk to some of the families I know. I should be able to find enough young bucks to make a respectable band of wild Indians. It's certain most wouldn't turn down a paying job, especially one on horseback."

Charlie grinned. "He'll probably want them to whoop it up, and fall from their horses; you know, act like they're shot. The usual stuff."

"Yeah. At least they'll look better than a bunch of white guys in make-up, black wigs, and feathers."

Charley snorted. "Just be careful. You and I both know something isn't right with that group out there."

The next morning, Sam drove to the El Rancho Hotel, and had a quick breakfast while he waited for Rance Wilder to come down from his room. Rance, wearing an expensive-looking pair of western slacks and a fitted shirt with pearl buttons, met him in the restaurant.

Sam smiled when he saw him. "You look like a wealthy rancher this morning."

"What did you expect? I come from the big city, but I do know how to ride a horse. I'll drive today, and you can ride with me. No need to take two cars."

As they drove out of town, Rance described the kinds of locations he was looking for. "Of course, we'll shoot the town scenes inside the compound where we built our western set, but we'll need places in the desert to stage our chases, and cliffs and rocks to climb around. I also want to find some running water if there is any out there—a dry creek bed would have to do if we can't."

Sam said, "I have a few places in mind. It would be easier to scout on horseback than to try to reach the more remote locations by car."

"I figured as much," Rance said. "That's why I wore these western duds. I ride quite a bit back at my ranch in California, but I'm still more at home behind a desk or a camera. The movie business is going to put Gallup on the map, Sam. I already have a dozen inquiries about locations and facilities from some of the other production groups."

Sam nodded, and let Rance do the talking.

"It looks like a nice day, but I heard someone say we might get rain late this afternoon. At least we'll get a chance to see the colors and the light before then. I'll have a photographer along to take reference shots of the places we visit."

A little after 9:00 a.m., Wilder and Sam reached Thoreau, and drove past Jake's Trading Post on the way north toward Crownpoint and the Chaco road.

Waiting for them at Blacksparrow, Red, the Foreman, talked to Bud and Artie in their barracks. "Mr. Wilder and the Navajo lawman should be along soon. He wants you two boys to stay out of sight until they ride out with the scouting crew. You two will ride with me and follow. He doesn't want Begay to get spooked before we show up to spring the trap."

Bud said, "I'm looking forward to using that smart-ass Indian as a target." He pulled out his .38 revolver and sighted down the barrel at a spot on the wall."

Red chuckled. "I'd advise you two tenderfeet to concentrate on staying on your horses until we catch up with them. Leave the rest to the real cowboys. Mr. Wilder says you'll get your chance to do some shooting when we join the group after they stop for lunch."

As Red walked away, Bud said to Artie, "I'd sure like to drag that smartass cowboy into a Detroit alley, and show him how we do business."

"I think that's what he was talking about Bud. Maybe we're all better when we work on our own turf instead of someone else's."

Bud turned his long face and glared at his partner. "Artie, it comes to me that I keep forgetting what a smartass you are."

Artie's eyes lit up when he saw the scowl on Bud's face.

Bud glared. "Keep it up, and you'll be laughing through some missing teeth. I'm tired of sitting around, sweating, and eating dust in this desert, shit-hole. Why the hell did Denocotti have to pick us to nursemaid this operation?"

"Bud, don't you remember? You're the one who volunteered us to go, so you could look for your wife and her kid while we're here."

"Well, sitting with the prairie dogs and cowboy, shit-kickers isn't going to help me find her. Jeez, this makes me so mad, I want to kill something!"

Artie giggled. "Then quit complaining. We'll get our chance today. What I really want to do is go to town, and sit in a bar that serves Irish whiskey, and I can watch some pretty girl waiting on the tables."

"You're dreaming, Artie. There's nothing like that within a hundred miles. Hell, I'd settle for a cold beer in a place that doesn't smell like horseshit. I swear Artie, don't even think of putting on that damn cologne of yours, because I might lose my head, and try something before I realize what I'm doing."

Someone outside yelled, "Here they come, boys. Get the horses and gear ready."

CHAPTER 60

Bud glanced out the window and saw Red walking to meet Wilder's car as it drove up to the dining hall. He watched as two men got out, and he recognized the big Indian. His thoughts quickly turned to filling the man's belly with lead.

Wilder introduced Sam to the cowboy who walked up to meet them. "Sam, this is Red Tyler, my foreman. Red, this is Marshal Sam Begay, the man I told you about."

Red stuck out his hand and smiled, his white teeth gleaming from his lined, sunburned face. "Pleased to meet you Marshal. You've got a real nice spread here. Thanks for letting us use it."

Sam nodded, and Red turned to Wilder, "The boys are saddling the horses right now, and packing the equipment you wanted. They'll also be carrying some lunch and extra water. Have you decided which direction we'll be riding?"

"That'll be up to Sam. I've described what I'm looking for, and his job is to take us to places that fit the bill." He turned to Sam, "Where do you think we should start?"

Sam looked at the position of the sun, and said, "We can head north from the gate. There's a small mesa past this one with some nice scenery on the northwest side. It's as good a place as any to start. We can continue north to pick up most of the other spots that might fit what you're looking for. We should be able to get back here before the afternoon clouds build up and bring some wind and possibly, rain."

"Good. Here come the boys and the horses now."

Three rough looking men rode over from the stable leading packhorses and saddled mounts for Wilder and Sam. Red said, "I'll stay behind to keep things running here."

Sam remarked on the rugged appearance of the three riders, and Wilder said, "They'd better look that way. These men are extras, as well as part of our set-up crew. The rougher they look the better. They'll take photographs today, and map the locations we visit."

Wilder introduced Will and Bob, both tall, lanky men, and a heavy-set guy named Frank. Sam said, "It's a good thing your men are armed, because we'll be traveling though some snake country. I always carry my own sidearm when I go into the desert." He opened the small pack he carried, and pulled out a belt and holster containing his well-used Colt .45. The men watched as he strapped it on his hips and checked the cylinder to make sure it was loaded.

Sam kept one chamber empty where the hammer rested to avoid accidental discharge. He knew some men who didn't, and suffered the painful consequences.

Red said, "Do you mind if I take a look at that Colt, Marshal?"

Sam handed it over, and the man did some trick twirling for Sam's benefit. "It's a nice, well-balanced gun, Mr. Begay. Maybe we can do some target shooting later—you could show us Hollywood cowboys how a real lawman handles a sidearm."

Sam smiled, and noticed a few wolfish grins from the others.

Fifteen minutes later, they were riding north along the mesa wall, across an expanse of rolling desert dotted by bunch grass, and greasewood. They passed a few stands of aspen and pine growing against the rocks, and then crossed several gullies and stands of yucca and cactus as they approached a smaller mesa to the north.

Heat waves radiated in the distance, and Rance looked up at the sandstone wall as they passed. He turned to Sam. "I noticed a road of sorts leading up the side of that smaller mesa. What's up there?"

"Nothing much, except for some scattered rocks that used to be an old Indian shelter and lookout post. There is a nice view of the surrounding desert up there, and I had a road built a few years ago, so some people from the University could explore the area. They didn't find much to make it worth their while, but there is a nice view."

Sam didn't mention the underground cavern they explored, and the unusual artifacts they found. He had closed off the entrance afterward, and he wanted to leave it that way.

"If we work along the west side of that mesa," he said, "we'll come to some bigger washes, and interesting terrain that might be suitable for your use."

Rance nodded and said, "Lead on, you're the guide. I just want to make sure we take advantage of the sunlight while we have it."

For the next hour, Sam took them along tilted, sandstone ridges and along the banks of a wide, dry wash that meandered across the desert like a snake. "Near those hills in the distance," he said, "there's some dogwood along the banks of a bigger wash. It doesn't fill up with water very often, because most of it flows down another branch to the north. We had rain a few days ago, so there might be some water in a few spots."

Rance had his men stop several times to take photographs, while unseen, behind them, another group of three riders kept pace with the group, but stayed out of sight.

After Rance stopped to let his people photograph a stretch of eroded cliffs and banded sandstone, they rode through a long, narrow valley that meandered through pink hills. When they reached an open area, Rance had the group stop.

"Sam, I want to take some shots here. There's a different vista in each direction, and it might be a good place for several scenes. We might as well break for lunch. By the way, what is that odd-looking line of rocks to the north?"

"You're looking at the edge of the Bisti Badlands. It's a place where the hard surface of the Colorado Plateau covers a layer of softer sandstone and volcanic ash. The hard rock cracks over time, and water seeps through to wash away the softer layers, leaving a kind of pedestal under the harder, cap rock. That's why some of the pillars have a wide knob or cap on the top. They're called hoodoos and fairy chimneys. Some people think they're spirits turned to rock."

"I want to get some closer shots of them after we rest and eat. Where are we right now in relation to Chaco Canyon?"

Sam looked around. "Chaco is off to the south and east about five miles."

"Good, I'll tell the boys to break for lunch."

They picketed the horses in a patch of grass near some cottonwoods, and the men passed around sandwiches and coffee. Most of them congregated near the trees while Sam and Rance ate a short distance away.

"What are they doing now?" Artie said to Red, who was watching the group ahead of them with his binoculars.

"They're taking a lunch break. That's our signal to get ready to join the party. We'll let them finish eating before we ride in."

Sam began to feel uneasy. He glanced around at the men, who took turns looking his way. They didn't seem to care that he noticed their direct stares. This could be where they would make their move. He expected something, and he was as ready as he could be, but a small voice in his head kept whispering a sour word of doubt.

After they ate, two men walked over to Sam and Rance. "Mr. Begay, we were wondering if you might show us movie cowboys some of your shooting skills. We could set up a target if you're interested."

One of them looked at Rance, and Rance turned to Sam with a smile. "How about it Sam? Are you willing to take on a Hollywood cowboy in a test of marksmanship? I know some of the boys think they're hot stuff with a six-shooter; it might be fun to see you take them down a peg or two if you're game."

Sam took a long look at the men and said, "Sure." Bob motioned to Will and Frank to set up some targets, and they picked up several flat chunks of shale, and stood them in the sand in a long row. Sam pretended not to notice a flash of reflected sunlight and a glimpse of movement in the distance behind them as he thumbed an extra cartridge into his gun. It looked like it was going to be a lot worse than he planned.

When they finished setting up the targets, Bob said to Sam, "Will thinks he's the hottest target shooter around here. What do you say we let him go first and try to impress us?"

"Okay by me." Sam stood aside and watched the thin cowboy step up to the line marking a rough, 30-yard distance. The man took his stance, squinted at the targets, and drew. He fired two shots at one of the rocks. A corner of the stone shattered from his first, the second hit the sand just in front it. He holstered his gun and drew again, this time hitting the rock twice and breaking it into pieces. He drew once more and broke the next rock in half.

Will stepped back and grinned at Sam like a bashful, young boy looking for praise. "I got a little excited on my first shot, but I calmed down for the rest. He ejected his spent shells and reloaded while Sam took his firing position. He stared at his target, drew, and fired all six shots at the

The Lightning Tree

next slab of rock, shattering it into several pieces. When he stepped back, he heard a hammer cock behind him, and he turned to see Bob with his gun aimed directly at him.

"Not bad shooting Marshal," the man said in his deep voice. Now, pass that Colt over to Will, and put your hands behind your neck. Be careful now, or you might make me nervous."

Sam had worried about something like this, but he didn't expect it so soon. "What's this all about Rance?"

"Sorry Sam, no hard feelings, but you've become an unacceptable risk to our operation. If anyone asks about you, I'll tell them I brought you back to Gallup this evening, and that I watched you drive away from the hotel. Of course, I'll have the boys drive your car somewhere out on the Reservation and dump it, and I suspect it'll be stripped or stolen within a few days.

I'll be shocked to hear of your disappearance, of course—a sad thing to happen to such a nice guy. Bob, you know what to do. Let's get this over with, and ride back to the compound."

Sam said, "Rance, what happened to change you from a popular movie star to a common criminal?"

Rance stared at Sam for a moment and said. "Popularity is an overrated and fleeting thing. When the bright lights diminish, so does the money."

"Is it just you, or does it include David Castor and your contacts in Michigan? I know about the two hoods. I met them when they first came here. Is it just opium and marijuana, or does it include amphetamines?"

"Sam, you surprise me. You are remarkably well informed, or at least a good guesser. It's everything you've mentioned, and more; like cocaine, for instance, and human trafficking. We'll start bringing in some girls from Mexico soon, and we might even pick up a few young Navajo squaws just to spice up the mix."

Rance had a smug look on his face. "Someone is going to do it, Sam, and it might as well be me. There's a market, and I plan to satisfy the demand."

Sam heard horses approaching, and he turned and saw the three riders who followed the group at a distance. Two of the men appeared uncomfortable in the saddle, and he recognized them as the two hoods he met at Jake's store in Thoreau.

Rance Wilder said, "The only thing I'll regret, Sam, is the tragic loss of a brave, Indian lawman. You're not such a bad sort of guy, but you stuck your nose where you shouldn't have."

He motioned to the men. "Bob and Will, leave your guns here so the Marshal isn't tempted to try to make a grab for them, and walk him out past the targets. I'll tell you when to let him go, and make sure you step aside so you're out of the line of fire."

"We'll give our two city boys a chance to show us westerners how they can handle their firearms. If they aren't up to the job, I'll have Big Frank standing by to finish it."

Bud and Artie were off their horses, walking up to where Rance stood. They both pulled their revolvers and checked their loads. Bud said, "Mr. Wilder, you might as well tell your country shit-kickers to go home, unless they want to grab a shovel and dig a Navajo-sized grave."

Sam had been in some bad situations before, but nothing quite like this. He knew it could be the end, and all he could do was to try to put some doubt into Rance Wilder's mind.

"Rance, I'm not going to tell you that you can't get away with this. You already know it. People know I'm out here right now, but what you don't know, is that I planned for something like this."

Bob and Will took hold of Sam's arms, but he didn't struggle. Rance said, "Save your breath Marshal. The only one who won't get away is you." He nodded to the two cowboys to march Sam away from the group.

Sam didn't say anything as he walked with a man on either side of him. They continued well past the rocks they used for target practice, and when Rance called to them, the two men stepped away, and began walking back toward the others.

Sam raised his voice to Rance and said, "They'll get you all before you make it back to Blacksparrow. Take a good look at that hill behind you to the south."

As one, they all turned, and Sam bolted away toward the deep wash he knew lay another two hundred feet ahead, beyond a rise. The drop was a good fifty feet or more, and the bank should be slanted enough, and mostly sand. He hoped for a soft place to land and get out of sight, but he was more concerned with avoiding the lead the others would soon be throwing at him as he ran.

He heard a shout from one of the men, and the gunfire started. Moving side to side, trying to make himself as difficult a target as possible, he dropped, dodged, and rolled with the terrain as lead buzzed past him

The Lightning Tree

like angry hornets. When he glimpsed the rim ahead, he jumped into a shallow gully that drained into the wash, hoping to use it for shelter as he scrambled along.

The gunfire stopped, and then began again as other shooters joined in. He was very close to the edge now. Rolling to his feet, he dodged in one direction and dove in another, still evading the flying lead. A bullet clipped his shoulder just as he jumped down a four-foot drop. He managed to roll to his feet, and felt a hard jolt on his hip when lead smacked the side of his gun belt.

He lost his balance and fell, then staggered to his feet with lead buzzing close to his ear. Gasping from his exertion, he saw he was nearly at the edge of the wash. He could see the ground open up and the sandy wall on the far side. The canyon was well over a hundred feet wide.

The gunfire stopped again, and as he ran toward the edge, he heard the sound of a projectile ripping past, and the unmistakable echo of a rifle.

The rifle meant more accuracy. His lungs wheezed for air as the ravine gaped before him. It looked like he might make it, and just as he realized the canyon was much deeper than he had anticipated; something slammed against the side of his head and knocked him off his feet. He lost consciousness, as the ground opened up and swallowed him.

Bob ejected the shell from his rifle and signaled for two men to run after Sam and check if he was dead. Big Frank and Will sprinted off, and stopped short of the deep, sandy cliff. Will picked up Sam's hat and saw blood and a hole on one side. Both men approached the edge and peered below, careful not to disturb the unstable sand and risk a fall.

"There's his body," Will pointed. All they could see was a boot sticking from a fresh mound of loose sand. Frank drew his revolver and fired three shots; one hit the heel of the boot, but it didn't move.

"He's a gonner," Will said. "That boot would have twitched if he was alive."

"Should we go down and check for sure? I can't see much else because of how the cliff sticks out"

Will looked at the other cowboy. "Just how do you think we're going to do that without breaking our own necks? He's dead, Frank. That fall had to kill him even if our shots missed—and they didn't."

Frank looked at the hat. "Yeah, it looks like we'll have to go further down the canyon to find a place to reach the bottom, and then make our way back here to see for certain."

Will stuck his fingers through the bloody gash in the hatband. "He's leaking brains for sure. Let's go back. If someone wants to spend a couple hours hunting a way down, let 'em."

CHAPTER 61

"He's at the bottom of the cliff buried in the sand, Mr. Wilder. We saw his boot sticking out, and Frank fired a slug into it. It didn't move. He's a goner for sure."

Wilder's face turned red as he glared at the two men. "Are you certain that boot isn't just lying there without a foot in it?" The two men glanced at each other, then looked down without answering. "Don't you think it would be a good idea to go down there and make sure he's dead?"

"But Mr. Wilder," Will said, "we have his hat with a hole clear through it, and it's covered with his blood."

Big Frank said in his high voice, "I know we hit him a couple of times, and then Bob nailed him with his rifle and knocked him off the edge."

"That's still not good enough. I want someone to find his body and make sure he's dead."

"Sir," Will said, "we can't climb down the embankment from here; it's too high, and it's all loose sand. We'll have to find another place to reach the bottom, and ride back to find the body. It'll take a while."

Bob overheard the conversation as he walked up. "Mr. Wilder, the clouds are building, and it looks like we're in for a wet ride back to the compound. If we send men into the wash with rain coming, it'll flood faster than you can imagine, and we can kiss them and their horses goodbye."

Rance glared at his foreman. *"I want proof Sam Begay is dead!"*

"Yessir, and if it rains as hard as it looks like it might, his body will end up in the Gulf of Mexico, or buried under the sand somewhere between here and there."

As if to underscore Bob's words, thunder rumbled in the distance.

Rance looked up at the dark wall of clouds approaching from the west. "Alright, chances are Begay is in the happy hunting grounds right now, but he's proven himself to be quite slippery. I still want to make sure we're rid of him for good. You and a couple of the boys ride back here tomorrow morning and make sure he's dead, or long gone. Ride as far downstream as you can, and take all day if you have to. If you find his body, bury it deep. If you don't find him, you'd better hope no one else does either."

"Yes sir, Mr. Wilder. The way those clouds look, we need to start back to the compound right away. The rain will fill every little gully in the area, and when it all collects in a wash this big, it'll carry every tree and boulder in its way. We'll ride back tomorrow, and let you know what we find, if anything."

While the riders headed back to Blacksparrow, and the towering thunderheads moved in, Sam Begay regained consciousness in the weird semi-darkness at the bottom of the wash. His head throbbed like a medicine drum, and he spit sand from his mouth, and blinked his grainy eyes as he brushed the dirt from his face. He heard thunder, and he remembered running, and something smashing against his head. When he attempted to sit up, pain shot through his shoulder and his skull, and he fell back as a wave of dizziness overcame him.

A sharp crack of lightning cleared his mind. He lay in a sandy depression in the side of the wash, and remembered falling. He was lucky to be alive.

It would rain soon, and that meant danger from a flash flood. He willed his body to sit up, and a wave of pain engulfed him. Wincing as he touched the side of his head, he discovered a sand-encrusted mass of dried blood covering his ear, neck, and shoulder. The exertion made him woozy, and he lay back, floating in and out of consciousness.

When he woke again, he tried to move. Everything was in a weird, shadowy darkness. He had no idea how long he lay unconscious, and he saw rain falling like a dark curtain. It took him several minutes to remember the danger he faced. A heavy rain could send a crushing wall of water and debris down every cut and channel that drained this part of the Colorado Plateau. He had to get to high ground immediately.

Bracing himself on one arm, he sat up and swayed with weakness. His head throbbed like a bell hit with a hammer, and his chest hurt with each breath. He was suddenly sick, and when he could lift his head again, he panicked when he saw several muddy streams snaking across the bottom of the wash. Desperate to move, he saw something across the open space, and it took him a moment to recognize the shape as a horse and rider.

They were coming for him! His only thought was to find a place to hide. His eyes lost their focus as he crawled on his hands and knees and passed out again. When he awoke, the rider was coming his way. He reached to his holster, founding it empty, and realized he was too weak to fight off an attacker. Is this how it would end for him? He struggled to get to his feet, fell back, and watched the blurry shape approach.

His eyes fluttered as he saw a lanky man dismount and walk toward him. He tried to make out the face in the shadow of a baseball hat, but he passed out before he recognized the rider.

Early the next morning, a group of men left Blacksparrow and rode north to make a thorough search for Sam Begay's body. They returned late that afternoon to report.

Red Johnson, dirty, and weary from the long ride, stood in front of his boss. "Mr. Wilder, we couldn't find a single sign of him. There must have been a lot of water running down that wash last night, because everything looked different this morning. The flooding must have pushed a mountain of rock and debris down that channel, and buried or washed away everything in its path. We couldn't even find our tracks from yesterday. We rode at least five miles down the wash, but all we saw was mud, rock, and broken trees. He's buried out there somewhere, but we couldn't find him, and I doubt anyone else ever will. That's what you wanted to hear, isn't it?"

Wilder appeared thoughtful. "Yes, I suppose it is. Very well. Get cleaned up, and have a couple of the boys ready to take a car and follow me back to Gallup. I want them to drive Begay's vehicle from the El Rancho parking lot, and ditch it somewhere in the boonies. I hope by the time anyone finds it, Sam Begay will be nothing but a distant memory. If anyone asks about him coming out here with me, I'll tell them he and I drove back to town this morning, and I haven't seen him since."

As the stars came out that evening, a small campfire flickered under a slab of rock, against a mesa several miles west of Chaco Canyon. The reflected glow lit the features of a tall, thin Navajo man in frayed clothing and a battered baseball hat. He sat facing a sleeping figure across the fire, and listened as a coyote howled somewhere in the darkness.

When a moan came from the prone form across from him, the thin Navajo said, "Are you awake? You're somewhere safe. When you feel like it, I have some hot broth for you."

Sam Begay's eyes felt grainy, and he blinked as he tried to focus on the seated figure across the fire. He tried to speak, but could barely manage a croak, "Water."

The thin man filled a tin cup and brought it over to Sam, who managed to prop himself up on one arm. He sipped, and then lay back and closed his eyes. A few minutes later, he opened them and said, "How did you ever find me, Dan?"

"First, have some broth. If you can handle that, I'll give you some stew. We'll talk later."

A gust of wind whistled through the shelter causing the fire to dance and release a shower of sparks. Dan Yazzie brought a cup of broth, and after Sam finished it, Dan refilled it with stew.

Sam savored each spoonful, and while he ate, Dan said, "The old man spirit told me where to find you, and he said to bring you here."

Sam thought about what Dan said. He'd known the man since he was a young boy. His parents were alcoholics, and after they were gone, his grandfather raised him. When he was old enough to have a wife and a child of his own, he lost everything because of his own weakness for alcohol. An automobile accident took his wife, and it sent him to prison for manslaughter.

Sam remembered the day Dan got out of prison. It was shortly after the deaths of his grandfather and daughter. When he'd picked him up at the bus stop, the man already knew of the tragedy. Prison had changed him, and Sam had helped him prepare for a journey to kill the creature responsible for their deaths, and regain his self-worth.

It was after that journey that Dan first spoke to him of the old spirit man who came to him while he was in the desert. Sam didn't understand at first, but now he believed the spirit was real. Too many strange things had occurred during the past few years, and the old spirit played a role in several of them.

"This is the second time you've come to my rescue, Dan. I'm glad the old spirit told you where to find me."

The Lightning Tree

Dan stared into the fire while Sam finished the last of his stew. After several minutes he said, "It wasn't the only reason I came, Sam. There is a danger here; something evil and powerful that you and I must stop."

Sam nodded. "Yes, I know about the men at Blacksparrow, and I know they are running a criminal operation."

Dan considered this for a moment. "There are many things we must face, and that is only one of them. There is something more dangerous, and the old spirit said I must kill it. He also said that I must have your help to do this. It is the only way." Dan paused for a moment. "Sam, the spirit also told me that you or I may die because of it."

Sam stopped eating. "Dan, you are my friend, and I will not let you face danger alone."

"Yes, I know this. You are my *good* friend. There is one other thing I will need to stop this evil." Dan reached to his waist and pulled out a homemade, iron knife.

"That looks like the same old knife you and Kip found in the desert last year, except that one had a broken blade."

Dan nodded. "I lost that one—one day it just wasn't there anymore. The old spirit told me I should make a new one, and he showed me how. He said I would need it someday. I tell you this because you are my old friend. There are things you must know, for there is a part for you. I have learned many things recently—things I found hard to believe."

Dan knew Sam needed rest. "Sleep now. I will speak more of this in the morning."

Sam awoke to the smell of stew, and as the sun peered over the tops of the distant mesas, he and Dan ate, and waited for the light of day to reach their shelter in the rocks.

"When I was young," Dan said, "my grandfather told me of two braves who came across a very large bear. They knew they would have a difficult time killing it with their arrows, so one man, knowing he was the swifter of the two, suggested they should run. Both knew the bear would catch the slower one, and allow the other to escape."

Sam grinned, having heard a similar story before.

Dan poked at the fire and said, "In the end, the two braves decided to stay and face the bear together."

Sam was surprised to hear this twist to the story. "So they were both good friends, and they decided to share their success or their fate?"

"No; they both decided to stay and fight when they saw the second bear."

They finished eating, and Dan said, "Do you remember a few years ago when I told you about the old man spirit showing up at my campfire when I was searching for Ye'iitsoh? I gave him a blanket, and he and the blanket were gone in the morning without a trace or track to prove he had ever been there."

"Recently, the spirit man came to me again, and he told me his journey had come around in a circle. He said his path now intersected with my future, and he said your journey is part of it. He told me that when I killed the monster Ye'iitsoh, he knew the creature would come back, and it would lead to our final test. He told me to make a new knife to replace the broken one, and you and I must work together to destroy the evil."

Sam felt the hair stand on his scalp as he listened to his friend.

Dan watched the heat waves shimmering against the mesas as he searched for the right words. "I asked the old man spirit if I was him—if he was me, and he said, no." Dan took a deep breath. "He also told me if you or I die before we fulfilled our destiny, the other will also die."

Sam rested throughout the day while Dan scouted the area. That evening, Sam felt better, and Dan told him he would take him to see a doctor tomorrow. They ate the last of the stew, and as Sam slept, he dreamed of seeing the moon through the opening of their shelter.

In his dream, he saw the campfire burning down to a few small embers, and he saw what he thought was Dan sitting across the fire with a blanket around his shoulders.

Sam said, "Dan, shouldn't you rest?"

An unfamiliar voice came from the shadowy figure. "I will sleep another time. You must understand that I will leave when you go to see the doctor, but I will be close by."

Sam lay back and closed his eyes. Dan's voice sounded strange. It sounded hoarse—and much older.

CHAPTER 62

Sam felt much better the next morning, but his head and body still ached from his wounds and his fall into the deep arroyo. He knew he was fortunate the sand near the bottom of the wash had prevented a more serious injury. Dan thought the pupils of his eyes looked normal, and he figured Sam would heal.

"Dan, I have to get back to town, but I don't want certain people to know about it. I figure the highway between Farmington and Gallup lies about twenty miles west of here, and if we head that way and follow the two-tracks, we're bound to run across someone who can give me a ride."

Dan nodded, and Sam said, "Where can I find you when I'm back on my feet?"

"I can't be sure. The old man spirit says he will help me prepare for what I must do. When the time comes for you and I to finish our parts, I will find you. With that, Dan saddled his horse and they rode double, heading west toward the highway.

It was late afternoon when Sam eased himself out of the passenger side of a pickup truck a few doors down the street from Charlie's house. He and Dan had been lucky to flag a truck down soon after reaching the main road, and even luckier for Sam to recognize the driver, Sonny, the same young Navajo who worked at Benny's garage in Gallup. The old white truck had a few more dents and scrapes on it, but it was easy to recognize by the metal bracing welded to the front bumper.

Sonny was sparing in his conversation on the way to Gallup, but Sam didn't care; he was tired and sore, and he just wanted to get to Charlie's house, and have his friend take him to get some medical attention.

Charlie wasn't home yet, and Sam took his time washing up and changing his bandages. His wound didn't look as bad as he feared, and just as he was thinking of finding something to eat, he heard the front door open.

When he saw Charlie's surprised expression at seeing him, he said, "Anything new going on in town?"

Charlie's eyes were big with surprise and concern. "Do you mean anything besides wondering what the heck happened to you, and why Decker called me today wanting to talk to you? Where's your car? Don't tell me you wrecked it again."

"It's a long story, Charlie, but as for the car, I left it at the El Rancho, Saturday, and I hope it's still there."

Charlie's forehead wrinkled with thought. "I saw it parked in the lot Saturday afternoon, but when I went by Sunday, it was gone. I figured you were out on the Res. looking for some Navajo boys to play movie Indians, like you told me. Sam you look like hell. What happened?"

Sam took a deep breath and said, "I took a fall, Charlie, and you and I have a bigger problem to deal with. Decker isn't going to like hearing about it."

Charlie groaned and sat down. "I'm not surprised. It's probably why Decker wanted to talk to you as soon as you showed up."

The two stared at each other for a minute, both wondering what was going on. Charlie said. "Before we do anything, I should take you to see a doctor. He'll want to do something about that head wound."

Charlie drove Sam to the hospital, and after stitches, a few shots, and some painkillers, the doc told Sam to go home and rest. Charlie picked up burgers on the way back, and said, "We can talk while we eat. You'll need to rest, but I want to write everything down first. Sure as hell, Decker will call again in the morning."

Sam told Charlie what happened over the past few days, and how the gunmen at Blacksparrow shot him, and how he fell into a ravine. He explained how Dan Yazzie found him, but he didn't mention anything about Dan's cryptic warning, and the dangers he spoke of.

Charlie shook his head after Sam finished. "Woo-wee, you sure stepped into something, Sam. I'm surprised you're still alive. Decker mentioned Rance Wilder's name, and he's going to be surprised to hear about this."

"You can bet on it," Sam said. "Charlie, we have to shut down the smuggling operation in such a way that we get our proof, and snare the top guys as well as the hired hands. I'm certain Wilder is one of the ringleaders, and David Castor is his local guy. I'm not certain how much his son Bobby is involved, but he undoubtedly knows what his father is doing."

"What about the two Detroit hoods you mentioned? Did you see them?"

"Yes, and I'll recognize all the other boys who rode into the desert with us. I'm sure most are from out of town. Charlie, not only are they bringing in illegal contraband, they're trafficking in young girls. I'll want to have a talk with Decker about shutting down the operation in such a way that we trap every one of the skunks red-handed. We need to start planning."

The two men thought for a moment, and Sam said, "Did Decker say what he wanted to talk to me about?"

"No, but it sounded important, and I got the feeling he might want to see you in his office in Albuquerque."

"Well, I don't have a car, and with my recent bad luck, I doubt anyone will lend me theirs."

Sam rode with Charlie to his office the next morning to call Decker. He made the call while Charlie fixed coffee.

"Sam Begay, it's about time I heard from you. I think you and I need to have a private talk. How soon can you be in my office?"

"Uh, that might be a problem."

"Look Begay, I'm not in a mood to beat around the bush. Why is it a problem?"

"Because my car was stolen."

"Well, can't you find someone who'll lend you theirs?"

"You don't understand sir; the stolen car was one I borrowed from a friend after my two other vehicles caught fire when my house burned down."

"So? Don't you have any other friends?"

"Not since my cars started getting wrecked, burnt up, and stolen, sir."

The line was silent for a few seconds. "I see." There was another pause on the line. "Listen; what I have to say to you must be kept in strictest confidence. I don't even want Charlie to know about it. That's why I need to speak to you privately, and as soon as possible." Decker took a deep breath. "There have been some thinly veiled threats made recently, and since they also seem to involve you, I think absolute discretion is called for."

After a few more minutes on the phone, Sam hung up and saw Charlie staring at him from his desk.

"Decker want's me on the bus to Albuquerque this morning."

CHAPTER 63

The bus ride to Albuquerque wasn't bad except for the heat, the noise, and the uncomfortable seats—the reasons Sam avoided this mode of transportation. The usual, listless passengers sat zombie-like watching the scenery, some nodded off in their seats; their eyes closed as their heads bobbed around. A few small children did their best to use their excess energy in a manner that made those passengers who couldn't sleep, wish they could, or at least, wish there were some way to render the children unconscious.

Sam ignored most of it, with his eyes closed under his Stetson. It was a long, three-hour trip, especially having seen the same countryside for most of his life.

He managed a few short naps in-between thinking about his recent experiences, and the loose strings of the wolf hair case. The identity of the person or persons responsible for the deaths was still a mystery. Several people had a motive, but when they ended up as victims, he had to go back to look for another string to follow. It had something to do with the ball players—of that, he was certain, and there was only one player left. Unfortunately, so far, that string led him nowhere.

He didn't like to think where one of the other strings led; it suggested someone from the Res. might be behind it all. It went against his people's beliefs, their system of values, and their way of life. The path led away from harmony, and to something dark and evil.

There was another thread, or at least a connection to something the whites seemed more familiar with; a criminal operation that reached across the country and into Mexico.

Sam shifted to get more comfortable. What could Decker want to see him about that involved both of them? The only connection he was aware of was the ongoing battle of their egos.

Eventually, they reached Albuquerque, and he walked through the lobby of the downtown bus station, and into the hot sun and sweltering streets. The FBI office sat a short distance away, and traffic was light after lunch. When he stepped into the familiar, multi-story building, he took an elevator to the proper floor, and told the receptionist his name. She asked him to take a seat, and said she would inform Mr. Decker of his arrival.

As he waited in the lobby, a noisy array of fans hummed in the background, moving the warm air around, and doing little to make anyone comfortable. He picked up a National Geographic and saw a picture of snow-covered mountains and a group of polar bears. It looked like a cold place, but it didn't help keep the sweat from dripping down his face.

He heard a buzzing at the receptionist's desk, and the young woman turned from her intercom, and called his name. "Mr. Begay? Station Chief Decker will see you now. Please follow me."

She was a different girl than the one who took him back to Decker's office the last time he was here, but she had similar looks and mannerisms; attractive, neatly dressed, and obviously competent.

She took him to a heavy door with 'Thaddeus Decker' and 'Station Chief' etched on a nameplate, knocked, and let Sam into the room. As soon as the door closed behind him, he noticed how cool the office was.

Decker surprised him by standing, and coming around his desk to shake his hand. "Thanks for coming today, Sam. What I have to say to you is going to sound unusual—to both of us. He waved to a chair in front of his desk. "Have a seat. Would you like some water?"

Sam nodded and sat down. Taking the offered glass from the man, he drank half of it before he placed it on the corner of the desk.

Decker folded his hands, and Sam noticed the uncomfortable, nervous way about him, much different from when he was here last as the target of the man's ire over him meddling in some agency business. The frames of the man's glasses looked familiar, as did the receding hairline and long chin. His suit looked cheap, clashing with the expensive-looking furnishings in the office.

"I'll get right down to it, Sam. Have you had any recent contact with Rance Wilder or David Castor?"

Expecting the question, Sam leaned forward and blurted out, "Yes, have you?" He narrowed his eyes and watched Decker, waiting for his answer.

Decker frowned, and then his shoulders sagged. "Sam, I know we've had our differences in the past, but right now I don't know who else to turn to. I'm not even sure I can trust my own people. The only reason you're here today is because I believe you and I may both be in the same leaky boat, and our only chance to save ourselves is to row together. The answer to your question is yes."

Sam saw the man's distress. "Yes sir, I've been in contact with both men, and I can't say I enjoyed the experience. Can you tell me why you're asking?"

"Very well, I'll give it to you straight, and I expect the same from you. What I say to you, must be kept in strictest confidence. Yesterday, I received a call from Rance Wilder that took me like a sucker punch. I won't beat around the bush; he's trying to blackmail me, and I suspect he may have something up his sleeve for you."

When Sam didn't comment, Decker said, "I played golf with the two men a few weeks ago. I've known David Castor since I took over this position a few years ago. We met at the Country Club, and we've played golf from time to time. At our last outing, he brought along a friend, Rance Wilder. The man talked about filming some western movies near Chaco Canyon, and he said he leased a place called Blacksparrow to use as his headquarters. That's why I asked if he's said anything to you."

A hard look crossed Sam's face. "Mr. Decker, Rance Wilder and his men shot me and left me for dead at the bottom of a ravine west of Chaco Canyon last week. It wasn't an accident; it was a deliberate attempt to kill me." Sam removed his hat, and he watched Decker's face grow pale at the sight of his bandage. "I managed to get back to town yesterday, and Charlie Redman took me to see a doctor. That's when he told me you wanted to talk."

Watching Decker's face turn grey with concern, Sam took a deep breath, and said, "Sir, I believe Rance Wilder and David Castor are running a criminal operation at the Blacksparrow Mine. I leased the place to Wilder so he could use it as a filming location, but I've recently seen evidence of possible drug smuggling and human trafficking. David Castor is also involved, but I believe Wilder is in charge. He and his men tried to kill me after he invited me to join them on a movie-scouting trip in the desert.

Decker sank back in his chair as he considered the scope of the events Sam described.

"That isn't all of it, sir. I have been investigating the Castor family in connection with some unusual murders that appear to have something to do with an old rape case involving his boy when he was attending high school. David has tried to stonewall my efforts, and I suspect he and Wilder decided to create a permanent solution to satisfy both of their concerns."

The men stared at each other across the desk for a moment, and Sam said. "What brought about your concern about blackmail?"

Decker looked at his hands for a few seconds, then took a deep breath and said, "A golf game, it would seem. Also, I learned I have a savings account that I was not aware of, and did not open. In that account, someone has deposited five-thousand dollars, and my signature is the only one on the account card."

Sam pursed his lips, and said with a wry smile, "All things being equal, sir, I think I would rather have your problem. How did you find out about it?"

"An anonymous phone call, and someone telling me I can either keep the money, with more to come, or I can do something stupid, like stick my nose where it doesn't belong in Rance Wilder's business dealings. The voice also mentioned a news reporter in town with a sweet tooth for stories involving corrupt, government officials."

Decker opened a desk drawer and pullout out an envelope. "Yesterday, I got this in the mail." He tossed it across the desk to Sam.

Sam read the postmark date and saw there was no return address. He opened the envelope and took out several photographs and a folded sheet of paper. Leafing through each photo, he counted five of Decker, Castor, and Wilder on the golf course. Sam figured someone took them from a distance with a telephoto lens.

"Read the note, Sam."

He set the photos down and picked up the printed note. "IT WOULD BE A SHAME TO RUIN A CAREER OVER A FRIENDLY GAME OF GOLF"

"That's curious," Sam said, "the note could refer to anyone in the photos. Wilder or Castor could deny sending it." He glanced at the rest of the note. "I HAVE ANOTHER SET FOR THE NEWSPAPERS."

Sam put the note and photographs back in the envelope, and Decker said, "I don't know if I can even trust my own people. Someone in this office could be involved. That's why I'm asking for your help—someone I trust outside of the FBI."

An hour later, with Decker's written authorization, Sam picked up a spare car from the agency's downtown lot and drove back to Gallup. The Ford sedan was a well-used vehicle with considerable mileage, but it seemed well maintained. It was good not to have to take the bus home.

He and Decker were both in a fix. After a half-hour discussion about how to counter the cards someone had stacked against them, they both agreed that discretion was called for until they could formulate a plan to stop the criminal operation, and to nullify the false evidence planted to force Decker's silence. Sam was lucky; as far as the criminals knew, he was dead; swallowed by a flood in a trackless desert. This was their ace in the hole, and it was his job to keep it that way until they could put together a better hand.

As he drove up 9 Mile Hill, headed west from Albuquerque, Sam gave some thought to Chief Decker's predicament with the bank account. He believed the man's story, but he knew there were many more who would presume the worst.

He felt a need for action—a swift, overpowering response to unbalance the opposing force, but it also must be decisive enough to stop the plans of the criminals, and counter the steps Wilder and Castor had taken.

He thought about this as he drove the old agency car past Laguna, and by the time he was through the lava fields near Grants, he had an outline of a simple but decisive offense. He must capture the men in the compound, and trap one of their cargo planes on the airstrip inside the gates. There would be gunfire, so he had to overwhelm them with more firepower. He was certain the defenders owned handguns and rifles, and possibly a few machine guns. They would make a desperate attempt to protect their illicit operation and their freedom—even more reason to plan a swift and overpowering attack.

He knew it would be a messy job, and not one to wade into without a definite plan. Decker would rather not send a large group of agents to attack a well-armed force; he would prefer the role of mopping up, and taking the survivors into custody. Sam knew he would have to count on Charlie Redman and any other resources he could muster.

Safety was his biggest concern, and the thought of facing machine guns inside the compound left him cold. He knew Decker had removed the automatic weapons usually kept at the Agency office in Gallup, some time ago. How could he counteract that kind of firepower? With dynamite of course; lashed to an arrow like he'd seen done before, and shot into the compound with a bow. It would provide enough accuracy and range to be a decisive weapon.

By the time he passed Prewitt and neared Thoreau, he decided to pay a quick visit to the trading post and see Eric and Jake before he continued on to Gallup.

Two Navajo families were just leaving the lot in their old trucks when he turned in, and he could see it was still busy inside. He heard the small bell ring over his head as he stepped inside, and he browsed around for a few moments to kill some time. He picked out a new Stetson, and made his way to the counter as the crowd thinned out.

Eric Nez saw him, and he ran up calling his name. "Sam, I got paid today—a whole fifty cents! It would have been more, but I drank too many bottles of grape Nehi this week."

The boy's grin was infectious. Sam ruffled his hair, and chatted with him until Eric hurried to the counter to pack a customer's groceries into boxes. As he waited for Jake to ring up the last group of shoppers, a new batch walked in, and Jake told Sam he might as well go to the back and talk with Eric for a while.

Brushing through the curtain to the living quarters, he and Eric talked for several minutes. When Sam said he had to go, he said he would stop back again next week and stay longer. He went back through the curtain, and saw the last customers leaving. Jake was at the counter reading some wrinkled pages from a magazine.

"What are you reading that's got you so interested?"

Jake looked up. "Oh, this? It's just part of a magazine that someone used for packing material. It must have come from some science publication. It says here that they use all kinds of mathematics to study the solar system. Not too many years ago, it says, that's how they discovered the planet Pluto, even though they couldn't see it with a telescope."

"You don't say."

"Yep, they couldn't see it, but they could tell something was causing the other planets to act in a strange way. Imagine that. They found it by noticing how other planets were reacting to it. Now tell me if that isn't some kind of fancy detective work. Even Sherlock Holmes couldn't figure out something like that. He-he."

Sam was halfway to Gallup, when he remembered what Jake said about the new planet; something about not being able to see it, but noticing how something else that they could see, was influenced by it. It got him thinking.

CHAPTER 64

Dan Yazzie rode east across the eroded hills and canyons of the Navajo Reservation north and west of Chaco Canyon. It was a lonely place of wind-scoured rocks and dry watercourses where dust devils jigged across the sand. As he rode, he paid special attention to the shadowy areas next to the cliffs.

The desert appeared barren of any wildlife except for an occasional coyote, jackrabbit, or high-flying scavenger. The small desert dwellers only came out at night to avoid the heat.

He saw glimpses of suspicious movement twice over the past hour, and when he came upon the blurred tracks of someone wearing moccasins, he stopped to study the prints. The person who made them was careful to travel over solid rock wherever possible, but still couldn't avoid leaving a faint trail.

His horse blew softly at some vague scent, and Dan thought he detected it too. It might belong to the one who made the tracks—small woman or an older child. He guessed at the direction the person was heading, and began to stray away from the path. He would return later to find where they had come from.

The tracks led into the eerie rock formations and haunted canyons of the Bisti badlands, a place many of his people avoided. Dan had his own medicine to protect him from wandering ghosts, still he was glad to have a swift horse to make a hasty retreat if he felt the need.

Questions swirled in Dan's mind. Who was this person, and why did they come this way? Why be so careful to hide their path? Was there a hidden destination—a hidden purpose?

Within an hour, he lost the trail completely. He stood on the edge of a rocky plain bordered by weird, eroded ridges. Ahead, a field of clam-shaped rocks the size of auto tires sat on short pillars of sandstone like a toadstool army marching to the far ridge. He made a widening search, and failing to locate the tracks, he gave up and headed back to where he first found the prints.

The pools of shadow were lengthening as he followed the faint trail toward their starting point. When the ridge opened on a rugged plain, he could see the outlines of the Sleeping Ute Mountains to the north. Shiprock stood alone like a sentinel, and to the west, the weathered Chuska range waited to swallow the setting sun. His eyes continued south to the Zuni Mountains beyond a series of low mesas.

He searched for sign of anything moving on the irregular ground below, and soon detected a thin trail of smoke in the general direction of the tracks. He presumed this to be the possible origin of the traveler, and within an hour, he came to a place close enough to observe a small, log hogan. Picketing his horse in some shade and grass, he awaited the person who made the tracks.

Sometime later, as the shadows grew, a young woman appeared, and approached the hogan. Dan watched as a bent, old woman stepped from the doorway and tossed out a pan of water. The two spoke for a moment, and went inside.

Dan continued his silent vigil, and within an hour, he noticed a plume of dust in the distance. A white truck approached, and losing sight of the vehicle several times as it passed behind outcrops of rock, it soon arrived at the hogan. As the wind carried the dust away, a man stepped from the vehicle and entered the hogan.

Another hour passed while the sun slipped low. Dan listened to the wind, and it whispered strange things, and hints of danger. Alarmed by what he was hearing, Dan abruptly returned to his horse and rode away. The animal appeared eager to leave the place.

The stars began to populate the indigo sky when Dan arrived at the sheltered place he sought. He gave the horse some water, and picketed it in a patch of grass near a small stand of pinon before he started a fire and put on some coffee. Warming himself from the night chill, he ate a piece of beef jerky while he thought back on his trek, and the events of the day.

Who was the Navajo girl, and why had she walked alone through miles of desert, always careful to hide her tracks? What part did she play in his visions? Who were the people she lived with? After a while, he lay back on his blanket to watch the stars gathering. Soon, the bright disk of the moon appeared, and the night sounds entered his dreams.

The small fire snapped and burned lower, and waking to the chill, Dan got up to search for more firewood. When he returned, he found the flames burning much brighter than when he left.

"I got tired of waiting for you to bring back more firewood," an old voice spoke as Dan emerged from the shadows, "so I brought some myself. The coffee smells good."

Dan waited for his heartbeat to slow down before he answered. "Why must you startle me like this?"

The old man chuckled, "Because I want you to know that I can still sneak up on you, even at my advanced age."

"Old man, you are a spirit. You move like a fart in the wind. Why shouldn't you be able to sneak up on me?"

"You're right. I guess it just pleases me, that's all. Come sit; let's warm ourselves, and talk. I have things I must tell you, and after that, I will give you a dream."

After building up the fire, the two sat with blankets over their shoulders, enjoying the warmth, and sipping coffee. The old man spoke. "You have seen the hogan across the valley to the west. Your eyes have rested on the old woman who lives there, and now I will tell you what she is.

"I will begin with the time of the long walk of the Navajo families from the old fort near Gallup. I was a young boy then, and the armies of the whites were fighting across the great river to the east. It was long ago, and many years before I was chosen by the spirits to serve another purpose."

"As many of our people still do, we raised livestock back then. We traded with each other and the Apache, and even some of the Utes to the north. We made treaties with them, and with the Spaniards, and the Mexicans. We also made war from time to time."

"When the whites came and built their forts, we fought them too. We made treaties, but they all failed. More troops came, and many people and livestock died. It was a time of raiding and taking captives. Men, women, and children were killed and enslaved, and in the end, our land was stolen from us."

"The Confederate troops came to southern New Mexico, and the Blue Coats told us we had to move from our homes to special settlements for

The Lightning Tree

our protection. Some of our people resisted, and started raiding again. The soldiers gave us the choice of extermination, or moving to another place. This is when the long walk began, and on the way, I witnessed the deaths of many people, including my parents."

"I think this was when the spirits first took notice of me. One day, I saw a young girl with an odd, red mark on her neck, being mistreated by the soldiers. We were both young, around 8 or 9 summers, and the men began to abuse her. I had a knife my grandfather gave to me, and when I tried to protect her, they broke my knife and beat me." The old man stopped and sipped his coffee.

"I felt shame," he said, his eyes looking into the darkness. "Some of our men were killed in retaliation, and the girl hated me for not being able to stop the soldiers from dishonoring her. She was too young to bear a child, but she was ancient in her ability to hate. I think she hated me more than she hated the Blue Coats."

An owl hooted in the darkness, and the old man was silent for several minutes. "When our people were allowed to return to our land, she was older, and her only thoughts were of revenge. Her hate grew, and she began to embrace the dark arts. I watched her from time to time, and I came to understand she was my enemy."

After a long pause, Dan said, "Did you ever try to speak to her again? What happened when you came home?"

Looking over at Dan, the old man said, "She killed me, that's what happened. She discovered some gold hidden by the Spanish long ago, and fearing that I would learn of the location and take it from her, she killed me to protect her secret. She still seeks revenge, and she has become a powerful witch. She wears the cloak of a skinwalker."

Dan shivered as he heard the old man's words; for who of the People do not fear the evil and blood lust of a powerful skinwalker?

The fire burned lower as the two men sat in silence and watched the moon paint pale shadows in the night.

The old man took a long, noisy breath. "You once asked me if I was you, and I said, 'not yet.' I did not mean it as if we are the same person, but I am here to guide you away from the path of self-doubt and shame that I traveled for many years. I would show you how to walk in beauty again. You have already learned much, but your final lesson is yet to come." The old man said nothing more, and shortly, he lay down in his blanket to sleep.

The fire burned lower, and as the old man's words swirled through his mind, Dan lay on his back to watch the stars. He remembered when he was younger, the troubled son of alcoholic parents. He learned to follow the same, self-destructive path after they were gone, and he relived the circumstances leading to the automobile accident that took the life of his young wife. The fault was his, and it sent him to prison.

Sam Begay came to visit from time to time, and though a lawman, he was the only one who believed in him. He brought news of his grandfather and young daughter, and sometimes he brought a few pictures.

On the day of his release from prison and his return to the Reservation, Dan found Sam waiting when he got off the bus. He had brought the terrible news of how the monster, Ye'iitsoh had killed his young daughter and his grandfather.

Dan remembered how broken and alone he felt, and how, without his family, he was as dead, as if pierced by an arrow through his heart.

CHAPTER 65

Thursday morning Sam drove to the bakery to pick up donuts, and met Charlie at the office to talk. He felt time was slipping away, and it called for some definitive action. He wanted to find a break in the wolf hair killings before Chief Decker considered moving against the criminal operation at Blacksparrow.

Last night he had tossed and turned for hours. He knew he needed to do something to take control of the events. After telling Charlie he wanted to talk with him tomorrow about everything he'd learned, he found himself shuffling through his mental clue cards again and again, but they still didn't expose anyone he felt certain to be behind the string of brutal killings. He tried to tie-in the people involved with the movie group, but the cards still didn't make a winning hand.

As far as a motive for the killings, he didn't see any of the remaining suspects fitting the profile needed to pull off such a brutal string of murders.

Edgar Dallas did exhibit some greed and bully in him, but he was a man too caught up in protecting his position in the community as school Principal. Sure, he could create some trouble, but when it came to getting his hands dirty, Sam couldn't see him stooping to such drastic action.

David Castor was a different story. Older and used to clawing his way to success, Sam had no doubt the man could justify killing someone to gain a tantalizing prize he wanted. He would be crafty, and think everything out before he acted. With much to lose, he would carefully balance everything against what he had to gain. Would he plan a campaign of murder over several years? Probably not. He might hire it done, but that left him vulnerable to the erratic mentality of a killer for hire.

Rance Wilder was the next clue card. He had already proven his willingness and ability to get rid of those he saw as a threat to his plans. He had a brutal crew taking his orders, and he seemed to have close ties to a large, criminal organization. The only problem was his absence when the string of killings first began.

Bobby Castor was an interesting suspect. He was a poser, to be sure, and Sam knew the man enjoyed the advantages of his position in the family business. He liked money and the expensive toys he could buy with it. Sam had no doubt the man could be cruel and manipulative, but could he be a killer? When he last spoke to him, Bobby appeared upset and concerned about the string of deaths of his teammates moving closer to him. Bobby was the last one living, and Sam suspected he was a coward, perhaps capable of a single, vicious act, but not planning and completing a string of killings. The man was certainly jumpy when he heard of the deaths.

Perhaps he could prey on that fear, and remind Bobby that he was the last ball player left alive. He could tell him about the tufts of wolf hair found with the bodies, and taunt him with stories about skinwalkers.

Taking his thoughts to an extreme, he considered Stacy Toledo. If she were alive, she would be Bobby's age. It would be unusual for a woman to kill in such a brutal fashion. Poison or some other subtle method would be much more likely, unless she had help, or if she was a skinwalker witch.

Sam frowned. No one had heard from her for 20 years, and the people he had spoken to on the Res. claimed to know nothing about her. She may not even be alive. Still, it was a lead, and some of the clues hinted at a reservation killer, for no other reason than the locations.

It was a weak thread, but he could check death records and birth information during the appropriate period after her rape. He vowed to follow it to an end today.

He parked his agency loaner in front of Charlie's office, and considered his last clue card, a joker. A serial killer has a method he or she prefers to use in dispatching their victims. It satisfies their need for revenge or gratification, and it becomes a time-trusted method for achieving it. When he thought back through the list of ball team victims, all the earlier deaths were due to random methods or by apparent accident.

He recalled a hanging, a rattlesnake bite, an automobile crash, and a shooting, but the six most recent deaths were by physical means—very brutal, and definitely not a result of any accident. They did have another thing in common; a tuft of wolf hair found on or near the bodies. It was as if there were multiple killers, one or more responsible for the earlier deaths, if not by accident, and another, methodical killer later on.

He walked into the office feeling a headache coming on from too little sleep and too much thinking. Maybe sugar and coffee would help.

He nodded to Charlie, and took the box of donuts to the back. As he poured his coffee and selected a donut, he remembered what Jake said about that article he was reading. It was about how the scientists found the planet Pluto. They couldn't see it, but they knew it was there because of the way the other planets reacted to it.

He sat down at his desk and thought about it while Charlie got up to refill his coffee cup and get a donut.

"Charlie, I may have a lead on the wolf hair cases. It's a long shot, but I'm going to check it out today. Regardless of what I find, if I eliminate a possibility, I'll be able to focus on a smaller group of suspects."

"That sounds good, but like you said, it still may not tell you who the killer is."

"I know. But it might tell me someone who isn't."

Charlie smirked and said, "That reminds me of a book I read when I was younger—in fact, it's what first got me interested in going into police work. I forget the author's name, but his character was from England. Have you ever heard of a guy named Sherlock Holmes?"

"Yes, and the author's name is Sir Arthur Conan Doyle. What makes you think of that?"

"I just thought of something he said in the book. I can't remember it exactly, but it was something like, 'If all the other suspects are proven innocent, then the one remaining, even though unlikely, is the guilty one.' Well it was something like that, but you get the idea. Spend your time winnowing through the suspects, and the one you have left, even though it seems far-fetched, is the guilty one." Charlie paused. "By the way, I checked schedules for the two Castor's, and they seem to be in the clear."

Throughout the day, Sam called every medical facility and courthouse north and west of Albuquerque that kept records of births and deaths. There weren't that many. He gave them the timeframe he wanted checked, and the name of the mother, Stacy Toledo. He cajoled the clerks to do an immediate search, and at the end of the day, he came up with nothing.

"So who is the killer?" Charlie said as they left the office for home.
"Probably someone else."
"Then why are you smiling?"
"Because, now I can focus on finding out who that someone else is.

CHAPTER 66

Saddle-weary from the rugged, wandering path he took across the Reservation, Dan Yazzie watered his horse at the end of the day, and picketed it in the grass near his campsite. He built a small fire under an overhanging cliff, and ate some jerky while he waited for coffee to get hot. When darkness came, he was already asleep.

He woke with a start in the middle of the night, surprised at the unexpected brightness of the fire. He remembered letting it burn down before he fell asleep. Without moving, his eyes explored the shadows around him, but he detected nothing.

An odd grogginess covered him like a heavy blanket, and when he struggled to free himself, he couldn't shake it off. Was this the dream the old man spirit had promised? His eyes focused on the fire until the dancing flames blocked out everything else. He heard the soft voice of the wind bringing whispered words, and he listened as the visions came.

Unfamiliar people and places appeared and faded in the writhing tendrils of the fire, and he saw a woman practicing some form of ritual as she sat naked on the top of a mesa. She chanted in a low voice, and after a short time, smoky figures began to swirl around her. To his surprise, she began to age before his eyes, and he noticed an odd birthmark on the side of her neck.

From her conjuring, a dark shadow began to rise against the rocks behind her. The shape soon towered over her and took form. Dan was terrified to recognize the features of the fearsome beast, Ye'iitsoh. His mind recoiled instinctively, but his body would not move. He couldn't take

303

his eyes off the apparition. He was certain the woman was a witch, and he knew the small golden disks she held in her hands were an offering for the creature to do her bidding.

In an instant, Dan was somewhere else. He found himself crouching on an outcrop of rock somewhere in the light of day. A young Navajo girl herded sheep in the field below, and beyond her, he could see the roof of a log hogan behind a low hill. He was startled to recognize the small dwelling as the house of his grandfather, where he and his young daughter lived before Sam Begay came to escort him to prison five years ago.

Every cell in his body seemed to hum, and he gasped for air as he saw a shadow creep out of a ravine some distance from the sheep. It was something large, and it moved in an unusual manner—*it was Ye'iitsoh!*

Dan gave a cry of anguish, for he knew he was looking at something that had happened just before he came home from prison. *The girl was his daughter.* He tried to shout a warning, but could not make a sound. He tried to move his arms and legs to come to her aid, but his body would not obey his desperate commands. As tears flooded his eyes, he knew he could do nothing but witness what he knew would happen—again.

Distracted by movement near the hogan, he saw his grandfather leave the dwelling and walk in the direction of the flock of sheep. The animals were milling about, and Dan saw his daughter react to the activity of the animals. She had not seen the creature yet, but she sensed some kind of danger.

Desperate to cry out a warning and run to her aid, but unable to move, Dan realized, it was already too late. Like a blur, the beast was upon her and the sheep, disemboweling and tearing their carcasses asunder. The girl died in an instant.

His lungs raw with his silent screams, Dan collapsed.

A short time later, Dan lifted his head, and with his face wet with tears, he viewed the carnage on the field below. He saw his Grandfather in the distance, running toward the hogan with the fearsome, gore-splattered beast loping in pursuit. Still unable to move, Dan eyes returned to his daughter's torn body, and he heard gunshots from the hogan. When the echoes faded, his vision blurred, and his eyes rolled upward as he passed out.

"Aahhhgh!" Dan screamed and threw off his blanket. His arms and legs jerked like a dancing puppet as he gasped for air, then he collapsed, sobbing with the pain of his remembered loss. Gradually, he awoke to the cool wind, and became aware of the darkness surrounding his small campfire. He gazed up at the stars, and let his thoughts drift away.

The sun was already climbing and warming the rock surfaces when he began to stir. He opened his eyes and smelled bacon. As he struggled to make sense of this, he heard a voice, and he sat up with a start.

"You have seen what the skinwalker witch has caused to be done. Now we will talk of avenging your family and bringing yourself back into *hozho*."

The old man spirit sat near the fire tending strips of bacon hanging from a stick. He said, "We will plan the death of the skinwalker witch who brought Ye'iitsoh back into this world, and I will show you how you must use your iron knife to kill her."

As they ate their meal and drank coffee, the old spirit explained how the witch had found a large number of Spanish gold coins many years ago as a young girl, after she returned home from the Long Walk.

"She spoke to no one about the treasure, fearing someone would take it from her. Soon, the gold corrupted her as it does the white man. She remembered the brutality of the white soldiers, and planned for her revenge. She also vowed to kill anyone who tried to harm her or attempted to steal her treasure."

After a pause, the old man sipped his coffee and said, "She learned the old secrets from a witch, and over time, she mastered the evil spells as she delved even deeper into the dark powers.

She had gained much power by the time she became a mature woman, and she knew her body would eventually become too old to allow her to enjoy all she wanted in her life. This is when she began to seek the knowledge of how to steal youth from another. Once she learned this, she began to covet the daughter of her sister."

Dan said, "How do you know this, old man? Did you see her?"

"Yes, I lived across the valley, and I watched her from a distance. She had no thoughts of me after our families returned to our homes, and I no longer wanted her to look upon me with favor. I saw her kill her sister, and take her place raising her young daughter. I decided to stay to watch over the young girl, and as the years passed, I saw the witch woman's mind become twisted beyond reason."

The old man spirit threw the grounds of his coffee on the fire. He looked up at Dan and said, "One day, I learned the young girl was raped by a group of whites in Gallup. She became pregnant and bore two children before she died. I watched the old woman bury her body, and raise the two children as their grandmother."

"For twenty years, I have done this as the two children grew, and five years ago, I stumbled upon the place she hid her gold. I did not wish to take it, but I gave in to my curiosity, and took a close look. I soon learned she saw me."

"Did she do something?"

"Yes, she killed me! It served me right, of course. She was a powerful skinwalker, and I should have known better than to trifle with her."

Dan looked at the lined face of the old man. "Is that when you became a spirit?"

"Yes."

The old spirit-man looked across the distant hills while Dan thought about what he had just heard. After a few moments he said, "Old man, in the dream you gave me, I saw the witch make Ye'iitsoh kill my daughter and my grandfather. Do you know why she did that?"

The old man nodded his head. "Yes. I wondered about it at first, but I learned it was because your daughter wandered near the place where she hid her gold. The girl was tending her sheep, and she didn't know it was there, but she was close enough that the witch decided to kill her and your grandfather. If you were living with them, instead of at the Santa Fe prison, Ye'iitsoh would have killed you."

"Hear me, old man, when I came back home, I killed the monster, and now I will kill this witch." Dan spoke through his clenched teeth, his face, a fearsome, scowling mask.

The old man turned and spat. "Yes you will, and I will teach you how, for if you do not, she will bring the creature, Ye'iitsoh back to this world. There is one other thing you must know. The witch raised the two babies, a girl and a boy, after their mother died, and she plans to take over the body of the girl now that she is of age. If this happens, the witch will have her youth again, as well as everything the gold can bring her. What she plans to do with the boy, I do not know—perhaps she will kill him when she has no further use for him."

"I will kill Ye'iitsoh again," Dan said, brandishing his iron knife. "I made this after I lost the broken one you helped me find."

The old man nodded. "It is good that you have done this."

Dan felt the sharp edge of the blade, "I will use this to kill the evil creature and the witch."

"You must do so, because under the witch's control, the beast will do her bidding, and will become more powerful than the first time you fought it. It may even gain the power to bring about the destruction of this fourth world of the Navajo People, just as the first three came to an end long ago."

The fire popped, and they listened to the wind rushing up the canyon. The old man said. "There is a better way you can use the knife. You can kill the witch before she summons the monster. You must prepare yourself for this, because the time is coming near."

"How will I know what to do?"

"I will be with you, and I will tell you."

CHAPTER 67

The old witch woman wore a traditional, full skirt and a velveteen blouse—both frayed and dusty, while she clutched an old shawl about her bony shoulders. Resting in her rocker under the brush arbor near the hogan, she gazed at the distant wall of rubble and red sandstone to the west. A fringe of pinon and juniper ran along the bottom of the talus slope, and above the rocks, cottony towers of cumulus clouds rose in the distance.

A faint breeze brought the smell of the desert, and with it, the first hint of evening. There was also something else; she sensed the presence of the ghost of the old Indian, and she wished she could rid herself of the troublesome spirit. Some things were difficult to do. She had killed him, and now, he was relatively harmless, though he did manage to disturb her from time-to-time. Recently, he had slipped into her hogan while she was away, and he left the stench of his flatulence behind to annoy her.

The problem was, he knew her full name; and with that knowledge, if he were to discover the path she walked, and confront her, he could use it to make her sick and die.

At the side of the hogan, Tessa sat in the late afternoon shade, peeling the skin from a rabbit while her grandmother dozed a short distance away. She heard the old woman mutter something unintelligible before she drifted off to sleep. Tessa ignored her while she finished gutting the animal for their evening meal.

When she stood to go inside, some instinct made her look toward the east. She saw a man running in the distance, and while she watched the steady gait and the fluid movement of arms and shoulders, her brother came nearer. She took the rabbit inside, and brought out a gourd of water for him.

The old woman awoke when she heard Sonny arrive, and she lifted her bony arms to welcome him. He took the water gourd and brought it to the old woman, kneeling at her feet as he offered it to her. After she drank, he finished the rest.

She reached her arthritic, clawed hands to his face, cooing something tender as she touched him, and Sonny kissed her shaking hands. "Grandmother, I will go to Gallup tomorrow and wait for the man who drives the small, black car. I will not return until I have finished this last task you have given me. Then, I will have avenged my mother."

His words seemed to please the old woman. She nodded and sat back in the rocker as Sonny stood and walked toward his sister.

Tessa marveled at her brother's strength, and she saw resolve in his eyes and in the set of his jaw.

"The old woman will make my medicine tonight," he said, "and tomorrow I will complete the task she has given to me."

"Will it be over then?" Tessa said, her doubt and concern showing on her face.

"Yes, and I will be done." He glanced at the old woman.

Tessa nodded and went inside as he walked back to their grandmother and sat at her feet. The old woman lifted her head, and began to mutter an ancient song.

Later, inside the hogan, Tessa served the rabbit stew, and the three ate in silence while the wind blew outside the door. Her brother grew sullen, though he didn't speak, and Tessa wished she were outside in the desert, alone with her thoughts. The old woman ignored them both.

When they finished eating, Tessa removed the bowls from the table, and the old woman spoke to Sonny. "Bring me the old book."

He stood without speaking and complied with her request. When he set the worn volume on the table, Granny pulled it close and began to leaf through the worn pages until she found the photo she wanted. She moved a gnarled finger across the boys standing in a group. Each had a penciled 'X' over the face except for one. She studied the last face, murmuring as she squinted, and then she spun the book around in front of Sonny.

"This one is the last," she said. "When he has suffered his punishment, it will be time to talk of other things." She glanced at the young woman

309

across the room, and shifted the book aside as Tessa turned toward the table.

When morning came, Sonny finished the remaining stew. His chiseled features hid the impatience that screamed inside of him. Pushing the empty bowl away, he said, "I will end this soon, old woman. Much time has been given to this task, and I grow weary of it."

"Patience, my grandson; a reward awaits us, and we must not weaken our resolve or our vigilance. Danger stalks our path, and we must not let it keep us from taking our revenge."

"Danger?" he said, "I fear it not. I am a warrior, and this danger is no more than I have faced before."

"Yes, my grandson, I see your courage and your strength, but you do not hear the voices that whisper to me. They speak of danger, and how unwary warriors fall before the actions of powerful spirits."

Anger flashed across Sonny's face. He jumped from his chair, overturning it as he stood. "Know this old woman. I am wary of tricks *and* danger from many places. I will have my reward, and I will be watchful of many things."

With that, he snatched the small bottle of potion from the old woman's hands, and strode out of the hogan. Tessa looked away, and the old woman watched through the open door as the vehicle roared to life and sped away. She took a deep breath, and ignoring the girl, she picked up her pipe, and shuffled out to her rocking chair under the brush arbor. She smoked as the rising sun brought out the colors of the desert, and she let her thoughts walk the path of her future.

She had waited long, and she was old. She had planned a life of wealth and comfort since she was a girl younger than Tessa. Her childhood had been full of hard work, though it did give her time to explore the desert around her. She had marveled at the stories of the ancient spirits, and she secretly hoped to see them one day. The wind spoke to her, and she wished she could answer it's call.

She was a young girl when she found the cache of gold coins. Believing the spirits led her to it, she felt chosen to use the metal for some important, future purpose. Above all, she understood the need to protect the secret location.

She remembered before then, when the soldiers took her and her family on the Long Walk to a place east of the river. Bad things happened, and it gave her a vision of her future as a powerful, medicine woman. She knew word of this would frighten those who knew her, so she kept her thoughts secret, and cherished the vision of having enough power so that no man could ever abuse her again.

She made sure the soldiers who caused her suffering, paid for their transgressions with their lives. Though still a young girl, she did it secretly, and by herself. She scorned the boy who attempted to help her but failed. He was weak, and he deserved to die.

These long ago events still lived in the old woman's mind, even after the years had hidden and blurred so many other memories. She saw herself in another time, when she could use her sister's baby daughter as a vessel for her own spirit. It was a small thing to kill her sibling, and take her place as the young child's guardian.

After that, she had groomed the girl, Stacy, to be a vessel for her own aging body one day. How she had hungered to be in control of the girl's youthful form, and for all the things she could do with it, and with the gold. The thought of wealth and youth sustained her—and then, the little fool became pregnant, and died giving birth to her twins.

"Bah!" The old woman spat and shook off her frustration. She had waited another twenty years to punish those who had abused the girl, and ultimately, caused her death. The death had forced her to wait for the girl's daughter Tessa to come of age so she could use her instead, to transform her aging body. The time was very close now, and there was only one more boy to punish.

She trained Tessa's brother to develop his strength, and do her bidding, and as his strength grew, so did her powers. She taught Sonny how to take the lives of those who dishonored his mother, and he willingly took to the task of punishing the ball players. Sonny preferred to act during the full moon, and he took the potion of strength the old woman prepared for him, and made the killing act a ceremony, leaving behind the sign of a wolf.

During this time, the old women increased her knowledge in the dark arts so that she could take over the girl's body and use it as her own. The time to act was very near, and she shivered as an electric thrill coursed through her ancient, wrinkled body.

Tessa appeared in the doorway, and when the old witch lifted a bony arm for water, Tessa brought a dipper. While the old woman drank, the girl looked to the east at the sun rising in a clear, blue sky. Her heart soared at the simple beauty, but then her brows knotted with darker thoughts and fears.

The old woman, sensing the girl's distress, gave Tessa the ladle and said, "Patience girl; I will be gone soon, and you will leave this place with the gold coins you watch over and protect.

Tessa stood quietly as the old woman closed her eyes for several seconds before speaking again. "A long time ago, your mother was wronged by a group of young, white men in Gallup. When she died giving birth to you and your brother, I trained him to be the tool of her revenge."

"She stared at Tessa for a moment, and said, "Your brother is a fierce warrior. He has struck down all but one of those who dishonored your mother."

Tessa had heard all of this before, and she looked away. "Grandmother, why must I watch over the metal disks? Why not just bury them so no one can find where they are hidden?"

The old woman shifted to get more comfortable. The lies came easy from her old lips. "Because, when I am gone, you *and* your brother will take the gold and leave this place. The power of the yellow metal will let you live in the white man's world, and that is why I have you guard it, to keep it from those who would steal it from you."

"But why must I keep the location of the gold from my brother?"

"Hush child. Do as I say. Soon, you will see that my caution is well taken."

Tessa left, and the old woman sat back and thought of where her long path began. She remembered how the death of her sister's daughter Stacy in childbirth, shattered her plans like a clay pot thrown against a rock. Only the two babies kept her from going mad.

Now, everything she had waited for was near, and Sonny and Tessa must never suspect what she really planned for them.

CHAPTER 68

Sonny drove from the hogan, west to the main road, and then south to Gallup. It was Saturday, and it annoyed him to think that Benny Ortiz expected him to work at the shop this morning before he let him have the weekend free.

The traffic was heavy, and it was busy in town with the Reservation shoppers. He knew this would allow him to blend in with the crowd when he finished work.

Sonny left work at mid-day, and he drove off to monitor Bobby Castor's whereabouts. He drove past Lone Mountain Trading and saw Bobby's small black vehicle parked behind the building; a funny-looking car, and much too low to the ground to handle the reservation roads.

He parked on a wooded hill a short distance from the building, and waited under the shade of some junipers and greasewood while he watched the parking lot. He had enough time now to pick the right opportunity to finish his final task. It had been several years since the first, after the old woman trained him, and he anticipated celebrating his final success after killing this prey.

The afternoon dragged on, and as the shadows of the junipers shifted, Sonny moved the vehicle to keep it in the shade. Traffic came and went from the trading post, and he noticed the large car belonging to Bobby Castor's father pull around to the back of the building and park next to the smaller one. It wasn't the old man he wanted; it was his son who would suffer the consequences of his own actions.

Inside the building, David Castor's arrival touched off a blaze of anger inside Bobby. He glared as the older man motioned with a curt hand gesture and a jerk of his head. Bobby exhaled his frustration and followed his father into the office.

"You act like the king of the world, and expect me to come at your bidding," Bobby said as he glared at the older man behind the desk. Choosing to remain standing, he said, "What do you want?"

David took some things from the desk and put them in his pocket. "I want the keys to your car. Mine's not running right, and I have to drive out to the movie set this afternoon." Hearing no response from his son, David looked up. "Don't just stand there, give me the keys. I'll bring the damn thing back this evening. If you're not here, I'll stop by your house in town."

Bobby's face turned red, but he kept his anger in check. "Just be careful with it, and keep your speed down on the back roads. The thing rides a lot lower than your Cadillac."

He tossed the keys, and David caught them with a swipe of his hand. "Boy, I was shifting gears long before you ever learned how to grab hold of your pecker. You can use the Caddy to get home, just watch the brakes, and see that *you* don't mess up *my* car while I'm gone."

With that, David left the room. Bobby stood there for a few moments, willing himself to relax. "Bastard," he said, and then walked out to the store.

When David Castor drove the Cord out of the parking lot, Sonny started his truck and jockeyed into traffic to catch up. Craning his neck to keep the small vehicle in sight, he saw it turn onto the main highway, and he followed it east through town. His breathing came faster as he kept his eyes focused on the distinctive, black sports car.

Traffic thinned outside of town and Sonny sped up; trying to hold his excitement in check. He willed his mind and body to be patient while he waited for the right opportunity to finish his long journey for revenge. He would stalk this prey, and follow the man like a ghost. When he struck, it would be without warning, and with no hope for escape. Bobby Castor would die today.

Several cars ahead, David Castor tried to adjust the seat to get more comfortable. Though he did enjoy the sporty feel and the responsive steering of the small car, the cramped legroom annoyed him. Having to fold nearly in half to climb behind the wheel, he felt odd driving it. Heck, it even lacked a running board outside. The ride left much to be desired, compared to his big Cadillac, but he did notice people in other vehicles looking at him with envy.

He couldn't help but smile. He remembered when his son brought the Cord home earlier this year, and how he drooled over the low-slung car, and talked incessantly about its features. It carried an 812 designation, even though it was identical to last year's model with an 810 badge. David snorted; anything to get some sucker to buy the thing. The instrument panel looked like it came out of an airplane, and there were hand cranks to open the headlights. He even remembered the boy's words in defense of paying far too much for it. Boy? Hell, Bobby was a forty-year-old man. When would he grow up?

As the traffic thinned, David put the pedal down. The front drive felt steady and sure, but the response of the low horsepower engine was a disappointment. Well, it did seem to get the looks, and he suspected that's what it was all about.

He turned off the highway at Thoreau and continued north through the village, unaware of the old truck following him since he left Gallup. He turned east beyond the small community of Crownpoint, took the turnoff, north toward Chaco, and then west on the side road to the Blacksparrow Mine. Pulling past the gate into the compound, he parked, and noticed some of the hands walking up to take a closer look at the black Cord, now grey with dust.

A mile back, Sonny turned around and retraced his route back to a place where he could hide the truck, and watch the traffic coming and going along the road. He would follow the small car when it left to return to Gallup, and he would take advantage of the long-awaited opportunity to strike.

He picked up the small bottle containing the potion the old woman prepared for him, and he remembered how quickly it filled his body with strength and euphoria. It made him feel like an avenging warrior, and he shivered in anticipation of what it would allow him to do when his prey in the black car returned to Gallup.

Inside the main house at Blacksparrow, David Castor said, "Now that I'm here, what is it you wanted to talk about?" He was annoyed at the curt way Wilder had summoned him, and all he could think about was that it had something to do with finding Sam Begay's body.

Wilder motioned Castor to a chair, and opened a decorative bottle sitting on a table. He poured two drinks, and said, "A little scotch to wash away the dust, David?"

Castor offered a thin smile. "That's exactly what I need. I had to drive my son's sports car, and I'm not built for something that small." He downed half of his drink, and felt the liquid burn all the way down to his stomach. He exhaled the heat, and said, "Any word about Begay's body showing up?"

"No. The boys spent all day following the watercourse downstream. I don't know how many miles they covered, but they found nothing. I haven't seen anything in the papers, either; have you?"

David shook his head and took another gulp from his glass. "He's probably buried under the sand somewhere, miles away. Forget about it. How's the shipment of the new merchandise coming along?"

"Very well." Wilder refilled Castor's glass and added a couple of inches to his own. "As a matter of fact, that's why I wanted to see you this afternoon. I believe the time has come for you and I to cement of our future working relationship. My people have big plans for you, and after the little ruckus Begay stirred up, I want to put the past behind us, and look to the future. It's time to move on to other things."

Wilder eased into his upholstered chair across from David. "I have made some inroads in compromising the FBI Station Chief in Albuquerque, thanks to the candid photos our man took of our golf outing with Decker. I have made him aware of their existence, and have discretely suggested he consider how appearances can negatively affect a man's career, especially in certain government positions."

Wilder smiled. "In addition, Thaddeus Decker is now aware of the significant balance he carries under his name at a certain bank, and he is, no doubt, considering how to manage a prickly situation known as bribery and blackmail. I expect his connection to the two of us will cause him to align his future path to one we can control."

"I hope so," Castor said, looking a bit uneasy. "What do we do next?"

"We plan your political campaign for Governor," David, "that's what."

Rance Wilder lifted his glass and raised it to Castor. "Here's to new, progressive leadership in Santa Fe."

"And more money in our pockets," David said, clinking Wilder's glass, and downing the scotch.

A few hours later, after discussing how to handle the new contraband soon to flow through their remote facility, and the finer points of planning a political campaign, David started the engine of the Cord and drove from the compound. The setting sun painted the western horizon with brilliant reds, but his thoughts were elsewhere.

Turning west toward Crownpoint, he didn't see the vehicle enter the road behind him with its lights off. Within a mile, headlights flared behind him as Sonny's truck began to close the distance.

Noticing the rapidly approaching vehicle, David hit the gas pedal. He cursed at the anemic response from the Cord's engine, and he let off the gas, and waited for the other driver to pass. Soon, a white truck flew by, dragging a thick cloud of dust. He lost sight of the truck as he drove on toward the improved dirt road that led south to Crownpoint, and the highway west to Gallup.

Reaching the intersection, ready to turn, the headlights suddenly glared from his left, and he saw the same white truck spin around to block the road. David could only turn right, and as he did, the road rapidly deteriorated into a rutted two-track that led toward the desolate Bisti.

He realized his error too late. While his chances of outrunning the truck on a well-maintained road were minimal, escaping a vehicle with better ground clearance and more horsepower on such a rough trail was impossible. The low-slung Cord lurched and bounced as the frame bottomed out on the rutted surface. Headlights glared through the back window, blinding him as he struggled to steer and build up speed.

His anger flared, and David was ready to hit the brakes and face the other driver, when the truck rear-ended the Cord, and propelled it sideways. Struggling to correct its path, David gave it gas again, and noticed something was wrong.

The small engine revved, and the truck mashed the rear end again, so hard, David's head jerked back and hit the roof. In his panic, he discovered the transmission slipped out of gear. He desperately tried to jam it back, but by this time, the truck began to push the small car, and it was all he could do to try to keep the front tires in the track.

They traveled a few hundred feet before the trail made a sharp turn, and while David struggled to make the Cord follow it, the crumpled body slewed to the right, darted off the track through some brush, and, careened off a rock. A moment later, the front end tilted sharply. The roaring truck engine drowned out David's screams, as the distinctive, rounded nose of the car dropped, and the headlights illuminated the bottom of a dark ravine.

There was no explosion when it hit, but dust filled the area like a fog. One headlight miraculously stayed on, but the crumpled mass of metal no longer resembled the sleek automobile it had once been. Something ran into David eyes, and he couldn't see. He heard weak moans, and knew they came from his own throat.

In the dark confines of the car thirty feet below the trail, a new sound came to his ears; the rhythmic pad of footfalls coming nearer. He heard breathing, and someone grunting with exertion, and then he detected the smell of gasoline. A bright flash of light followed, and fiery heat was his last sensation—that and the eerie howl of pain that escaped from his mashed lips.

CHAPTER 69

A Navajo family visiting relatives east of Standing Rock, drove home on a breezy, Sunday afternoon, taking the long way toward the Chaco Valley, and south on the unimproved trail to Crownpoint and Thoreau. High, wispy clouds passed overhead, while the children enjoyed watching the occasional roadrunner and jackrabbit dart across their path, and listening to the jays calling from the scattered greasewood and scrub pine.

The six children in the back of the pickup dozed, bellies full, and senses numbed by the rocking motion of the vehicle. Ten miles north of Crownpoint, Mrs. Shorty noticed a smudge of smoke off the road on their left. She made a noise, and lifted her chin in that direction as she twitched her lower lip.

Tommy Shorty looked where she indicated, then stopped near some vehicle tracks and churned up sand off the side of the trail. Curiosity and the lazy pace of the afternoon made him decide to stretch his legs, and his two eldest boys walked with him to investigate the smoke.

As they approached the edge of an arroyo, they saw where two vehicles had careened through some rocks and brush. Mr. Shorty's interest, now increased by creeping concern, made him hurry to the edge of the wash to see a smoldering, wrecked automobile.

Three o'clock that afternoon, Charlie Redman and Sam Begay interviewed Mr. and Mrs. Shorty at the Thoreau Trading Post, and then drove north to the location of the wrecked vehicle.

They stood at the top of the arroyo, and waited for the Medical Examiner to arrive, both recognizing the distinctive shape of the car below. Charlie said, "Do you think Bobby Castor was inside it when it burned?"

"Only one way to find out," Sam said, and he rigged a rope to lower himself down to the wreck. When he reached the smoldering vehicle, he found it impossible to identify the badly burned body inside. It would have to be Doc. Beeman's job.

He recoiled from the smell as much as the gruesome condition of the corpse, and he yelled to Charlie. "It's hard to tell anything, except that the body is human. He turned back to the car, and pulled out some charred bits of clothing to look for a wallet or some other identification. Noticing a watch and a ring, he carefully removed them before he continued to search for a wallet. He found it under the body, and gingerly pulled the crispy lump of burned leather from the car. He gave it to Charlie when he climbed back to the top so he could put it somewhere safe.

The two investigated the ground above the crime scene, measuring tire tracks and a few boot prints, and noting the fresher prints of Mr. Shorty and his boys. Then, completing a slow circle of the area, Sam noticed a plume of dust coming from the south. "I'll bet that's Beeman now."

They finished marking off the tracks while they waited for the M.E.'s van to pull up, and then watched the familiar form of the examiner step out. His shaggy blond hair framed a sunburned face beneath a tan Stetson.

Charlie said; "Doc looks unhappy about something, Sam."

"Yeah, I've seen that face before. He's probably wondering how it is that you and I keep finding these dead bodies."

Doc. Beeman walked up to Charlie's car with his instrument bag in hand. "I was just telling myself it's been quiet these past few weeks—too quiet. I figured you both must be on vacation, and I thought this might be a perfect time to take a trip back east—but then the phone rang."

"Honest Doc, we didn't find this one. Charlie and I were just talking about how we hoped you'd get a chance to do some fishing, and then someone called us."

"Forget it, Begay, I'm not that naive. Let's get this over with. Maybe I'll get back to Gallup in time to see a softball game this evening, but somehow I doubt I'll be that lucky."

"It's a bad one Doc," Charlie said as he adjusted his Stetson. "It looks like there was a car chase, and a collision causing one vehicle to fall into the arroyo. It caught fire with the driver inside, and the other vehicle left, and let it to burn."

Charlie started taking some notes, while Sam went down to the wreck with Beeman. He joined them later, and walked around the scene looking

The Lightning Tree

for more clues. A half-hour later, when Doc was ready to lift the body from the arroyo, Charlie noticed Sam pick up something from the sand and blow away the dirt.

"Find something?"

Sam held a small stick between his finger and thumb, and said, "Yeah, a match."

"Maybe that answers the question of how the fire started."

"Could be. I found something else stuck in that bush off to the side." Sam pulled a small, folded envelope from his pocket and opened it for Charlie to see."

Charlie looked up, "Wolf hair?"

"Uh huh, it was stuck to a broken twig about eye level. Someone left it for us to find, Charlie."

After they pulled the bag with the charred remains up the bank, and secured it in Beeman's vehicle, the doc said, "Any idea who the victim is?"

Sam took off his hat and wiped his forehead with his sleeve. "Well, I'm pretty sure the car belongs to Bobby Castor, and there seems to be a connection to the other deaths we've found over the past few years. He was a baseball player back in high school just like the others."

"The corpse isn't Bobby's," Beeman said. "It's an older man. I noticed signs of arthritis in his bones. Bobby is about forty, and I'd say this man was closer to sixty years old. I'll know for sure when I complete my autopsy. Did you say you found some jewelry and a wallet?"

"Yeah, but the wallet is mostly charcoal; I doubt we'll be able to read anything inside it. Our best chance of confirming the identification is from the watch and ring."

Charlie said, "Maybe it's Bobby's father. I don't know of any other car like this in the area, and I doubt Bobby would lend it to a friend."

Beeman nodded. "Good point. I'll let you two know when I finish the autopsy Monday. In the meantime; let me know if you find out anything more about who it might be."

The two watched as Beeman turned his van around and drove away. Sam said, "What do you want to bet someone *thought* it was Bobby Castor inside that car?"

Charlie had a dubtful look on his face. "Just because the car might belong to Bobby, doesn't mean someone tried to kill *him*. That piece of wolf hair could have blown there in the wind, or rubbed off when an animal walked past it."

Sam shook his head. "Charlie, neither one of us believes that. It makes more sense that our killer mistook who was driving the car, and since Bobby is the last ball player still alive, I have a hunch who the killer is."

"Don't be too sure without Beeman's autopsy findings. We've seen car accidents before—even some with wolf hair at the crash sites. Wait a minute; do you think Bobby is the killer?"

"No, I think he was the intended victim. But I remember seeing some tire tracks like these before." Sam pointed to the tire prints behind him. Do you carry a bag of plaster in your trunk?"

"Sure, and some water. I'll get it."

CHAPTER 70

Sam and Charlie returned to Gallup, and left the plaster casting of the tire and boot prints they found at the scene, in the back room of the office to dry. Charlie shuffled a stack of papers at his desk, and took a deep breath and exhaled. "I guess I'd better get to work on these reports."

"Why don't you let me do it?" Sam said. "You can drive over to Strong Mountain Trading and talk to Bobby Castor. I still don't want him to know I'm around, just in case he's in communication with the men who tried to kill me at Blacksparrow. He should recognize the watch and ring as his father's, and if he does, ask him how his dad came to be driving his car. You'll have to tell him about some of the details, of course, and when you come back, you can put his statement in the report."

The trading company was busy that afternoon, but the traffic was starting to thin out as the Reservation folk started heading back to their homes. Charlie pulled into the lot and drove around the building just to make sure there weren't two black Cord convertibles. He saw David Castor's Cadillac, and parked.

As he stepped inside and made his way down the center aisle to the pawn counter, he noticed Bobby Castor talking to a customer. Charlie stopped to look at some new boots until the customer left, and Bobby glanced up as he approached the counter.

"Well, if it isn't Agent Redman, I never thought I'd see you working on a Sunday. Are you looking for something, or is this an official visit?"

Bobby's voice had an edge to it, and it appeared he had other things on his mind.

"I'm surprised to see you working today, too. I didn't notice your sports car outside."

"You didn't see my car, because my father borrowed it yesterday and didn't bring it back like he promised. I'm almost mad enough to report it stolen."

"Mr. Castor, can we talk in private?"

Bobby stared at Charlie Redman, wondering what could be on the Agent's mind. "If you wish. We can go back to the office."

Bobby called to one of the employees to watch the counter while he stepped away for a few minutes, and Charlie followed him down a short hall to the office. Bobby shut the door, and offered Charlie a chair.

Settling behind the desk, Bobby said, "What's on your mind Agent Redman?"

"Mr. Castor, I think we found your car." Charlie reached in his pocket and set the watch and ring on the desk. "Can you identify these items?"

Bobby frowned, obviously surprised and suspicious. "They look like my fathers..." His voice trailed off.

"I'm sorry to have to tell you that I believe your father died in an automobile accident last night. The coroner is looking into the exact cause and time of death, and I hoped you could identify the items. I'm very sorry."

Bobby spoke in a whisper, "Are you certain it's him?"

"No more than you are Mr. Castor. We found the wreckage of the car, with a body inside, burned beyond recognition. The Medical Examiner is trying to confirm the identity right now. Can you tell me how your father came to be driving your car, and where he was going last night?"

Bobby Castor leaned forward on his elbows with his head in his hands as Charlie waited in silence.

Bobby slowly sat back in his chair, eyes unfocused as he spoke. "He asked to use my car yesterday because his wasn't running right. He said he'd return it that evening, and when he didn't show up...I became angry."

Charlie watched the man's lip quivering. "Mr. Castor, did he tell you where he was going?"

"Yes, he said he was driving out to the movie site north of Thoreau to talk to Rance Wilder about some business matters. Have you talked to him yet?"

"No, I wanted to notify you first, and I had no way to be certain it might be your father without talking to you."

Bobby blinked his eyes. "Can you tell me what happened?"

Charlie said, "A call came in to my office around mid-day. A Navajo family found the wreck in an arroyo off the trail north of Crownpoint, and they stopped in Thoreau and had someone call my office. When I got to the wreck, it appeared some other vehicle rammed into it, and may have pushed it off the trail. I don't know if it caught on fire from the crash, or if someone deliberately set it, but it was out when I arrived. The medical examiner is doing an autopsy right now."

"Do you want me to make the identification?"

"Yes sir, that's why I brought you the watch and ring. The condition of the body is…I'm afraid it would be difficult for anyone to identify him."

Charlie returned to the office with a somber expression on his face.

"Did you talk to Bobby? Did he confirm the car and driver?"

Charlie sat at his desk and looked at Sam. "Yes to both. He said his old man borrowed the car to drive out to Blacksparrow yesterday afternoon, and he never made it home."

Charlie gave him the details of the interview, and said, "I think if your ball team theory is running true to form. Bobby Castor may have escaped his own death by shear, dumb luck."

Sam said, "Yes, and it will mean it's still not over yet. If Bobby isn't the killer, the real one will probably make another attempt on his life."

"What if we kept the identity of who died out of the papers? Would that help?"

"It might, but I doubt it's even possible. The presses are probably rolling right now, and soon, everyone will know about the accident."

"You don't think Bobby could be the killer, do you? It doesn't make sense, and besides, he told me he was playing baseball yesterday evening with some friends. He said they played cards after that, and he didn't get home until midnight. There are witnesses, and besides, why would he want to get rid of his father and destroy the car?"

"Good point. It should be easy enough to verify Bobby's whereabouts, and all we know is that the last person who spoke to David Castor alive is probably Rance Wilder."

"Would he have a reason to kill him?"

"There's only one way to find out. Charlie, I'm not ready to let anyone know that I'm still alive, so why don't you pay a visit to the El Rancho and see if Wilder is in. When you tell him about Castor, it should be enlightening to see his expression and hear what he has to say. If he's still out at Blacksparrow, maybe you can find out when he's expected back in town."

"While you do that, I'll stay here and work on the report. When I see Wilder face-to-face again, I want it to be in such a way that I make as much of an impact on him as possible. I'll call Beeman and make sure he keeps my name off of the report. I'll also ask him not to mention it to the press. I'll lock the door and draw the shades, and I won't answer the phone until you get back."

Charlie left, and returned twenty minutes later. "Wilder wasn't at the hotel, but I had the manager call him at Blacksparrow, and I arranged for an appointment here in his room tomorrow morning."

"Did you tell him about finding Castor and the wreck?"

"I didn't have to. He said Bobby called him fifteen minutes earlier."

CHAPTER 71

Monday, a Gallup Independent reporter interviewed Bobby Castor about the death of his father. When the same reporter approached Charlie Redman, he refused to comment about any ongoing investigation. Charlie suspected the reporter would try to corner the medical examiner to garner any other details he could.

Tuesday, the death and accident made the front page of the Independent. He threw the paper down. "Darn it Sam, how did they get so much information?"

Sam shrugged. "People talk—the Navajo family that reported it, or someone they talked to, maybe even someone overhearing something at the Trading Post. That doesn't take into account Doc. Beeman, Bobby Castor, or a dozen others who just like to flap their gums. News travels fast, and bad news travels faster."

"Well, it doesn't make our job any easier. They should call it the Gallup *Indiscreet*."

"Sam chuckled, "Relax, and try think of it as the Gallup *Insignificant*. Don't let it bother you. You checked out Bobby's alibi yesterday, so all we can do now is wait and see what kind of activity the news draws out."

"Yeah I guess. I have my meeting with Rance Wilder at the El Rancho in twenty minutes. I'll get his statement, and try to press him on what David Castor was doing out at Blacksparrow that evening, just in case he makes up a story we can refute later on. I'll talk to you when I get back."

Later, when Charlie returned from the El Rancho, his posture told Sam he had come up with nothing solid to work on. Charlie hung his hat on the rack, and sat behind his desk flipping through his notes. "Wilder says they talked "movie business," and that Castor left Blacksparrow a little after 9:00 p.m. He said he didn't know of any concerns David had, except that his son wanted the car back as soon as he returned to town."

Charlie chuckled, "He did ask about you."

"Oh?"

"Yeah, he said if I saw you, to tell you to let him know if you found any young Navajo men to act as extras in his movie."

Sam's grin was full of malice. "That's clever of him. What did you say?"

"I just said I hadn't heard from you since you went to Blacksparrow over a week ago. I told him when I noticed your car was gone from the El Rancho parking lot later that day, I presumed you were doing some work out of town."

"Hmm, good thinking."

"I thought so too. Rance said to remind you to give him a call when you get back."

Sam nodded as he thought. "I'll call him alright. And when I do, I want someone standing there to tell me what kind of look comes on his face when he hears my voice. Better yet, I'll go see him in person with you as a witness."

"By the way, I called Beeman while you were out. He says he estimates the time of Castor's death was between 8:00 p.m. and 11:00 p.m. Saturday night, but he said to give-or-take an hour or so either way because of the condition of the body. Based on drive time, I'd say the accident and fire took place somewhere around 9:45 p.m."

"That figures, but we've still got nothing but that plaster cast of the tire print for a clue—that and the tuft of wolf hair you found." Charlie slouched in his chair. Is the coffee still hot?"

"Nah, it's cold by now. I think I'll drive out to the trading post in Thoreau and see how Eric is doing. While I'm out there, I'll check with Jake to see if any other customers came in with some gossip. You know how us Navajos like to talk. Are you going be around today?"

"Later in the afternoon, but I'm not sure when. I have to be in Ft. Defiance to meet with a council member about a family feud over some cattle. When we get back together, we should start making plans to take down the operation at the movie site. We have enough information to get

The Lightning Tree

a warrant, but I want to talk to Decker about using the agency's resources for support."

Sam nodded, "All I want to do is figure out how to set up the raid when they have some contraband at the site we can use for evidence."

Sam left by the back door wearing an old baseball hat and jacket as an impromptu disguise. He still wanted to be an unexpected, wild card, and keep surprise on his side. He started the unmarked car Decker let him use, and drove out of town toward Thoreau. There were long lines of trucks on the road today, but the traffic moved fast enough for him to get to Jake's by lunchtime. He parked at the side of the building and walked in just as Jake was saying goodbye to his customers.

"Sam, am I glad you showed up."

"Why? Do you need help with something?"

"Yes...maybe. Oh, I don't know, but...Sam, Eric hasn't been around all morning, and the last I saw him was when he went to bed last night. I called him for breakfast, and when he didn't show up, I checked his room and found it empty. His bed was made, and I don't know if he left last night or this morning. I figured if he didn't show up for lunch, I'd call you. Where do you think he would go?"

Sam stood there thinking. "Was anything wrong? Was he mad about something?"

"No nothing like that. We get along fine, but I remembered something I heard him say yesterday that made me think. I wish I'd called you earlier."

"That's alright, what did he say?"

"Well, he was talking to a pretty little Navajo girl at the counter, and she was smiling at him and looking at some small carved totems under the glass. She seemed to find them interesting, and I heard Eric tell her that he had some, and he could get them for her if she really liked them.

Now Sam, it's not a secret how a young boy likes to impress a pretty little girl. The more I think about it, I'll bet when she showed some interest in what he told her, he decided to get them and give them to her as a gift the next time she was in the store."

"Do you know where he kept them?"

"Not exactly." Jake had a sheepish look on his face. "He talked about it once before, and I believe he said he hid them someplace at Blacksparrow."

"Blacksparrow?"

"Yes. I started worrying he might get into some kind of trouble, so I tried calling you at your friend's house and at his office. There was no answer, and I couldn't think of anything else to do but try calling back after lunch. Sam I'm sorry."

"Don't worry about that. I was planning to do some nosing around out there tonight, and this just makes it more urgent."

While Jake rang up purchases for another customer, Sam used the phone to call Charlie's office. There was no answer. Charlie was on the road to somewhere on the reservation.

Sam took Jake aside when he was done with his customer. "Jake, I'm going out to Blacksparrow to look for Eric. Just so you know, he could get into some bad trouble out there, and that's not something to repeat to anyone besides Charlie."

When Jake pressed for more information, Sam said, "Jake there is something bad going on out there. I'm going to have to make some arrests, and probably shut the place down. Before I go, I'll need to get some equipment to take with me. I want you to keep trying to reach Charlie Redman in Gallup. He may be out of town for most of the day, but I want you to keep calling until you reach him. Call his office and home number, and I'll write down what I want you to say."

"Tell him I'm at Blacksparrow looking for Eric, and tell him I'll try to stay out of sight of the guards. I want him to call the FBI in Albuquerque and have them send out some help, pronto. Tell him to meet me out there around dusk, and tell him to come armed for bear. Maybe he can block the gate and keep everyone inside. I'll either be waiting for him outside, or I'll be hiding inside the place. I'll try to find a way to let him know. Tell him not to let anyone escape. By the way, I don't know when, but if any FBI agents stop here for directions, tell them to get out there right away."

Jake started to say something, but Sam stopped him. "One more thing, I need to make a call to Washington, before I go. I'll reverse the charges."

After a short wait, Jack Whorten's familiar voice came on the line in Washington. Sam pictured the man's piercing, grey eyes and his tailored suit. "Sam Begay—I was hoping to hear from you."

"Jack, I just have a few minutes to brief you before I need to take off. I believe I found that mob connection you told me to watch for when we spoke a while back. It seems I leased Blacksparrow to a group of crooks

The Lightning Tree

without knowing it, and I think they're smuggling drugs, and some other stuff. Do you have any other information or instructions for me?"

"As a matter of fact, I do. I just received a full report, including testimony from a member of the old Purple Gang that your pal from Michigan, Jason Bigwater, helped put out of business."

"There was some interesting information about an operation in New Mexico, and I'm putting a lid on it here to keep it from floating around the Washington gossip circuit. I can tell you this; one of your local businessmen is implicated—his name is David Castor. There also seems to be a connection to someone in the movie industry from California who's helping set up the operation. Maybe you've met him, his name is Rance Wilder."

Sam was not surprised to hear that Jack Whorten was on top of the clandestine operation. "I've met both men, sir, but Wilder is the only one in a position to cause any trouble."

"What about Castor?"

"David Castor died when his car burnt up Saturday night. We don't know if his son Bobby is involved, but right now I'm more worried about Rance Wilder and the group of thugs he has with him at Blacksparrow."

Whorten was silent on his end of the line for a moment. "Sam, I don't have anyone nearby I can send to help you."

"Don't worry, sir, I'll try to get the FBI to cover my back. I'll let you know later, what happens."

Twenty minutes later, after purchasing some equipment, ammunition, and a modest amount of dynamite, Sam repeated his instructions for Jake to keep calling Charlie Redman, and tell him to get out to Blacksparrow with some help as soon as possible.

He drove away with a mind full of worries, and he had to keep remembering to ease his foot off the gas; after all, he was carrying enough dynamite to scatter pieces of his car, including himself, over several acres of desert.

His biggest concern was for Eric. He knew the boy was resourceful, but the men in the compound were killers. He tried to think about how he would go about finding Eric. Knowing he couldn't approach the place until dark, he would have to avoid the gate, and try to climb the cliff somewhere. Then he would have to climb down the inner wall of the compound. If he succeeded without someone noticing him and setting off the alarm, he would then have to locate the boy. He didn't even want to think about what the odds were of finding him.

At the very worst, he would have to wait until Charlie and other agents from Albuquerque arrived to confront the guards. He would then set up his own distraction, and he had more than enough dynamite and ammunition to keep their attention.

In spite of his best hopes, he knew there a thousand things that could go wrong. What if he couldn't find Eric, and someone else already did? He gritted his teeth and focused on the road. He would not let fear be his enemy; he would turn it, and use it to make him stay alert and cautious of the dangers he would face.

CHAPTER 72

That morning, Sonny woke late, still groggy from the potion the old woman gave him to enhance his strength and endurance; he was also tired of her telling him what to do. She was taking advantage of him, and a portion of the gold was his. It was clear that she withheld the knowledge of its location from him for a deliberate reason.

A gust of hot wind blew through the yard as he stepped outside the hogan. He gripped his hat as he confronted the old woman napping in the brush arbor. "I am tired of this. I have killed the white men who dishonored my mother. They are dead, and I am finished. I want what is mine. You have promised me gold, and I will have it now."

The witch glared at her nephew. She seemed to find a reserve of strength, and rose from her rocking chair and took a step toward him. Her dark eyes held his, and when she spoke, her words were like the hissing of a snake. "Yapping dog, I will give you what I choose, and when I choose. Your work is not done, and you will have nothing until it is. I will tell you what you must do, and when it is finished, we will talk of what I shall give you."

Sonny clenched his fists, his face red with anger. "I do not fear you old women. I walk my own path, and I will no longer do your bidding. I will have my own hogan, and I will take my sister with me. She knows the place of the golden coins, and she and I will have them. She will cook for me, and you will live here until you die."

Sonny took a step closer, but froze as a strange, subtle transformation washed over the witch. He wondered if his eyes were blurring, because her face seemed to change shape into something impossible for a human being to mimic.

He stepped back to clear his mind, and though the trance was broken, fear overcame him, and he turned and ran to his truck. He jerked the door open, started the engine, and glanced back at the witch as he let out the clutch, and tore out of the yard.

Surrounded by miles of eroded hills and mesas, Dan Yazzie watched the activity outside the hogan from his vantage point on a ridge a half-mile away. He saw the young man step from the hogan, and walk to the old woman who arose from the brush arbor. He could see agitation in the man's posture and his gestures, but the distance was too great for Dan to make out any words. He saw the man turn abruptly, and run to the old, white truck parked in the yard.

As the vehicle left, Dan noticed another movement from the doorway. He recognized the girl, and he watched her step outside, only to be shooed back into the building, followed by the old crone.

He sat back, perplexed by what he saw. He recalled the spirit man telling him the old woman was a skinwalker witch; the most dangerous kind there could be. That meant she would have to be childless to become a skinwalker, therefore the young man and woman who lived with her were not her children. Perhaps they were relatives, but if so, why would they choose to stay with her?

Were they captives? It didn't appear so. Dan had seen anger and fear in the young man gestures, but only subservience in the girl. Both had their freedom, so how could they be prisoners? What could it all mean?

Remembering the whispered stories, he knew a skinwalker was entirely evil and self-serving, a creature who could read your thoughts, and if you came upon one, it must kill you.

Dan knew time was running short, and he remembered what the old man spirit told him to do. He must find the path of the skinwalker. With that, the spirit man could confront the witch, pronounce the evil one's name, and make it sick and die. Unfortunately, the witch instructed the young girl to walk the path for her, and to make it more difficult to follow, the girl took a different route each time.

He took a breath, and exhaled his frustration. The girl was also good at hiding her tracks. He had been unable to follow her, losing the trail each time as the terrain became rugged enough for her to drop out of sight.

"Woah," Dan gasped as the door of the hogan burst open, and the old woman dashed outside with such speed and agility that he couldn't believe his eyes. He focused on the wild form sprinting across the yard, shedding clothing as her shape changed to something that resembled a large crow, and flew off.

Dan blinked his eyes, scarcely believing what he saw. He saw the black bird in the air, and then noticed the young girl dash out of the hogan writhing as if in horrible agony.

Nearly a mile away, Sonny bounced and jostled in the cab of the truck as he careened down the trail. He dodged and braked for potholes, and drove around several spots that were so eroded they could barely be consider part of the track. Reaching a long, sandy stretch, he stepped on the gas, and risked a glance behind him. His eyes caught the shape of a dark bird, and a desperate cry of dismay sounded from his lips.

He must escape. He knew the old woman to be a shape-shifter and a witch, and in the form of a crow, she could easily follow his vehicle. He risked another glance behind him, and saw the large bird settling to the ground near a dead tree.

Instead of relief, he now feared the worst, for the witch could take on many shapes. He concentrated on the rough trail again, and when he glanced in his rearview mirror, he saw a large creature running behind him. The hairy beast was something spawned by a nightmare, and the thing was gaining on him.

Fear distorted his sense of time, and he saw his surroundings in jerky, slow motion. His hands gripped the steering wheel without feeling, and as he bounced on the broken seat springs, the growling and hooting of the engine made a discordant background noise. He soon detected a moaning sound, and was startled when he realized it came from his own mouth.

He slewed the truck around to avoid a ditch, and the vehicle angled away in a tangent as the tires sank into some deep ruts. It bounced free, but slowed as the engine stalled. With desperate fury, Sonny tried to restart the vehicle, all the while glancing around for his pursuer. His breath came in ragged gasps as he kicked at the gas pedal and ground away at the starter—until it stopped, and left him in brain-numbing silence.

Sonny lost sight of the animal, and he froze, fearing it would jump out at any moment. He expected death from every direction. It came from the open passenger window.

Two muscular, clawed hands appeared at the edges of the door and ripped it from its hinges. As Sonny recoiled from the sudden assault, two fur-covered arms reached in, and the claws slashed at his face, blinding him, and nearly tearing off his nose. It was too late to scream, but he managed a short, high, yelp before the claws tore open his neck, exposing his spine, and then dragged his twitching, bloody corpse across the seat and away from the vehicle. The fearsome beast tossed the broken body around like a toy, and then left it to bleed in the dirt next to the trail.

As the creature ran away, it alternated between a two, and four-legged gait.

CHAPTER 73

"Man it's hot," Artie slammed the door and felt the relative coolness inside the small barracks at the Blacksparrow compound. He took his hat off and hung it on a peg. "It's at least 90 degrees out there."

Bud Thomas, awake from his nap, looked up and said nothing.

"Just think Bud, if it was this hot in Detroit we'd be ringing wet and panting like dogs. They say it's not just the heat, it's the humidity."

Bud closed his narrow eyes and took a deep breath, "Artie, if you say that one more time—if you tell me it feels hotter back east because of the humidity—I'm going to throw a bucket of coal oil on you and strike a match."

"He-he-he, that'll just make it hotter, and besides, you'd have to catch me first. You know you can't run more than ten feet without gasping for air because of the altitude. I still can't believe we're a mile above sea level, and we're just standing on level ground."

"There you go again Artie."

"What? I didn't say anything about the humidity. Can't a guy have an intelligent conversation without being yelled at?" Artie knew he was egging his partner on, but he didn't care. He felt like taking his own frustration out on someone, but Bud would only stand for so much, and he sounded close to that now.

Bud sat up and reached for his shirt. "Artie, I'm too hot to kill you right now. It's not that I don't want to; the trouble is, our boss in Detroit would probably send Fish-lips or Jerky Lou to take your place, and I can't stand either of those two pricks."

"Then quit your whining; you're lucky you got me. Bud, it's almost six o'clock, and there's nothing going on out there, unless you call Big Frank and his horse trying to out-fart each other something interesting. You couldn't tell them apart in the dark, from the noise or the smell."

Bud put his shoes on, and groaned as he stood. Reaching for his hat, he said, "You know what gets me the most, Artie? It's these cowboy, shit-kickers giving us razz berries about that Indian cop jumping off the cliff before we could plug him. Maybe I'll have to do something about it." With that, he walked to the door and stepped outside.

The heat pushed back at him, and his thoughts were dark as he walked toward the mess hall. That damn Helen! First, she and her kid run off with my money, and now I'm stuck in the middle of the desert, with an idiot for a bunkmate, and a dozen assholes in cowboy boots for company.

It was all her fault. If she hadn't run away, I'd still be in Detroit sipping a cold one with some pleasant company. He let his thoughts wander as he imagined what he would do with Helen and her kid if he found them. The kid would be easy, but Helen deserved some special attention. Maybe he'd use his switchblade. A few slashes for effect, and then bury the blade, and watch her eyes go blank. Heck, he might even let Artie watch—the sick bastard liked that sort of thing.

When he returned to the barracks, the sun was touching the mesa, and shadows began to reach across the compound.

Later, atop the sandstone cliffs surrounding Blacksparrow, Sam Begay looked down on the open spaces and the buildings. Darkness covered a good part of the grounds now, and he scanned each section with his field glasses, looking for movement, trying to count and fix the locations of the guards.

Directly below him, the false fronts of the movie sets cast angular shadows, and to his right, the darkened shape of an old mining structure stood near the end of the railroad spur. To the south, beyond the movie sets, he saw stacks of building supplies, some covered with tarps. Farther along, on either side of the narrow airstrip that ran east and west through the compound, two old hangars stood near the west end by the cliff, and across the strip, he could see the stables, barracks, and the mess hall. Near the gate, he could see lights in the small house where he used to stay when he lived here.

He saw little movement from his vantage point 100 feet above the ground, until he noticed the two guards at the entrance gate. The rest of the men were probably eating dinner before they went back to their evening activity. He knew most of them would stay on the far side of the compound, and he focused on the barracks and stable beyond the airstrip. A few other lights were on, and he saw someone walking from the dining hall. That made three men so far.

A few vehicles drove away earlier, and he guessed that would leave maybe six guards behind. He saw two trucks and a dark car, but there could be more vehicles parked behind the buildings. The car could be the Cadillac he saw with the two men at the trading post a while back.

He decided to wait a little longer before he dropped his rope and started searching for Eric, and as darkness came, he thought back on the events of the day, and the instructions he gave to Jake. He hoped Charlie would get his message.

He had left his car in a ravine a few miles south, and walked the rest of the way with his duffel full of gear to a spot where he could climb the mesa. He remembered thinking that this was the second time he had planned an assault here; the first, three years ago when he and some others had flushed out a nest of Nazi spies, and rescued some captives.

He took over ownership of the mine; given to him by the head of a shadowy, government agency because of his help in exposing the spy ring. The property belonged to him, but the responsibility of ownership, was becoming a suffocating burden. He should have known better, and he regretted ever hearing about the place.

He was a Navajo, and the traditional ways of his people did not recognize the concept of ownership of the land. After all, the earth and the sky gave him life, and it nurtured him, so how could he say that he owned it? It was more reasonable to think that it owned him.

It was nearly time to move, and when he thought of the dynamite he carried, it reminded him to pay attention to his footing. Earlier, while climbing the cliff, he had slipped on a loose stone, barely catching himself before he fell. Every move he made since, he did with extra caution. Reaching this spot above the movie set, he had discovered something that made him grin. This was directly above the place where he'd found Eric's tracks when he first met the boy, and this is where he would drop his rope.

He remembered how the boy seemed to disappear up the cliff wall, and how baffled he was that someone could do that. He had looked for a rope hanging somewhere, but found nothing; not even a tree stump to secure a rope. Still, he knew all the boy could have done was to throw a lasso and try to snag something above, and then hope it held his weight when he climbed.

Sam shook his head when he found this spot earlier. Three feet in front of him, he looked at the wooden stake, as thick as a baseball bat, and knew that Eric must have hammered it into a gap in the rocks. Unable to see it from below, someone who knew where it was could reach it with a good throw. Smart boy.

Once inside the compound, Eric could shake the rope free, hide it, and no one would ever know he was inside—except for noticing faint tracks he left in the sand below.

It was dark enough now, and time to go. Sam could only hope Charlie had returned to Gallup, got his message about what was happening here, and called his boss in Albuquerque, and that Chief Decker would send agents to help. It was a long, thin thread.

Taking a last look below, Sam looped his rope on the stake, and dropped it down the side of the rocks. He shouldered his gear, and began to slip down to the ground. The dark fronts of the movie set offered enough cover to move about without anyone noticing from across the compound.

When his boots touched the ground, he carried his gear to a place where he could put on his moccasins. Did he dare remove the rope looped around the stake on the cliff? No, if he needed to make a hasty escape, it would be best to leave it right where it was. He would not have the time to toss a rope and hope to find it in the darkness.

He edged along the false buildings until he found a route where he could sneak across the open area behind the stacks of supplies and equipment.

Shivering in the chill of the evening, he studied the lights ahead, and moved to a building near the airstrip. How was he going to find Eric? Where could he be? The boy could move like a ghost, and he was a master at hiding. If he came here to pick up something, it must be in or near the barracks where he used to sleep.

With nothing better to go on, Sam crept toward the small hangars near the west end of the airstrip, where he hid the bulk of his gear and explosives.

The Lightning Tree

He would have to be careful crossing the open space and approaching the other buildings.

Charlie Redman walked up to the front door of his house, and heard the phone ringing. He used the key, and dropped his papers on the couch as he hurried to the phone.

"Hello?"

"Charlie? Charlie Redman? This is Jake Jasperson at the trading post in Thoreau."

"Yeah Jake, this is Charlie. What's up?"

"Boy I'm glad I finally reached you. Sam told me to call you. He needs your help."

"Oh? What's he up to, Jake? Is he in trouble?"

"Most likely. He's at Blacksparrow right now, and he's planning to raise some hell. He left here this afternoon with a bunch of dynamite, and he went there to look for the young Navajo boy who's been staying with me. The boy disappeared last night, and we figure he was going to sneak into Blacksparrow to pick up something he left behind. When I told Sam about it, he took off, and said I should call you and tell you to get some FBI agents to help out, pronto."

"Help? At Blacksparrow?"

"That's what he said, Charlie, and he's planning to sneak inside and look for Eric. He took enough ammunition and explosives to do something drastic, and he made me promise to keep calling until I reached you. He wants you to bring in some other agents from Albuquerque to help, and he's been gone since this afternoon. Charlie, he said to tell you to show up with your guns ready."

"Jeez! I'll make the call right away, and head out there. I'll stop at your place first, just in case he shows up."

Charlie hung up and called Albuquerque, When he spoke to the agent on duty, he learned that Decker and most of the other agents were in Phoenix at a conference, and wouldn't be back in time. He explained his need for back up, and the agent said, "I have an agent in the office right now I can send; Agent Jensen. That's all the help I have until I can locate someone else to come out. Where do you want to meet?"

"Have them stop at the Thoreau Trading Post just off the highway in Thoreau for directions. The owner's name is name is Jake, and he'll send them on their way. I'll take any help you can get, as long as it's fast. What's

341

the Agent's first name? Al? I'll be waiting near the destination. We'll just have to make do with what we can get."

Charlie hung up the phone, and swore under his breath. He made several, quick sandwiches and a thermos of instant coffee, and stopped at the office to pick up some additional firepower. When he headed out of town, he figured he would reach Thoreau about a half-hour before the other agent showed up.

CHAPTER 74

The lights inside the compound made the shadows even darker, providing Sam with ample cover as he moved from building to building. He kept track of how many guards he saw, and counting the fifth one, he presumed there may be another one or two indoors somewhere.

As he approached the barracks where Eric used to stay, he heard talking and movement inside. At least one person wore hard-soled shoes, and made clopping sounds as he walked across the wooden floor. This would be persons six and seven. He still hadn't found Eric, and he figured if the boy was around, he might find him first.

He circled the building, and was about to dash to the next one when something went "*hisst*." Sam froze, and as he turned his head in the direction of the noise, he saw a small hand reach out from the darkness underneath the building and wave.

Eric crawled out from between the pilings where he had been hiding, and Sam, motioned for silence as he took hold of the boy, and hugged him. Eric breathed with relief, and Sam motioned for him to stay, while he took a few steps around the building. He could still hear voices inside, and he noticed an old bench he could stand on to take a quick glance in one of the windows. When he looked, he saw the back of one man and the legs of another sitting on a cot.

"Artie, why do you think we are here? All we do is watch what comes and goes, and make sure these cowboy, shit kickers don't steal something."

"That's about it, Bud. Mr. Doncotti doesn't want anyone cheating him out of his share."

After tipping back a bottle of whiskey, Artie set it down and exhaled. "Whooh, that's raw. I'll be glad when we can leave this place and get our hands on a decent bottle of booze. Artie's eyes watered as he glanced toward the window, and to Bud's astonishment, the man yelped, and rolled off the cot, and started to choke.

"Ahhh! (cough) That face—*It's him!*"

"What was that all about, Artie? What are you doing spitting that booze on the floor? It's the last bottle we have!"

Artie was still choking, trying to talk. "I saw him. *(cough)* I saw the Indian!"

What Indian? Are you seeing ghosts or something?"

"I just saw that big Indian we shot in the desert last week!"

"What?" Bud spun around. "Where?"

"He was looking right at me in the window, I swear it Bud! You gotta believe me!"

"Believe you? Hell I don't even like you." Bud walked to the window, but couldn't see anything in the shadows. "There's nothing out there." After he spoke, Bud felt a small twinge of fear. "If it'll make you feel better, I'll go outside and have a look. Come to the door and keep an eye on me."

"Bud, be careful—take a flashlight. I'm not kidding! I saw him as big as life."

Drawing his revolver, Bud followed the beam of his light down the steps and over to the window. He saw the bench, and figured if someone looked inside; he would have to stand there, and might have left some tracks. He listened for any sound of moment, and turned his light on the packed ground. He saw no marks or footprints.

Turning off the flash, he walked back up the steps. Artie you're nuts. You better lay off the booze. There's nothing out there; and no footprints."

"But Bud, I…"

"Zip it Artie! Close your eyes and go back to sleep. Don't forget we have that important shipment coming in tonight—opium, and a lot of it. The plane is supposed to take the three Mex. girls when they leave."

Sam swore under his breath, and he grabbed Eric and hurried into the shadows of next building.

The Lightning Tree

They waited in the darkness a few more minutes before he and Eric moved away from the barracks. The two men he saw were the same ones he had seen at Jake's last month with the black Cadillac—the same men with the group of cowboys in the desert when he was shot.

When he and Eric were far enough away to talk, he said, "I counted seven guards, are there any more?"

"No that's all; the rest leave for the night, and won't be back until morning."

Sam took a deep breath. "That's a relief. Did you find what you were looking for when you left the trading post?"

Eric grinned and nodded. "Yes." He reached in his pocket and showed Sam two small carvings of a turtle, and a rabbit. "I made them myself, and I was going to show them to a girl that comes into the store."

Sam gave him a knowing smile as Eric put them back in his pocket.

"I found something else when I got here, Sam,. They have three girls locked up in a building over there." He pointed across the airstrip to the second hangar. "It's also where they store most of their other cargo. We have to do something to help them."

Looking at the placement of the lights around the buildings, Sam figured they would have to approach from the back. "Do they keep a guard inside?"

"Not over there. They stay around the other buildings closer to the gate. Sam, I think the girls are from Mexico. Are we going to help them escape?"

"Yes we are, and after we do, I'm going to plant some dynamite. I'm expecting some company of my own, and I want to get you and the girls out of way before any fireworks start. We may not have much time."

"That's good, because I heard some men talking about a plane landing tonight to take them away."

Gritting his teeth, Sam said, "Then we better get moving."

As they slipped away from the building, keeping to the shadows, Sam hoped the help he asked for would arrive in time, if it arrived at all.

They found the back door of the old hangar unlocked, and verified there were no guards inside. Eric said, "They keep them locked in a little room over there."

Sam knew the layout of the building. "Good, you go up to the door, and try not to startle them. Tell them to stay quiet, and that you and your friend are here to help them escape. I'll find something to break open the lock."

Within ten minutes, the three girls were free and ready to leave. Sam's heart nearly broke when he saw the tears and fatigue in their dark eyes and faces.

Before they left, Eric said, "Do you want to see what else the planes are carrying?"

Sam looked at the boy. "What is it?"

"I'm not sure, but it smells funny. It's in those boxes over there."

Walking to the other side of the building, Sam detected an unmistakable odor from one of the crates someone had opened.

Confirming his suspicions, he returned, and said to Eric, "We'd better get going. I'll tell you a secret; I found out where you used to climb up the cliff. That's where we're going, and I want you to help me get everyone up there so they'll be safe."

They moved through the darkness to the far side of the compound, and when they reached cliff near the movie set, Eric noticed a rope hanging down the rocks. He gave Sam a big grin. "I guess you found out how I hid my rope when I used to sneak in here."

"Yes I did. You were clever to place that hidden post up there."

Sam's face took on a darker look. "Eric, I don't know when help will get here, and we may not have much time before the next plane comes. I'm going back to the airstrip to plant some dynamite. I won't set anything off until the plane arrives, and I'll try to trap it on the runway. I'll also disable the generator and knock the power out."

He gripped the boy's shoulders. "Don't let the noise bother you. I know you can handle yourself, and I'm giving you the job of keeping these young women safe. When we get everyone up the cliff, I'll go and finish my work. The FBI is supposed to send help, but I don't know exactly when that will be. Just stay here until they show up."

"Sam, you're coming back here, aren't you?"

"Yes I am, but not until it's safe for you and the girls to come down. Don't worry; just keep an eye out for me when I come to get you."

With that, they helped the three young women climb the cliff. When they all were safe above, Eric pulled up the rope, and Sam disappeared into the shadows. Eric kept watch, and saw Sam's dark form moving toward the buildings across the way.

The Lightning Tree

When Sam returned to the two hangars at the end of the dirt airstrip, he began to work his way along one side, hunkering down behind some barrels and an old tarp to plan his next move. He had enough dynamite to crater the runway and destroy several buildings. He hoped to disable the plane when it landed, and if not, at least prevent it from leaving.

First, he needed to get rid of the nearest guards. He knew the plane could show up anytime, and he hoped the FBI would do the same.

Taking care of the first man was easy. Never expecting an attack from inside the compound, the sentry barely had time to react. The only noise he made was an abrupt gasp of breath that turned into a soft snore. Sam tied and gaged him, dragged him under a tarp, and then began placing his explosives.

He worked in the shadows, setting the charges for maximum effect. He hid several bundles along the airstrip and near the buildings, and then made his way to the electrical box.

Careful to make sure he was unobserved, he took out his wire cutters. It wouldn't do just to cut the electricity, he also wanted to make sure it would take some time to get to the generator started to provide a backup. The noise and chaos caused by the explosions would mask his other activity, and hopefully, the eventual arrival of the FBI.

He figured a plane was certain to arrive soon, and as he worked on finishing his task, he thought he heard a faint noise in the sky. Thinking quickly, he knew if the plane landed, all he had to do was prevent it from taking off again. He would set up a distraction, and with all the explosions going off, he hoped it would confuse the guards enough to delay them from discovering the missing hostages. Well, that's why he brought the dynamite.

He wore a grim smile as he set his charges. Where was the FBI? Help should be on the way, but would it would arrive in time? His attention turned again to the faint noise—it seemed to come from the darkness west of the mesa, and it sounded like an aircraft engine. As he listened, it occurred to him that it might be too late to count on the FBI, and he would need to put the dynamite to work.

With several extra charges placed and ready to bring into play, he cut the power, and waited for the guards to investigate. They would have to fix the fuse box first, and with the lights still out, they would have to figure out what was wrong with the generator.

Hoping the lack of lights would buy him some time, Sam waited in the darkness for the help to arrive. Several guards moved about, and he heard the engine of the plane, louder now. It was close, but he figured it wouldn't land until the men found the problem, and had the airstrip lights on again.

As the plane began to circle the compound, his spirits dropped when the generator popped and coughed, and roared to life. The noise drowned out the sound of the aircraft, and the lights were on again.

All of this activity took the attention of the guards off their post at the main gate, and he hoped they wouldn't find his dynamite. The next few minutes were agony for him. He moved to other cover, and tried to stay focused on what he planned to do when the plane touched down.

Hunkered behind some barrels, prepared for the worst, he thought he noticed a light flash beyond the gates. Was it the help from the FBI? He didn't see the light again, and all he could do was hope the agents were here, and had doused their headlights as they drew nearer.

When the action began, everything seemed to happen at once. Amid the loud snarling of the aircraft engine, the lights of the plane came on and lit the end of the runway. The small craft touched down with a rush of air, just as the headlights of two approaching vehicles lit the entrance gate. Sam was relieved, but concerned he saw only two cars. The agents would need all the help he could give them from his position inside the compound.

He lit the first series of charges to disable the runway behind the plane as it tore past his position. By then, the guards were dashing for cover, firing their guns at any shadows they could find.

The plane was still moving, and Sam watched it slow down and turn at the far end of the runway near the mesa wall. The engine roared, and it was obvious the pilot was going to try to gain enough speed to take to the air again. Sam ran to another spot, touched off several more charges, and as the explosions lit up the night, the pilot passed his position. The pilot must have noticed the craters and debris on the runway, and apparently deciding the portion of the strip was too torn-up to use, he spun the craft around, and roared back toward the mesa wall.

Sam had a fleeting thought; was there enough room for the plane to become airborne before it reached the rocks? He grabbed his bow and a handful of arrows rigged with sticks of dynamite tied to the shafts, lit the first one, and aimed it several dozen yards in front of the aircraft. Lighting another, he let loose, and turned to fire two more toward some guards who were firing from behind cover. He flushed out two of the men and saw them run behind another building.

With flames burning, and explosions shattering the night, Bud said to Artie. "Try to hold them off at the gate until the plane stops. There's bound to be guns onboard, and we can use the extra firepower, or better yet, maybe we can use the plane to escape."

Artie turned to Bud. "I don't think the pilot plans to stop."

Over the noise and chaos, a megaphone called out from behind the gate for everyone to drop their weapons and surrender. The voice was Charlie Redman's, and Sam heard him say he would shoot the plane out of the sky if it tried to leave the compound.

When the gunfire continued, he spoke again. "This is your last warning. This is the FBI. Throw your guns out, and step into the open with your hands up."

A barrage of pistol and rifle fire answered his words, and at the gate, the other agent looked over at Charlie, and they both pulled the cocking levers of their Thompson machine guns. Charlie nodded, and a few seconds later, a hot stream of lead raked the nearest building where most of the gunfire came from. The roar of the Thompsons, and the dozens of impacts of .45 slugs, silenced their gunfire.

Charlie said to the other agent, "Are you out of ammo?"

"Nope, I'm using a 100 round drum. I've still got another 50 rounds or so."

He lifted the megaphone again. "This is the FBI speaking, and you have one last chance. We have more agents on the way. You can surrender now, or be cut down by enough firepower to turn your hides into hamburger."

His words brought silence this time, and over the sound of the droning aircraft dodging the potholes down the runway, Charlie heard a car engine. He turned to pinpoint the noise, and saw a dark vehicle careening around a building, stirring up a cloud of dust as it headed toward the gate.

The headlights of the two agency cars lit up the speeding vehicle, and the big body of the dark Cadillac bounced and swayed as the driver dodged debris. When flashes of gunfire came from the passenger side of the car, the agents lifted their Thompsons and sprayed it with .45 slugs. The Caddy slewed left, bounced through some potholes, and lunged toward the gate.

The other agent turned to Charlie to say something, when a loud explosion sounded, and a huge fireball lit the cliff wall at the far end of the compound. In the attempt to escape, the aircraft had lifted off, but failed to clear the rim of the mesa, and exploded against the rocks in an angry ball of heat and flame.

Knocked down by the explosion, Sam staggered to his feet shaking his head as the sound of the huge blast echoed away. Flaming debris began to fall on the buildings, igniting the dry wood. He couldn't see much from where he stood, but the flames lit the dark car as it careened toward the gate. He heard more, rapid gunfire, and then a crash of metal against metal. Dust rolled over the area, hiding everything from view except for the remaining headlights.

The Caddy must have hit one of the agency vehicles with a glancing blow, and Sam could see the bouncing taillights of the big car escaping down the road. It appeared to stop for a moment, and he thought he saw the passenger door open before it sped off again.

A moment later, Charlie's voice boomed over the megaphone. *"Anyone who doesn't come out with their hands up, NOW, I personally promise to shoot out of spite! Put your guns down, and walk toward me with your hands in the air."*

As the flames caught hold and spread through the compound, casting tortured shadows, and sending the horses running in terror from the stable, Sam watched four men limp into the light with their hands up. He hollered out. "Charlie, this is Sam. I've got four of them covered from this side. I think there's one more still tied up. I'm stepping out to check right now. The rest are yours."

In a few minutes, Charlie had the prisoners searched and handcuffed. When he saw Sam walking up, he said, "Did you find the other one?"

Sam nodded, "Yeah, and he's dead."

Charlie took a deep breath, and said, "By the way, Sam, let me introduce you to Al—Alice, a new agent from the Texas side of the state. She says two more agents should be on their way by now."

Sam touched the brim of his hat, too tired to speak or show surprise. The agent looked sturdy enough, and he noticed a lock of red hair showing under her tan Stetson. "While you two secure things here, I'll go and bring back what these guys were planning to ship out tonight. It'll take me about twenty minutes." With that, he turned and jogged away.

The Lightning Tree

Alice said to Charlie, "Agent Redman, you should call him back until we can secure the area. He might stumble into more trouble. There could be other men hiding somewhere."

"Relax, Agent, I've worked with Sam before. He knows what he's doing. He was born sneaky, and he can move like a ghost. He once told me his mother didn't even know she was pregnant until he popped out one day and introduced himself."

A short while later, Sam, Eric, and three young women approached the gate, their features backlit by the flames.

"This is my friend Eric Nez, and I'll let him introduce you to his three new girlfriends." Sam turned and gazed at the flames across the compound. In a moment, he said to Charlie. The movie people told me they flew their equipment in overnight, but I'll bet that plane was carrying something else. Eric can show you where they stored the opium they hauled in earlier. These young ladies are an example of some of their other cargo."

Charlie tipped his hat to the girls, and turned to Sam. "Is there anything we can do to keep the fires from spreading to the other buildings?"

A frown crossed Sam's face as he looked around. "No, let it burn—let it all burn. Can I borrow your car? I left mine out in the boonies, and I just had a bad feeling about that car that got away. I want to check in with Jake at the trading post."

"It's got a flat tire, Sam. If you'll hang on a few minutes, I'll see if the spare is alright."

"No time, Charlie, I need to get over to Jake's right now."

Sam strode to Alice's car, jumped in and started the engine, and tore off into the night.

Alice ran up, hollering after him. She stamped her foot as she watched her car disappear down the road. "Agent Redman, I hope he has a good explanation for his actions. Who does he think he is stealing FBI property?"

Charlie looked up after he removed the spare tire from his trunk. "Agent Jensen, he used to be a Reservation Cop—a good one, and now he wears a U.S. Marshal's badge. I've worked with him for three years."

"Well I don't care if you share a bed with him, or if he's the damn Governor of this state," she stamped her foot again. He's taking Government property without proper authorization."

Charlie tipped his hat up, and said, "Well, you can authorize it right now, or I will. By the way, when I talked to the agent on duty in Albuquerque, he told me he was sending out a new agent named Al Jenkins—you don't suppose he was trying to pull my leg do you?"

Alice gave Charlie a scorching look. "Don't try to change the subject."

CHAPTER 75

Bud Thomas slewed the big Caddy around the gravel curves, pedal to the floor, on his way south to the highway. It was too dark to make out the terrain, but he knew there were several ravines along the side. His upper arm was on fire from a bullet wound that grazed his skin, and he could feel the tear in his shirt. He was lucky to get away with only a scratch. Too bad about Artie, he took a bad one, and there was blood all over the passenger seat where his partner died before he shoved him out the door. Artie was road-kill now, and he would clean the car later.

"Geez, what a screw-up," he said under his breath. He was lucky to get away, and he knew he damaged one of the cop vehicles at the gate. Maybe, they'd be too busy to follow him. He slowed down for some tight S-curves, and he kept glancing in his rearview mirror, but he saw no other vehicle lights.

He wanted to get away before more cops showed up, but he had to take a few minutes to stop and grab some bandages, and some food and drink somewhere. That trading post by the highway might be a good place. If it wasn't open, he'd break in and take what he wanted, and if anyone objected, that would be their problem.

Following several miles behind, Sam's biggest worry was Bud stopping at Jake's for money and food before he made his getaway on the highway. If the lights were on in the store, he almost certainly would stop. He would find Jake in his usual, cantankerous mood, and there was no telling what a desperate man in his position might do. He might take him hostage, or he might even kill him.

A rush of blood warmed his face, and Sam felt his guts tighten. Fortunately, he found the man's partner dead on the side of the road when he left the compound, and he had just one man to apprehend. He was still far enough behind the other car that he couldn't see lights; just a little dust from its passing. He did notice skid tracks off the shoulders, and it told him how desperate the man was to get away. He gritted his teeth and drove with fear gnawing at his thoughts.

After nearly a half-hour of desperate driving, Bud slowed as he motored through the small town of Thoreau. He saw the lights on at the Trading Post, and pulled into the lot. With Route 66 just ahead, he figured he would do a quick job of grabbing the cash from the till, and picking up whatever else he needed before he beat it to the highway.

Parking near the door, he shut off the car, checked his .38, and replaced the spent cartridges before he walked into the building.

Back in the living quarters of the store, Jake heard a car pull up. He set aside his newspaper, and heard the tinkling of the bell above the front door. He walked past the curtain, hoping it was someone with news about Eric."

The man walking toward the counter was an Anglo, and a stranger. Jake started to say something, but Bud reached out, and shoved the revolver in his face. He hissed his words. "Don't even think of making any noise old man; I'll knock what's left of your teeth so far down your throat, you'll never get 'em back."

Bud looked around to verify no one else was in the store. "Now listen to me. If anyone is hiding behind that curtain, I'm liable to shoot first and find out later. Who's back there?"

"Nobody. I live here by myself."

"So you're alone, eh? Let's just take a little walk and see for sure."

Bud stood behind Jake with his hand clutching the old man's neck. He jammed his gun barrel under his ear as he pushed him forward. Jake moved the curtain aside, and when they stepped into the back room, Bud took a quick look around the small kitchen and said, "If you make a move, I'll blow your head off." Then he raised his voice and said, "If there's anyone else back here, you'd better come out right now. If I have to tell you again, I'll kill the old man first, and come looking myself."

Jake said, "I told you there's no one else here."

Bud rapped him across the temple with his gun, and Jake fell to the floor. "Stay put while I take a look. You move—you're dead."

After a quick look in the bathroom, Bud glanced back at the old man on the floor, and brushed back the curtain to the bedroom.

The small room was empty. Bud turned to the man on the floor, and it looked like the old geezer wasn't going to move. He stepped into the bedroom looking for something worth taking, checking the closet first, and then glancing across the room. He saw a small, framed photo on the dresser, and froze.

"HELEN?" Bud grabbed the picture, obviously a recent one of his wife and her daughter Clara.

He bellowed his rage and dashed out of the room to confront the old man. Jake was sitting on the floor holding his head.

"WHERE ARE THEY?" Bud screamed, and kicked him.

Jake gasped, and curled up holding his side. Bud kicked him again, and threw the picture on the floor, cracking the frame. He strode around the room kicking the furniture. "Wherever they're hiding, you'd better tell me or I'll kill you."

Jake saw the broken glass, and managed to speak through his pain. "There's no one else here. She mailed the picture to me a week ago, and I put it in a frame."

Bud spun around, spit showing in the corners of his mouth. "Mailed? From where? Don't lie to me or, so help me, I'll beat the truth out of you." Bud fired his gun into the cupboard near Jake's head to get his attention.

"I don't know," Jake said through his pain. "It was somewhere in Michigan. There's an envelope in the top dresser drawer. Go see for yourself."

The sound of the gunshot seemed to cool Bud's rage. "You're lying to me old man. I know she and her daughter took a train out here. I'm her husband, and I just want to talk to her. There isn't anything wrong with that is there?"

Jake said nothing, and Bud walked into the bedroom to look in the dresser. He found the envelope and saw the return address as Rural Route 3 in West Branch, Michigan. He swore, and muttered, "Well I'll be; she left a fake trail, and headed north." He stuffed the envelope into his pocket.

While Bud was distracted, Jake found the strength to slide across the cracked linoleum floor. Hissing through his effort, he reached around the cupboard for his cane. Jake wasn't even sure what he would do with it, but he had to do something. He heard Bud cursing from the other room as he pulled himself to his feet, gripping the end of the wooden shaft, and when the man appeared in the doorway, Jake swung the cane at his head.

Bud dodged, taking the blow on his shoulder, and he grabbed it from Jake's hands. He yanked so hard that it smacked the edge of the doorway and broke in two. Bud tossed the pieces on the floor and screwed the gun barrel into the old man's face.

Jake, wilting from his effort and the smell of Bud's stale breath, went limp and glared.

Bud said, "I'll give you a choice; you can die right now, or you can relax while I get some rope and tie you up. I'm going to clean out the till and grab some things before I go, and I don't even want you to think of doing something stupid. If you cooperate, I may just let you live. Try something stupid like you just did with that cane, and this place will need a new owner."

Bud returned with a coil of clothesline, and pushed the old man to the floor. He tied his hands behind him, and looped the remainder around his feet before cinching them back toward his hands.

"Now stay put, and you might live a few more years."

Bud grabbed the cash out of the till, and filled a sack with iodine, bandages, a few bottles of soda, and some things to eat before he returned to the back room. He smiled at Jake and said. "I figure you must keep more money around here than what was in the till. Where is it?"

Jake was in no position to resist. "It's in a box behind a panel in the counter."

"Good. Tell me where, or I'll drag you out on your face so you can show me."

A few minutes later, Bud opened the panel, and as he reached to grab the stack of bills, the headlights of a vehicle flashed in the store windows. He pulled the money out, and said, "Stay quiet back there if you want to live. Pretend you're fast asleep. I'd hate to think that you'd do something stupid, and get someone else killed, too."

Sam saw the dented Caddy parked next to the building when he pulled in, and he remembered the man who harassed a customer in the parking lot over a month ago. He knew the gunman was a hard case, and probably had Jake hostage inside. He cut the lights, and parked the agency car out of sight around the building.

The Lightning Tree

Knowing the man would recognize him, he jammed his hat down, pulled out the tail of his shirt, and shuffling like a drunk, he pushed past the screen door. He shaded his eyes as he made out the situation inside. He saw no one.

The first thing he wanted to do was make sure Jake was safe. He pretended to stagger, caught his balance, and looked around as if drunk and confused.

Bud stepped out from behind the curtain and said. "The place is closed. Go home and sleep it off."

"Wassum...uh...I furgot m-moneys. Inna-car." Sam turned and walked with an unsteady gait back to the door. "Be back inna minn..." and he stepped outside. The instant he was out of sight, he ran around the building toward the back door of the living quarters.

Bud kicked the counter. "Shit." He didn't know what to do. Maybe he should just run out the door and let the drunk come back and wander around the store. The guy would probably never recognize him, as drunk as he looked and sounded, but the old geezer in the back would.

Bud was getting nervous as he waited for the customer to return. Standing in the store next to the curtain, he said to himself, "Where is that damn Indian? He said he had to get some money from his car, and I didn't see him drive away, so he must still be out there looking for it."

He thought aloud, "Okay, club the drunk when he comes back in—take his money, and put a bullet into the old man's head."

Sam moved as quickly as he could around the building. It was very dark, and he tried to be careful and not make any noise. When he reached the rear door, he saw a faint light through the curtain, and knew he had to risk a quick look inside before he took any action. He didn't want to endanger Jake.

He pulled out his revolver. There should be only two people in the store: one hostage—hopefully alive, and one gunman. Both were likely to come to harm if he didn't do things just right.

When he peered inside back door, he saw Jake lying on the floor, tied up with rope. He saw him move, but he couldn't see Bud. The gunman might still be in the store, waiting for his Indian customer to return with his money. Sam weighed his options. He didn't have much time. He wanted to avoid a gunfight, and he wanted to remove the hostage from the equation.

The back door made a small noise when he opened it, and Jake looked up and saw him. The man's face had blood on it, but he smiled and nodded as Sam opened the door and crept inside. Sam motioned for silence while he turned to close the door.

When he faced Jake again, he noticed a blur of movement, and his head exploded with stars.

Bud tied Sam next to the old man, and he was thinking he might just as well kill them now, when the bell jingled again at the front of the building.

"What the hell? Is this rush hour?" he said under his breath, stepping to the curtain. When he peered out, he saw a man in slacks and a sport coat walking to the counter. He looked like a cop.

Bud was sweating, trying to think. "Be out in a minute. Have to finish what I'm doing first. Take your time and look around."

"That's okay; I'm just looking for directions."

Bud knew he might have to shoot it out, but he thought he'd try to get rid of the guy first. He hid his gun behind his belt, and straightened himself up before he stepped around the curtain.

"Look, my uncle's asleep, and I'm just visiting for a few weeks. I'll try to help you, but I'm not very good at directions around here."

"I'm just trying to get to a place called Blacksparrow. Know where that is?"

"Sure, that one's easy, just head north through town."

Sam regained consciousness, and heard the last part of the conversation. He nudged Jake, and when he saw him open his eyes, he whispered, "Lay still, and I'll try to work on the ropes. The guy is talking to someone in the store, so we'll have to be quiet." Sam worked himself around to reach the knots on Jake's hands. Struggling for a moment, he said, "I think I've got it. Can you reach the rope around my hands?"

Jake grunted as he worked at the knots. After a few minutes, Sam felt the rope loosen. He could still hear the men talking.

"I think you've got it Jake—say, did you just fart?"

Jake freed the last knot, and gave him a feeble grin. "Sam, at my age, all I can do is hope."

With his hands free, Sam reached for the ropes on his legs, and heard voices behind the curtain again.

"Well, I guess I'll be leaving and heading out to that Blacksparrow place. Funny name for a ranch, isn't it? Thanks for the directions and the candy bars. Too bad you didn't have any coffee left. I hope I didn't make too much noise and wake your uncle."

"That's alright. He's a pretty sound sleeper. I need to get back to what I was doing, Thanks for stopping in. You should find the place pretty easily."

Sam waited as he heard footsteps.

Bud stuck his head into the back room, and glared at the two men on the floor. Deciding to leave them in no condition to be a problem—ever, he pushed the curtain aside, and entered the room. He stooped close to Jake, and Sam saw him lift his gun, and knew what was coming. Hoping his tingling muscles would respond, with his legs still tied, he made a desperate lunge. His arms were moving, but he knew his reach would be short.

Bud jerked away, and Sam saw the gun barrel waiver as the man cartwheeled backward. Then he heard a muffled gong that sounded like a church bell struck with a rubber mallet, and in an odd, puppet-like motion, he saw the man collapse unconscious.

Sam glanced at Jake, to see what had happened, and he noticed a cast iron pan lying on the floor next to the old man. He took a deep breath, and lay back exhausted. "Jake, he said, it's nice to meet someone who knows how to use a fry pan."

He picked up Bud's gun, and confirmed the man was unconscious before he helped Jake untie the last of his bonds. Using the rope to secure his prisoner, He said, "It looks like he slipped on your broken cane. Are you alright?"

"I'm fine, Sam, but I've felt better."

There was a loud rap on the back door and a voice said; "FBI, put your weapons down and get on the floor." Another voice came from the opened curtain as the other agent came in with his gun.

"I'm Marshal Sam Begay, and this is my friend Jake. We have a prisoner for you."

"Glad to meet you," the one at the curtain said. "We're agents Richmond and Peters. We were told to stop here for directions to a place called Blacksparrow."

"You're in luck. I'll lead you there, and you can take the prisoner with you."

Ten minutes later, with Jake wearing a bandage and Bud handcuffed in the agent's car, Sam explained briefly, what happened at Blacksparrow. He said goodbye to Jake, who assured him he was O.K., and led the agents out of town to assist Charlie and Alice.

CHAPTER 76

Sam drove Alice's agency car back to Blacksparrow, followed by the two agents and their prisoner. When he pulled up near the gate where Charlie and "Al" stood, he noticed Eric and the three female hostages sitting in Charlie's car out of the cool wind.

A few fires still burned in the rubble of the buildings, and wisps of smoke drifted around like low clouds under the pale moon.

Alice walked up to her car looking for any damage. She glared at Sam, and he held up his hands and gave her an apologetic grin, "I'm sorry ma'am, for having to take your vehicle. It was an emergency."

Alice placed her fists on her hips. "Officer Begay, you can consider it the *first and only* time I'll ever let you get away with something like that. Next time, I'll shoot first, and slap the cuffs on you just in case I missed something vital." She held her stare for a moment. "Agent Redman has a Navajo man who says he's a friend of yours, and he seems eager to talk to you."

As Sam joined Charlie, his friend pointed to a tall, gangly figure and two horses standing in shadows fifty feet behind him. The man wore an old baseball hat.

Charlie said, "Did things work out alright?"

"Yes, Jake is fine, and we caught the crook who escaped. Is that Dan Yazzie standing with the horses?"

"Yep, and he says he needs to talk to you."

Sam approached his Navajo friend, and said, "You're out a bit late for a ride aren't you?"

Dan said, "We must go now. I saddled an extra horse for you, and packed some food and water. It is time for us to face the evil one. We will talk to the spirit man, and he will make some magic to protect us."

Sam nodded without speaking, and turned to Charlie as he walked up. "Rance Wilder is behind all of this, Charlie. It's a shame we didn't catch him here."

"Do you want me to pick him up in Gallup?"

"No, you can tell him what happened here, but don't mention me. Tell him not to leave Gallup until the FBI completes their investigation of the compound; say it'll take two or three days. I have to leave right now, and I should be back by then. I want to confront him in person, and see the surprise on his face when I walk up to him."

"You can place him into custody after that. Right now he thinks all we have is circumstantial evidence against him. He'll claim he knew nothing about the activities of *some* of the men out here."

Sam looked around at the damage in the compound. "He'll think you don't have anything solid against him, so just keep your eye on him until I get back. By the way, could you have someone bring my car inside the compound? It's a mile south on the Chaco road, parked behind some trees on the right, next to a shallow wash. The keys are in it. I'll be in touch when I get back to Gallup."

Charlie said "okay," and watched Sam and Dan Yazzie ride out of the compound.

Alice came up to Charlie as the two riders left. She shook her head and said, "I don't think he'd ever make it as an FBI agent; too impulsive and undisciplined."

Charlie took a deep breath and said, "Yes, that's what Chief Decker keeps telling him."

Miles northwest of Blacksparrow, an old Navajo woman sat inside her hogan smoking a corncob pipe. Her eyes squinted as the smoke curled around the deep lines on her face.

Tessa Toledo lay on her side on a narrow sleeping platform across the room. "What will we do now, Grandmother? Our enemies are dead—my mother is avenged." When the old woman didn't answer her, she sat up with a frown. "You have read the white man's newspaper; the old Balagaana is dead. Does he not take the place of his son? I am tired of this hogan, and I wish to leave. Don't forget what you have promised me."

"I forget nothing, impatient one." The old woman glared at her with pale eyes as she set her pipe down. "You will get what you deserve when I decide to give it to you. The young Castor still lives, and Blood Law says we must punish those who kill someone of our clan. Those boys killed your mother, even though it took months for the circumstances to cause her death. Just be glad she gave you and your brother life before the spirits called to her."

"Listen to me now. Your brother has been the weapon for their punishment, but now he has failed." The witch woman, tried to keep her anger to herself. "He killed the wrong man in the burned automobile, and he has paid the price of his error."

The old woman remembered how Sonny had been unusually quiet and subdued when he brought the newspaper home, and after she had finished reading the article; *Gallup businessman dies in flaming vehicle,* she'd thrown it in his face. Sonny's failure ended his usefulness, and when he had responded with strong words, he brought about his own grisly death.

The younger Castor was the last link in her long chain of vengeance. Alive, he represented an obstacle to the completion of her plans. She could not allow him to live, and she vowed to finish the deed herself. The old witch felt the heat of her anger rise on her wrinkled, leathery neck and face.

There was much to prepare, and she must maintain her control of the girl. Tessa would be her vessel. She had nurtured her and protected her all these years; keeping her out of harm's way until the proper time came about. Soon, the girl would have her own role to play, but now, the old witch would sleep and build her strength for what she must do next. She sighed, and collapsed back in her chair.

Miles south, beyond the dark canyons and mesas, the moon cast grey shadows on the two Navajo men on horseback. The pale light was enough to allow the riders to find their way, trusting their horses' senses in the night.

Sam Begay let his mind wander as the night air chilled him. He thought of the group of students who had met their deaths—under a full moon, according to Joyce Dobson. By some cruel trick of fate, Bobby Castor was the last one alive: his own father a victim, instead of him.

Sam was certain he and Dan would be facing the same killer, or killers. The danger would be unlike anything he had confronted in the past. Instead of thugs and criminals, they would be facing an unnatural being with unimaginable powers. Any person who could carry such hatred and a lust for vengeance for so long, and then act upon it with such uncommon brutality, could scarcely be someone considered human.

Dan must have been thinking along the same lines, because he stopped and pointed to the outline of a dark mesa across the valley. "We will spend the night there. It will be safe, and tomorrow we will find and kill the skinwalker."

Sam said nothing, and Dan turned to face him. "It is not someone playing a deadly game of mischief; it is a real witch. We must not underestimate its power, and the evil it can do. The old spirit-man told me he would try to weaken the creature, but he feared she may be too powerful for him."

An hour later, on the other side of the valley, Dan led them up a path to a sloping bench covered by some grass and a few stunted pines. He said, "We will leave the horses here. There is a sheltered place for us in the rocks."

It took a short time to gather enough wood to build a fire, and while Dan put on some coffee, Sam opened a can of stew. They spoke only a few words as they waited for the food to heat.

As they ate, Dan said, "Tomorrow morning, we will have a ceremony to make us strong. We cannot take lightly what we must do. The old spirit-man showed me where the witch lives, and I have seen the beast in the form of an old woman. She is also the one responsible for the death of my daughter and my grandfather several years ago. The beast Ye'iitsoh killed them, but it was the witch who led the creature to them."

Looking at the stars above the dark outline of the mesa, Sam listened to the night. He heard the horses munching the tough grass, and he turned when an owl hooted down the canyon. Across the way, a coyote howled its soulful song to the moon.

Dan became silent, and Sam reached for the coffee pot. He refilled their cups and when he sat back again and sipped his coffee, Dan spoke again.

"The old man spirit told me he has tried to find the path of the skinwalker, but he has failed. She does not leave tracks, or perhaps someone else walks the path at her bidding." Dan paused, and looked at Sam. "The witch is very dangerous. Her eyes glow in the night, and if you should see them, she will kill you. When you lock eyes with the witch, it can absorb itself into your body."

Both men considered the dangerous task ahead of them. Dan finished his coffee, and poked at the fire with a stick. As the flames grew, he said, "The spirit-man says he must confront the witch, and pronounce its full name to make it sick and die. The witch knows this, and she has taken some of his bones to use as charms to protect herself from him. Unless he can find her path, he cannot use her name against her."

"What kind of path was he talking about?"

A long silence passed before Dan replied, "I am not sure, but he told me he will be the bait while you and I seek the witch. He also mentioned something else. He spoke of the Spaniards from many years ago who marched through this land after the Chaco people were gone. The men wore metal shells, and they carried much gold. He thinks the witch has a path to a place where she found their treasure."

In his mind, Sam saw the image of Spanish royalty on the face of the gold coin Eric Nez gave him two months ago. Eric found it with the remains of Harold Borden, and the place could not be far from the path Dan mentioned.

CHAPTER 77

Dan & Sam rose early, as a pale glow defined the eastern horizon. They watered and saddled their horses, ate some jerky, and while they rode away in the chilly, pre-dawn hours, neither spoke, but listened to their own thoughts. They traveled for an hour before the sun showed itself.

Seldom speaking as the morning progressed; they rode through miles of greasewood, sand, and rock, while the sun drew the sweat from their bodies. It was after mid-day when Dan led them up a faint trail to some higher ground to get a better view of the witch's dwelling. The place overlooked a wide expanse of hills and low ridges, and Dan pointed out the small hogan in the distance.

"There lies the dwelling of the skinwalker. A young woman lives with her, and also, a young man with a white truck, but the witch has killed him."

Sam adjusted his binoculars, shading them so the sun wouldn't create a reflection noticeable to anyone below. He grunted in surprise when he recognized the place. He had stopped at this very dwelling last month, where he saw a tire print with an unusual cut in the tread. He was certain now, that it matched the plaster casting he made recently near Castor's burnt car. Never suspecting a connection at the time, he marveled at how close he had been to the center of the mystery.

He lowered the glasses and said, "I have been to this place before. It is the home of the man who dove me to Gallup the day you took me to see a doctor. The driver's name was Sonny, and he worked for a man at a garage in town."

Dan said, "I see someone moving down there."

Sam looked, and passed the binoculars to Dan. "Yes, she is the old one I saw. There was a girl—there, she just came out of the hogan."

He gave the glasses back to Sam. "Remember when I told you the old spirit man said I needed your help? Well, I didn't mention he spoke to me again in a dream last night."

Sam lowered the glasses and gave Dan a wary look.

"He said, you and I would need each other's help to destroy the witch, and he told me death would be watching us."

"What did he mean by that?"

"I am not sure, but he said the witch is in league with a very ancient and evil spirit." Dan paused for a moment. "It is not a human thing, and it cannot interact in this world without taking some other creature's form—just like it took over the body of the large beast that killed my family. The evil spirit is Ye'iitsoh."

"Does Ye'iitsoh control the witch?"

"Yes, though she may think otherwise. "The old spirit told me something else. He said I should keep my iron knife with me, but he didn't say why."

Sam frowned as he considered Dan's words. He lifted his glasses toward the hogan again, and he saw a young woman standing outside next to the old one. They appeared to talk, and then both went inside the building. He put the binoculars away and said, "Dan, can you take me to where the witch killed the man who drove the white truck?"

A half-hour later, they reached some high ground that allowed them to see across a large stretch of desert cut with dozens of twisting gullies and arroyos. Sam was able to make out part of the trail where Dan had seen Sonny driving his truck.

Finding an easy route that would take them down, they rode through a narrow canyon, and emerged to find they were standing on a low bench above the trail.

Dan led the way down through some fractured rocks, and after several minutes, they located the dented body of the white truck.

"There it is." Dan pointed at the vehicle tilted off the side of the trail.

Reaching the abandoned vehicle, Sam peered into the driver's side. There was no body, but he saw dried blood on the inside of the doors, and seat.

Dan walked to the passenger side, and leaned in through the opening. "I wonder what happened to the door—oh; there it is back on the trail."

Sam said, "I don't know how that happened, but there's a lot of dried blood in here. I'd sure like to find the body."

Dan looked along the rocks near his side of the vehicle, and after a few minutes, he said, "Over here Sam."

Sam briefly examined the mutilated corpse, and since they had no shovels, he and Dan piled rocks to cover it. Sam identified the Navajo male as Sonny.

With the grisly work done, sweating from their exertions in the heat of the day, Dan said, "It is time we prepared for our battle."

Sam looked at the dark bank of clouds moving in from the west. "In that case, we had better find some shelter."

The cumulus clouds had been gathering over the Chuska Mountains to the west since morning. Powerful up and down currents gradually changed their puffy, fair-weather, shapes into towering thunderheads, and the wind was picking up. If they didn't hurry, they would be caught in the middle of a cloudburst and some dangerous flooding."

Dan glanced up at the high ground. "I noticed a place we passed not too far back that looked promising. It should provide enough shelter to keep out most of the rain, and allow us build a fire. We must prepare to battle the skinwalker, and I must ask the spirit man to help us."

"Good, let's go."

They mounted their horses and rode away from the damaged truck, as the wind rushed past them in strong gusts. The bursts carried enough loose sand to sting their faces, and force them to protect their eyes. As they hurried through a long, twisting canyon, Dan said, "It is good we are nearly there; I just felt some rain."

They reached cover not a moment too soon. The sky opened and released a grey curtain of water just as they entered the shelter of two big slabs of rock leaning against the wall of the cliff. The space had enough headroom for a man on horseback, and it went back about twenty feet before it ended at a rock fall that sealed most of it off.

Sam said, "I'll look for some dry wood to make a fire."

Twenty minutes later, the rain stopped, and the sun brought out the colors of the rocks around them. Dan said, "There are more clouds coming, and this place looks as good as any to spend the night."

"That's fine with me," Sam said, "Do you think the old man spirit has confronted the witch yet?"

Dan thought for a moment. "If he did, and he was successful, he will tell me."

"And if you don't hear from him?"

"Then the witch may have killed him. If that happened, she will know about us, and we must be watchful. I still have the iron knife, and he told me I should use it to kill the witch. He also told me I would need help from lightning."

Feeling unsettled, Sam brought out the makings for coffee, while Dan dragged over more wood. He picked up a large chunk, then, tossed it away.

Sam noticed. "Is something wrong?"

Turning to Sam, Dan said, "It was hit by lightning."

Sam nodded, and returned to making coffee. His people considered burning wood hit by lightning to be bad luck, and it could cause illness. "I'm glad you noticed it before one of us picked it up in the dark. We don't need any bad luck now."

After bringing up enough wood, Dan stood in the opening of their shelter and looked out across the valley. "I'm going to find a place higher up, and have a look around. I saw a crow flying, and it made me uneasy."

The old witch sensed the presence of the two men, and it made her think of the fear she felt, knowing the old man spirit was also nearby. She must make medicine so she could deal with this threat.

She knew the old spirit watched her constantly, waiting for a chance to follow her path, and confront her by calling her name. This was the only way the ghost could harm her. It could make her sick and die, and she avoided him by sending Tessa to watch over the gold coins. She would continue this until she could put an end to the danger.

Changing back to her human form when she returned to the hogan, a thrill passed through her aging bones as she envisioned taking control of the young girl's body, and leaving the reservation with the gold. The long years of waiting for Tessa to grow and become a suitable vessel were nearly over. Soon the old woman would shed her wrinkled skin, and leave this place of poverty to enjoy her youth again. With the gold, she would live as she long wished. Having plotted and planned for so long, a giddy feeling overwhelmed her.

The time was here, and she no longer had the patience to continue her cat and mouse game with the old spirit. She made her preparations. First, she would return to kill the two riders she saw, and then she would rid herself of the spirit man for good. She would use his bones, taken when she killed him years ago, and make an amulet for her protection. After that, she would savor her final act of revenge, the death of the younger Castor.

A small cloud of concern entered her mind. She had made a bargain with the evil beast Ye'iitsoh many years ago, and it meant that his fearsome, dark presence would also be near.

CHAPTER 78

Dan noticed the black shape of a crow flying beyond the canyon, and he backed away from the ridge and made his way down to where Sam waited.

Covering the last twenty yards in a rush, he spoke in a low voice when he entered their shelter. "The witch is looking for us. She has taken the form of a crow, and we must leave right now. Forget our things, and make for the horses. We need to get to level ground where we can maneuver and put on some speed."

They ran to the horses and pulled the picket stakes. Saddling the animals, they were both away within minutes. As they rode down the hill toward the trail and the abandoned truck, Dan kept glancing around while the horses stepped sure-footed through the rocks. Nearing the canyon floor, he said, "I think I saw that crow again. It flew into a clump of pines across the valley."

They raced their horses down the two-track. Sam glanced back from time to time, and saw the sky becoming darker. When the first drops of moisture hit him, he looked back again, and it was his undoing. His horse lost its footing and fell. Fortunately, Sam pulled his boot out of the stirrup in time to roll clear, but the horse was injured, and struggling to regain its feet. He could tell it had bruised one of its legs.

Dan reined in and came to Sam's aid. "Hurry, take my hand and climb up. Your horse can't make it, and we need to get out of here."

Sam stood with his eyes on something in the distance. "Forget it Dan, we'll never get away with your horse carrying both of us."

Dan followed Sam's gaze, and saw a large, fur-covered animal dash from the trees heading in their direction. It ran like a wolf, but when it changed to a two-legged gait, both men stared with wide, fearful eyes.

Sam noticed Sonny's truck sitting on the trail ahead of them. "Maybe I can get it started. I'll try, and if it doesn't work, leave me and get out of here. From what you said, there is no use trying to make a stand. We can't kill the wolf-thing with a bullet, but I can try to slow it down and distract it."

Dan didn't argue, but he would not leave his friend behind. They rode to the vehicle, and Sam jumped in the cab, and fumbled with the ignition, but the engine wouldn't fire.

"We'll need to give it a push. There's a slope here, and as soon as we get it rolling, get on your horse and ride out of here."

As they rocked the vehicle, Dan caught a good look at the loping animal crossing the open space. It was a large wolf, and it was heading directly toward them.

They both heard the awful howl of the creature as they pushed and rocked the truck until it began to roll downhill. "Go Dan. Get on your horse and ride out of here."

Sam jumped behind the wheel, and as the truck gained speed, big drops of rain began to splatter on the windshield. He popped the clutch, and heard a feeble sputter from the engine. He depressed the clutch again, and when it picked up more speed, he let it out and heard a ragged backfire, and then a roar from the engine. He put the pedal to the floor, and had a fleeting thought of the absolute futility of his effort.

Heavy rain began to slash across the bouncing truck as Sam tried to avoid any large rocks that could stop his headlong race to level ground. He saw where the two-track came around, and he knew the trail would allow him to put on more speed. He must stay ahead of the horrifying creature that pursued him to allow Dan to get away. He couldn't see it in the rearview mirror, but he knew it was closing in somewhere behind him.

As Sam concentrated on reaching the trail, he was unaware that the beast had turned away and began to pursue the horse and rider.

Dan saw Sam speed away, and he let his horse choose its own path. Trying to gain some distance from the beast, he knew his mount wanted to run from the fearful creature as much as he did. The dark sky closed over them creating a surreal backdrop for their desperate escape. The rain turned the clay soil greasy, and Dan's horse stumbled and slid in the mud several times, making his escape even more difficult and dangerous. He struggled to stay in the saddle, until a crushing blow from the large, pursuing animal knocked him off his horse. Dan slipped as he tried to regain his feet, and he found himself looking directly into the eyes of the fearsome beast.

He watched as the creature shook the rain from its fur, and then shift its form to that of the old, witch woman. Dan's rifle was with the horse, and he reached for his knife just as the witch blew a handful of corpse powder in his face, temporarily blinding him. His lungs burned, and he fell to the ground in a fit of coughing. When he tried to stand, his limbs would not obey, and he felt his world fade into smoke.

Fishtailing down the muddy trail, Sam kept the pedal to the floorboard as much as he dared. The windshield wipers flapped like slashing wings, but were largely ineffective against the onslaught of the rain. Clouds blocked out the sun, and the desert became a surreal landscape of noise, punctuated by jarring explosions and blinding bursts of lightning. Rock formations and gnarled trees leapt out of the gloom, and took on sinister shapes, as he expected the beast to leap out at him at any moment.

Desperately concerned for Dan's safety, he noticed the dip in the trail too late. The truck nosed down and plowed through a foot of water. Fortunately, momentum carried him to the other side of the narrow arroyo. He feathered the gas, and the engine sputtered to life again.

Soon, ice crystals driven by the fierce wind, hammered against the windshield, and he nearly jumped out of his skin when a mass of tumbleweed blew in through the missing passenger door. The thorns tore at his shirt and face, and he lost his hat while shoving the wet, prickly brush back through the opening. He wiped some blood from the side of his face and neck, and kept on driving.

He hadn't seen the creature, and he worried about Dan. Did the fiend go after him instead? Did Dan get away? As if in response to his silent query, the beast appeared in his path. He had no time to react, and it was all he could do to stay on the trail.

Sam heard a noise, and felt the truck jostle as something large jumped into the bed of the truck. Reacting more on instinct than fear, he slewed the vehicle off the path and back again in an attempt to dislodge the fiend. A dip jarred the truck on its frame, causing it to leap like a bucking horse, and he noticed a dark, hairy shape fly over the cab onto the side of the trail.

The darkness was nearly complete as the storm thrashed around him. Rain came in heavy bursts, and the trail felt like a wet slide. He watched his speed around the curves to avoid skidding against the boulders bordering the trail.

Sam had no idea where he was, other than somewhere near the edge of the Bisti. As if to reinforce his guess, a series of explosive, lightning bursts lit up a line of eerie, rock gargoyles standing nearby, watching him. If it ever rained in hell, he was sure it looked like this. Braking by reflex, he dodged a boulder in his path, and his fears come to life.

A large hairy form leapt upon the hood of the truck, struggling for something to grasp as it slid against the windshield and over the cab. Sam jerked the wheel, and risked losing traction as he tried to dislodge the creature. He fishtailed, and as he struggled to stay on the rutted trail, a hairy claw burst through the glass in his door and raked across his shoulder, tearing away part of his shirt and a large patch of skin. Sam screamed in pain, and then gasped when lightning struck so close, it shook his body, and caused his eardrums to ache.

In wild desperation, he focused on the trail. His arm burned, and he struggled to breathe in the charged air and surreal, semi-darkness. Sam heard the beast scrabble on the roof of the cab, trying to keep its balance, and he steered side-to-side, hoping to make it lose its grip. His head crashed into the roof, flattening his hat around his ears, and the fiend slashed at him again through the broken window.

After a hard, careening impact that mashed his left fender against some rocks along the edge of the trail, he realized it must have also dislodged the beast. He aimed the truck down a hill, and a flash of lightning lit the road ahead of him. His eyes grew wide when saw a dark gulf of open space on the left, and a dead tree at its edge, with its bent and boney limbs grasping for the sky.

The next instant, he was fighting for his life, trying to avoid the snapping teeth of the creature entering the open passenger doorframe and reaching into the cab. Sam fumbled for the door handle, and shifted his body, desperately trying to get away from the beast as it pulled itself across the seat.

He fumbled for the latch, and sensed more than saw the large boulder directly in the path of the truck. He dove out of the driver's door, hit the ground, and rolled, and when he looked up, the entire area exploded in a huge burst of lightning. The thunderous detonation drowned out the sound of the head-on impact of the vehicle, and he saw the creature thrown through the shattered windshield, cartwheeling through the air, and hitting the dead tree.

Sam passed out for a moment, and when he came to, he found himself wet and covered with mud. He struggled to stand, and saw flames engulfing the vehicle, casting writhing shadows on the tree. Halfway up the gnarled trunk, he saw a broken form impaled upon a sharp, twisted branch.

It was a scene from a nightmare, and Sam was too numb to do anything but watch, and try to catch his breath. He saw the creature writhing in the flames licking up the dead tree, apparently attempting to remove itself from the shaft of wood sticking from its chest. As the rain diminished, to his horror, the fiendish creature transformed into the shape of an old woman—the witch.

Cold and shivering, Sam sat there, and thought he was hallucinating when he saw someone running toward the tree.

Dan Yazzie staggered up to the jagged branches, wet, and at the end of his endurance. He reached for his iron knife, and climbed toward the writhing form. The spirit man told him all would be lost if he could not force the blade deep into the breast of the witch. He knew what he must do, and as he lifted the weapon, the old witch turned her hollow eyes and hissed at him. She slashed with her nails, driving him back until he fell to the base of the tree.

Out of breath, and at the end of his endurance, Dan struggled to his feet, and somehow found the strength to do what he must. He climbed again, and as he drew back his arm to thrust with his blade, the strange amorphous form of the old man spirit enveloped him. Dan heard a voice whisper the name of the witch-creature, and he felt a ghostly hand guiding his iron knife deep into the heart of the witch.

Dan collapsed to the ground, and when he lifted his eyes to the impaled creature, the air exploded in a blinding fireball of electricity. Thrown back by the blast, and deafened by the noise, Dan shivered and lost consciousness.

After the sound of the thunderous blast echoed down the black canyon, Sam stumbled toward the burning tree to help Dan. He recoiled from the acrid smell of the blackened body of the witch, but what he saw next made him jerk back in horror. The charred and disfigured remains of the creature began to writhe and twist as if it were trying to escape the knife and tree that impaled it. He fell across Dan's prone body to protect him, and he hoped the iron blade captured the witch's Chindi—her evil spirit.

Heavy rain engulfed the area, and when it subsided, Sam put his ear to his friend's chest and checked for signs of breathing. He lifted the lifeless form, and staggered as he carried it a short distance away. Checking again, he detected the faint flutter of a heartbeat. He knew he must get his friend to shelter and warmth.

Glancing back at the tree, Sam saw the charred figure, now reduced to a cinder. Small pieces began to fall away, and as the wind scattered the ashes, he saw the broken blade of Dan's knife.

CHAPTER 79

Sam found Dan's horse, and it took nearly an hour of riding double to find adequate shelter and build a fire. He worried about his friend, and knew he had suffered greatly from his ordeal.

Tending their wounds after building a fire, he heated a can of stew and helped Dan get comfortable before they ate. The blaze warmed the rocks around them, and when Dan gave in to sleep, Sam watched over him until his own fatigue took him and he closed his eyes.

Over the hills and ridges, the moon peered through the clouds and cast a cold light on the lightning-struck tree. Wind had scattered most of the ashes of the witch's body when a young wolf came to the place and sniffed around for a scrap of meat. It jumped back when a burnt limb fell, jarring free the last bit of charred flesh stuck to the tree.

It returned in a moment, and ignored a piece of metal that fell to the ground, as it resumed its search for food. Soon, the wolf started to act in a very odd manner. It jumped back and sneezed, and then it began to twitch as if it had lost control of its own body. Hair fell away in clumps, and as it shivered and whimpered, the pitiful creature crawled away into the haunted spires of the Bisti.

Dan woke during the night. Warmed by the fire, but still aching and weak, he drew a deep breath, and thought back to what he remembered of their ordeal. He shifted to ease the aches in his body, and he heard a voice speak from the shadows across the campfire. It wasn't Sam.

The old man spirit's lined face appeared in the glow of the fire, and he spoke to Dan. "You are out of danger now. I have made a spell to ward off the sickness the witch gave to you. It is time I must leave, but before I go, I will speak to you of something you may not fully understand."

"Know this; there is still a lingering danger from the witch, and it is fed by a hidden treasure of Spanish gold."

Dan listened, waiting for the spirit-man to explain. The old spirit looked up at the stars, and Dan could see sadness covering the man's face like a mask.

The spirit looked at Dan's prone form. "You must rest, but first, know this; our two spirits have always been tied together—that is why I came to you. We both carry a burden in our hearts, and we have found it easier to lift together."

"You bear the sorrow of an accident that took your wife, and also, the event that took your daughter and your grandfather. Know that as your friend, I have shared this burden."

"Old Spirit, I know all I can do is walk a new path forward."

"Then waste no more time wishing for what cannot be. Your family is gone, and they cannot come back to you."

Dan said, "I have wished it was I who died in the wreck instead of my wife."

"And if you had, you take away everything you did today, and what you will do tomorrow—perhaps an even greater tragedy. My friend, you are not me, but you are like me. We have made mistakes, and we bear the scars wrapped in the muscle of our hearts. This will be the last time you will see me, but before I go, I have a favor to ask of you."

Dan winced with pain as he lifted himself on his elbows. "The last time? Where do you go?" He waited for an answer, and then took a weary breath. "I am sorry; I meant to ask what favor I may do for you."

The spirit smiled, "You have already done it."

Dan slept and dreamed, and when he awoke, he heard Sam moving around the campfire. The smell of pinon smoke wafted past him while he lay on his blanket, and from their sheltered place in the rocks, he watched the rays of dawn touch the hills across the valley.

"I let you sleep," Sam said. "I feared the witch may have poisoned you."

Dan thought about this. "How did we get here? I don't remember."

"Lightning hit the tree, and I thought it killed you along with the witch. When I reached your side, I found your pulse, and I put you on

The Lightning Tree

your horse and brought you here. It was strange—I saw a small fire from a distance, and I thought lightning may have started it. When we drew closer, I found a campfire burning, and more firewood stacked to the side. Someone else made the fire, but I didn't see any tracks."

Dan knew it was the old spirit-man.

"How do you feel, Dan? Would you like some coffee?" Sam saw his nod, and poured him a cup of hot brew.

Dan held the steaming cup, and spoke between sips. "The old spirit made the fire for us. I talked with him while you were sleeping, and there is something I must do. I ask that you help me."

After they ate some bacon and biscuits, Dan felt stronger, and he led the way along the side of the hill into a narrow gap where the high walls blocked most of the light.

"Here," Dan said, and he lit a match to some dry grass and sticks he piled up. In front of them, sheltered under an overhanging rock, the flickering light illuminated a scattered pile of bones lying in the sand next to an ancient, frayed blanket.

Sam waited for an explanation as his friend built up the fire. After a few moments, Dan said, "They are the bones of the old spirit-man. I promised I would cover them with rocks. I shed no tears, for he is a spirit, and he does not need them."

Some minutes after they finished, an eagle screeched somewhere in the rocks above them, and they saw it fly across the sun.

It was obvious that they both needed more rest, and Sam said, We will stay here today, and tomorrow, we will ride to the old witch's hogan. I have a feeling I will find the proof of who was responsible for the killings over the past several years. Maybe then, I will understand why they happened in the first place."

Beyond the valleys and sandstone ridges to the west, Tessa stepped from the old hogan. She glanced up to confirm the time of day, and began the trek she had taken many times before.

She chose a variation of the path that would lead her to the small cave deep in the land of the spirits, and she carried enough food to spend the entire day in the strange and beautiful country she loved.

The old woman did not return last night, nor did her brother. Tessa wasn't certain what that meant, but she sensed things would soon change for her.

She had always been obedient, and she feared the old woman who had used her. There were times when she thought she would come to harm, but now she felt something new had happened—something that changed her prospects for the future. She felt differently about her brother. He had treated her well enough, but never as an equal. She had seen the two argue, and Tessa feared one or both of them were dead. That could mean one could come home soon, and if so, she did not know what it meant for her.

She would stay near the small cave with the gold today, and return at dusk. That would give her a chance to watch the hogan to see if someone had returned. Perhaps then, she would know what to do.

As she walked away, her anxious thoughts offered another solution. What if she removed the gold coins, and hid them in another spot? If she were careful not to leave any trace of the new hiding place, only she would know the location.

She shivered with excitement at the chance to create a much different future for herself. There may be danger, but she now felt she could control her own destiny.

Later, when she reached the low cave in the eroded folds below the sandstone pillars, she took off her pack, and crawled into the dark space. An odd, musty smell came to her, and she struck a match to see her way, and to find out what may have caused it. What she found in the flickering light made her recoil in horror.

Lying on its side in a far corner, a disheveled, nightmare creature stirred as it watched her. Tessa recognized the fur of a wolf, but the animal appeared horribly disfigured and sick. Patches of fur were gone, and the bare skin oozed pus and blood. Dark, haunted eyes held nothing in focus, and the creature wheezed as it panted for air. Ever the practical girl, she reached for a large rock to brain the beast and put it out of its misery.

As her hands moved, something resembling a fluid smoke erupted from the animal and swirled around her. She had a brief sensation of choking before she collapsed, unconscious.

CHAPTER 80

The sun reached the small opening of the cave in the Bisti as the young Navajo woman crawled out and stood in the cool morning. She brushed sand from her clothing, and gazed across the eroded cliffs in each direction before she began walking.

Her one purpose was to return to the hogan to retrieve her personal things before she abandoned the place for good. She anticipated standing in front of the mirror to confirm what she could already feel.

As Tessa stood there, the last bastion of her mind fell, and she accepted her fate. She felt the cold, twisted mind of the old woman creep inside hers.

Knowing she would reach the hogan in a few hours, she walked at a brisk pace in spite of the weight of the pack full of gold coins. The coins were vital; they would buy her a new life, and a new home.

When she reached a vantage point where she could look upon the old log dwelling, she scanned the hills and dry watercourses before satisfying herself that no intruders were in the area.

The girl spat in disgust when she reached the rough cabin, hating what she had endured for the past twenty years. It would be different now. Not only did she have her new body and a new life to experience, she had the white-man's gold. It would all allow her to live in wealth and privilege. Her considerable, dark powers would increase over time, and she would soon control the lives of others to do her bidding.

First, she would gather the few belongings she wished to keep, and then walk to the highway to catch a ride to Farmington. It was imperative that she exercise great caution, and seek only temporary lodging while she planned her new life. She would change some of the gold to dollars, and purchase a vehicle and clothing before seeking a suitable place to live.

Inside the hogan, the witch-Tessa changed clothes and packed her few personal belongings. She moved the coins into a different pack to make it easier to carry, and in her haste, spilled several onto the dirt floor. She cursed as she watched them roll away, and she scrabbled on her hands and knees to retrieve them. Finally, when they lie hidden among the rest of her belongings, she stepped to the door and gave a final thought to what she carried inside her bag.

A small concern crossed her face. Was she forgetting something? She smiled when she caught her reflection in the small, scratched mirror by the door—a young woman, attractive enough, and with a lifetime to live. Her eyes glowed as she noticed the red birthmark on her neck. One final look around, and she chuckled as she reached for the corncob pipe, and walked outside.

A few hours later, two riders on a single horse approached the old hogan. Sam jumped down, favoring his injured arm, and Dan Yazzie dismounted, careful of his own wounds. Both men studied the surroundings and the deserted look of the place.

Dan carried his rifle as they walked up to the building, and Sam peered inside and stepped in first. The place was vacant, and showed signs of a hasty departure. He noticed drawers pulled out, and their contents carelessly tossed on the dirt floor.

"It looks like she just took what she wanted and left—maybe for good," Sam said.

Dan grunted in agreement. "I'll go outside and see if I can find some tracks while you finish looking around in here."

"Okay, it shouldn't take long."

When Dan returned twenty minutes later, he found Sam sitting at the battered kitchen table with an old book and some papers. Sam didn't glance up when Dan spoke. "I followed some tracks, but they faded out. Did you find anything?"

"Yes, and it's making my hair stand on end. Come over here and look at this. It's an old Gallup High School yearbook from twenty years ago. Take a look at the group photo of the baseball team."

"What's so interesting about that?"

"I've seen the same photo at the school, but in this book, someone has crossed off the faces of the ball players. I still recognize them, and I know they're all dead—except for one. He operates a trading post in town. I also found a stack of newspaper clippings about the deaths of each player."

"It seems odd to collect that kind of information on a baseball team."

"It's more than odd, Dan. What would you say if I told you that the same person who saved these clippings had a hand in the murder of each one of the players?"

"I'd say only an Anglo would ever do such a thing." Dan's expression changed after he spoke. "Or a Navajo witch." He looked around the room. "You don't think the young girl is involved in this, do you?"

Sam didn't answer. He turned a page, and picked up an old envelope he found in the book. As he pulled out the brittle contents and read, his eyes widened. Now he knew why other families in the area seemed not to remember Stacy Toledo. She lived with a witch, and the neighbors were too frightened to speak of it to a stranger. They would fear that the stranger might also be a witch, and do them harm.

Sam spoke two names aloud. "Sonny Toledo and Tessa Toledo."

"Huh?" Dan turned. "Who are they?"

"I believe they are the names of the young man and woman who lived here with the witch. I suspect they were brother and sister, and likely the children of Stacy Toledo."

When Sam gathered up the papers and stuffed them back in the envelope, he didn't mention the other item he'd found; a Spanish gold coin, apparently misplaced when it dropped and rolled under a gap in the log wall.

"I don't think we'll find anything else here, Dan. I need to get back to Gallup and take care of some business. Let's ride back to Blacksparrow so I can pick up my car."

Dan nodded. "After you drive off, I'll stay and rest for a few days, and then ride back here and search for any fresh tracks leading toward the Bisti. I saw the girl walking in that direction before, but I always lost her trail. Maybe I'll find something this time."

The two rode for Blacksparrow, each keeping to their own thoughts, and planning the next steps they would take. Sam was certain that Stacy Toledo was dead; probably buried in the hills somewhere. If she were alive, she would have no reason to leave her young children, or do them harm. He also had a good idea that the old witch used the children, or at least the boy, as a tool of vengeance against the students who brutalized their mother.

Vengeance was a strange concept for most Navajo, but a witch would embrace it as an outlet for her anger. The old woman must have trained Sonny since he was a child to prepare him for the role she planned for him. For the girl, it seemed unlikely she would train her to take part in the murders. Did she have a different role for Tessa to play? If so, what was it? Sam shook his head. Each answer led to more questions.

When he and Dan reached Blacksparrow, it was still light enough to see the damage to the buildings in the compound. Every structure bore the scars of bullets, fire, or dynamite. Half of the dining hall was gone, but a good portion of the main house was still standing. Nearly all of the other structures were nothing but scattered piles of ashes and rubble.

Even the old hangars at the far end of the runway were gone, and he noticed the twisted tail section of the small aircraft sticking out from a pile of debris next to the mesa wall. He took a deep breath and shook his head.

"Dan, I'll hunt up some food and water, and some blankets you can use. You can take off when you're rested. My car is here, and I'll drive it back to Gallup. I have a feeling the next few days are going to be very interesting. By the way, do you still carry a small knife you can use for whittling?"

"Sure, why?"

"Well, I remember you were always handy at carving wood, and I wondered, while you're catching up on your rest, if you could carve a cane for someone I know. He is a brave old man, and he needs a new one. Could you make something special to replace the one he broke?"

"Sure. It should't take long."

"Good. There's lots of wood around. Maybe I'll see you when I get back in a few days—if you're still around."

"Sure, and if I leave, I'll put the cane on the porch of the house."

Sam left a short while later. As he drove west on the paved highway to Gallup, he reviewed his mental deck of clue cards, and added some new information. One fact kept popping up; Stacy Toledo was not just the innocent victim, as he had once believed. She had acted with deliberate intent to attach herself to Bobby Castor and his family's money. Somewhere along the way, when Bobby's father became involved, she had seduced him with her youthful willingness, or allowed the older man to seduce her.

Had the witch encouraged her efforts? Was Stacy following the instructions of the old woman who raised her? There was no way to be certain, and no clues in the papers he carried from hogan, just the mention of an aunt who claimed to be her guardian.

Knowing fatigue would soon affect his ability to think, he would stay at Charlie's tonight and catch up on his sleep after checking what was going on with the pending arrest of Rance Wilder. Tomorrow, he would tell Charlie what he found out about the wolf-hair case.

CHAPTER 81

Sam woke to the sound of an alarm clock, and it took him a moment to remember where he was. Lying there half-asleep, he saw sunlight in the window, and heard Charlie walk downstairs, probably to heat some water for coffee.

A short while later, Charlie knocked on the door of the guest room and said, "Sam, it's after 6:00, and we'll be meeting the agents guarding Wilder at the hotel at 7:00 a.m. sharp.

Sam yawned and said in a ragged voice, "I'm awake. I'll be glad to get this over with. If you buy donuts afterward, I'll tell you what I found out about our wolf-hair case."

"Do you think you solved it?"

"Most of it, but I ran into a few things I still have trouble believing. It'll take a while to explain. In the meantime, let's get this over with. I want to see how surprised our friend, Mr. Wilder is to see me alive. If it's O.K. with you, I'd like to have the honor of putting the cuffs on him when the agents take him away.

On that clear Saturday morning, a few minutes before 7:00 a.m., Sam and Charlie walked inside the lobby of the El Rancho Hotel. One of the FBI agents was waiting for them. He stood and introduced himself to Sam, and then went up the curved stairway to the second floor to tell his partner it was time to bring Wilder down from his room. Charlie and Sam waited near the fireplace, and Charlie watched the stairway while Sam faced him with his back to anyone coming down the stairs.

The Lightning Tree

After ten minutes, they heard Wilder's blustering complaints as he walked down with the two agents. Charlie stood, and with a cheerful smile, said, "Good morning Mr. Wilder; we've arranged a nice trip to Albuquerque for you this morning. I'm sorry you had to wait these past few days until we completed our arrangements. I hope you enjoyed your accommodations during the delay."

Wilder acted belligerent and said something under his breath.

Charlie glanced at Sam, and said to Wilder, "Someone asked me if I thought you wouldn't mind if they said goodbye to you before you left. Since you're something of a celebrity, and probably used to that kind of thing, I didn't think it would be a problem." Charlie nodded to Sam, who stood from the couch and turned to face Rance Wilder with a grin.

Sam's dark eyes watched Wilder's stern expression sag as he recognized him. The man's lips began to quiver, and his face turned grey. It looked as if Wilder wanted to say something, but couldn't think of anything appropriate.

"That's alright Rance," Sam said, "I guess neither of us has much to say to each other. We might as well save it for the courtroom."

Sam's mild expression turned into a wolfish grin when Charlie handed him the handcuffs, and while the two agents held Wilder's arms, he placed them on the prisoner.

Charlie wore a smug expression as the agents escorted Wilder from the hotel to their car. "How did that feel, Sam?"

Sam grinned. "It felt so good, *I'll* buy the donuts. When we get back to your office, I want to call Jack Whorten in Washington to give him a briefing on what went on."

"It's Saturday; do you think he'll be in?"

"Charlie, from what I can tell, that man probably lives at his office, and I suspect he rarely sleeps."

Charlie left to get the mail, and Sam called Whorten after finishing his second cup of coffee and two donuts. Waiting for the call to go through, he wondered what it was like to work directly for the President.

He and Whorten spoke for fifteen minutes about the recent events at Blacksparrow, and near the end of the conversation, Sam said, "I'll let you know if anything else comes up, but there is one small thing I need to ask your help with. It has to do with a personal problem the FBI Station Chief in Albuquerque, Thad Decker, brought to my attention. This is what he told me…"

Ten minutes later, Sam put the phone down, and took a deep breath as Charlie returned to the office. "Well, it's over with. Whorten told me to personally, thank you for accommodating my absence on the reservation these past few days, and holding your prisoner until I returned."

Charlie smirked. "Believe me, it wasn't so easy. Rance swore he had no knowledge of any illegal activities carried on by the men at Blacksparrow. He professed his innocence, and even threatened a counter-suit against the FBI. He had some slick-talking attorney show up after we arrested him, and the guy threatened us, and said we'd all end up in jail, or in the poor house so deep in debt, we'd forget what sunlight was."

Sam leaned back in his chair with his hands behind his head. "It seems more likely Rance is going to be the one missing some sunlight." "The government boys don't play games with someone involved in drug smuggling, human trafficking, or racketeering."

Charlie selected another donut, and filled their cups with the last of the coffee. "I'll admit I had some concerns that you might not show up today. Rance swore we had no proof, but thanks to your timely arrival, his story turned into hot air. Hee, hee, hee, I'll never forget the look on his face when he saw you—him thinking his boys killed you that day in the desert."

As they finished the last of their coffee, Sam mentioned a few things he learned on his call to Jack Whorten. "It seems Rance has connections to some of the old Purple Gang in Michigan, as well as Capone's boys in Chicago. He stays away from the enforcement end of the business, but he pulls the strings out west. He had the contacts for the merchandise and the shipping, and he took a share of the profits from the organizations back east who handled the distribution. His business was never just about making movies."

"It makes me wonder if he lost his shirt on a couple of bad films and needed the money," Charlie said, "or maybe he just got greedy."

Sam shrugged. "Maybe both. Whorten also mentioned something implicating our local businessman and politician, David Castor, but I told him it was a dead issue since he went up in flames inside his car. By the way, has Station Chief Decker said anything to you about my involvement in all of this?"

Charlie tilted his head with a quizzical expression. "Now that you mention it, no, and that seems a bit odd. He hasn't mentioned you at all. In fact, I heard that one of the agents complained to him about your behavior during the Blacksparrow raid—something about you commandeering an

The Lightning Tree

agency car without permission—and he told the agent to back down. Do you have any idea who that could have been?" Charlie's smile was full of mischief. "Hell Sam, a few months ago, Decker was ready to have your hide tacked to his wall, now it seems you can do no wrong. Do you have any idea why?"

Sam sipped his coffee in silence. He knew exactly why, and he knew Whorten came through on his promise. In a moment, Charlie shook his head and changed the subject. "Are you going to tell me what you came up with on the wolf hair case?"

Sam set his cup on the scarred surface of the desk. "Charlie, from what I've seen and learned the last few days on the Reservation, I could talk for an hour, and still not cover everything—much less believe most of it."

"So?" Charlie slouched behind his desk, "Start talking, I don't have anything else to do, and the phone's not ringing."

Sam shifted in his chair to get more comfortable. "Okay, believe it or not, it all seems to lead back to some things that happened several decades ago—some even as far back as the Civil War, but I got that part on hearsay. Don't ask me where or how."

"The first thing that brought me into all of this was when you told me about Orville Baxter's death well over a year ago. Someone reported it, and you found him with a crushed skull lying near his car off the Zuni Road. You mentioned finding a tuft of wolf hair in the broken glass of the car. A year later, there was Charles Wacker's car wreck, and you said you found knife wounds on the body, and another tuft of wolf hair. I also remember you mentioning both deaths happened during a full moon."

"Yes," Charlie said. "I had no idea what to make of the killings, and you offered to snoop around since you carried your new U.S. Marshal's badge."

"That's right, and I was living at Blacksparrow when a Navajo boy showed up and told me he found a body out in the Bisti. I brought you into it, and the dead man turned out to be Harold Borden. The boy told me he found an old, Spanish gold coin on the body, and shortly after that, I learned Borden's uncle was killed in town around the same time."

"Then I found out Borden had ties to the two men who died earlier, I discovered they were all classmates in school and played on the same baseball team. Bobby Castor was one of them, and that's when I found out that Bobby knew something about Borden and the gold coin."

"You called me out to the scene where Alan Sandoval, another ball player, died in a car wreck, and shortly after that, I discovered there were only two old baseball team players still alive; Louis Montoya, and Bobby Castor."

"Oddly enough, I had a run-in with Montoya a short while later when I was serving court orders for Judge Reilly. I figured he might know something about the killings, but when he came up dead in a car wreck, all I had left for a suspect was Bobby Castor."

Charlie said, "Yeah, either a suspect or another victim. He's still around. Do you think he's the killer?"

"Nope."

Charlie's eyes widened with surprise. "Do you think he's going to be the next victim?"

"I doubt it."

Sam's bland expression annoyed Charlie. He sat up and said, "Then who is the killer? Don't tell me you think they were accidents; we both saw enough evidence to know they couldn't be."

"You're right Charlie, and if you stop rolling your eyeballs, I'll tell you a story that I'm going to ask you to forget you ever heard."

Charlie frowned and folded his arms. "O.K. Go ahead."

"To begin with, we have to go back to the time of the "Long Walk."

"What? Wasn't that was back in the 1860s? Sam this is 1937. Are you serious?"

"Yes, and I want you to forget everything after I tell you. Actually, it began when the Spanish explorers traveled through here with their gold in the late 1400s; that's where the coin came from—and I found another one at an old hogan—and a piece of wolf pelt—but let's forget about that for now."

Charlie looked like his head was going to explode, and Sam grinned and said, "Do you remember me telling you that Dan Yazzie claimed to talk to a ghost—an old spirit man? Well, he told me that when the old man was still a boy, he was there when the Union soldiers took all the people to a place east of Albuquerque. During that march, the boy witnessed the soldiers abusing a young girl, and some years later, that same girl became a powerful witch. Our people would call her a skinwalker."

"The girl blamed the boy for not being able to protect her from the soldiers, and she took to learning witchcraft so she could exact her own revenge against them. She also used it against the boy when they relocated back to their own lands after the Civil War, and she eventually killed him.

The Lightning Tree

Dan told me the boy's spirit kept watch on her all these years." Sam looked at Charlie to see if he was following along. "About Fifty years later, in 1913, Stacy Toledo was raped by some boys on the Gallup High School baseball team. And, in 1932, the Gallup police found one of the boys hanging from a noose in his yard. Since then, eight more ball players from that team died by suspicious accidents or brutal murder. Bobby Castor is the last of those ball players still alive, and when David Castor died recently in his son's burning car, I believe the accident was meant for his son."

"Just a minute," Charlie said. "What does all this have to do with the witch and the spirit-man?"

"Nothing that I was aware of, until my friend, Dan Yazzie showed up after the Blacksparrow raid. With his help, and some guidance from the old spirit, we followed some dim clues surrounding the deaths, and found ourselves on the trail of the witch. Everything led to an old Navajo woman living on the reservation with a young man and woman.

There was something unusual about the three of them, and I believe now, that the old woman was a witch, and she transpired with the two children of her dead niece, *Stacy Toledo*, to kill the men who abused and raped their mother 20 years ago. I admit I have only circumstantial evidence for some of this, and I don't believe I can bring in an old spirit to testify."

"So you think the old witch killed all of them?"

"At least the first ones; I think she taught the boy do the dirty work later on."

Charlie looked stunned. "What makes you think that?"

"Because I know who was responsible for the later deaths. It was Sonny Toledo; Stacy's boy, now around 20 years old, and he drove an old truck and ran the victims off the road before killing them. He worked at Benny's body shop, and that's where he fixed the damage on his truck each time he used it." Sam leaned back in his chair.

"What about Louis Montoya, the guy who blew up your house, and tried to run you off the road? I thought he was a suspect."

"That was something else. He was one of the victims, remember?"

"Oh yeah."

"Charlie, I think the witch did the earlier killings—maybe using them to train the boy until he was old enough to take over."

"How do you figure that?"

"I'm not positive, but there were differences in the methods used in the first four killings. There was a hanging, a rattlesnake bite, a car accident, and a shooting—and none of them showed any evidence of wolf hair clues. In the last six deaths, including David Castor's, we found a tuft of wolf hair on or near the bodies. I think Sonny used it as a sign of his work—something to let those still alive, know that their time was coming. It was either that, or maybe he used it to misdirect the police."

Charlie appeared thoughtful. "And David Castor was driving Bobby's car when he was killed. It was a mistake. Bobby was supposed to be the victim!"

"Yes, and when the witch and the boy became aware of their mistake, they must have made plans to kill him too. By the way, I saw a cut on one of Sonny's truck tires, and I'll bet it matches the plaster cast you made at the scene of Castor's death."

"Wow, we'd better get on it right away."

"No, there's no need."

"What? Didn't you just say they were going to kill Bobby?"

"Not any more, Sonny is dead. Dan Yazzie saw it happen a few days ago, north on the Res. The man drove away from his hogan after an argument with the old witch, and she chased and killed him. When Dan came to take me to see the body, the witch found out and came after us."

Charlie's jaw dropped. "Holy cow!"

"We were in the boonies on horseback, and after my horse came up lame, Dan decoyed the witch while I got Sonny's abandoned truck started. I drove off, and she came after me in the form of a wolf. Charlie, I've never been more frightened in my whole life. It was a nightmare. She chased me through the desert during a thunderstorm, and after dark, she caught up to the truck and tried to kill me. Charlie, I saw her transform herself into a wolf-like creature right before my eyes."

I was driving for my life with lightning crashing all around, and when she caught up to me and crawled into the cab, I aimed the vehicle at a boulder and bailed out. The truck hit head on, and she went through the windshield. She ended up in a dead tree just as a bolt of lightning hit it, and everything blew up, and caught fire. She burnt to ashes, and the wind blew her away."

Charlie stared at Sam with his mouth open as Sam continued. "Dan showed up, and the next day we went back to search the witch's hogan. I discovered some evidence that shed light on the past events, and I found an old, High School yearbook with a photo of the same baseball team from back then. Someone had crossed off the faces with a pencil, as if keeping score as they died, and I also found some old newspaper clippings mentioning each death—that is except for Bobby Castor."

Sam glanced at Charlie, who appeared stunned. "Weird huh? Here's the best part. I found an envelope containing a report card and some identification papers of a Navajo girl who attended school in Gallup in 1915—Stacy Toledo. There were other scraps of paper with the names of two children, twins judging by the date next to their names. Their birthdays were the same as the date shown for Stacy's death.

"Are you saying Stacy Toledo died giving birth to twins? Do you think the children were the result of the high school rape?"

"Yes to both, and that's when I realized something else." Sam leaned forward on his elbows and ran his hands through his hair as he formed his words. "The witch lived with two young adults; a girl and a boy. They were much too young to be her own kids by decades, but about the right age to be Stacy Toledo's children—the right age to make one or more of the high school boys their father."

"Holy Cow." Charlie sat back and shook his head. "That's what all the killings were about; revenge, and all of it planned by a witch."

"That's what I figure; a vindictive, skinwalker witch, probably their grandmother, with enough patience and hate to span a lifetime. It's a moot point now, because Sonny is dead, and so is the witch. I can only guess what may have happened to the girl—she's missing, and Dan is out there trying to find her."

Charlie shook his head. "How are you going to write a report about all that? Are you going to say a witch was responsible for the killings, and now her ashes are blowing across the desert?"

"It sounds like a tall tale, doesn't it?"

"No, it sounds like a drunken nightmare. Sam, I believe you, but I don't think anyone else on the planet will."

"Yeah, I was afraid you'd say that."

CHAPTER 82

Sam was still thinking about the cause and effect of the whole Stacy Toledo incident when he fell asleep that night. Did he have all the facts? Did he make all the connections? Was anything missing? He knew the case wasn't closed until he found the girl, Tessa, and spoke with her to confirm his conclusions, and put the case to rest.

Saturday morning, the birds in the big cottonwood outside the window next to his bed, called to each other as they came and went, inspecting the bark and leaves for a quick morsel. The cicadas were in fine voice this year; the mating calls rising and fading like the scream of a power saw.

He was tired beyond caring. Lethargy seemed to take over his body and mind, and all he wanted to do was sleep. Listening to the noise outside, he closed his eyes for another half-hour, and eventually dragged himself out of bed.

As he splashed water on his face and brushed his teeth, he heard Charlie moving around in the kitchen. At least the coffee would be ready.

Charlie heard him come downstairs, and said. "Want some coffee? For a while there, I didn't expect to see you until noon."

"Was I snoring?"

"According to the neighbors, you were."

Sam snorted. "Very funny. I guess I needed some sleep."

"Pour yourself some coffee; it'll wake you up. I want to show you what I found in some of Rance Wilder's papers he left in the safe at the El Rancho. The manager called this morning, and I went to pick them up."

Charlie left the room for a moment, and returned with a thick manila envelope. He dumped the contents on the kitchen table in front of Sam, and went back to the stove to scramble some eggs and heat a pan of leftover chili.

"How does a breakfast burrito sound to you?" Charlie looked over his shoulder for Sam's response.

Sam's attention stayed on the stack of random papers. He yawned and lifted his coffee cup, sipped, and set the cup down before he reached into the pile. "It sounds good to me."

Charlie rolled his eyes, and turned back to the stove.

Leafing through the papers, Sam found a copy of his lease agreement with Wilder for the use of Blacksparrow. Underneath it, he found an envelope full of receipts and payroll information. In another, lists of equipment and personnel. There were some photos of people and places, and Sam recognized several shots of the buildings and layout at Blacksparrow, as well as some of the surrounding desert.

He sipped his coffee again, identifying some of the workers he'd seen and met. There were other photos of people he didn't recognize, as well as some larger, promotional shots of actors and actresses. When he came to one photo, he nearly dropped his coffee cup. The picture was of an attractive young woman in a seductive pose. He could see some Indian blood in her features.

"Find anything interesting?" Charlie said, stirring the eggs with his back to Sam.

"Did you look through this stuff already?"

"No, I just glanced at a few things, and brought it back here for both of us to look at. Why, did you find something interesting?"

When Sam didn't answer, Charlie stepped to the table and looked over his shoulder.

Sam heard Charlie's sharp intake of breath, and a surprised, "Ho-lee cow."

"Sally Whitefeather." Sam said in a soft voice as he stared at the photo, still reacting to the unexpected surprise. Her hair was different, but it was her. He spoke in a monotone voice. "She said she went to California last winter to teach school, and she came back here in the Spring. It looks like she found something more interesting to do while she was out there."

Charlie said, "It looks like a promotional photograph that movie stars give to their fans. Do you think she knew Wilder?"

Sam thought back to last spring when Sally returned from California. He remembered her tired looks and jumpy mannerisms. She said someone gave her a ride from the highway to Blacksparrow, and she was obviously glad to see him, but there was something different about her—something that haunted her and made her look tired and hollow.

He said, "No wonder Rance Wilder knew about Blacksparrow. She must have told him about the place; after all, she stayed with the rest of us through the summer while we excavated that site at the small mesa."

Charlie, sensed the awkward moment, and went back to the stove. He worked his spatula to hide his unease, and said, "Eggs are almost ready. Do you want some hot sauce?"

Sam ate slowly, and Charlie had the good sense to pay attention to his food and not try to force a conversation that was bound to bring up some bad memories that still haunted his friend.

After breakfast, they both finished going through the papers. When Sam put everything back in the envelope, he said, "Now that I'm up and awake, I think I'll call Joyce and see how things have been going on at the school."

"Okay, while you do that, I'll put this stuff in the safe at the office. I'm going back there to do some paperwork."

"Good. I'll probably run around town a bit, and check in with you later."

The phone rang three times before Sam heard Joyce Dobson's voice on the line. "Hi Joyce, it's Sam. I figured it was time I gave you a call and asked how things are going with you and Principal Dallas."

"Figured it was time? Sam Begay, where have you been? Probably in the hospital, since you obviously haven't been well enough to call me before now."

"Joyce, can I come over and make amends? I promise to tell you all about it, unless you're busy with something else—you aren't are you?"

"Well, if you're asking me if I'm sitting on the back porch sipping a mint julip, reading a movie magazine; I'm not. You can come over and keep me company if you like."

Sam pulled into her driveway fifteen minutes later. Joyce gave him a brief hug at the door and led him into the kitchen where she was mixing a pitcher of lemonade.

He looked at her soft, red-brown hair as she moved around, and he could see she'd touched up her lips with some color. "It's good to see you Joyce," and he knew he really meant it. "How are things going on at the school? Has Dallas been treating you alright?"

"Yes he has, although he's been a bit abrupt at times. Mostly, he leaves me alone." Concern crossed her face as she looked at him. "Look at you; you've lost weight, and you look tired."

"I've been trying to catch up on my sleep the last couple of nights, but I figured it was time to check-in with you and get busy again."

She stared into his eyes while he spoke. "No you don't Sam, you're not leaving here until you tell me everything you've been up to these past few weeks, and I don't care how long it takes you."

They took the pitcher and their glasses outside on the shaded porch, and sat across from each other.

Sam took a long pull from his drink and smacked his lips. "You must have read about some of it in the paper, but I'll tell you the expanded version. Rance Wilder asked me to come out to the movie site at Blacksparrow and help his crew scout some filming locations. Several miles away in the desert, they pulled their guns on me. I managed to get away, but I was hit. My friend, Dan Yazzie found me and took me to safety before the men could finish me off."

Joyce's eyes were big with concern. "Is that a scar on the side of your head?"

"Yes, but I feel fine now."

"When I got back to town, Charlie Redman and I went out to investigate the car crash that killed David Castor. Later, I went back to Blacksparrow to find a missing boy, and all hell broke loose. To make a long story short, there was a plane crash, and some gunfire, and explosions, and the FBI showed up to make the arrests."

Joyce stared at him with her mouth open.

"I know it all sounds pretty dramatic, Joyce, but it turned out alright. The rest, you probably read about in the paper. FBI agents took Rance Wilder into custody and charged him with smuggling, human trafficking, and attempted murder. He's in Albuquerque now, awaiting trial."

Joyce's forehead knotted up, and she turned to look across the yard. When her eyes came back to him, she said, "Stay for dinner Sam." She paused for a moment, and said, "I read about his arrest, and I just couldn't believe it. I met him years ago after I lost my fiancé in the big flu epidemic in 1918. Rance Wilder was a big movie star then, and he was a friend of David Castor. He was in all the movie magazines. In fact, he was in some of them last year, too. I still have a few copies in the living room. Would you like to see them?"

At Sam's interested nod, Joyce left the porch to retrieve the magazines. When she returned, she set three issues in front of him. "Now you know I'm just a girl who likes to dream about Hollywood movie stars. Each magazine has an article about Rance. One even tells about the big scandal last winter—something about a young woman who tried to rob him before she disappeared. There's even a picture of her in the article. Try the middle one in the stack."

Sam's heart began to beat faster. He picked up the issue and started leafing through the pages. He found the article near the front.

At the top of the page, he saw a photo of Wilder walking into his office past a row of reporters and their cameras. The caption read, *"Movie producer thwarts robbery by a young actress."*

He started reading the article, and learned the woman and a male accomplice attempted to swindle and blackmail the aging movie star. There was an altercation, and they tied him up, and attempted to steal the contents of his safe. Fortunately, a bodyguard interrupted the robbery, and after firing shots at the two, they escaped and were still at large. Sam turned the page and saw a small photo, identical to the larger one he saw this morning in the envelope with Wilder's other papers.

"What's wrong Sam? You look like you've seen a ghost."

He looked up at Joyce with a blank expression. "I have."

When it became obvious that Sam wasn't going to offer any more information, Joyce said in a soft voice, "Do you want to talk about it?"

"Not right now. Maybe another time."

Joyce accepted his wishes for now. She had no doubts she would get the whole story out of him eventually, whether he wanted to or not.

CHAPTER 83

There was and unseasonal chill in the air Monday morning. September always seemed to bring some warm weather, but today, the flannel shirt and old leather vest he wore barely compensated for the cool breeze. Sam grabbed his Stetson to keep it from blowing away and ending up somewhere in Texas, as he walked across the parking lot at Strong Mountain Trading. It was warm inside the store, and he made his way to the pawn counter.

Bobby Castor noticed him from behind the wood and glass counter, and he frowned, as if detecting an unpleasant odor. "What do you want?"

Sam's face showed no emotion. He let the sharp words pass, and said, "I came to give my condolences for the loss of your father. I also wanted to tell you who I think killed him, and why."

The scowl on Bobby's face softened with uncertainty. He looked to the side for a moment, making a half-hearted attempt to straighten a stack of catalogues.

Sam said, "Would you like to talk here, or would you rather go back to your office?"

Bobby didn't make eye contact. "I guess we could go to the back. It's more private." He motioned to a clerk to watch the counter, and led Sam down the hallway.

When Bobby shut the door, he motioned for Sam to take one of the chairs in front of the desk. To Sam's surprise, Bobby sat next to him, ignoring the high-backed chair behind the desk.

After a brief silence, Bobby said, "Tell me."

"It's a shame it happened like it did, but I think you know it was supposed to be you in the car."

"What do you mean?" Bobby had a wary look on his face as he waited for Sam to explain what he already knew was true."

"You were the last one, Bobby. Everyone else is dead. Peter Borden wasn't the first; it was Robert Tibbits five years ago, then Steve Seller, John Damon, Mel Stewart, Orville Baxter, and Charlie Wacker. Now, after Alan Sandoval and Louis Montoya, it leaves just you alive from the old high school baseball team. I came here today to try to keep someone from killing you."

"What can you do about it? You couldn't help my father, or any of the others. Besides, what makes you think you're right about what happened?"

"Bobby, I know all about what you did twenty years ago, and I think someone saved you for last. I imagine the killer was surprised to learn that your father was driving your car that night."

"You know who killed him?"

"I have an idea, but before I talk about *who*, I want to tell you *why*."

"I already know why; it's because of that damn party out in the boonies when we were in school. Don't you think I wished a million times that it never happened? I can't do anything about it now!"

Sam took a deep breath before he spoke. "There's no need to wish anymore. I think the killer is dead." Bobby's eyes grow wide as he stared at Sam, trying to decide if he should believe him.

"Who was it! *Tell me!*"

"Not until you tell me something that I want to know."

It was a stare down, and Bobbie blinked first. "What is it you want to know?"

"First of all, you're right, you can't do anything about what happened that night back in high school. I won't be filing any charges, but I do have a few questions that need an answer before I can close my file."

"Like what?" Bobbie appeared sullen, but somewhat relieved.

"I know Stacy Toledo lived with your family while she was going to school here. I also know you were angry at your father, and why." Sam saw Bobby's eyes shift away for a second. "What I don't know, Bobby, is who was responsible for convincing Edgar Dallas to bury the information about the girl." Sam waited for an answer, and after a moment, he watched Bobby's shoulders slump.

400

"It was dad. He talked to Dallas, but I think it was Rance Wilder who helped him to bury everything in the first place."

Sam nodded. "Who bought the beer for everyone that night? Don't tell me it was one of your friends."

"No, it was some guy who worked for Mr. Wilder. Look, it was a long time ago. I don't remember much else about it. If it'll make you happy, I was very angry with my father. Stacy was a pretty girl, and I liked her, but when I saw her in bed with him, well, I figured I'd teach them both a lesson."

Sam nodded again. He understood the need to balance things—how an injustice needed closure and resolution to allow everything to come back into harmony. Unfortunately, one injustice cannot resolve another.

"Bobby, Stacy became pregnant, and I believe she died giving birth to two children." He watched the surprise on Bobby's face. "It was her son and an old woman, probably an aunt, who planned the killings. Both are dead now, and I guess that makes you safe."

After a long silence, Bobby said, "Is that all you want from me?"

Sam saw wariness on the man's face, and he decided not to tell him about the girl who was Sonny's sister—her current whereabouts unknown. What could he say that would change anything? "Bobby, all I want from you, is for you to remember how everything always seems to come around and seek some sort of balance. You do something wrong, and it'll eventually bite you back. If you want a clear conscience, the only thing that will bring it to you are your actions and words now."

When Sam drove away, he realized that Bobby had not asked anything about either of Tracy's children. Returning to the FBI office, he noticed Charlie's car was gone. He used his key, checked the coffee pot to find out if it was still warm, and poured the last of it in a clean cup before taking it to the spare desk to think.

Rance Wilder seemed to be a common thread to several of the events. Although he didn't cause the Castor family problems, he was behind the alcohol-fueled party in the woods, and he pulled the strings to convince Edgar Dallas to bury Stacy's school records afterward. He protected David Castor and his son twenty years ago, and he probably groomed David to be his associate in his illegal smuggling operation in New Mexico.

Wilder was behind the attempt to kill him in the desert near Blacksparrow, and he tried to blackmail the FBI Station Chief in

Albuquerque. When Sam looked at everything, he realized Wilder even played a part in Sally Whitefeather's return to New Mexico that ended in her tragic death.

He decided to talk to Principal Edgar Dallas next, and when Dallas came on the line, he told him he had to speak to him right away. The man seemed reluctant, but when Sam mentioned he would try not to implicate him in any of the fallout from the arrest of Rance Wilder, Dallas agreed to see him.

Edgar Dallas appeared subdued and visibly nervous when Sam took a chair in front of his desk at the school. "Just what is this you were saying about me being implicated in the illegal actions of Mr. Rance Wilder? I don't see how any of it has a connection to me. It's true, I do know the man, and have spoken with him from time to time in the past, but what kind of a ridiculous charge are you trying to place on me?"

Sam told him of the deaths that occurred over the past several years, all because of Stacy Toledo's rape twenty years ago. Dallas turned pale and began to sweat. Sam told him at least some of the responsibility was his because of the role he played in covering up the assault.

That evening, he and Joyce Dobson had a quiet dinner at her house. Sam brought wine and flowers, and during their meal, they talked about small things. When the topic came to Principal Dallas, Sam waived it off until they finished eating. After he helped clean the table, Joyce poured two cups of coffee, and they went outside on the porch to continue their conversation.

He explained the part Dallas played in the cover-up of the actions of the baseball players, and he answered her questions about a few other details, before he said, "Joyce, I told him that I wouldn't put up with any action taken that might affect you at the school. I made him understand his part in what transpired, and I didn't want to put your job in any kind of jeopardy by doing it."

Joyce looked up and smiled. "Sam, I'm not afraid of that man. If he feels any heat from his own actions, I have enough backbone to tell him to get his own fire extinguisher. Who knows, maybe he'll feel bad enough about this to quit, and I can apply for his job."

Sam grinned. "I'll bet you'd make a great Principal." Turning solemn, he said, "Joyce, I'm going to tell you why I acted evasive about that story in your movie magazine. Maybe I've chosen a poor time to talk about it, but I want you to know who I am, and what I think I stand for. I don't want anything to come up and surprise you in the future."

He looked into her eyes. "Joyce, I know the girl in the photograph in that article about Rance Wilder. She was with a group of people who stayed with me at Blacksparrow while we did some archeological work last year. She left over the winter, but returned this spring, and she died in an accident at the compound. We were…close for a while."

Joyce smiled, and reached out to hold his hand. "Sam, I already know about that." When she saw his surprise, she said, "Never underestimate a woman's curiosity. You and I have something in common, Sam. We both lost someone we cared for. It wasn't our fault, and it doesn't stop us from going on with our lives." She paused to let her words sink in. "Thank you for telling me. I know you are a man of character."

She patted his hand before she released it. Sitting back, she sipped her coffee, then smiled and said, "And don't flatter yourself. I'm not looking for a husband—but I do see something in you that I find interesting. I know I can count on you, and as far as I'm concerned, that's pretty sexy. By the way, I may need some work done around here from time to time—especially on my ego."

Sam drove back to Charlie's place that evening, thinking of Joyce, and still feeling her lips on his when they said good night at her door. He was just pulling into the driveway when an errant thought made him forget everything else.

"Why did Harold Borden die? He was there with the other boys, but he didn't participate in the rape. If anything, he was a reluctant bystander, and he took her home. Sam's eyes opened wide with understanding. The gold of course, Borden found the gold. He had a Spanish coin with him when he died.

CHAPTER 84

It was Sam's turn to buy donuts the next morning. He walked in the office, and dropped the bag on Charlie's desk on his way to the back to get a cup of coffee. While he poured, he heard the phone ring.

When he walked to the front, Charlie pointed to the phone on the other desk, and mouthed "Chief Decker."

Sam picked up the phone, and when he heard Decker's voice, he pictured the man's dark framed glasses, big forehead, and long chin.

"Sam, I'm glad I caught you before you headed out somewhere. I've just heard some bad news; Rance Wilder is free on bond. We couldn't convince the Judge that he was a flight risk, so he let him post bail and go free until his trial. He had a smart lawyer from the West coast come out and portray him as an innocent bystander to anything and everything that happened."

The words surprised Sam, and he couldn't speak for a moment. "But... he ordered his men to kill me, and I signed a statement to that effect."

"I know Sam. Don't worry, we're going to keep a very close watch on him to make sure he shows up for trial. We tried to do the same with the hood you captured at the trading post after he got out on bail, but I heard they found him dead in an alley somewhere in Detroit. In the meantime, I'm catching all kinds of hell, and I need your help. Can you drive to Albuquerque this morning so we can talk with one of our people from Washington?"

Sam took a deep breath, and scratched his head as he let it out. "Okay. I'll head out in a few minutes. I should be there around noon. Is that alright?"

"Yes, yes. I'll have lunch brought in for us. Thanks Sam, I consider it a personal favor."

Sam put the phone down and looked at the clock. He swallowed his coffee in two gulps, and heard Charlie say, "What's going on?"

"Decker says he needs to talk to me right away. He also mentioned some slick, West Coast attorney got Wilder free on bail."

"The hell you say."

Sam grabbed his Stetson on his way to the door. "Stay out of trouble while I'm gone, and save me some donuts."

"I'll save one, but that's it." Charlie said as Sam closed the door behind him.

He made a quick stop first, and gassed up on the way out of town. What kind of problem would make Decker want him there in his office? He didn't even work for him. Did it have something to do with the banking problem he mentioned a few weeks ago? If so, Jack Whorten told him he would take care of it.

Deciding he would just have to find out when he got there, Sam drove east into the sun, reflecting on how he straddled two different worlds. It wasn't just his Marshal's job, and how it occasionally tied in with the FBI, it applied to him being Navajo, and trying to live within the customs and expectations of the white man's society. With one foot in each world, he struggled to define his place and his values.

The thought seemed to sit in his mind more and more lately. He ignored it, or tried to for many years, but it was still as unresolved as it was back in college when he studied law enforcement and Native American history. Where was his center—his balance—and what could he do to find *hozho?*

The sky showed only a few clouds when he parked the car in the downtown parking lot of the FBI office. A gentle wind blew the scent of the river to him. He checked his watch when he got on the elevator—a quarter to twelve—and when he walked into the office, a polite, young woman acknowledged him by name and asked him to have a seat while she informed the Station Chief that he had arrived. Five minutes later, the man called for him, and the secretary led him back to his office.

He shook Decker's hand, and sat in the offered chair in front of the big walnut desk. The room looked the same as when he was last here. The plaques and framed photos were in their familiar places, as was J. Edger's portrait on the opposite wall. The only thing different was the other man sitting on the couch, with an expensive suit, slicked hair, and a leather briefcase on the floor next to his glossy shoes.

Chief Decker's smile seemed pained, but at least it was there. "Thanks for coming Sam. Let me introduce Mr. Jones. He's a government attorney from Washington, and he has some papers for you to review and sign."

The slick-dressed man stood and walked over to shake Sam's hand. "Mr. Begay it's a pleasure. Rather than explaining the document, please just take a few minutes to read it."

Sam did, and as he finished the last page, a small grin crept across his face.

The attorney cleared his throat. "Mr. Begay, does this document accurately describe how you understand the events took place?"

Sam nodded, "They seem okay to me."

"Good, it's regrettable that this banking error has caused some concern for Mr. Decker, and I wish to thank you for contacting us in Washington as quickly as you did. Fortunately, we were able to clear it up before any negative fallout occurred. We will have the funds in question placed in a charitable account for the benefit the Rehoboth Mission Hospital, per Mr. Decker's wishes."

Jones placed the signed document in his briefcase, and shook hands with both men. "Good day gentlemen, I'll leave you to attend to your other business."

When the man left, Decker stared at Sam from behind his desk. "Am I glad that's over; I've been stepping on eggs around here for weeks. I don't know how you did it, Sam, and I certainly don't want to know how you came to acquire such important friends in Washington, but I do hope someday I can return the favor."

There was a soft knock on the door, and Decker said, "Come in."

The young secretary walked in with two box lunches and coffee. She set them on the corner of the desk after Decker cleared a space. "Thank you Margaret. That will be all. Please see that we're not disturbed. I'll buzz you if we need anything else."

He sat back and exhaled, while Sam, being from a stoic race, merely stared at him. Decker took off his glasses and started the conversation.

"Dammit Sam, don't you have anything to say?"

"Sure, let's eat."

As they ate their sandwiches, Sam said, "That was a nice touch to have the money donated to the hospital. I know they can use it."

Decker shrugged his shoulders. "Your friend, Mr. Whorten, said they would probably need it because of the way you keep getting banged up and shot at, and then showing up at their door." His expression turned serious. "Sam, I don't know how you did it, but thanks." He gulped some coffee. "I'm sorry we got off to such a bad start back when I first took over this position. I hope we can put it all behind us. How are you and Charlie getting along sharing an office?"

The question surprised Sam. "Oh, pretty good. We worked together in the past, but now we go our own ways most of the time. It's convenient to share the space, and It's good to have someone to cover the phone, and to bounce ideas off from time to time."

"That's pretty much what he told me. I figured it also might be time to send someone else out there to learn from the both of you. It would be Charlie's responsibility, but I'm sure you could provide valuable insight to a new officer. Decker smiled. "I have someone in mind, but I haven't made my decision yet."

It was Sam's turn to smile. "Does Charlie know about this?"

"He will when I tell him." Decker chuckled. "Sam, I've never doubted your ability or your honesty, it's just that some of your methods grate on my nerves like fingernails on a chalk board. If you'd ever consider embracing our rules and procedures, I could use someone with your background and experience on my team."

Sam sipped his coffee before speaking. "Mr. Decker, I appreciate you saying that, but I found that I do better working on my own. Procedures and rules sometimes seem to do more harm than good on the Reservation." He set aside his food wrapper and sat back. "I'll tell you one thing, sir; I know you're a good man, and you do a good job of running this operation. I'll be happy to back you up whenever you need it, but I just think it's better if we keep some jurisdictional distance between us."

Decker nodded and said, "Do you remember the time last year you were in this office?"

"Yes sir I do." Sam's eyes beamed with humor. "You were sounding like a human buzz saw chewing some butt, and as I recall, I was eyeing one of those special chocolates your mother sent you on your birthday."

Wilder raised his eyebrows for a moment. "Yes, and I remember you snitched my last one when I wasn't looking. I was very upset with you Sam."

They stared at each other to see who would flinch first—it was Sam. He reached into his jacket pocket and brought out a small box of wrapped chocolates. He set it in front of Decker, and said, "I guess I owe you for having your people help me out at Blacksparrow."

Decker was quiet, obviously moved by the gesture. He reached for the box of sweets and held it in his hands. "Where did you find these Sam? It's the same kind my mother sends me."

Sam waived the question aside. "Consider it a peace offering, and if you don't mind, I need to get back to Gallup. I'll return the agency car you loaned me in a few weeks, as soon as I can find a replacement. You don't need to bother to see me out."

Decker stood, and they shook hands. "Well, goodbye Sam, and thank you."

After Sam closed the door, Thad Decker picked up the box of chocolates again, and turned it over. He read the printing on the box aloud. "One dozen fine chocolates." He opened a drawer to put it away, then changed his mind, and slowly lifted the lid, savoring the anticipation. He felt the cardboard top slide up along the sides, and saw the wrapping folded over the nest of individually wrapped morsels. He gently opened the paper, and blinked. It took ten seconds for him to give voice to his surprise, and when he did, the laughter spilled from the room and down the hall.

Through tears of surprise and mirth, he saw *eleven* beautifully wrapped chocolates, each in their proper place, with one space containing an empty, crumpled wrapper.

CHAPTER 85

On the way back to Gallup, Sam thought of how he stood with each foot in a different world, not certain where he really belonged. He remembered growing up, and stepping out of the family hogan, facing east across the mesas toward the rising sun just as his father had taught him. Greeting the day, and feeling the sun warming his body, he knew his place with the land and the sky that nurtured him.

When he grew older, and lived in the city while attending the white man's college, he felt as if he were inside a hive of bees. The city was noisy, and filled with people and vehicles, and it made him long for the peace of the open desert. He learned how to live and survive in both worlds, but now he didn't know which one was really his.

He took the Thoreau turn-off, and drove past the trading post on his way to Blacksparrow, hoping Dan Yazzie finished carving the special cane, so he could give it to Jake on his way back to Gallup.

When he drove through the gates, he saw Dan sitting on the porch at the main house. He pulled up, and stepped from the car, and said, "I picked up some groceries before I left Albuquerque. How are you feeling?"

"Rested," Dan said, "and hungry. The cane is in the other room. I'll get it for you."

Sam gazed upon his friend's handiwork, and he couldn't help but smile. He touched every detail of the design, and marveled how Dan used a small amount of paint to accent a few of the carvings on the shaft. It was beautiful, and a fitting gift to give old Jake.

After they talked, Sam said he needed to get back to Gallup. "Thank you my friend, I'll deliver this on my way, and I'll be back in a few days with more groceries. If you're still here, maybe you can help me figure out what to do with this place."

The small bell rang above the screen door as Sam open it for some customers leaving the trading post. He stepped inside the cool interior, and held the cane behind him as he shuffled along the worn boards toward the counter. Eric saw him first. He called his name, and ran from behind the counter to greet him.

Sam ruffled the boy's hair. "Ya-ha-tee," he said to Eric and then smiled at Jake who was watching, and repeated the greeting.

Jake said, "We were just talking about you, wondering where you've been keeping yourself."

"Mostly in Gallup, but I'm just on my way back from Albuquerque. I stopped at my old place to check on Dan Yazzie. He's been staying there to keep an eye on things. I figured I'd see how you two were doing before I made my way back to Gallup."

"Sam," Eric said, "Jake told me you know how to do a rain dance."

Jake stood with his thumbs in his favorite pair of red suspenders. "What I said was, 'he's been *trying to learn how* to do a rain dance.' The Hopis are the ones who usually get it right, but it just doesn't come as easy to a Navajo. Oh, I know he's tried it a few times, but he told me all it did was make him pee."

Eric glanced at Sam, then back at Jake.

"Well it's true."

Sam shook his head and rolled his eyes. "I have something I think you could use, Jake." He brought the carved cane from behind his back and handed it to his old friend across the counter. "I figured, since you broke your other one in that scuffle with the gunman, I'd have this special one made to replace it."

Jake was stunned. Sam was his good friend, but he never expected to receive such a beautiful gift as this. His eyes devoured the intricate carving as he held it in his hands, feeling the weight. "I don't know what to say Sam."

Eric moved closer to see the work, and Jake showed it to him. "It's not just a cane," he said. "It has an eagle head for a handle. You hold on to the beak here."

The Lightning Tree

Sam took Eric aside as Jake admired the gift. He stooped down and spoke for a few minutes while Jake stepped back and forth behind the counter with his cane, trying it out, and showing off. After a minute, Eric nodded his head to Sam.

Sam straightened up and returned to the counter. "I've got to run, Jake, but I'll be back in a few days."

"You'd better," said Jake. "We'd enjoy your company." Jake stuck out his chest, and his face beamed with pride. "I guess people don't expect to receive a gift like this, even when they do something brave."

They said their goodbyes, and as Sam walked toward the door, he heard Jake talking to Eric about the cane.

"A person has to do something special to get a gift like this," he said. "People will think I have the heart of an eagle."

"Uh, uh," Eric said, "Sam told me he had it made, so when the old ladies come into the store and ask to see your beak, you'll have something to show them."

A shadow of perplexity crossed Jakes whiskery face, then his head came around so fast, Sam though he could hear it snap. Eric stepped back and began to suspect something was amiss. He turned to Sam for support, but saw him duck out the screen door in a rush. Turning back to the counter, the boy saw Jake standing there in shock.

When Jake noticed Eric's pained expression, he couldn't hold a straight face. A wide grin spread from ear to ear, and he chuckled. "Boy, you and I are going to have to figure out a way to get that big ol' Indian's goat. It may take us a while, but we got it to do."

Sam drove out of the lot with haste, grateful for his timing in exiting the building. He knew he would have to be careful for a few weeks—Jake had a good memory, and many more years of pay-back experience.

It was after 5:00 p.m. when he drove past the hogback into Gallup. Charlie would probably be home by the time he drove up, and if he knew his friend, he would want to hear all about his meeting with Decker.

"So, you gave him a box of those special chocolates? I can't believe it. Next thing you'll be telling me you two kissed and made up."

"In a way, I guess we did."

"Hmm," Charlie said, "I'm not so sure I would trust that man to be happy for long. It just isn't in his nature."

411

Sam smiled as he remembered the empty candy wrapper. "You're probably right, but I might as well enjoy it while I can."

"How about I go out and pick us up some burritos for supper?" Charlie said. "It's my turn to buy. I think I still have some beer in the fridge."

"It sounds good to me. I'll give Jack Whorten a call while you're out, and I'll let him know how things turned out."

Sam heard the phone ringing in an office somewhere in Washington, DC, and Jack Whorten's voice came on the line with a non-committal "Hello."

"It's Sam Begay; do you have a few moments to talk?"

"Sure, Sam, what's on your mind?"

"I want to thank you for handling the delicate matter of the mystery-money in Thaddeus Decker's bank account. Your offer to make a donation to our Indian hospital was a nice touch."

"Yes," Whorten said, "it did seem like the thing to do, seeing as how you're one of their regular customers."

"Jack, if I may ask, what are your thoughts about Rance Wilder posting bond until his trial?"

"All I can say Sam, is it's a shame how our system works sometimes, but don't worry, he'll receive his ultimate reward after the judge and jury hear the whole story. I should tell you that the FBI is also investigating his mob connections. The Purple Gang may be a thing of the past in Detroit, but some other groups are popping up. Chicago has some of its own people there, as well as the East and West Coast. It seems when you cut off one head, two more take its place. Is there anything else?"

Sam didn't want to go into what he and Dan Yazzie went through recently, but he did have one other thing on his mind. "Jack, remember when you and I first met after the Blacksparrow battle a few years ago, and how I pressured you to give me ownership of the property?"

"Like it was yesterday, Sam, and I'd say it was more like blackmail, why? Are you going to tell me you finally figured out I had plans for you all along?"

Sam made a face into the phone. "No, I figured *that* out some time ago. I don't think anything happens without your advance knowledge and approval. It's just that I've been thinking that owning Blacksparrow may not be the right thing for me."

"Just a moment Sam, you're not trying to slip out of our working arrangement, are you?"

The Lightning Tree

"No, it's not that. I'm happy with our bargain, it's just that I don't want to be responsible for the place anymore. My people don't abide by the concept of owning land. They think more along the line of being part of it, like caretakers. They use it, but they don't own something that already owns them. Does that make sense?"

"I understand what you're saying, Sam. Why not just think of yourself as a caretaker and use it?"

"Use it for what, Jack?"

"I don't know. Raise some sheep or horses. If you want, you can sell it, or give it to someone else. You can even walk away and let it go back to nature, but there's one thing you can't do; and that is, give it back to the government. Just imagine the mountain of paperwork, and the thousands of dollars of payroll it would take to accomplish such a thing—not to mention the years of planning."

Sam frowned, "I see your point, Jack."

When Charlie returned with the burritos, Sam told him how his conversation went with Whorten. Charlie listened, and offered his own suggestions about how to use the place.

"Like I said, I think you should keep it. You don't have to live there, but someday you'll find a good reason to sell or give it away. Until then, why not just enjoy it whenever you feel you want to?"

"Charlie, the place is a disaster. It's been torn up by a plane crash, and dynamited, and shot to hell—on top of all that, I have some very unpleasant memories."

"Sure you do, Sam, and I know you've got some good ones, too. Don't fight it; just find a way to live with it. Isn't that what the 'Navajo Way' is all about?"

That night, Sam lay in bed and thought about Charlie's suggestions. Maybe he should consider some other options with Blacksparrow. As he waited for sleep to come, he took a long look back at his footprints. He saw the places where he took a wrong turn, and he awoke in the morning with a clear path forward.

CHAPTER 86

When Sam woke up Wednesday morning, he knew it was time to do something about Blacksparrow. He heard Charlie leaving the house for work, and as he lay in bed, he realized he had some thinking to do, and people to see before he could put a definite plan into action.

As he washed and dressed, the image of a tree struck by lightning popped into his head. He thought of the dramatic events he and Dan Yazzie had experienced with the skinwalker witch, and he remembered why his people had always avoided places where lightning struck. They said it was dangerous, and it could bring on sickness. A damaged tree became the property of lightning, and it was bad luck to use the wood to build with, burn for heat, or use for cooking.

Pondering this, he also remembered something strange Joyce Dobson told him the other day. She spoke of a book where a man wore an albatross, hanging from his neck. It was a punishment, and a reminder of something unworthy he'd done. In a moment, it dawned on him that Blacksparrow was *his* albatross—*his lightning tree*.

So many of his experiences there, were full of sorrow, danger, and bad luck, it was as if a bolt of lightning had infected the place. Sure, he had made some good friends, and there were many good memories, but overall, the place was the home of too much death, *and too many bad things*.

When he left the house, it was with a newfound purpose, and a feeling of connection. The sky was clear, without a cloud in sight, as he drove across the tracks to Benny's garage.

The Lightning Tree

Noticing his friend's stocky form partially hidden under the raised hood of a car, as he walked in through the open, bay door, he said,

"Hey Benny, when you can take a break, I need to talk to you."

Benny grunted. "Gimme a minute, okay?" He finished turning a bolt before he lifted his head and took off his smudged, baseball cap. He set his wrench down and grabbed a rag to wipe his hands.

"It's been a while since you've been around, Sam. I'm busier than a bug at a picnic, but go ahead and talk; this is as good a time as any to take a quick break." He dragged a hairy arm across his sweaty forehead. "Whew, it's hot. I've got business stacked up, and I haven't seen my helper in a week."

Sam grimaced at the thought of Sonny's fate. "Benny, it's just like you to complain with all that money rolling in."

"Sure," Benny said, "but my wife takes care of that end of the business; I'm just the one who crawls under the cars and tightens the nuts. Sometimes I think she's working on me the same way."

Sam chuckled. "Benny, you're so full of it. If there's anything she's known for, it's her sweet disposition—and her ability to put up with you. On the other hand, if that's what she's doing, maybe you should feel lucky."

"Benny grinned. Yeah, I guess you could take that two different ways. Maybe I am lucky."

Sam rolled his eyes as Benny sat down on a nearby crate. He motioned for Sam to sit on an old folding chair nearby. "What's on your mind?" He continued to wipe the grease from his hands as he waited for Sam to talk.

"Benny, do you remember the layout of my place north of Thoreau?"

"Sure do. Why?"

Sam hesitated as he thought of how to explain what had recently happened. "I had some trouble out there, and most of it got blown-up or burned down."

"*What?*"

Sam adjusted his hat. "There was a plane crash, and a bunch of dynamite got touched off. Right now, it looks like a tornado went through it. The point is; I want to clean it all up, and let it go back to nature. I know there's a lot of trash, but I figure there's also some scrap metal around, and maybe some other useable material. I thought your boys at the junk yard might be interested in taking a look—maybe we can work out a deal to clean it up."

Benny pursed his lips and looked thoughtful. "It's possible. Scrap prices are going up with all the stuff going on in Europe right now. Why not go over and talk to them? I won't be able to help, with all this work piling up, but I know they can put a crew together if there's a sizable project. I'll give them a call right now if you want to go over and talk."

An hour later, Sam left the junk yard and drove north from Gallup toward Shiprock. Benny's boys said they would meet him at Blacksparrow Friday morning, and that gave him a day or two to do something he should have done months ago; drive to Farmington, and look around for anyone who might have known Eric's, missing mother. He remembered her name was Rosemary Nez, and the boy said she worked at a restaurant and motel in Farmington, where she stayed during the week, and came home on weekends. It was a small town, and there couldn't be that many motels and restaurants.

Eric said she hitchhiked each way after walking to the main road from the house, but she didn't come home the last time. How long ago was that? It must have been late March or early April. Assuming she didn't just run away, which seemed very unlikely, something must have happened to her on the way to work, at work, or on the way home.

He envisioned the road to Farmington, and he made a mental list of possibilities: Kidnapped, a serious automobile accident, or some harm coming to her where she worked or stayed in Farmington.

This gave him something he could check. He could get police records of any automobile mishap along the route, or any reports of abduction, or someone finding an unidentified body around the time of her disappearance. He could also canvas the stores in town to locate where she had worked, and perhaps find some other useful clue.

He reached Farmington early that afternoon, walked into the Sheriff's office, and found the answer to his inquiry so fast, he felt embarrassed not looking into it sooner. The officer on duty had records of four deaths in their jurisdiction during that two-week period—one was a white male, but the other three were Navajos—two males, and a female. The female appeared to be approximately the right age.

The officer pulled the file, and Sam found it contained a physical description of the deceased, but no mention of any possessions found with the body to identify the woman. The police photo showed severe injuries—an apparent victim of a hit and run accident. Her facial features were mostly unidentifiable.

Sam noted the description of her clothing, and the location of the final disposition of the corpse, and when he left, he gave the officer the name of Eric's mother, Rosemary Nez, as a possible name of the victim.

He needed more information, and the only way to get it was to start at one end of town and inquire at every restaurant and motel to ask if they recently employed a woman by that name. This also turned out to be embarrassingly simple. Within 30 minutes, he was speaking to her employers; a middle age couple, who ran a husband and wife business near the west end of town.

The lunch rush was over, and the owners sat down with Sam to talk. They told him Rosemary worked at the restaurant, cleaning tables and washing dishes. She also did housekeeping work at their adjoining motel, where she stayed during the week. They said when Rosemary didn't return after going home one weekend, they were concerned, and after more than two weeks went by, they gathered her things and stored them in a back room.

Sam explained what probably happened to her, and they took him to the storage area and let him go through her personal belongings. Among the small assortment of combs and toiletries, he found what he was hoping for: a small case containing a name badge, and some other personal effects, including a photo of Eric. He also found a small, wooden talisman that he suspected the boy carved for her.

When he carried the bag with her things to the office, the owners expressed their condolences, and gave Sam an envelope with some money in it. They also gave him an employee photo of her in her uniform and apron. The woman said, "The money is what we owe her for the last week she worked, and some extra for her boy. We are so sorry to hear what happened, and we hope the extra money will help in some way. She always talked about how much she loved her son."

Her husband added, "She was a good worker and a very likable person. We'll miss her."

Sam thanked them, and took the belongings to his car. There was only one other thing left to do. He wanted to find her grave; not because his people were likely to visit such places, but so he could tell Eric about it, and take him there if he chose to see it.

On the long trip back to Gallup, he decided to drive to Blacksparrow Thursday to talk to Dan about what he planned to do, and see Eric on Friday, after Benny's boys came to have a look around the place.

CHAPTER 87

While they ate supper that evening, Sam told Charlie what he'd found out in Farmington about Eric's missing mother. He still didn't know how he was going to break the news to the boy.

Charlie said, "Are you certain it was his mother?"

Sam thought for a moment, and said, "Yes. Even though the facial features were unrecognizable, the few, small items found with the body, and the circumstances of her disappearance and not showing up for work, all seem to fit. The boy should remember the description her clothing, and I have some personal items he should recognize."

Charlie didn't envy Sam for what had to do. "The poor kid. Are you going to take him to where she's buried?"

Sam had thought about this all the way back from Farmington. "I'm not sure, Charlie. If he's like most traditional Navajo, he won't need to see her resting place. Most of our people place no value on a body once the spirit leaves it—they consider it a worthless shell. I'll ask him, and if he wants to go, I'll drive him up there and maybe, help him get a marker."

As the sun went down, and the desert gave back the heat of the day, they sat on the porch and talked. Sam described what he wanted to do with Blacksparrow.

"The Ortiz boys are going to meet me out there Friday morning to see about cleaning up the place. I've pretty much decided to let it go back to nature."

"Sounds like a good idea. As I recall, there wasn't much of the place left standing anyway."

The Lightning Tree

Sam nodded. "Just my house; it didn't suffer as much damage. I could fix it up. Who knows, once they clear up the mess, it might be a nice place to stay on the weekends. It's quiet, and I can keep some horses. I'll have to think about it."

"Dan Yazzie is out there right now; maybe he wouldn't mind sticking around after all the work is done. With winter coming, he might appreciate a warm place to stay until Spring. I'll be out there until sometime Sunday. Is there anything you need me to do before I go?"

"Nope. Just as long as you promise not to do something that would make me have to write another report like the last one I did."

Sam grinned and said, "Charlie, all I can do is try."

Thursday morning, Sam drove to Blacksparrow after an early breakfast with Charlie. Dan Yazzie was waiting on the porch of the main house when he drove through the gate.

Sam said, "It looks like you did some work on the house. What do you think about sticking around while I have some workers clear up all the rubble? You could even stay here over the winter."

Dan nodded. "I was thinking about how cold last winter was, and how warm this house would be. You saved me from having to ask. Coffee's on if you want some."

They brought their cups out to the porch, and as they looked across the compound, Dan said, "Last night I walked around the place waiting for the stars to come out. When they filled up the sky, they looked so close I thought I could hear the noise they made."

Sam nodded, and Dan spoke again. "I asked the stars, 'Why am I here?' And do you know what they said? 'Don't ask us—why should we care?'" Dan took a sip from his cup. "It was then I realized that I was the only one who could answer the question, and since I didn't have an answer, I decided to stick around and see if I could find one."

After they refilled their coffee cups, Sam said, "Dan, there's a lot of salvageable lumber; and some is stacked across the way near the movie set. I think I can use it to repair the house and build a stable for the horses."

As they finished the last of their coffee, Sam realized he was putting off something he had to do. He had to talk to Eric Nez.

"Dan, do you remember that Navajo boy I was telling you about? The one I found hiding in the compound? He's staying with Jake at the trading post, and I need to talk to him about something personal. I might bring him back with me, along with some groceries."

Eric saw Sam the moment he walked in the trading post, and he ran to great him. Sam didn't want to delay telling the boy the sad news, so he greeted Jake, and took Eric aside.

"Eric, how would you like to come out to Blacksparrow with me for a few days? Do you think Jake could spare you? One of my good friends is out there too, and I think you'll like him."

The boy seemed excited, and when Sam talked to Jake at the counter, the old storekeeper said, "By golly Sam, this boy has things running so smoothly around here that all I do is sit back and eat candy. I'm getting' fat and lazy, and it'll do me good to fend for myself for a few days." Jake looked around and whispered, "You don't plan to keep him away very long, do you?"

Sam grinned. "Jake, I'll bring him back Sunday on my way back to Gallup."

Eric packed a few things, said goodbye to Jake, and Jake told him to hurry back before he forgot how to play checkers.

As Sam and Eric drove north, the boy talked about the trading post, and working with Jake, while Sam fretted about how to bring up the topic of the boy's mother. After a few miles, he decided just to say it.

"Eric, there's something I need to tell you, and I'm sorry, but I don't know how best to do it."

"The boy turned his big eyes to Sam, and then lowered them. "Did you find out what happened to my mother?"

Sam had been holding his breath. He let it out, and with a lump in his throat, he said, "Yes. I know she loved you very much. She would have come back to you if she could."

Eric nodded, and Sam told him everything he knew.

That evening, after meeting Dan, and walking around the compound with them after supper while they discussed plans, Eric went to bed early.

Sam cooked breakfast Friday morning, and a short while after they finished eating, a truck with three men pulled into the yard.

Benny's boys spent two hours with Sam as he walked them around the place, pointing out the demolished structures and other debris. The men

The Lightning Tree

had a good look at the wreckage of the small plane, and the damage to the large hangar door on the far wall of the mesa. When Sam showed them the open space behind it, they seemed impressed by the size of it, and by the heavy equipment stored there.

Seeing their interest, Sam said, "I won't go into it all, but before I took over, this was a dirigible hangar. I suspect they widened and roofed over a natural cleft in the rocks to build it. Now, I just use it to store the equipment I brought in by rail a year ago."

Arthur, Benny's oldest boy, said, "What do you want us to do with it?"

"I want to tear off the damaged door and the roof, and make everything like it was before they built it."

"What about the equipment? You've got some pretty new stuff; a dozer, a grader, a nice crane, and some trucks."

"I'll probably sell it. Do you know anyone who can use this kind of stuff?"

Arthur grinned, "Yeah, us."

The Gallup men took nearly two hours to walk around the compound and assess the work Sam wanted done. When they met back by the gate, they stood off by themselves and talked while reviewing their notes for fifteen minutes.

Walking up to Sam after they finished, the oldest boy said, "Mr. Begay, I think we have an offer that you may find attractive."

The deal they roughed out involved no cash changing hands for the demolition, clean up, and landscaping. The Ortiz boys got some badly needed, heavy equipment in the deal, and Sam would have the compound cleared except for the main house and some building supplies. Sam also kept the grader for maintenance of the road.

The boys said they would arrange to have some rail cars brought in on the spur leading to the far side of the compound, and use them to haul out the scrap. They promised to remove the tracks after they loaded the cars and left.

Sam felt good about the deal, and after the men left, he noticed Eric sitting by himself, looking subdued. He asked if he would like to drive up to Farmington, and Eric said he didn't need to see his mother's grave; he knew in his heart that she never left him.

Sam understood, and he put his arms around the boy. For some reason, he thought of the words a wise uncle told him about family. 'Family is a powerful thing. It is always a part of us, and it is what makes us what we are. It can nurture us, cheer us on, and pick us up when we fall, or it can cut us off at the knees, and poison us.' Sam's experiences this year brought him clear examples of this.

As the three ate lunch that afternoon, they discussed what the place would look like after the work was completed. Dan suggested Sam could hire some locals to help build a stable for the horses and make some house repairs in exchange for the extra building supplies. He suspected many were experienced carpenters.

Sam said, "I noticed a small trickle of water seeping from the rocks across the way, near the hangar doors. Dan, I believe this place could become a haven for the animals. Grass will grow, and the horses will have a place to run. I think it is how it should be."

Dan said, "Eric told me he likes it here, and I told him he was welcome to stay with me whenever he wants while the work is being done."

"Good." Sam said. "By the way, what are your plans for staying over the winter?"

"I think I'll take you up on that, Sam, but before the work gets started, I want to saddle a horse, and ride back to that old hogan to see if anyone has been around since we were there. I'll let you know if I find anything."

Saturday afternoon, Sam brought Eric to the trading post on his way back to Gallup. He promised the boy to pick him up to watch the work when it started. He told Jake about his clean-up plans, and that Eric was always welcome there.

Jake smiled and nodded, "It'll be good for the boy. He misses being outside in the desert."

As Sam left, Jake turned to Eric and said, "Guess what the soda-pop delivery man brought while you were gone? I got us six cases of RC Cola!"

Eric's eyes lit up. "Can we have some right now? I bet I can burp louder than you can this time."

Jake said, "You wanna bet? We'll just have to see who beats who."

Eric came back with two bottles, and Jake popped the lids off, and set one in front of the boy. Gripping the other, Jake said, "Ready? One, two, three, GO!"

In unison, the two tipped their pop bottles up, and their throats worked as they chugged. Jake finished first, and he belched with so much force, his false teeth came loose and popped partway out of his mouth. By then,

Eric was in full voice. Caught in mid-belch, he was so surprised to see Jakes protruding teeth, he laughed and blew pop through his nose.

When they could stop laughing, Jake grabbed his teeth and repositioned them, and said, "Boy, maybe we should call this one a tie—let's not mention any of this to Sam, O.K?

CHAPTER 88

On the drive back to Gallup, Sam brushed away his other distractions, and mentally retrieved the odd assortment of wolf hair clues he'd collected through the summer. One-by-one, he reviewed them.

He knew the roles of Bobby and David Castor, and of the other students on the baseball team. Lingering over the uncanny revelations of Dan Yazzie and the old spirit man, he also knew of the motivation of the skinwalker witch and Sonny, her accomplice. After all the deaths, what did that leave him?

Bobby Castor was still alive, and the young Navajo girl who lived with the witch was missing. There were two other things; the Spanish gold coin found clutched in the bones of Harold Borden's hand, and the matching one he'd found at the old hogan. It was a connection, but was it a viable clue? He may never know, and perhaps it was time to forget it all.

Saturday afternoon, back in Gallup, the Reservation traffic swarmed through town. Sam stopped at the FBI office, and found Charlie filling out his reports.

Charlie said, "Decker called and mentioned he was sending out a new agent Monday. He said things seemed to be getting busier on this side of the state, and he wanted the agent to get some Reservation experience."

Sam said, "Things are always changing, Charlie. By the way, I made a deal to clear up all the mess at Blacksparrow, and I'm thinking of building a new house on my property outside of town. If I can get a crew together quick enough, I might be able to complete it before the weather gets too cold."

"No need to rush, Sam. You're welcome to stay with me over the winter. I heard we might get an early cold spell and snow, and if you make your plans for the spring; you'll have more time and less stress, and the workers will do a better job. Besides, we never did figure out who's the best checkers player."

"Charlie, maybe I'll take you up on that—and just for the record; you and I both know it's me."

Monday morning, while the sun took the chill out of the air, Sam and Charlie sat in his office drinking coffee, wondering when the new man Decker was sending out would arrive. Sam told Charlie he was thinking of doing some work for Judge Reilly, bringing in fugitives.

Charlie said, "You can still use the extra desk here. I asked Decker, and he said it was all right with him."

Sam nodded, sipped his coffee, and twirled his gold coin on the top of the desk.

"Is that the coin you found on Borden's body?"

"Nope, this is another one. I found it at an old hogan where Dan Yazzie and I saw the witch."

"Do you think the two coins came from the same place?"

"Hard to tell, but probably—you know how us Navajo like to believe all things are connected. Charlie, I've been thinking over the weekend, and I have a feeling the young girl who disappeared from the hogan still has a role to play in this."

"How do you mean?"

Sam downed the last of his coffee. "It just makes sense. I have no doubt the old woman was a skinwalker witch; and they say for a female to become one, she must first kill a family member. Charlie, I wonder if that old woman killed Stacy Toledo's mother, and maybe she was the woman's sister? What if this woman, Stacy's aunt, wanted to take over her body so she could enjoy her life again as a young woman?"

"But," Charlie said, "I thought you said Stacy died giving birth to her two children?"

"Yes, she must have, and it would mean that the witch would have no body to take unless she raised Stacy's kids, and waited for the female to grow up, so she could use her body."

"I don't know. That's quite a long time, and it sounds like a stretch of the imagination to me."

"Maybe, but it fits all the other facts we know. What else could make the witch angry enough to plot the deaths of the ball players, if it wasn't linked to Stacy's pregnancy, and her death? Something else fits too. Do you remember how some of the first boys died by different means than the later ones? We know Sonny did the last killings, but he would have been too young to commit the first ones. The witch must have started the killings, and Sonny took over when he was old enough."

"I guess that's possible, But he died before he could finish off Bobby Castor."

"Yes, and don't forget, Charlie, a witch would never give up on her revenge. She may have to delay it, like in this case, but she would still find a way to finish it. And there is one other thing; the old witch watched over a large hoard of Spanish gold coins she found as a young girl."

"How do you figure that when you only found two coins?"

"Dan Yazzie said his old spirit man told him. He also told a story about how a young Navajo girl became a witch after suffering an atrocity during the "Long Walk." He said this was all about her revenge, and it took her 70 years to complete it. There's just one thing that bothers me; I know the witch is dead, but the young girl, Sonny's sister, has disappeared."

Charlie caught on to what Sam was saying. "Do you think...?

"Yes, and that's what still bothers me." Sam picked up the coin and spun it again.

Charlie went to the back for a refill, and said over his shoulder. "Do you want more coffee?"

"No, I'm done. You can finish it. Did Decker tell you when the new guy is supposed to be here today?"

Charlie's voice came from the back. "Nope, he just said the agent would be here. He did mention he hoped you would be available to help out because of your Reservation background."

A small furrow formed on Sam's brow. "I guess that's alright. It's good to know he wants to be thorough."

"Yeah, I thought so too."

The phone rang, and Sam said, "I'll get it."

Charlie heard him talking and asking questions. When he heard Sam hang up, he said, "Who was that?"

Sam appeared thoughtful as the furrows deepened on his forehead. "The manager of Strong Mountain Trading Company up the street said Bobby Castor hasn't been in for the last part of the week and all weekend.

The guy said he didn't show up this morning, either, and he still doesn't answer his phone."

Charlie said, "Maybe he went out of town for a long weekend."

"Maybe, but he said the last he saw of him was Wednesday, talking to some Navajo girl at the back counter. He said he remembered her because she had some kind of red mark on her neck, like a birthmark, and she was pawning some gold coins. He said Bobby gave her quite a bit of cash, and the funny thing is, Bobby left with her, and no one has seen him since."

"That is odd," Charlie said as he poked his head out from the back.

"The manager says he's been calling him on and off, and he even went to his house in town, and the one out by Ramah on Sunday, but the doors were locked, and Bobby wasn't around. He figured his boss took off with the woman, but when Bobby didn't call or show up today, he decided it was time to call someone."

Charlie gave Sam a questioning look. "Do you want me to go over there and interview him?"

"Nah, I'll go. You might as well stay, and make a fresh pot of coffee for when your new agent gets here. There's something about this that I don't like."

Sam returned an hour later, and found Charlie on the phone. He sat at his desk, and while he waited for Charlie to finish so he could tell him what he found out, a strange, sixth sense tickled his scalp.

He was about to get up to see if the coffee was on, when he heard a noise from the back. Glancing at Charlie, who was doing his best to avoid Sam's look, his jaw dropped when he saw a young woman with curly red hair step into the room.

Agent Alice Jensen said, "Don't bother standing on my account, boys. I can put up with the dust, and the smelly bathroom, but I'll be damned if I'll drink this crappy coffee."

With that, she grabbed her Stetson, and headed for the door. "If you two will spend a few minutes to clean up this place, I'll come back and make you a *good* pot of coffee."

It was Wednesday before someone discovered Bobby Castor's car, abandoned in a wooded canyon south of town. His body wasn't found until two days later.